D1292186

B. F.'s DAUGHTER

BY
JOHN P. MARQUAND

B. F.'s DAUGHTER

BY JOHN P. MARQUAND

LITTLE, BROWN AND COMPANY · BOSTON

1946

COPYRIGHT 1946, BY JOHN P. MARQUAND AND
ADELAIDE H. MARQUAND

ALL RIGHTS RESERVED, INCLUDING THE RIGHT
TO REPRODUCE THIS BOOK OR PORTIONS
THEREOF IN ANY FORM

Published November 1946
Reprinted November 1946 (seven times)

PRINTED IN THE UNITED STATES OF AMERICA

Foreword

One purpose of this novel is to depict certain phases of American life during the last few years. To create an illusion of reality the names of a few nationally known characters have been mentioned, although none of these personages actually appears in any scene. The active characters and the scenes are, as they always must be, a sublimation of the writer's own experience. If they are artistically successful, they must naturally also appeal to facets of the reader's own experience. The persons depicted in these pages, however, are known to the author only in his creative mind. No one who exists here is intended to represent even remotely, either accurately or in caricature, any actual person either living or dead. If any character bears the name of a real person, this is a purely unintended coincidence, and one almost impossible to avoid considering the number of persons in the United States all of whom are identified by names.

For courteous permission to use the lines from various songs quoted, grateful acknowledgment is made to the following: —

To Mr. John Golden, and Chappell & Co., Inc., Music Publishers, for lines from "Goodbye Girls I'm Through." Copyright MCMXIV by Chappell & Co., Ltd.

Lines from "Don't Change Horses" are used with the permission of Drake-Hoffman-Livingston, Music Publishers.

To Chappell & Co., Inc., Music Publishers, for lines from "I've Got Plenty of Nothing." Copyright MCMXXXV by George Gershwin, published by Gershwin Publishing Corp.

Contents

B. F.'s DAUGHTER

I

All in Its Original Condition

ONE NOON in mid-December when Tom had been called suddenly to Washington, Polly took the train from New York to spend the night at their country place in Pyefield. She had not wanted to go particularly, but she believed that it would be a good idea to see how Mr. and Mrs. Brewis were getting on, and you never could tell what caretakers were really doing unless you dropped in on them without warning.

It was always a long and tiresome train ride to the Berkshires. The single Pullman on the twelve o'clock, a car that must have been built near the turn of the century, was overheated and half empty. The porter remembered her and asked for Mr. Brett. Tom was always very good with porters. Polly said that Mr. Brett was down in Washington helping someone write a speech, and it occurred to her that this was what she was always saying about Tom lately. The porter said he could give her some beans and brown bread from the kitchenette, but Polly replied that she did not want any lunch, thank you. Polly had purchased the *Nation*, the *New Yorker*, and the *New Republic*, but the car swayed so that she did not want to read them. There was nothing to do but sit for hours and think.

You always forgot, when you lived in New York, how much snow there was in the country, and when Polly realized that she was wearing open-toed shoes, she thought it might have been better after all if she had asked Mr. Brewis to get out the Packard and meet her at the junction. He would have had enough gas with his B card, but then if she had done that, there would have been no possibility of checking up on the Brewises. Now she could only hope that

3

Mr. MacMahon and his taxicab would still be meeting trains there. Otherwise she would have to go to that little hotel near the station, and call up Mr. Brewis or some friend in Pyefield — but there would not be anyone in Pyefield, except perhaps the Ellises. Peggy and Arthur Ellis would be in the old tavern, war or no war, because Arthur made his living by doing etchings of birch trees on the mountains in winter.

At any rate there was no use making plans until she reached the junction; so she had time to think about all sorts of other things. She thought about her father. He had been very busy lately, and her mother had said he was not sleeping well, but when Polly had asked him to come up with her to Pyefield, just to get away from things, he had only half listened because he had been trying to get a priority call through to San Francisco.

"Well, it's nice you want me," he had said. "Yes, I'm waiting, operator. . . . The name is Fulton, Burton Fulton. . . . If he isn't at his office, ask where I can reach him. . . . You go ahead by your-self and have a good time, Poll."

As far back as Polly could remember he had always been telling her to go somewhere and have a good time.

"Polly, dear," her mother had said, "if you're going away up there, I wish you'd wear something warm underneath. When I was a girl at Willett, we all wore long woolens."

"A girl can go anywhere," Polly had answered, "if she believes in herself and has a mink coat."

Her parents never seemed to realize that she had grown up, and this delusion of theirs became more and more of a problem as she got into her thirties. They never thought her brother Harry was grown up either, but then, neither did she. He had been at Biak, and now he was at Leyte, but she still thought of him as a sort of Eagle Scout — like the one Admiral Byrd once took with him to the South Pole. She had not been able to get time and values straight since the war started. A bland, impervious curtain was always drawn between her and all that was going on. She had never even heard a gun go off except in the newsreels. When a ship was sunk in the Pacific, she did not hear of it until weeks later, and when the sons of older friends,

4

who had always seemed impossibly young, were killed or missing, she heard it mentioned at some dinner party as an event that had happened long before.

It used to be wonderful to leave everything behind in New York and take the train to Pyefield. She and Tom used to love the quietness and isolation of a winter's night in the Berkshires, and now they had not been there together for three years, in winter or in summer either. Tom was never able to come because it was too far away from Washington, and no matter how carefully they planned it something always came up. It had once been like going home whenever she went to Pyefield, but now it was like going back to some scene in one's childhood, to some place that had only remote associations. She could even wonder what it was that Tom and she had ever seen in Pyefield, and why they had chosen to live any-where that was so far away. The thought made Polly lonely and frightened. She seemed to have no more roots than a displaced per-son in Europe. She kept wandering among disconnected thoughts, telling herself it would surely be all right when she got off the train.

It was dark when she reached the junction, but a rising moon made everything white and cold. The clean, dry air clutched at her throat for a moment, and then she saw the lights of a car at the place where Mr. MacMahon's Buick always stood.

"Mr. MacMahon," she said. "Why, how are you? I began to be afraid you might have been drafted."

"Why, hello, Mrs. Brett," Mr. MacMahon said. "No, the Board hasn't got me yet."

It did not sound very patriotic, but then Tom always said people in the country did not know what the war was about.

"Pyefield? It's too tough on the car," Mr. MacMahon said. "If you stopped at the hotel, you could get the bus in the morning, or maybe you could call up Brewis. If I'm to take you there now, I've got to get twenty dollars."

Mr. MacMahon implied that he was under a personal moral obli-gation to get twenty dollars, and she knew he would never have asked anyone else such a price.

When Polly and Tom had first seen Pyefield, saplings had cov-

5

ered the hayfields, and the population had dropped to almost nothing, but there were still some beautiful deserted houses around the village green, and the church and the old tavern were still standing. The Ellises had bought the tavern for a song, and they had wanted to start a summer community of congenial people who did something. It had been like founding a colony when she and Tom, just after they were married, had bought the old parsonage. Half the roof had fallen in, but the timbers were sound, and the old woodwork was beautiful, and the only reason the Metropolitan Museum had not bought the staircase for the American Wing was because they had not seen it. It was just the sort of life that Tom had liked — getting friends of his to come to Pyefield and buy the other houses, and forming a co-operative association to maintain the church and the green. There it was, ten miles from anywhere, but not hard to reach before the gas rationing.

When they left the main highway and took the mountain road, she could see Pyefield in the moonlight, looking like an American primitive with its boxlike church and its bare trees and houses in cold black and white. It had never seemed so remote; it no longer seemed to be alive. It might have been better, she was thinking, if Pyefield had simply been allowed to disappear when its usefulness was ended — if the houses had been allowed to fall as other houses had into the cellarholes of forgotten New England hill towns. It never helped, perhaps, to resurrect a past that had no connection with the present, and yet she and Tom and all the rest of them had once had a definite purpose in restoring the houses on the village green. They had done so as a revolt from other environments, so that they could live without the usual social pressures. But then, no one could be an individualist really. When Polly thought of it, they had all been like everyone else in a certain social group, the liberal intelligentsia, all wearing the same clothes and adopting the same manners, and all somewhat self-satisfied. It was remarkable how pleased they all used to be with themselves there in Pyefield.

High banks of snow surrounded the green, but the driveway to the house was open, and she was pleased to see that Mr. Brewis had

6

dug the paths, showing that it had paid to have them know she might arrive unexpectedly. The snow had even been cleared from around the four-car garage — an addition they had made in early 1941. The house looked in fine condition, as it should have, considering what she had spent on it. It was a good thing Tom had never seen the bills, because he would have objected. Tom was always telling her she must not throw her weight around simply because she was a rich girl. She had never wanted to be ostentatious either, but at least she had a good business head and wanted to have things right, the best material, the best paint, the best plumbing, and the best nursery stock. She could see the outlines of the sunken garden which had been built on the foundations of the old cowbarn, and the fence, with the pineapple posts that had been designed to follow the motif of the front door, looked very well, just as though it had been there always.

Mr. Brewis had opened the kitchen door even before the car stopped, and he was standing there, in the cardigan jacket Polly had given him last Christmas, holding an electric flashlight. When you came to think of it, Mr. Brewis was really quite a treasure, and so was Mrs. Brewis. When Polly got them at that agency in New York, two nice, middle-aged people, they said they liked the country and never got lonely. Mr. Brewis said he never drank — all he did out of the ordinary was to smoke a pipe after supper — and he liked puttering around a place and keeping it shipshape. Mrs. Brewis came from a Vermont farm, and she said she liked nice things and liked to keep things nice. The beauty of it was that it had all turned out to be perfectly true.

"It's wonderful to be back," Polly said. "Everything looks perfect."

"And you look well, too," Mrs. Brewis said, "a little thin, but real well. I hope Mr. Brett is keeping well. He should get time to come up here. We surely do miss Mr. Brett."

"Everything looks perfect," Polly said again. "Perhaps I could have supper in front of the living room fire, just a little something and some tea, and don't bother about me at all. I'll just walk around."

For a few minutes at least everything was secure, just as it should have been. The house and the Brewises seemed untouched by out-

7

side circumstance, perhaps because the Brewises had no contact with the war, no children, and no relatives as far as Polly knew — just two sweet old people with nothing to think of but keeping the house in order. They were not liberal or conservative, or anti-British or anti-Semitic. They cared nothing about the rights of labor or private enterprise, and they were not concerned with winning the peace after winning the war.

The house was warmed and dusted and all ready to move into, just as though Polly and Tom had been there yesterday, and Polly had arranged it all by herself without anyone to help her — certainly not Tom. Tom was always completely useless when it came to selecting and placing furniture or pictures, and negotiating about pumps and septic tanks and copper roofing. He always said just to do it, for God's sake, and for Polly to work it out herself with the septic tank man, as long as she kept it simple and as long as they did not have too many possessions. No children, no possessions. He wanted to be able to get up and turn the key in the lock and move away any time. That was what Tom had said, but of course it was a pose. No one made more of a row than Tom when his bed was not comfortable, or when the cooking was not right or when anybody misplaced things in his study. The house did look simple too, but thank heaven Tom did not know what it had all cost, or he would have been wild. Actually, he had no idea about values, and that was just as well, since this obliviousness of his made it possible for her to get him those shirts and socks and ties without his knowing they were expensive. Everyone said she managed Tom very well. It was not so difficult either if one was careful. It was all a matter of understanding.

Polly gave her coat to Mrs. Brewis and walked to the front of the house. As she went through the pantry with its Monel-metal sink she glanced at those lovely yellow plates that she had bought in China, at the set of Sandwich glass from the Halsey collection in New York, and at the pink luster tea set. The swinging door to the dining room had lost its squeak. The dining room was small for big dinners, but then she and Tom both hated big dinners, particularly Tom. The collection of glass bottles in the pine corner cupboard was all dusted, all ready to glow when you turned on the switch of the little inside light.

"I do one room every day," Mrs. Brewis said. "That's my rule — and air everything every morning." Polly made up her mind that she must really do something nice for the Brewises.

The house looked almost alarmingly neat. In fact, it reminded her of one of those houses run by a historical society. Mrs. Brewis might have been a hostess at Williamsburg in a mobcap and possibly a bustle, opening the front door to visitors.

"You are now about to go through the Brett House," Mrs. Brewis would be saying, "all in its original condition, just as Mr. and Mrs. Brett left it. The articles which you see on the tables — and which visitors will kindly refrain from touching — were all the possessions of Mr. and Mrs. Brett, once used by them in their daily life when they resided in Pyefield and restored what is still known as the Pyefield Parsonage. The surprising perfection of all these objects, the lack of thumbprints and pencil marks upon the wallpapers, is due to the fact that Mr. and Mrs. Brett were fortunately childless. The clothing in the closets on the second floor, all in its original condition, and even the medicine in the cabinets of their individual bathrooms, was all used personally by Mr. and Mrs. Brett.

"The ell to the right is not original. It was constructed by Mrs. Brett for a study. Here Mr. Brett once pursued his writing, assisted often by Mrs. Brett. Although new, it was designed carefully to conform to the older parts of the residence, and in it you will see the pens, stationery and typewriter used personally by Mr. Brett, placed on his long writing table exactly as he left them. The built-in bookcases, besides containing Mr. Brett's personal casual library and volumes of reference, also hold the manuscript of his Ph.D. thesis on 'American Criticism in the Nineteenth Century,' and the manuscripts of his lectures delivered while an instructor at Columbia University . . . before he married Mrs. Brett, who was then Miss Polly Fulton, daughter of Burton Fulton the industrialist. His files also contain letters to the press and various half-finished, unpublished works, started while Mr. Brett was associated with members of the New Deal 'brain trust' — so-called. On the wall you will see Mr.

9

Brett's diplomas, and a personally signed photograph as well as a personal letter of thanks from Franklin Delano Roosevelt. Also upon the wall appear similar signed, framed photographs of Paul V. McNutt, Bernard M. Baruch, Harry Hopkins, Henry A. Wallace, Thomas Corcoran, Raymond Moley, A. A. Berle, and others.

"The bookcase near the door contains a personal library collected by Mrs. Brett, begun during her days as a student at Bryn Mawr College, all in its original condition. On a lower shelf, you will note a set of scrapbooks, pasted and arranged by Mrs. Brett herself, one volume for each year, which Mrs. Brett kept in lieu of a diary, showing, in photographs, news clippings, and mementos, the activities of herself and friends before and after her marriage to Mr. Thomas Brett. Beneath this shelf of memorabilia, in the locked compartment, are certain personal letters of Mrs. Brett's which she never made up her mind to throw away, including letters by Mr. Brett himself written during their brief courtship, and also some selected letters from her former fiancé, Mr. Robert Tasmin, who later married Miss Mildred Knowles and who now is an officer in the U. S. Army. The block-front desk in the living room contains Mrs. Brett's personal ledgers of household expenses. The whole residence was completely restored before World War II; its heating is indirect, and it is air-conditioned. But in a tour of the house let us start with the fine front hall which runs from east to west . . ."

There was not a disturbing sound from the winter's night outside, but inside the tall clock was ticking on the landing, and so was the banjo clock in Tom's study. In their bedroom the glazed chintz curtains were up, and all Polly's things were out on the dressing table, in the original condition, and Tom's military brushes were on his high bureau, also original. The twin beds, of course, were reproductions because Tom had said that he did not want to feel that he was living in a Noah's Ark, and he particularly did not want any Currier & Ives prints of kittens around, or any Staffordshire dogs either.

"Mrs. Brett," Mrs. Brewis was calling, "supper's ready and there's a lovely fire, real birch logs that he cut last winter."

Original birch logs, cut by Mr. Brewis.

It was better when the fire was burning, because there was always something elementally symbolic about an open fire. After she had eaten the scrambled eggs and bacon that Mrs. Brewis had cooked for her, Polly began to think her mood had been the result of an empty stomach. The tea was perfect, that smoky tea which you could not buy any more, and she was glad she still had several pounds of it. Tom had always especially liked that tea. After she had finished a second cup, she decided to call him in Washington.

The telephone was in the study, one of those old-fashioned upright telephones, and you had to turn a crank on the wall to get the operator. First, she lit the fire in the study, because another fire made everything still brighter, and then she sat in the green leather chair where Tom always sat when he called Washington. You never were quite sure the telephone would work at Pyefield. The sound in the receiver when you rang was always discouraging, and the operator's voice saying, "Number, please" always sounded like someone's voice in a country store.

"I want to speak to Washington," Polly said. "It's a person-to-person call. Mr. Thomas Brett, Monroe 3000. . . . Yes, that's it. Just call me when you get him."

If she could get him, it would be almost as though Tom were at Pyefield too. She could surely reach him if she were to wait and call him at his office number in the morning, but still there was a chance he might be at the club, where he had a room when he was in Washington alone.

She had given more thought to that study of Tom's than to any of her other projects. She had furnished it with all the things he had wanted whether she liked them or not, so that it would be his room, a man's room, a place where he would like to work. The only things of hers in it were the books — there was no place for them anywhere else — and now that she was waiting for the call, she looked over at her scrapbooks.

Polly had started them years before when she was a senior at Heatherbloom Hall, and scrapbooks had been a fad with a lot of the girls. They were large and uniform, with leather backs like ledgers, each with its own year printed on it, all in a row on a lower shelf. She had not been through them for a long while, and now she pulled one out at random — the year 1925. It had been Polly's idea that the individual pictures and clippings in those books did not matter as much as their indirect associations. She found herself examining a snapshot of three girls by the edge of the swimming pool at Gray's Point, certainly the Gray's Point swimming pool because of the yew trees in back of it, and underneath she had written in a round hand that scarcely looked like her own, "Three Little Maids from School." She must have just come out of the pool, judging by the moist appearance of her archaic bathing costume, and by the wet fringe of hair coming from under the edges of her bathing cap. There were snapshots of picnics and of a fishing camp, and snapshots of her Uncle Herbert and Aunt Martha at Willett . . . static, half-forgotten moments. One was entitled "B. F. Eats an Apple" and another "Mother in the Garden," and another "Harry Home from Camp."

She took down more of the scrapbooks until they made a disorderly pile on the floor. In 1928 there was picture after picture of Bob Tasmin by the swimming pool and by the Duesenberg and by the tennis court, and then a clipping from some sports page, "Tasmin Again Wins Singles at Mill River." In one of the books were clippings with her own pictures, "Polly Fulton Bows to Society in Gala Scene." In another, "Tasmin, Runner-up at Southampton," "Tasmin Heads Squash Racquets Team," "Burton Fulton, Industrial Genius," "Production Is Answer, Says Burton Fulton" — everything was there, all her life. Next there were the accounts of the lecture that Tom Brett had delivered at Wisconsin, "Brett Gives Wadley Lecture." . . . "Polly Fulton Wed to Thomas Brett." . . . There were pictures from France, pictures from around-the-world cruises, views of the house at Pyefield as it had been when they had bought it. She and all her friends had apparently spent their lives standing in formal gardens, or on decks of steamships, always casually dressed and squinting at the sun.

There were the play programs and the engraved invitations to dances and weddings. The marriage pictures all seemed like duplications — the wedding party on some lawn with the ushers in their cutaways and the bridesmaids in their picture dresses. She saw herself and Tom standing on the lawn at Gray's Point. Her wedding dress had come from Lanvin, and she did not look so badly, but Tom in his cutaway looked wretched. He had not wanted to wear one, nor had he wanted to have the wedding at Gray's Point, but he had accepted the inevitable.

She turned the pages rapidly and it was like a *montage* — unrelated scenes blended together to indicate the passage of time. There was another wedding announcement a year after her own. Under it she had written "Happily Ever After." "Mr. and Mrs. Morgan Knowles announce the marriage of their daughter Mildred to Robert Tasmin." She had pasted with it a clipping from the *Times,* ". . . Miss Knowles is a granddaughter of the late Jason Knowles, former member of the United States Senate and author of the Knowles Tariff Act. Miss Knowles attended Miss Spence's School and is active in the Junior League. Mr. Tasmin, graduate of Groton, Yale '25, Harvard Law School '28, rowed on the Yale second crew. He is a partner in the law firm of Barstow, Barstow and Bryce. His New York Clubs are the Racquet and Yale. After some months in Europe, Mr. and Mrs. Tasmin will reside in New York."

There had been a time when Polly had thought of pasting some of Bob Tasmin's letters in one of the earlier volumes, but instead they were locked in the lower compartment of the bookcase. "Dearest Poll," they always started, and they always ended "I love you always, Bob." "I wonder if you have that mustard yellow dress with you, the one you wore when we went walking Sunday," she remembered his writing. "It goes so well with your hair. There's nothing like your hair, darling, and your eyes. I hope you have the Navajo pin with you too, just to remember me by." That had been one thing, he had always noticed what she wore. "A tough time in the office. Willoughby was asking about you. Squash with Sam Melcher. I think about you all the time."

Everything was very still, except for the banjo clock on the wall, an Aaron Willard because Tom had always wanted one.

That was the way Bob Tasmin's letters used to go. They said exactly what he meant, and there never was anything to read between the lines. The telephone was ringing, and though she had been expecting it, she nearly dropped the scrapbook she was holding.

"Hello," she said, and she could hear Tom's voice. The connection was very good.

"Hello. Is that you, Poll? Where are you?"

"I'm in Pyefield. I just came up."

"My God, what are you doing in Pyefield?"

"Don't you remember? I told you I was going up to look at it."

"Well, now you see it, how is it?"

"It's beautiful, but I miss you."

"I should think you would in Pyefield," Tom said. "How is it? Cold?"

"The heat's on," Polly said. "It's beautiful. It's like a museum. I'm in your study and the banjo clock is going."

"What clock?" Tom asked.

"Don't you remember? The one I gave you. The banjo clock. The house is like a museum."

"What's like a museum?"

"The house, I said, the house. Tom, are you all right?"

"Yes," Tom said, "I'm fine. I'm pretty busy down here. I won't be back until Thursday."

"Do you miss me?" Polly asked.

"What's that?" he asked. "Do I what?"

"Can't you hear me? I said — do you miss me?"

"Oh," Tom said, "I miss everything down here. You and sleep and everything."

Then the operator was speaking. "Please confine your call to three minutes," and Polly realized that the call had meant absolutely nothing.

"Wait a minute, operator," Tom was saying. "I'll be back Thursday. Well, it's fine you're in Pyefield, Poll. Give my regards to everybody. It's swell of you to call me, Poll."

"What are you doing?" Polly asked. "Are you having a good time?"

"Listen," Tom said. "I wish you wouldn't keep asking whether I'm having a good time. Nobody has a good time. We're all run

14

ragged. Listen, Poll, they can't keep the circuit open. There's a war on. It's swell you called up. Good night, Poll."

Polly hung up the antiquated receiver very carefully, though she wanted to hurl the whole instrument at the wall. Then she pushed herself up carefully from the green leather chair and walked softly to the center of the green carpet in front of the open fire. With part of her mind she was thinking of the carpet's texture — it was one of those soft, downy carpets from Sloane's, and its color was light and cool. For a moment she did not feel weak or strong, or sad or angry — there was nothing but complete emptiness. Then she felt waves of heat and cold, just as though she were about to be sick. All sorts of little things were joining together into a large and inescapable conviction that she was useless where she wanted most to be useful. She felt as empty and meaningless as the house.

At the same time, her reason was telling her to take hold of herself, that she was only going through the restlessness and uncertainty that everyone was facing. There was no reason to take those few words seriously, for any voice was brittle and artificial over the telephone, particularly Tom's. Just because she had expected something which she had not received, just because she had been in one mood and he in another, there was no reason for her to make interpretations, but still she was making them.

If she had not been in that antiseptic country house with everything so still, if she had been in New York, she could easily have gone to dinner with some man just to show Tom how she felt about it. There were plenty of men at loose ends in New York, mostly officers on leave. Though she had never gone in for that sort of thing or behaved like some women she knew, there were plenty of men in New York. There had been an infantry major the other night, for instance, who had a wife and three children in Ohio and who had just been ordered back to France. He had asked her to keep talking, just keep talking "like crazy" about anything at all so that he could hear her voice. He had called her up three times to ask her to see him before he left. There were plenty of men in New York, and if Tom was bored, other men found her attractive. She was pulling herself together. It would be better if she were not in the house.

There were overshoes and a heavy coat downstairs. Polly put them on and opened the front door into a cold clear starlit evening. All the lights in Pyefield were out. She must have walked for nearly half a mile to the bridge by the creek.

"My goodness," Mrs. Brewis said when she got back. "Out walking in the dark? I was just going to send him after you. New York's been calling. Ask for New York Operator 32."

Polly was sure that something terrible was going to happen.

"It's Mrs. Brett," she was saying, "Mrs. Thomas Brett."

Polly looked at her watch, the diamond and platinum one that her father had given her. It was only a little after nine o'clock.

"Do you know what New York number could be calling?" someone was asking. The telephone service, like everything else, was getting worse all the time.

"Is this Mrs. Brett?" A man's voice was speaking. "This is Dr. Williamson. I'm speaking for Mr. Fulton. I want to say first there's no immediate reason to be alarmed."

That was the way those damned doctors always talked, and that was how Polly heard that her father had suffered a heart attack. He had been in the library with two men from the office going over something just after dinner, and he had slumped over in his chair, but he had recovered by the time the doctor came. He had said that those salty oysters someone had sent him from Virginia had given him indigestion. It was Dr. Williamson, internist from the Presbyterian, who had said it was not oysters.

"He wants to speak to you himself," the doctor said, "but I don't think it would be wise. . . ."

It was much better to have something happen than to think of something which might, for at least you could meet it face to face, or "face up to it," as they had been saying lately.

"Well, if he wants to speak to me, he'd better," Polly said. "Give him the telephone by his bed, and press the red button."

She could see that tall four-post bed and her father lying on it, and her mother, the doctor, and a nurse near him. His voice sounded as strong as ever, with all its old nasal, vibrant tone. She felt like crying. At least it meant that she was useful again.

"Hello, Poll," he said. "How is it in the sticks?"

"B. F.," she said. "Oh, B. F., darling."

"I'm in bed with two trained nurses," B. F. said. "At least, I am . . . they're not. It wouldn't be proper, would it, with your mother here?"

"B. F., darling," she said. "You ought not to talk so much. I love you."

"They've given me a shot of something," B. F. said. "How's everything up there?"

"Never mind it, darling," Polly said. "It isn't like anything up here. If I can get the gas, I'll drive back tonight."

"Isn't it like anything?" B. F. asked. "Well, it isn't like much of anything here either. Don't let it get you down, Poll. There's no reason to hurry back."

"I'm coming right down," Polly said. "Please do what they tell you. How are you feeling?"

"Fine," B. F. said. "It was only indigestion. We were in there after dinner and . . . I just want to say this, just this."

"Never mind it now," Polly said, but there was no way of stopping him.

"Don't say it isn't like anything. You're wrong there. Everything's like something. Even this is something. Here's the doctor. All right, Doc."

Then his voice was gone. He had wanted to speak to her, just in case there would never be a chance again.

There was a train leaving the junction at 6:05 in the morning, due to arrive at Grand Central at 11:15, but that was not soon enough. It was better to be doing something instead of waiting until six, better to leave the house at once instead of trying to sleep. She was in the kitchen in her mink coat before she had thought it out clearly, telling Mr. Brewis to get out the Packard. Then she was calling up Mr. MacMahon. Mr. MacMahon knew who she was and knew that she was good for it, which was one good thing about money.

"Stop arguing," she was saying to him. "You're driving me to New York. I've got my own car and it's better than yours." It *was* better, too, a 1941 Packard which had gone only ten thousand miles. She remembered how Tom had complained about having a Packard on the place instead of a cheaper car, and she wished Tom could listen to her now. She was not Mrs. Tom Brett any longer, but Polly Fulton who was used to having things done as she wanted them, and used to making people do them. "Don't argue," she was saying again. "Don't tell me you haven't any gas. Find some, and we'll put another can in the car." She had always hated rich, imperious people who threw their weight around, but she was doing just that. "Tell me how much you've got to get," she was saying to Mr. MacMahon, "and then multiply it by two if you want, and you won't have to work all winter." Tom was always talking about helping small people and small business, and she was doing that, too.

When the Packard was out she said she would drive it herself to the junction, and she took some bills out of her purse because she had not forgotten to do something nice for the Brewises. She put her foot down on the accelerator to warm the motor and remembered to powder her nose. It was only when she reached the turn on the mountain road which gave the view of Pyefield and the valley that Polly wondered whether she and Tom would ever live at Pyefield again.

II

It's Up to the Boss

POLLY'S FATHER and mother had purchased a thirty-room apartment on Park Avenue after they had given up spending the winters at Gray's Point. Entering it usually gave Polly an oppressive sense of being poured back into a mold, as though all effort had gone for nothing. She was always worrying for fear a trace of that atmosphere would cling to her and someone would look at her at a gathering of interesting people and say "Park Avenue."

Somehow Park Avenue did something to women, so that they all looked alike and had what she called a "kept" quality. You could also tell a Park Avenue dog, no matter what its breed, from the sheen of its coat and from the way it lifted its feet. You could tell a Park Avenue woman whether she was a bootlegger's wife, or a chorus girl, or someone from the Colony Club. All the jewelry looked alike, and there was even some indefinable quality about Park Avenue flowers and about Park Avenue books from Dutton's. Even if those books had been imported from a British gentleman's library, it seemed to Polly that their very leaves rustled in a certain way when they got to Park Avenue. The women were all trying frantically to be different, but they all tried in the same way at the same time. Polly had once made an effort to have a tweedy, country look on Park Avenue, only to meet dozens of other girls in tweeds, alighting from station wagons with the names of country houses painted on the doors. You could try and try without its doing any good. It was the strongest environment in the world.

It had been a long while since she had arrived at the family's apartment at two o'clock in the morning — not since those parties in the years after she had come out. If you weren't careful, you could go into any of those apartment houses in the sixties and mistake it for yours. The doormen all had the same paternal look, and the carpets and chairs and mirrors and durable art objects were almost interchangeable.

She had the illusion that she was coming back from another party, even after the long, cold ride from Pyefield. She recognized the same night watchman who had been there when she had gone to dances. If he and the elevator man knew about B. F.'s illness, and they must have, for those people were familiar with the health and frailties of everyone in their buildings including the dogs, they were too polite to mention it.

In the little hall outside the elevator there were the white azaleas which were brought in fresh every week from the hothouse, and Polly had a key to the apartment because her father had always wanted her to keep one. There was a dim light burning in the front hall, just as there had been when she got back from dances. She had the old instinct not to awaken anyone, so that the family would not know she had been out so late. The Lawrence portrait of the red-coated Army officer looked shadowy and disapproving in its heavy gold frame, and the lady in the blue dress by Gainsborough had her old, enigmatic, two-o'clock-in-the-morning simper. There was no time to distinguish objects, but she had the impression that everything was where it should be in the shadows. There was the usual clean, soapy smell mingling with the exhalations of fresh flowers, and no sign at all of illness.

She had a feeling of deep relief as she tiptoed up the stairs, for she was sure the apartment would not have been like that if anything more had happened. She knew without anyone's telling her that B. F. was still alive, holding it all together. When she was half-way down the hall, a trained nurse opened the door of her father's bedroom noiselessly, throwing a vague shaft of light across the hallway. She was a plump girl and she had the sleepless look of all night nurses.

"I'm Mrs. Brett," Polly whispered, "Mr. Fulton's daughter. Is he . . ." She stopped because there was no use finishing the question.

"He's doing very nicely," the nurse answered. "He's sleeping."

"Is my mother asleep?" Polly whispered.

The nurse nodded. The doctor had given her something, she said.

"Can I see him?" Polly asked.

She could see him if she was very quiet, and she put down her suitcase softly. B. F. was asleep in a hospital bed which must have been brought in that evening. A shaded light from the corner of the room threw the shadows of his own Elizabethan four-post bed across him. He was lying on his side, brushed and neat, and he looked as though he were having a pleasant dream. He opened his eyes just as Polly bent over him, but Polly was sure that no sound from her had awakened him.

"Hello, Poll," he said.

"Mr. Fulton," the nurse whispered. "It would be better not to talk."

"It isn't anything, Poll," B. F. said. "How are the roads?"

"The main roads were all right," Polly said. "Just go to sleep."

"It's funny, running into something like this," B. F. said. "It's a little out of my line."

He was wearing blue silk pajamas, and he looked as well as he ever had now that his eyes were open.

"What car did you have?" he asked. "That Packard?"

"Yes, the Packard."

"All right," B. F. said. "What time is it?"

"It's half-past two. Darling, go back to sleep."

"All right," B. F. said. "I'll see you in the morning."

"Yes, darling," Polly whispered. "Please go to sleep. There'll be plenty of time to talk."

"That depends," B. F. said. "That depends on the Boss, but I guess He'll let me see you in the morning."

"You do what the Boss tells you," Polly whispered. "Now please go back to sleep." But his eyes were still wide open, and he was smiling.

"I don't mean the doctor, I mean God. He's got a lot on His mind, but I guess He'll let me see you in the morning."

It was the first time she had heard him mention God since she was a very little girl.

"A thing like this makes you think," B. F. said. "Poll."

"Yes, darling," Polly said.

"Don't worry about things not being like anything. Nursie, I think I'll have a glass of water. How many of you girls are there here?"

"Two, Mr. Fulton," the nurse whispered. "Night and day."

"Night and day," B. F. repeated. "Make a note to have the phonograph brought up here tomorrow. I want to hear that record. It's a nice song, 'Night and Day.'"

The nurse followed Polly into the hall and closed the door softly behind her.

"Mr. Fulton's so funny sometimes, isn't he?" she whispered. "Now don't you worry about him, Mrs. Brett."

B. F. could always get on with people.

"I'm not worrying," Polly said.

There was something about her father that made her feel as if he would always be all right anywhere — sick or well, alive or dead. She never had worried about B. F., and now she knew she never would.

Nothing in Polly's room in the apartment had been moved since her wedding day. She had never wanted anything from it except her clothes, because she had felt it would be confusing to have things around her which had other associations. It was like the room in stories which was kept for the erring daughter in case she should ever return. There she was again, and for a while nothing that had happened since she had left to sleep elsewhere seemed to amount to much. She was Polly Fulton again, sitting by her dressing table, brushing out her hair. Instead of feeling married she was almost wondering who might call her up in the morning or whom she might call up. She had been alone too long, and she was dead tired. It was not until she was in bed and half asleep that she thought of sending word to Tom in Washington, and by that time it did not seem to matter.

Polly saw her mother at ten the next morning. She seemed more bewildered than upset — as if B. F.'s sudden illness were another of his unpredictable impulses, like the time he had bought a private plane or the house at Bar Harbor, or had added that wing of an English country house to Gray's Point.

Her mother was wearing a plain skirt and shirtwaist which was like an unconscious rebuke to the rest of the establishment. When she put her arms around Polly and kissed her, she began to cry, and then she wiped her eyes with a lace handkerchief.

"Well, it's happened," she said, "and I always knew it was going to. Please hurry and get dressed, dear." And she sat on the edge of the chaise longue. "I don't see why you don't freeze to death, dear, in those underthings."

Even that morning they were back on the subject of underwear, but not for long, because her mother wanted to tell why she knew it would happen. When they were first married and living in Willett, she said, Burt would never wear any long underclothes either, but only those things they used to call B. V. D.'s before everyone talked in initials; and he would go into that steamy mill in Willett and out again without an overcoat. Even then, he always forgot meals, going to bed at any time, waking up in the middle of the night and reading, and it had grown much worse lately. There would be a telephone call and off he would go to Pittsburgh or Detroit, to one of those meetings, or else to one of those places with initials in Washington. You could not do anything with Burt. Generals, admirals, secretaries and office managers, had been using the apartment like a hotel. You could never tell how many there would be in to dinner, or there might not be dinner at all. It was something about some metal, she thought, though Burt never told her anything. Burt always wanted her to meet those men, though she never knew what under the sun to say to them. She never knew when Burt might want to show them his old silver, or who was going to stay for the night, or whether they would all suddenly call the airport and take a plane for one of those places. There never had been anything anyone could do with Burt.

Polly must hurry and dress because the doctor was there now, and maybe the doctor could make Burt see it was serious.

"I've told Burt he's got to be sensible," she said, "and now you've got to tell him."

B. F.'s room was bright with the peculiarly brilliant winter sunlight. From the window there was a view of the bridge and the East River, so free from haze that you might be looking at it through binoculars. B. F. lay in his hospital bed, but now the back had been raised. The doctor was seated beside him, and the day nurse, a thin, blonde girl, was standing near the open door of the dressing room. B. F. looked more rested than the doctor — in fact, he hardly looked sick at all.

"Hello, Poll," he said. "This is Dr. Williamson. He's a specialist in broken hearts."

The doctor laughed in a placating manner.

"I've never heard it put quite that way," he said.

"Now you listen, Doc," B. F. said, "and you, too, Nursie. I want you both to run out of here for a little while and close the door."

"Just for half an hour," the doctor said, "and you're not to get excited, Mr. Fulton."

"Darling," Polly said when they were gone, "I wish you'd try to do what they tell you."

Polly sat down on the straight chair beside the bed, and he took her hand and held it tight.

"You're a damned nice girl," B. F. said. "Now don't start crying."

"I'm not crying," Polly said. "It's just — it's just dreadful."

"Go over to the table and get a cigarette and light it," B. F. said. "Doctors and nurses always make a room smell. This isn't bad at all, Poll."

"How do you mean it isn't bad?"

He turned his head and looked out toward the river.

"Well, it might have been cancer or something else. A lot of people are dying these days, Poll, and this thing didn't hurt at all. I was dictating a memorandum, and suddenly I wasn't there."

"If you do what they say — " Polly began.

"Don't interrupt me for a minute," B. F. said. "I'm facing it. I'll have a damned good time, maybe quite a lot of time, to think.

Maybe I'll get some idea of what everything's been about. It's going to be fine to put my mind on another whole set of problems."

"What problems?" Polly asked.

"Personal ones," B. F. said. "Now, I've been pretty lucky, materially speaking, and I don't think I've done so badly. Of course, I wouldn't say that I've been socially conscious. You and I have never quite got that straight."

"Darling," Polly said. "I wish you wouldn't worry about that now."

B. F. took her hand again. "I wasn't born into a controlled economy," he said, "but I don't think I ever cheated anyone, not much. Maybe I was paid more than it was worth for what I did, but I've given a lot of work to a lot of people. The boys have always liked me, even the C.I.O."

The great thing about her father was his complete simplicity. He could make anything clear when his mind touched it. She had thought at times that he oversimplified, but now she was not so sure.

"Phil Murray likes me," he said. "Of course, our ideas don't always mesh, but I can understand him. It's all right if you just think of people as people. Everyone's a person, Poll."

She had heard him say it so often that she knew exactly what he was going to say next.

"As long as people have an equal chance, I don't care where they begin. That's about all there is to it. An equal chance for every American boy."

This was the embarrassing phrase that he always used, but he seemed anxious to summarize everything.

"Of course, I'm old-fashioned, Poll," he said. "There's a different model now."

He stopped and cleared his throat and Polly gave him a glass of water. "Where's Tom?" he asked.

"He's in Washington." Polly tried to answer casually and brightly. "I called him up from Pyefield. That was before I knew you were sick. He was coming back on Thursday. I'm going to call him again this morning and he'll drop everything."

"He needn't drop anything," B. F. said. "What's he working for now? The O.W.I.?"

He had asked the same question before, and it was difficult to answer because Polly was never sure herself where Tom was working.

"He's in a great many things," she said, "and they all keep changing."

B. F. moved his head toward the window again.

"He's kind of a funny boy," he said. "I don't see why you ever married him."

"He isn't so funny," she said, "and if you want to know why I married him, I married him because he's like you. Every good daughter ought to be in love with her father."

He looked interested, which showed that it must have been a new idea.

"Maybe I've been in love with you myself," he said. "I've never thought of it that way."

"It's perfectly natural," Polly told him.

"All right," B. F. said. "But Tom isn't like me. He's a different make. He's bright, but he isn't stable. I wouldn't hire him for the office."

"But you never had to hire him."

"No," B. F. said. "I've just been thinking."

Polly moved uneasily in her straight-backed chair. This criterion of B. F.'s that he would not hire someone for his office had always seemed to her narrow and unfair.

"Hasn't it ever occurred to you," she asked, "that there are a great many useful, important people who wouldn't fit into your office? How about President Roosevelt?"

"That's right," B. F. said, "he wouldn't do. He'd overload the organization." But his mind was on something else. "It's a peculiar thing," he went on, "the number of people around who don't know anything and think they do. Now take these boys down in Washington who think they know all about business."

"You mean the ones that you say never sweated out a payroll?" Polly asked.

26

"I wouldn't mind their not knowing anything," B. F. said, "if they only wanted to learn; but they don't even ask questions from people who know. It's a new mental attitude. Tom's like that."

"Now, B. F.," Polly said, and she felt her voice grow sharper. "You don't understand Tom, and you don't try. You'd love his mind if you ever talked to him."

The maddening thing was that B. F. had never tried, and only because Tom was someone he would not hire for the office.

"He discounts me," B. F. said. "He puts me in a category the way all those boys do. There's no such thing as categories. I've been thinking about you and Tom."

"What have you been thinking?"

B. F. closed his eyes for a second, but she knew he was not tired. It was that old habit of his of being able to relax at odd moments, and then of picking up everything just where he had left it.

"About why you two ever got married," B. F. said; "what you see in each other. I guess it's been a little tough on Tom. I guess you're not an easy girl to be married to, Poll."

"You're wrong there," Polly said. "I'm awfully easy. I do everything he wants."

He seldom spoke about Tom and herself, and she dreaded his doing it because she thought it would be emotionally difficult. Yet now surprisingly enough she felt relieved, for he seemed to be nothing more than a disinterested bystander.

"You're like me," he said.

"I'm not like you at all," Polly said. "If you want to know, you've always been a lesson to me in everything not to do. If you want to know, I don't know how Mother's ever stood it."

"I don't know how she ever has either," B. F. said. "But she has." No matter what you said, nothing ever made him angry. "I've never asked you many questions, have I? Not lately, anyway. Do you mind if I ask you one now?"

She minded, but she had to say of course she didn't.

"Are you and Tom happy?"

There it was, and she was sure it was why he had wanted to see her alone.

"Now take Harry," he went on. "Harry's just what he is, and he'll always get along. Harry's married to a nice, peaceful girl, and he isn't restless. I'm not worried about Harry, but I wish you'd tell me. Are you and Tom happy?"

She leaned toward him and stroked his hand.

"It's awfully sweet of you to ask," she said, "but it's a very broad question, isn't it? No two people are completely happy all the time, are they? It all depends on the definition."

"It's something inside you," B. F. said. "That's the only way you can answer it. Your mother and I have been pretty happy. I wish you'd tell me, Poll."

For some reason she was blushing.

"All right," she said, "I'll tell you. We're not very happy right now, but it doesn't mean anything. It's the war. It's — " She found that she was twisting her handkerchief between her fingers and she stopped. "No one has a normal life with this damned war. Everyone will tell you. It's just as though — "

"As though what?" B. F. asked, and now that she had started, she wanted to go on, because it was so much better to hear herself saying it than just to think it.

"It's just as though nothing that used to count counts now. All those things you did and thought — they don't keep two people together any more. You can't go back to them, and you know there's going to be something else, but you don't know what it is."

"Yes," B. F. said, "it's a little like dying, isn't it?" Sometimes he said the most amazing things. He was looking straight in front of him at the silver bamboo design in the Chinese paper on the wall. "You don't know what's going to happen afterwards. You're starting on something new. The main thing is not to be afraid. You're not afraid, are you?"

"No," Polly said, "I'm not afraid."

"Well, that's fine," B. F. said. "That's all I wanted to know."

The whole mood of the room had changed. He was able to move from one subject to another as though his mind were a filing system.

"Aren't you getting tired?" Polly asked.

28

"No," he said, "I'm feeling fine. Where's Bob Tasmin, Poll? I'd sort of like to see him. I've always liked Bob."

"Now wait," Polly said. "Isn't it pretty late to bring Bob Tasmin up? He's in the war. I think he's somewhere down in Washington with his wife."

"I always liked Bob," B. F. said again. "Maybe you should have married Bob."

"Well, it's too late now."

"I was just thinking out loud," B. F. said. "Why didn't you marry Bob?"

"Do you really want to know why?"

"Yes," he said. "I really do."

"Because he was the sort of man you would have liked to hire for the office." She had never thought of it in that way before. "And he wasn't like you, B. F. My God, he wanted me to live in Gray's Point. All he wanted was one of those brick houses in a new development, and dogs, and exercise and dancing. Darling, I'd have been on a committee at the Club. He was everything I wanted to get away from. He isn't intellectual."

"Bob has a good legal mind," B. F. said. "I wish he were here now to do some work on my will."

"I hate legal minds." Polly's voice had risen.

"He knows what he's talking about," B. F. said.

"Who cares what he knows?" Polly answered. "He was absolutely conditioned by the time he was five. He's an anachronism, darling, even his clothes. Yale Club, Mill River Club, and then that exercise."

Just then the nurse tapped on the door.

"The half hour's up," she said.

"All right, Nursie," B. F. answered. "Well, that was quite a talk, Poll. Now I've got time to put my mind on you, we'll have to talk some more. Look, Cutie, I want to leave a thought with you."

"Don't make it sound like one of your letters," Polly said.

"All right," B. F. said.

"And you can only leave the thought," Polly said, "if you don't call me 'Cutie.'"

29

It must have amused him because he always called her Cutie after that.

"Now, Cutie, you go out to the Colony with someone for lunch, and try to see some men tonight, if there are any men left. Try to have a good time. That's my thought." He held her hand tight when she kissed him.

"And don't be afraid. Understand? Have a good time, and don't worry. Come around tomorrow and tell me about tonight."

"I ought to stay here," Polly said. "I don't want to go running around when you're . . ."

B. F. beckoned to the nurse. "Are there any reporters downstairs now, Nursie?"

The nurse looked anxious and she stammered.

"Dr. Williamson talked to them," she answered. "They've gone now."

"Well," B. F. said, "if they've gone, you go too, Poll. Those boys know better than the doctors. That means I'm not news yet."

The office was in charge by this time, and downstairs in the bare little room with the telephones and filing cabinets, where B. F. talked business when he was in the apartment, Miss Silver, his private secretary, was answering calls. She was saying he was much better this morning and that it was too early still to give a definite report. Every time she hung up the telephone it would ring again.

Polly was always good at arranging things and taking over, as they called it — opening flowers, talking to the doctors and to the secretaries, and then to callers. A great many people dropped everything to come and inquire personally, and you had to know just how to treat them and to remember who they were.

They were mostly from those different directors' boards. Mr. Royall, president of the bank with which B. F. was connected, although he was sick with the grippe, got out of bed and came. Homer J. Lovelace, the president of the Bulwer Machine Company, dropped everything and flew from Pittsburgh, bringing with him his own special osteopath in case B. F. should want him. Mr. Lovelace said he knew you could not monkey around with doctors, but he had brought him and he was going to leave him at the Waldorf in case B. F. felt cramped or uncomfortable. Mr. Lovelace had been suffering with stitches in the side himself, and that man was the only one who could take them out. He didn't look like much, but he could straighten out anything. Arthur Murcheson, who was down in Delaware seeing the Hercules people, had left a meeting right in the middle, and he had called up his house at Miami to have everything there all squared away in case B. F. wanted to move South. Mr. Blossom was in town from Toledo, the one who owned Blossom, Jones, Ohio Glass, and with whom B. F. had been working on plastics. If B. F. wanted to go to Arizona, Mr. Blossom was ready to have him flown there.

They all referred to Polly and her mother as "you girls," and they all wanted to send up word to B. F. that they were in there right behind him. They wanted the girls to know there wasn't anything good enough for old B. F., and they wanted B. F. to know that he could relax and that they were all taking over. There was no reason to move B. F. to any hospital because the hospital could move its works right up to the apartment and they could attend to it personally. The thing for B. F. to do was to relax. Then they all sat together in the library, drinking Bourbon and talking to Polly and her mother about B. F. They wanted the girls to know that B. F. was not only a genius but a sweetheart and they all loved him, and they all kept saying "Remember the time — " Remember the time B. F. changed that assembly line at Detroit. Remember the time B. F. established research at Bulmaco. Remember the time they were all in that car playing poker. Something about the poker game made Mr. Lovelace begin to cry.

"I love him," he sobbed. "You can't help loving the old sonofabitch." And then Mr. Murcheson told him there were ladies in the room.

"Excuse me, girls," Mr. Lovelace said.

No one could help loving B. F. The girls would never understand, they couldn't, what B. F. meant to an organization. There just wasn't anybody like B. F. Do you remember what he said, do you remember what he did?

They were right: it was all something that Polly could not understand. They were all beings from another world, beings with only
primitive powers of self-expression. They all came from plain backgrounds with the exception of Mr. Royall, and she remembered that
B. F. had said bankers had to have manners. They were all there
because they were fond of B. F., and their affection made them soft
and awkward and wordy. They just sat there repeating themselves. No one could get production moving like B. F. Put him anywhere for an hour and all the boys would get going, and that was
genius when you thought of labor nowadays. By God, B. F. could
talk to labor better than those conciliators in Washington. B. F.
knew everybody's language.

But they were not speaking Polly's language. That was why she
was so glad when Apples Sandler called her up in the afternoon.
Things were quiet then, and she told Apples she would stop in to
see her at Sutton Place, and besides she had to go to her own apartment sometime to get some clothes if she was going to stay at the
family's. If everything was all right, they might even have dinner
somewhere. . . .

III

Encore les Martinis

IT WAS refreshing seeing Apples and her apartment at Sutton Place with all its glass and mirrors and modern, whitish furniture. There were glass-topped coffee tables, and Steuben glass fishes on the mantelpiece, and wire sculptures with little beads that you could move up and down, and three abstract pictures by a new man who, Apples said, kept growing on you.

"Oh, darling!" Apples said, after they had thrown their arms about each other. "You look simply dead. A Colonel Beyers is coming up, an Air Force one, and that commander — you know, the submarine one who knew Arthur at Nouméa. I couldn't find where they were to put them off, but we can talk ourselves out before they come. Would you like tea, or a drink?"

Polly sat down in a curved chair that was also half a bookcase. It was so low that she almost fell into it, but once she was there she felt comfortable.

"Just a long, cold glass of water," Polly said. "That's the way I feel."

Apples pushed a bell beside the fireplace.

"I do wish they weren't coming," she said, "but when Father was sick, everyone treated me like a cloistered nun, and you've got to keep on living."

"That's what B. F. told me," Polly said.

"And Chuck's only going to be here for three more days," Apples said. "He's got his orders."

She was referring to her submarine commander. Apples was always too obvious to conceal anything; she might as well have told Polly that she was crazy about him and be done with it instead of

33

being transparently devious, and it made Polly sorry for Arthur out there in the Pacific.

"Marie," Apples was saying to her maid, a grim Norman-French girl in a starched apron, who never smiled, "*apportez une verre de l'eau pour Madame Brett.*" Apples' French was rudimentary, but she loved to speak it.

"*Bonjour,* Marie," Polly said. Her own French was very good.

"*Bonjour, Madame,*" Marie said.

"She still doesn't know what happened to her farm," Apples whispered.

"What farm?" Polly asked.

It was very hard to keep up with everything, particularly after that day.

"Her family's farm near St. Lô," Apples told her.

Polly could never quite accept the change in Apples since their schoolgirl years together at Heatherbloom Hall. Apples had been a dumpy, clumsy girl then, but now she had a lacquered hair-do and plucked eyebrows, and a made-up mouth that changed her whole expression. Her figure, too, in a carefully preserved green Schiaparelli dress, was svelte and graceful, but underneath this deliberately cultivated surface, she was still Apples to Polly, dear Apples. Polly would always remember when Apples had not been quite honorable at Heatherbloom Hall, when Apples had kept a boy's picture on her bureau when such things weren't allowed, and had said it was her brother. Apples had been summoned before the Senior Council and made to apologize to the class. No matter what her latest phase might be, Polly always thought of her as Apples, which, of course, was not her name. Her real name was Olivia, and she had married a Yale boy six years before named Arthur Paxton, a friend of Bob Tasmin's, and Polly had been the matron of honor.

"I've been thinking about you all day, precious," Apples said.

It was a relief to talk to an old friend, to be able to say what you wanted without having to be careful. She could tell Apples all about her worries at Pyefield and the drive down without having to explain too much.

"He doesn't look sick at all," Polly said and her voice choked. "He's so damned brave. I don't know how to say it. He's so — he doesn't seem to mind it."

She could tell Apples anything.

"Polly darling," Apples said. "Don't you want some Scotch or a Martini?"

"No, thanks," Polly said. "Not now."

"Well, you mustn't let it get you down."

"It doesn't," Polly said, "but it's just as though he could see everything. He wanted to know if Tom and I were happy."

"Now precious," Apples said. "Are you sure you don't want a Martini?"

"I wish everything weren't so mixed up," Polly said. "How can anyone be happy?"

"Where's Tom now?" Apples asked.

"Where he always is, down in Washington."

Apples lighted a cigarette. "I wish lipstick didn't come off on everything," she said. "Poll, do you think there's anyone down in Washington? I don't want to worry you. I'm just asking."

Polly tried to sit up straighter, but the functional chair was not made for it.

"Apples," she said. "Have you heard anything? If you have, don't pretend you haven't."

"Why, Poll, if I had, I'd have told you right away."

"Then why did you ask?" Polly felt annoyed and very edgy, but then Apples was her best friend and she had a right to ask.

"Now don't be upset, precious," Apples said. "I was just thinking everybody's getting to be so emotionally unstable. You can't keep your love-life all tied up and in a box. At least I can't. It keeps readjusting itself. At least, you have Tom right with you. He isn't an abstraction."

"All right," Polly said. "Let's not talk about it any more. I'm sick of thinking about Tom."

"And I'm sick of thinking about Arthur," Apples said. "My God, Poll, I can't remember what he looks like. I can't remember the reason for anything."

"I'm sick of thinking of reasons," Polly said. "You just keep going over them, and they never get you anywhere."

Apples pressed the bell again.

"Marie," Apples said. "*Apportez deux Martinis.* I'm going to have one if you're not. Poll, who do you think I saw yesterday, right outside the Ambassador? I saw Will Tasmin. He's in some sort of Public Relations at some flying field in Miami. He didn't remember me at first."

"You can't expect anyone to recognize you," Polly said, "when you keep doing yourself over."

"It's better than staying the same and just looking at yourself," Apples said. "Poll, I wish you'd let me take you to Elaine's. She gives a personality diagnosis."

"Never mind my personality," Polly said. "How was Will looking?"

"Just the same," Apples answered. "He has that same squint. The uniform doesn't change him. He doesn't look a bit like Bob."

"Did he say how Bob was?"

"He said Bob's in the Pentagon Building," Apples answered, "and he keeps going around on missions. Something to do with Intelligence. I always adored Bob."

His name had come up again. It was like shaking pebbles in a bottle and having a certain pebble persist in rising to the top.

"If you adored him, why didn't you marry him?" Polly asked.

"Why, precious," Apples said. "How could I when you had him all staked out?"

In the distance the apartment doorbell rang, and the faint sound made Apples jump from her chair and take a quick look at herself in the mirror above the fireplace.

"There they are," she said. "Poll, let's forget everything." She sounded just the way she used to at Heatherbloom Hall. "We'll all go somewhere to dinner — you can have the colonel — and then we'll go to the Stork Club or somewhere."

"I can't," Polly said. "Not in this dress. And besides I ought to go to the apartment and pack." But it was not such a bad idea to forget everything.

"Why, darling," Apples said. "You look just right. You're beautiful." B. F. had honestly wanted her to go somewhere that night, and it might upset him if she didn't.

There was nothing reasonable or constructive in having cocktails and going out somewhere with Apples and two strange men. Neither she nor Apples would have dreamed of doing such a thing before the war. She would have felt like one of those unattached girls who keep giving men their telephone numbers. Now you were always being asked to do something about someone who was in New York at loose ends for a few days. Somehow, the nation's uniform made all men look very much alike after a year of service. Even their backgrounds were erased by the uniform, and by a few months in the European or Pacific theaters, so that you were always completely in the dark about them at first. Still, it was patriotic to go on the assumption that all officers were gentlemen, particularly when they got to be colonels and commanders.

"Polly," Apples was saying. "This is Colonel Beyers and Commander Wildhaus — Mrs. Brett."

Wildhaus, the one that Apples called Chuck, was dark, saturnine, and discouraged. His eyes were narrow, and he wore the insignia of the submariner. Colonel Beyers was one of those young Air Force colonels with a lot of ribbons.

"What a lovely room!" Colonel Beyers said. "I'm always partial to glass. Lovely."

That speech made him, at least, the sort of person who used the adjective "lovely." Commander Wildhaus made no comments on the room. He had obviously been there often.

"You'll forget the glass when you get around a couple of these Martinis, Mike," he said. "Mrs. Paxton really makes them. Colonel Beyers is one of these wine and food boys, aren't you, Mike?"

"Oh, not really," Colonel Beyers said. "But there's nothing more lovely than a Martini. They're rare in London. Are you familiar with London, Mrs. Brett?"

"Yes," Polly said, "I used to be." And she smiled. "But I haven't been there lately. Have you, Colonel?"

"Back and forth. Leaving for there the day after tomorrow," the colonel said. "Back from leave to the old 86th, but let's skip it."

"I didn't bring it up. You did," Polly said.

The colonel had finished his Martini.

"Darling," he asked, "what has kept us apart all these years?"

"I wouldn't know," Polly said. "Where can you have been?"

"Right here in this terrific city," the colonel said, "before this fuss started. Right in the National Broadcasting Company."

He threw the name in lightly as though he expected her to be impressed.

"Oh, you were one of those people, were you?" Polly said, and she tried to imagine him in civilian clothes. The colonel was like the men who had come to the apartment when Tom had done a piece on "The Critics' Fifteen Minutes." If he were not in uniform he would be wearing a hand-painted tie.

"Why do you say 'one of those people'?" the colonel asked. "Do you know about radio?"

"My husband has something to do with it sometimes," Polly said. "Speeches."

The colonel looked at Polly in a way which indicated that he was one of those men who know they have a faculty with women. He was not the misunderstood, little-boy type, or the strong, silent type, or the man who was about to go back there and face death alone, although she supposed that he might eventually use some of these poses. Now he was only intellectual and world-weary. At any rate, he was handsome in a way, with dark eyes, a straight nose and a firm but temperamental mouth, and a dimple on his chin. Polly wished he did not have that dimple.

"Brett . . . You don't mean — you're not Mrs. Tom Brett?"

He asked the question incredulously, showing clearly that Commander Wildhaus must have told him that they were just going up to an apartment to see a hot little number he knew. It made Polly angry at Apples.

"Well, well," he said. "Tom used to be quite a pal of mine. We worked on some hush-hush stuff for the Air Corps before they wanted me in uniform."

"Tom's always working on things like that," Polly told him.

"To think of your being a friend of Chuck's girl," the colonel said.

"It's a small world, isn't it?" Polly answered, and the colonel laughed.

"It's a world that's full of a great number of unexpected concatenations of circumstances. To think that I should be wandering lonely as a cloud talking to Jack and Charlie and end up in a hall of mirrors with Polly Fulton. You must be *the* Polly Fulton if you're Mrs. Brett. Aren't you?"

She was sure by now that he was not even café society, just one of those people who pretended to know everyone.

"Tom always knows everybody," Polly said.

"Tom has a lovely way of making friends," the colonel answered. "I know another personal friend of yours too. You don't mind if I call you Polly, do you? And you call me Mike."

"No," Polly told him, "I don't mind particularly."

"Well, that other personal friend, Polly, is Milton Ouerbach. Good old Milt. He's not only an ace commentator, but he's an integrated person, and he knows his Public Relations."

That was what Mike was, of course — not a real flyer, but one of those Air Force Public Relations officers, who went to England to handle policies and stories. At the same time, though, Polly had never been so glad to be desirable to someone. There was nothing like it to change one's whole point of view. He was a real New Yorker, he said, although his roots were in the Middle West. Did you ever notice how real New Yorkers all came from somewhere else and fell in love with the city and made it home? He had started, just a kid from the Middle West, on a newspaper, then advertising, then radio. He had a good spot in N. B. C. before the war, and they simply had to have him in Public Relations. Ask him about anyone. He knew everybody in SHAEF. Eisenhower, Spaatz, Tedder, everybody.

"But let's skip all that now," he said. "My mind just goes around in circles."

She saw Apples and Commander Wildhaus on the other sofa, sitting close together, whispering, and Wildhaus was patting Apples' hand.

"Let's talk about you," the colonel said. "Frankly, I'm simply fascinated by — you."

It sounded painfully juvenile, but as long as someone was fascinated, Polly did not mind it for the moment.

"Why are you fascinated?" she asked, and she spoke in that timid, husky voice of hers that men always liked.

"Do you really want to know, Polly darling?"

He was settling into the "dear" and "darling" stage, and another time she would have put him in his place, but now it was relaxing and it took her mind off everything.

"I'd like to know," she said.

"We're both ships without rudders, aren't we, Polly darling?" he said. "I have an appearance of assurance, but I'm frustrated really. The women I've known, the things I've done, sometimes they seem to amount to so little."

"I suppose you must have had a lot of women in your life," Polly said.

"You can see that, can you, darling?" Mike said. "A moment of loneliness, a moment of surcease. Oh God, women! But I'm not referring to you, darling."

"It's charming of you not to. Why aren't you?" Polly asked.

"Because you're real, a real and lovely and honest person, but frustrated and lonely, drifting. I know that beautiful butterfly look. You're not secure, you're not happy, any more than I. Do you know what I think?"

"No," Polly answered, but of course she knew what he was going to think.

"I think we might both be a great help to each other."

"It's sweet of you to think so, Colonel Beyers," she said.

"The name is Mike."

"All right," Polly answered. "Mike."

Then Apples was speaking.

"Children," Apples said. "We're all going to Chambord for dinner, and then we'll go to the Stork or somewhere afterwards. Right?"

"Right," Mike said. "But couldn't we have another round of Martinis first? Giulio never mixes them to suit me. Those Italians."

"Marie," Apples called, "*encore les Martinis.*"

Then Commander Wildhaus thought of something.

"Do you remember Byron's poem on his birthday?"

"What are you, for God's sake, an anthology?" Colonel Beyers asked.

"If you're not educated, I am," said Commander Wildhaus. "Besides, it's my birthday too."

"Oh, Chuck, darling," Apples cried. "Why didn't you tell us?"

"I'm telling you now," Commander Wildhaus answered, "and I'm trying to think of a poem to fit my own personal status. Don't stop me. How does that Byron thing begin?"

" 'Through life's road, so dim and dirty,' isn't it?" Polly asked.

"That's it," Commander Wildhaus said. "There's an educated gal. Now don't stop me."

No one stopped him. The commander stood up, groping at the air, as though he were walking in his sleep.

" 'Through life's road, so dim and dirty, I've reached the age of six and thirty.' "

"Yaa-a-ay," Colonel Beyers called. "That's telling them, Chuck, that's putting it on the line."

" 'And there's naught in this life to come up nex', except some braid and maybe sex.' How'm I doin'? That's my birthday poem."

"Oh, Chuck!" Apples began to giggle, and Polly saw that all the three were laughing. "He ought to put it in the *New Yorker*. It's just like Thurber, isn't it, Poll?"

"Exactly like Thurber," Polly said. "The same unworldly ring."

"Now don't go sour on us, sweet," the colonel said. "Don't look now, but Chuck's a lovely person."

"Well, let's be going," Apples was saying. "Polly and I are going to powder our noses, and the Navy can show the Army where it goes, won't you, Chuck?"

Polly wished she could get into the spirit of it. Before she was married, she had gone to all sorts of speak-easies and night clubs, and it had been part of an accepted convention, but now she felt like a little chippy being taken on a party. The colonel was sitting very close to her in the taxicab. Suddenly he took her hand, and she did not draw it away because that would have seemed stuffy.

"You don't mind, do you?" he asked. "Such a lovely little hand. You're not happy, are you, sweet?"

"I'm not unique in that, am I?" Polly said.

"You're so utterly brave," the colonel said. "You don't know it, but I'm going to make you very happy."

Polly did not know it, and yet it was nice to have someone make the effort. She only wished he were more like people she was used to and understood, and she wished he would not show off. He would have been much more attractive if he had stopped pretending that he knew everything about New York, and that he was an important factor in winning the war. He was admitting that Tooey Spaatz could not get on without him, and he was talking about food. He could eat a K-ration or a C-ration if he had to, but good food was a part of culture. He was talking about the more important dishes at Chambord, and about the other restaurants they might have gone to, this French one or that Italian one, and he was telling about the headwaiters. It seemed that all the headwaiters knew him because he liked food and service. It was not so much the tips you paid them as having something intelligent to say about the wine and the pressed duck . . . but Polly was only half-listening.

She was thinking of other nights when she had sat in taxicabs and had gone to other dinners and dances. It was Bob Tasmin who used to take her out to places like Chambord or the Silver Slipper, something that Tom had done very seldom, because apparently you never did that sort of thing after you were married. Tom had always been indignant about the godawful price you paid for an evening's entertainment, but Bob Tasmin had never spoken of it, though it must have meant that he had skimped somewhere when he took her to those places. Bob would have paid the taxi driver without calling him Buddy and telling him to keep the change. He would have spoken more quietly to the waiter, and he would not have told her that she was a lovely, lonely character. He would not have waved to other people, and he would not have tried to exhibit her; instead he would have made her feel that she was the one person he wanted to see. He would not have indulged in free lectures about love and life, and he would have been able to drink without becoming noisy, and he certainly would not have tried to play footie under the table.

She was angry at herself for thinking of Bob Tasmin because they all were not having a bad time really, and she and the colonel were saying things that made them both laugh — but what on earth would she do about Colonel Beyers when the party was over? She was almost certain that he was not going to say good night easily, and at moments she was not sure that she wanted him to. Sooner or later she would have to go down to her own apartment and pack her bag before she went back to Park Avenue, and she supposed the colonel would go down there with her. And then what was going to happen, and what would she do if it happened?

It was not fair to keep comparing him to Bob Tasmin, but when they got to the Stork Club she thought of Tasmin again. Bob would not have called the headwaiter by his first name, or if he had, he would not have made it sound as if they were both in the same college fraternity. He would not have fussed about the table or fussed about champagne.

"Isn't he adorable?" Apples said in the dressing room. "I knew he'd be mad about you, darling."

At any rate, he danced better than Bob Tasmin. He held her close and kept saying they were made to dance with each other. He was talking about going back to the Squadron again. Bob Tasmin would never have mentioned it. He would never have used that line about rudderless ships, either. At the same time, when she was in the colonel's arms on the dance floor, she forgot everything else now and then, and she was not bothered in the least by what Tom might think about it.

As far as she could remember the champagne had no great effect on her, and besides, if she had not taken some, she could not have stood those night clubs. She could not imagine where all the patrons came from or what they did in the daytime or how they had the money to spend on such an evening, or why. They were trying in a sad sort of way to manufacture a romantic moment, and naturally this was all that night clubs were for, unless you were very young.

43

You danced about on those crowded little floors, or listened to those entertainers, only in order to push beyond your mental horizon things that would happen to you inevitably.

The colonel had said that he was unhappy, that his wife had left him six months ago just like that. They had been married in '41, and suddenly they had realized that there was nothing to hold them, and it was better, wasn't it, much better, just to call it off. The colonel said he was footloose now, which was why meeting a lovely character like Polly meant so much to him, because just seeing her made him feel that there was a future and not a past. The colonel was dancing with her beautifully and telling her that there was nothing like kids to make a home, and he was asking her whether she had any, and when she said she hadn't, he asked her why. She was surprised to find herself telling him that Tom had never wanted any, and she could not understand why she should go into such details with a stranger.

"He's a heel if he doesn't want kids," the colonel said. "Kids and roller skates and tricycles make a home. I want a home. I'm tired of sleeping around."

A few years ago no one would have said such things, but now people blurted everything out with such disregard for amenities that they talked about sex and intestines as easily as they talked of the war.

"What are you thinking about, my sweet?" the colonel asked her.

"About a man who used to take me dancing."

"What did he have that I haven't?" the colonel asked.

It must have been at about this time that Polly said she was tired. She had been up late for two nights, and she had to go to the apartment to pack a few things before going back to the family. It was not hard to get away because Apples and the commander made no objections — in fact, they seemed relieved. Of course, it was only courteous for the colonel to say he would go with her, and there was the usual tiresome business of saying that she could go downtown perfectly well by herself, and the colonel's saying that she certainly could not. Then there was the tiresome business of not being too emphatic about it. She was not sure how Colonel Beyers would

44

behave alone in the taxi, but he behaved very well, considering. He was suddenly so considerate and silent that Polly found herself saying those things that everyone always said.

"I've had an awfully nice time," she said. "I'm sorry I've been so *distrait*."

"You've been lovely," the colonel said. "You're a lovely character." And he put his arm around her.

It was such a conventional gesture nowadays that it would have been very gauche if she had drawn away.

"You're tired," the colonel said. "Just try to forget what's bothering you."

"All right," Polly said, "I'm trying."

"You see," the colonel said, "out of our lives this is a moment that belongs to you and me. No one can take it from us."

He was right. Such as it was, it was their little moment, but she was thinking about Bob Tasmin. It was ridiculous because she had never thought of Bob in the role of a great lover. Bob Tasmin would never have talked about a moment. Instead, he would have sung one of those old songs he knew. He had always been very reticent about physical contacts, not at all like the colonel.

"Why do you live down on West Twelfth Street?" asked the colonel.

She was glad to have him say something impersonal.

"We like it down there," she answered.

She was too tired to tell him that Tom was always self-conscious about being married to a rich girl, and that he had insisted on a small walkup apartment in one of those brick buildings downtown, the rent of which he had started to pay himself . . . but he had not been doing so lately.

"That's all right, Buddy," the colonel said to the taxi driver. "You keep the change."

The apartment was on the second floor of a late Victorian house. The living room was high-ceilinged with a black marble fireplace and tall windows. It was a part of old New York, Tom used to say, and they did build beautiful houses then. The big sofa in front of the fire and the comfortable chairs and the books made the spacious room dignified and livable, and very little had been done in the way of remodeling except for a newly built hall that led past the single large bedroom to the dining room and the kitchen.

"This is a charming, natural place!" the colonel said. "Do you mind if I light the fire? There's nothing so lovely as an open fire."

He looked very handsome with his ribbons as Polly lit the candles.

"I'll get you something to drink," she said. "What would you like?"

"Oh," the colonel said, "just a skitch and soda. Here, let me help you, sweet."

He went with her into the kitchen, saying, as of course he would, that he was wonderful in a kitchen. Then there was that usual business of holding the ice cubes under the hot-water tap and of having them fall into the sink and washing them.

"Here," the colonel said. "Pour yourself a real drink, sweet."

Then they went back into the living room and sat side by side on the sofa, looking at the fire.

"How stupid," the colonel said, "to spend a hundred bucks when we could have been here all the time. It's out of this world, isn't it?"

"Yes," Polly said. "It's certainly out of this world."

If it had not been for that telephone conversation with Tom and for everything else, she would never have considered entertaining a man in her apartment at half-past one in the morning. The colonel set down his glass and put his arm around her, and she knew he was going to kiss her.

"Do you mind, sweet?" he asked.

"No," Polly answered, "not particularly."

No one had kissed her that way for a long while. She wished she did not think of all those phrases in books, "he kissed her carefully," "he kissed her lingeringly," "he kissed her savagely." At any rate, as far as Polly could recall, she did not mind it.

"Oh God," the colonel said, "you lovely, lovely, lonely character."

It must have been then that Polly said she had to put some things in a bag because she really had to go uptown, but the colonel's arm was still around her.

"Don't go yet, sweet," the colonel said. "Take some more of your

46

skitch and soda. This is like a real voyage of discovery, isn't it?" And he kissed her again, carefully or tenderly or fiercely, or however he did it.

"Mike," she said. "You stay here. I've just got to throw a few things in a suitcase, and then I'll be right back."

She felt somehow that everything would be under control and conventional if she once had her suitcase packed and had it standing in the living room.

"Let me help you, sweet," the colonel said. "I'm the world's champion packer-upper."

"Please, Mike," she asked him, "just stay here. I won't be a minute."

She did not know very clearly what she was packing, but she knew that she had to occupy herself. Her hands were trembling as she opened her bureau drawers and her alligator-skin suitcase. It was an impossible situation, and she could not even remotely imagine herself being carried away by it. Yet for the first time in a long while she felt that she was alive and living. She was leaning over her suitcase when she heard his step in the hall, and then before she even saw him, he had her in his arms. He was kissing her again, and her knees were weak. At least she was living, at least she was doing something. She was even thinking that it might not be entirely impossible.

"Mike," she said, "don't, please." But what was it they said about women? They always said no when they meant yes. It was not impossible at all. She could call the family and tell them that she was staying in the apartment for the night.

"Mike," she said again, "don't. Please." And then she thought of Bob Tasmin. That must have been what stopped it. Suddenly the whole thing became a sordid, vulgar, meaningless surrender and she wrenched herself away.

"That's enough of this damned nonsense," she said. "Go in the other room and finish your drink, and then we're leaving."

She had never been so close to doing anything like that, and she wondered whether the colonel knew how near she had been to saying something else.

47

His face grew brick-red. "Look here," he said, "you gave me every reason to suppose — and don't say you didn't, because I know."

The humiliating thing was his knowing it, and it was only fair to acknowledge it.

"Well, it's different now," she said. "I'm sorry." And it was true. She was sorry about everything.

"But what happened?" His voice was hurt and incredulous. "What did I do wrong?"

She could not very well tell him that a memory of someone whom she had hardly seen for years had been what happened. It must have started with looking at those scrapbooks. Actually there was nothing she could tell him, but she was fair enough to understand how he felt.

"I'm awfully sorry, Mike," she said. "I wish you'd let me pay you for the dinner and the champagne and everything. I'm really sorry. I guess I'm not the type."

Then he was what he had been before — a dreadful, harmless sort of person, but not so dreadful either.

"It's very lovely of you to put it that way," he said, "but it's merely money. The evening has been a real pleasure anyway, and Polly, you're a lovely, enigmatic character. I'll just get back to my skitch and soda and write it off to experience."

"Yes," Polly said. "Let's both do that."

"A thing like this is the basis for a sincere friendship actually," the colonel said. "Somehow I never can be friends with anyone I sleep with, can you?"

Polly found that she was blushing.

"I don't suppose you'll believe it," she told him, "but I wouldn't really know."

"You're a very, very funny and lovable character," the colonel said. "Yes, I believe you."

She almost wished she could tell Bob Tasmin sometime, but she never could. It would always be one of those things that you kept only to yourself and thought of before you went to sleep. She would have liked to tell him that he had saved her from something worse than death, or at any rate, from something.

48

IV

They All Turned Up There Sometime

WHENEVER Bob Tasmin traveled to the war theaters for G–2, as was happening again when he went out to the West Pacific as an Intelligence officer in Lieutenant General Waldron G. Bogart's team, he was invariably surprised when he met someone he knew. After all most of the people in his own age group had something to do with the war. If they were not in the line combat forces, they were in Supply or Military Government, or they were writers or news commentators, or they were something. Still, he was always incredulous about those encounters.

It was all a little like meeting people at those old unwieldy subscription dinners or testimonial banquets or whatever they were called that used to be given before the war, to raise funds for indigent musicians or for the control of parenthood, for race equality, or to greet someone who had lived to be eighty, or someone who had just returned from Tibet. He had to go because Mildred had bought tickets at ten dollars a head. It was a nice way to pay back people, Mildred used to say, by getting up a table, or someone else would pay back Mildred by getting up a table. Each of those occasions was like every other.

There almost always seemed to be snow and slush, and Mildred would never wear overshoes. The taxi would take you to the side entrance of one of those large New York hotels that used to be having trouble meeting its bonded indebtedness, and once inside, you would find yourself moving with a mass of moist people in a sort of migration that was beyond your own volition. You would find yourself jammed in one of those gilded elevators — direct to the Grand Ballroom, no other stops, this way to the Save Finland

49

Dinner, and have your tickets ready, please. The ladies' cloakroom to the right. The gentlemen's checkroom to the left. Cocktails now being served in the Fontainebleau Room on the Mezzanine. You began to labor under a paralysis of dull resentment at finding yourself in a place like that, particularly when it was your own fault partially. You used to say to yourself that this was the very last time you would ever let yourself, so help you, get into anything like this. You said it, though you knew very well that you would get into something like it again some day.

"You will have a good time when you get there," Mildred always said, "and besides, you may meet someone useful."

He used to ask Mildred in what way she thought that anyone they met there could be useful. No one was ever impressed by him at those functions, no one ever offered him a job or even a small loan. There was no use being cynical about it, Mildred used to say. How would it look if they sat at home when everyone they knew was going and when they were sponsors?

Then, invariably, just when his senses were blunted by the noise and the motion, he would see someone whom he had known quite well at some time or other, someone he had met on a ship, or at Gray's Point, or in college. First he would have some doubts, but then the face would become more and more familiar.

"Hello," he would say. "How did you ever get into anything like this?"

He would ask because he really wanted to know the answer and he also wanted to explain why he was there, too, and make it clear that he could not help it.

You could not help being in the war either once you were in it. He had not wanted to be on Bogart's staff. They had started out for Guam from Washington, all Regular Army except himself, and even after a month together the general was still disconcerted by Bob's civilian background. The general had asked him at least three times how he had been assigned to such an operation. He wanted to tell the general that it was not his fault. In the early days when everything was expanding, they had sent him to staff school because he was good at papers and reports. He had been placed in the Japanese section by accident, and he had been made a lieutenant colonel because rank was necessary. The office at the Pentagon was very much like a club, but he could not tell the general that.

"I don't see why they didn't give me Hokey Smith," the general said several times. "I asked for Hokey Smith — not that I'm criticizing you in the slightest. This is a big opportunity for you. Get me Map A for Operation Blue."

Tasmin knew how to sit at table and laugh at the general's jokes. He knew just where to stand and when to speak and when to keep his mouth shut. He had been on the same sort of party several times before. He had been sent to London to work on Operation Peaches, he had been in Casablanca by order of the Joint Chiefs to work on Chariot. The mission to Guam would be another of those jobs involving volume after volume of secret documents. He would be more of a librarian than a soldier, a consultant waiting outside the conference room with the other consultants, to produce the maps and orders when the admirals and generals called for them.

It was perfectly obvious that most able-bodied persons would arrive sooner or later at some such place as Guam, but when he saw Harry Fulton just outside one of the Quonset huts, he felt that old bewilderment at seeing a friendly face. Harry looked unfamiliar to him in a uniform with captain's bars and he did not belong in that light yellow sticky mud that was steaming in the sun. It was necessary for Tasmin to make mental adjustments and to pull memories into order, for all sorts of recollections of home and of other people appeared when he saw Harry.

"Well, Harry," he said, "how did you ever get into anything like this?"

Harry Fulton's staff insignia showed that he also was attached to some general, and Harry was just the sort of boy that a general would want. Tasmin could almost hear the general talking about Harry to some other general.

"I have a new aide. Young Harry Fulton. Yes, that's the one. Burton Fulton's son, and he is a good kid. Just like any other kid. Now when I was at dinner in New York at the Fultons' . . . Oh, Harry, get my field jacket, will you?"

Harry was staring at him through dark glasses of the General

51

MacArthur type. From his dress and deportment, it was obvious that he must have seen General MacArthur somewhere. In some subtle way, he was assuming the manners and attitudes of the general. There was a similar outward thrust of the jaw, the same dauntless tilt of the head, the same half-careless and photogenic, but military, way of standing. If Harry had been carrying a cane or swagger stick, he would have been a small model of MacArthur saying, "I shall return." But then, you had to imitate someone if you were not a professional soldier.

"Why, Bob," Harry said, "is that you? Long time no see." And they shook hands.

The expression annoyed Bob Tasmin slightly. It reminded him that Harry had been picking up the glib phrases of the moment ever since he was a kid, and Harry still looked pretty young.

"Who did you think I was," Bob asked, "General Sheridan?"

Harry laughed, and Bob remembered that Harry had always had an embarrassed way of laughing, as though he was not quite sure what the joke was about and wanted to be nice but was still anxious not to make too much noise.

"Of all the people I least expected to see here," Harry said. "Well, well, this is quite a shock! When did you blow in?"

A hint of patronage in this remark made it also annoying. Harry was being a battle-scarred veteran from the great open spaces over there. He was wearing a yellow ribbon with three stars on it, and he had three service bars on his left sleeve for eighteen months overseas, but even so, a second of mental arithmetic reminded Bob Tasmin that Harry was not quite thirty yet, and he himself was forty. It also occurred to him that he outranked Harry. A lieutenant colonel might mean anything or nothing, but still he had the rank. He found himself looking at Harry in a calculating, supercilious way that he had copied from other officers who had served with troops.

"You're not a flyer, are you, Harry?" he asked.

"No," Harry said. "Good God, no!"

"Then how do you get to wearing one of those floppy caps?"

"Oh, that," Harry said, and he pulled the visor a little more over his right eye. "The general has the staff wear them."

"What general?"

"Old man Pinkham," Harry answered. "He's tough, but he's a nice old guy when you get to know him."

Perhaps they were all nice old guys when you got to know them.

"Any relation to Lydia Pinkham?" Bob asked.

Harry laughed again.

"Haven't you been in this man's war long enough to learn not to make cracks?" he asked.

"Haven't you been in this man's war long enough to get over calling it 'this man's war'?"

"Well, you tell me then," Harry said, "whose war is it? I flew over with the old man. Luzon. There's a lot going on here, fella, in case you don't know it."

"You have learned a lot of words, haven't you?" Bob said. "If you don't mind, don't call me 'fella,' and I do know there's a lot going on."

"More damn brass," Harry said, "and whistle-stop boys. What brass are you with? When did you blow in?"

"This morning," Bob told him. He was already getting over being annoyed by Harry. They were getting back to a half-forgotten relationship which had existed between them once. "I came along from Washington with General Bogart. I am attached to him for the trip."

Harry was looking at him with respect.

"Gosh," Harry said. "I didn't know you were in with the Joint Chiefs. Are you stopping at headquarters?"

Bob nodded. "They've got us all over there."

"Well, well, that's wonderful!" Harry said. "Let's get together at the club tonight. It's been a long time no see."

There was a fine view of the ocean and a gentle breeze was blowing. They were standing on a bare hill in the sun near a greenish two-story prefabricated building with an outside staircase. Ammunition carriers and jeeps and reconnaissance cars and small touring cars with generals' stars on the plates were all parked in front of it. The air overhead hummed with planes and from the distance there came a series of dull explosions.

"They're still blowing out the coral," Harry said. "It's out of this world, isn't it?"

53

"How is Polly?" Bob asked.

When his sister's name was mentioned, Harry took off his dark glasses and put them in his pocket, and then he looked just as he used to, with brown eyes and a thin, anxious face, not confident like his father, but with the same high forehead and the same long and rather delicate hands. He looked like a newer version of his father — more streamlined, and at the same time, more fragile.

"Poll?" he said. "Oh, Polly is fine. When did you last see Poll?"

"Not for quite a while," Bob said. And there was a short and embarrassed silence.

"That guy she is married to . . ." Harry said. "Well, Poll can always work things out. Did you know I'm married, too?"

It was curious that you could drift away from old associations so completely. You would become involved in some new crisis or in some new interest, and it would be like turning the page of a book to new names and another chapter. Those old friendships were back somewhere among the turned pages, but there was never much time to review them. The war had knocked everything galley-west. It blotted out the past the way a smoke screen erased the horizon. It drew you into yourself, confining you to a few essential contacts only.

"Yes, I remember," Bob said. "I always mean to write letters about things like that, and I never do. Let's see, when was it you got married, Harry?"

"August 15, 1942. Period!" Harry answered.

He was a little uncertain what Harry meant by "Period!" — whether it meant joy or resignation, or simply nothing.

"Let's see — August 1942," Tasmin said, and he found himself looking at the flagpole by the green headquarters building. All those headquarters looked alike, even when they were established in Grosvenor Square or at the Saint George Hotel in Algiers. There were always the same jeeps and touring cars, the same signs on the doors, the same orderlies and the same M. P.'s. "August — That's why I didn't do anything about it."

"Were you in the North African show?" Harry asked. "You really have seen this man's war."

Tasmin looked at the flag again. It was rippling beautifully in the breeze, like the flag in a technicolor film.

"Who was it you married, Harry?" he asked. "I don't remember."

"Elsie Hollister," Harry said. "Susy's younger sister. Do you remember what Polly used to think of Susy Hollister?"

Tasmin looked again at the headquarters building. It was time to go inside and meet those officers known as his "opposite numbers." He could see himself entering the office of some strange Naval Intelligence captain. They would look at each other suspiciously like two strange dogs; then they would shake hands. The captain would be wondering exactly who in hell he was, and he would be looking at the captain's Annapolis ring and wondering why the Navy always felt that it knew everything. If it wasn't the Navy, it was the British — they both adopted the attitude that Papa could fix it by himself without bothering the bungling United States Army. The orders were that they were to indulge in a free exchange of information, but the captain would look at him dubiously, as though he were not sure that Tasmin was quite up to receiving important secrets, and Tasmin would be feeling the same way about the captain.

He should be going inside to establish cordial relations and instead he was like a circus rider standing on the backs of two different horses — trying to remember Elsie Hollister. He knew whom Harry meant, and, of course, she was just the sort of girl Harry should have married.

A formation of Corsairs flew low over them, so low as to give the impression of incredible speed, and the multiple roar of their motors blotted out every other sound and every other thought. It was over in a few seconds, but that sudden pervading sound was like a wet cloth over a blackboard, washing everything away.

"I'll try to see you tonight," Tasmin said, "and if I don't, we'll get together sometime."

"Oh, yes, we'll get together," Harry answered. "Long time no see."

Then Tasmin felt the meeting had been too casual.

"Oh, Harry," he said, "I forgot to ask. How's your father?"

"B. F.?" Harry said, and he no longer looked like General MacArthur. He looked as though something had hurt him. "Haven't you heard about B. F.?"

"No, what about him?"

"I thought of course you'd heard. He's dead. He died about a month ago."

The news was like the destruction of a solid, personal belief, even in a place where life expectancy was short.

"No," Bob said, "I hadn't heard. I've been out of touch with everything for a month. I'm awfully sorry, Harry."

"It was very sudden, a coronary," Harry said.

"I'm awfully sorry," Tasmin heard himself repeating. "He was always very kind to me. He was — " but he could not think how to end it.

It was like one of those letters of condolence that he was never good at writing. There were all sorts of things in his casual friendship with Harry's father that suddenly assumed new values now that it was too late to do anything.

"He was," he began again, "a great — " and then another flight of Corsairs went over them and his words were gone. After all, there had been nothing specifically great.

A sentry by a Quonset hut near them snapped to attention. There was a sharp call that brought drivers and orderlies up standing. A door had opened and a major general stepped carefully to the muddy road, a spare, medium-sized man with a tanned face that was molded into careful, authoritative lines. Lieutenant Colonel Tasmin and Captain Fulton were saluting.

"Call the car!" the general said.

"Yes sir," Harry Fulton answered, but there was no need to call it. An Army car with a two-star plate had backed out of the row and had stopped in front.

"Who's your friend?" the general asked Harry.

"Colonel Tasmin, sir, attached to General Bogart."

"Oh," the general said. "How's Washington?"

"About the same, sir," Tasmin answered.

"We keep hearing it's still there." The general smiled bleakly and Harry followed him into the car.

"I'll see you later, Bob," Harry said. The driver closed the door, and the car was gone.

V

Pass the Papers Clockwise

The operation was called "Operation Vanity," and for purposes of convenience it had been divided into two sections known as "Homer" and "Horace." Even the waters around the islands were divided into specific areas, each of which bore its own code name. Some of the best naval and military minds in the country had been working on those names, and they had pretty well run through the dictionary.

Work had been begun on Operation Vanity months before. The information had been collected from a hundred different sources, and facts and requirements had been sifted and checked in a hundred different ways. Even the flora and fauna had been listed, down to the sawgrass and the scrub typhus mites and the poisonous snakes. Reports had been reduced to one-page abstracts and also enlarged to include other reports; documents, all Top Secret, were jamming up the files; but Operation Vanity was still only a castle in the air which might still be discarded and replaced by another operation. They were simply there to explore the possibilities. Bob Tasmin was thinking, as he talked to the captain in Naval Intelligence, that many of the preliminaries to Operation Vanity were like the preparations for a lawsuit or a corporation contract.

He and the captain were establishing a cordial personal relationship — as had been directed. The captain's name was Murphy and he had played fullback for Annapolis in '25.

"Did you ever know Red Grange?" Captain Murphy was asking, but Bob had never been acquainted with Red Grange.

"Red was quite a Joe," Captain Murphy said. "I wonder where the hell Red is now. He ought to be with our muscle boys. There are ten big-league ball players here right now, and Dempsey was here a while ago. Do you know Jack?"

Bob Tasmin had never been acquainted with Jack either. "What do you do on the outside, Tasmin," Captain Murphy said, "when you're not being a soldier boy?"

"Oh, I was a lawyer."

"Oh," Captain Murphy said. "How do you keep it down, here?" And he slapped his stomach.

"You mean food?"

"No, no. What do you do for exercise, Tasmin? . . . But you don't look as though you needed to lose weight. How do you keep it down?"

"By worrying mostly, I guess," Tasmin answered.

"If you worry, you get ulcers. What's your first name, Tasmin?"

"Bob," Tasmin answered.

"All right," Captain Murphy said. "I'll call you Bob, and you call me Spike."

They had reached a cordial relationship, and Captain Murphy stood up.

"I guess we'd better get going to the Room, now. They ought to all be there." Captain Murphy picked up a typewritten list of names and folded it carefully.

The Room was guarded by two Marines who checked them against a list when they entered. There were several Army and Navy officers in the room, and an angular British colonel with a close-clipped, gray mustache. They were all standing by a long table, talking in low voices. The table, some chairs, and a blackboard were the only furnishings. Captain Murphy walked to the head of the table, and a young lieutenant commander placed two briefcases before him.

"Pass out the sheets, Bill," said Captain Murphy, and then he raised his voice.

"Let's all take our weight off our feet, gentlemen. The admiral has ordered me to conduct these meetings, and I imagine everybody knows everyone else, and everyone knows security or he wouldn't be here. But just in case everybody doesn't know everybody else, and as long as we're going to be thrown pretty closely together for some days, I'll ask each gentleman to rise when his name is mentioned, so you can all have a look at him." Captain Murphy began reading from a list. "I'll begin with our English guest first. Colonel Smythe Smythe . . . Is that right — two Smythes?"

The British colonel looked up, startled.

"Yes, right, Captain," he said. "Quite."

"Colonel Smythe Smythe Dawson."

Colonel Smythe Smythe Dawson stood up and inclined his closely clipped head. He looked thin, and Tasmin wondered whether Murphy was wondering how he kept it down. Captain Murphy continued reading from his list.

"Brigadier General Sandburg, Colonel Robinson, Commander Howland, Lieutenant Colonel Gasser, Commander Krock, Lieutenant Colonel Rollo, Lieutenant Colonel Tasmin. Is everybody here? Then we're squared away."

They all sat silently about the table, studying their mimeographed sheets.

"All right," Captain Murphy said, "just before settling down, I'd like to say if there's anything I can do about your rooms at the B. O. Q., or if there's anything you want, just make your gripes to me. If you haven't anything better to do, come to my quarters at 1730 and I'll have a little something to put hair on your chests. And now, let's go."

He pulled a folder from one of the briefcases that contained photostats and typewritten sheets carefully bound together.

"A–7825. Got it? A–7825. Check it and pass it on to your neighbor on the left. That's the one about Beach Blue for an alternate landing if the wind blows hard from the northwest. 70823. Here are those captured Jap documents. 70828."

His voice went on and the papers began to move around the table. Bob Tasmin had often thought that a good part of the war consisted of checking Top Secret papers. He could tell that everyone there was trained to do it automatically from the rapid, expert way they flipped through the pages. He could see that Captain Spike Murphy knew his job, simply from the contemptuous way he held the papers in his heavy hands.

The faces of the officers were like the faces of poker players. There was silence except for Captain Murphy's voice and the rustling of the papers. Colonel Smythe Smythe Dawson was sitting at his right, and the brigadier general, with the sunburst of the General Staff, sat on his left.

"Bill," Captain Murphy said to the lieutenant commander, "turn on the fan over there, will you? I'm sweating like a pig."

"Pigs don't sweat, do they, or do they?" Colonel Dawson asked.

His question broke the concentration of the others, but instead of being amused by it, they were all seriously considering whether or not pigs did sweat. The general leaned toward the right so that he could see the Britisher.

"That's right," he said. "They don't. I ought to know. I was raised on hog and hominy."

There was an uncertain silence, and then everyone laughed politely.

"Well, anyway," Captain Murphy said, "*I'm* sweating." The fan made a drowsy humming sound.

"70829. This one is new. A report on Beach Blue. Some of our demolition kids landed there in a rubber boat. They made contact with guerilla forces."

The general tapped his pencil on the table.

"What about air reconnaissance?" he asked.

Captain Murphy's voice changed, not because it was a pertinent question, but rather because he was answering a general.

"I'm glad you asked that one, sir," he said. "The plan is to examine the latest photographs this afternoon, and frankly they're not satisfactory."

"What's the matter?" the general asked. "It ought to be easy to get −38's over from Area 300."

There was a stir of interest. It was like the question about the pigs.

"They've been having bad luck, sir, with the dicing," Captain Murphy said. "It's safe to count on overcast, but everything is getting shot up that comes in low. They've got twenty millimeters behind every palm tree, and as Japs go they really know how to shoot. Five planes went over last week, and the only one that got back had the cameras full of holes. They don't want us taking pictures."

There was enough in what Captain Murphy said to make Tasmin feel cold and uncomfortable.

"But we're going to get those pictures," Captain Murphy was saying. "We're going to try from here."

"From here?" the general asked. "How from here?"

"Well, frankly, sir," Captain Murphy said, "we've asked for a B-24 from Pearl. One came in this morning with a picked crew and they're going to try that beach tomorrow — low obliques. B-24's can take a lot of punishment. Does anyone want to go?"

"Frankly, no," the general said. "I'd rather sit right here." And everybody laughed.

It was work that you could do with half your mind, and Tasmin was thinking of the Fulton family and how well he had known them at one time.

"Don't call me 'Mr. Fulton,'" Harry's father had said once. "You're around the house too much. Why don't you call me 'B. F.'?"

He and Mildred, soon after their marriage, had gone to dinner at the Fultons' apartment on Park Avenue.

"I wish you wouldn't call him 'B. F.,'" Mildred had said. "It doesn't sound a bit like you, darling. He's so obvious. Don't you see he's obvious?"

A good part of Bob Tasmin's life was spent with obvious people. He often wished he were as sure of what he was doing as obvious people were. . . .

"If no one has an objection," Captain Murphy said, "I suggest we break off for five minutes and stretch."

They all pushed back their chairs. Bob saw that the general was looking at him, and he glanced quickly at the general's ribbons — he had learned how to absorb ribbons at one glance — the Croix de Guerre with a palm, and the World War ribbon with three stars, and that would make him a flyer in the last war.

"I've seen you somewhere," the general said. "Wait a minute. Don't tell me."

Bob could not have told him even if he had wanted, but he had seen a great many people exactly like the general.

"I know," the general said. "You worked on Drumhead, didn't you? I did some work on Drumhead."

"That must be right, sir."

"Who are you with now?" the general asked.

"I'm attached to General Bogart, sir." It was a singular way of putting it because he did not feel attached to General Bogart.

"Oh," the general said. "Do you like gin rummy?"

"Yes, sir," Bob answered.

"Well," the general said. "I'll take some money off you some-time."

"If you gentlemen are ready," Captain Murphy called, "let's get on with it. We've got about another half hour, I think. We'll meet this afternoon to do what photographs we have. All squared away? 7038!"

The officers around the table were being drawn together already, not because they were mutually congenial, but in an artificial, enforced sort of intimacy, because they were all dealing with dangerous military secrecy. They could drink together and play cards together without that stultifying, ever-present dread that they might say something inadvertent which would give the show away. They stole appraising glances at each other as they passed the papers. They were all cleared and absolutely safe, but that was all they had in common. Their private lives and their aspirations would all be hidden beneath a polite veneer.

"Well, that about ends it," Captain Murphy said. "Are there any questions, gentlemen?"

They all raised their left wrists to look at their watches. It was five minutes past noon.

"All right," Captain Murphy said. "We'll break off. We'll meet here again at three."

They all filed through the open door, past the sentries, into a large outer office where yeomen in their undershirts were pounding on typewriters. The guard locked the door of the Room behind them, and at the same time they all closed the doors of their own minds on what had gone on in there.

"I always find these little gatherings a bit on the trying side, don't you?" Colonel Dawson asked.

"Yes, sir," Bob answered. "They always are a strain."

"Now there was a chap I knew in Delhi," Colonel Dawson said, "rather a good chap, too, who never for the life of him could recall whether he had read something in *The Times* or whether it was a future operation. He had to confine his conversation entirely to the caste system to avoid taking the bowler, or to tigers. Do you know tigers?"

"I knew a man who trained them in the circus once," Bob answered.

Captain Murphy laid a heavy hand on Bob Tasmin's shoulder.

"Let's get out of here before this gets any more screwy than necessary," he said. "Come on to lunch. I've got to stop in at the office first."

Bob knew that Captain Murphy was asking him to lunch because he was attached to General Bogart, but still, it was kind of the captain. Bob followed him into his office.

"Those British are all whacky," the captain said. "They're always acting as though the U. S. A. is a government in exile. Say, wait a minute." He had picked up a typewritten memorandum from his table. "Here's someone who's been calling to see you. Say, I don't like this. It's one of those damned correspondents."

"Who is he?" Bob Tasmin asked, and he did not like it either. It was a good idea to avoid columnists and the press, particularly at such a time. They were always hanging around at cocktail parties, and cropping up at Washington dinner tables. They were always friends of someone whom you did not want to offend, and they were always putting two and two together and adding it up to something.

Captain Murphy made a face, as though he had tasted something unpleasant, and spoke in a slow, careful voice.

"The name is Milton Ouerbach," he said.

"Milton Ouerbach!" Tasmin repeated after him. "Good God!"

"Do you know him?" It was obvious that the captain was changing his opinion of Bob fast, now that he realized Tasmin knew undesirable people.

"Yes," Bob said, "I went to college with him."

Captain Murphy pursed his lips and made an uncomplimentary sound.

"It's Public Relations," he said. "It's that goddam office of so-and-so's right around the corner. Those little sundowners don't know what security is. This Ouerbach. Who is he? What's he covering?"

"I don't know," Bob told him. "I haven't seen him for a long while, but I hear him pretty often."

"What's that, a riddle?"

"The radio," Bob Tasmin said.

Captain Murphy looked startled.

"He's done pretty nearly everything in the writing line," Bob said, "but lately he's been an inspirational commentator."

"You mean like Gabriel Heatter?"

"He has a very large following, Spike," Bob said. "He runs a program — you must have heard it — 'A Quarter Hour with Ouerbach.' I don't know how he heard I was here."

Captain Murphy sat down heavily.

Bob Tasmin took the memorandum and read it. The time was 10:25.

"War Correspondent Milton Ouerbach wants to get in touch with Lieutenant Colonel Tasmin. He says he is a friend of his. He is staying at B. O. Q. 6."

"I don't see how he got out here," Bob Tasmin said again.

"We'll damn well find how he got out here!" Captain Murphy said. He picked up the telephone. "Get Lieutenant Sweeney here from Public Relations. Tell him to report on the double!"

Captain Murphy put down the telephone and stared in front of him.

"I can't help who I know on the outside, Spike," Bob Tasmin said.

Captain Murphy sighed.

"That's all right, Bob," he answered. "I know. If he didn't know you, he'd know someone."

Neither of them spoke for a while, and Captain Murphy leaned back in his swivel chair, and the springs groaned and complained beneath his weight.

"How do you get the boys to keep their mouths shut in Washington?" Captain Murphy asked.

It was very hard to maintain security in Washington, Tasmin told him. Most people when they learned a secret invariably felt that they were obligated to impart it to someone instantly. Give them a few drinks and they wanted to be important. If you only knew what I know!

The captain agreed. The best thing to do was to get them drunk and watch them. "One yap out of them, and put them on report," and he didn't give one good hot damn how much rank they had either. Now take that officer in the E.T.O. who spilled the date of D-Day at dinner in London. And they took the officer in the E.T.O.; and then they took an officer at Pearl Harbor who used to play water polo with Captain Murphy, and then a knock on the door interrupted them.

It was Lieutenant Sweeney from Public Relations, a pale, dark-haired boy, who, Bob Tasmin thought, might once have been an advertising copywriter, or a section man in an English course at college.

"Did I interrupt you in a sonnet, mister?" Captain Murphy asked. "Didn't you know I'm in a hurry?"

"I'm awfully sorry, sir —" Lieutenant Sweeney began.

"Haven't you been in the Navy long enough," Captain Murphy asked, "to know it doesn't do any good to be 'awfully sorry,' mister? Don't you boys in Public Relations know there's a war on?"

"Yes, sir," Lieutenant Sweeney said.

"Oh, you do, do you? Well, thank you for reassuring me," Captain Murphy said.

It had never seemed to Bob that such painful scenes did much good, but at the same time he reluctantly admired Captain Murphy's technique. It took years of experience to bawl out a junior officer properly.

"I'm sorry, sir," Lieutenant Sweeney answered. "I was on the telephone."

Captain Murphy nodded and smiled icily.

"Thanks, thanks a million, mister. That explains everything. Who was on the telephone with you, son?"

"It was the Flag Secretary," Lieutenant Sweeney answered. "I couldn't very well cut him off, sir."

The captain rubbed his hand across his forehead.

"All right," he said. "Sit down, Sweeney."

"Thank you, sir," Lieutenant Sweeney said, and he sat down.

"This is Colonel Tasmin," Captain Murphy said. "There's a character here, one of these characters you boys bring out, one of these civilian radio belchers. His name is —" Captain Murphy scowled. "What did you say his name was, Bob?"

"Milton Ouerbach," Bob answered.

He wished Milton Ouerbach might be present to hear himself discussed so frankly.

"He's just one of these people who's winning the war single-handed," Bob Tasmin added. "He takes it very hard."

"The point is, what's he doing around here?" Captain Murphy asked. "You know we're dealing with future operations, don't you? And I'm responsible for security, and we don't want any correspondents around. Do you know him, Sweeney?"

"Yes, sir," Lieutenant Sweeney answered. "He's out to visit the war theaters. We were very glad to get him."

"My God!" Captain Murphy said. "Glad?"

"He's perfectly trustworthy, sir. He has a very wide following. Don't you know him, sir?"

"It just happens, mister," Captain Murphy said, "that some of us around here, not all of us, and I'm not mentioning any names, are pretty goddam busy with this war, and we don't have time to meet fascinating characters that privileged guys like you used to see around the Stork Club."

66

"He's done a lot for us," Lieutenant Sweeney said. "He's done a lot to make people Navy-conscious."

"What's that one? Come again. What's that one?"

"I don't suppose it's seagoing, sir," Lieutenant Sweeney said. "I just said Navy-conscious."

"You mean so people back home will know we've got a Navy, is that it?"

"Well, that's what we're here for, sir," Lieutenant Sweeney said.

Captain Murphy looked at Bob Tasmin, and then he looked at the ceiling.

"He has a very high priority, and the Secretary's interested in his trip," the lieutenant went on.

Captain Murphy stood up.

"All right, all right," he said. "You'd better see him, Bob, and have lunch with him. Take him out, Sweeney. I'll see you later, Bob. Remember, the Room at three o'clock."

The glare of the sunlight on the bare ground was momentarily blinding, but the light gave Tasmin a sense of relief and a feeling of gratitude for unrestricted space. Lieutenant Sweeney smiled at him.

"As you gather, the P.R.O. is rather on the hind tit here."

"Someone always is," Bob said. "How long have you been in the Navy, Lieutenant?"

"For about two hundred years, sir," Lieutenant Sweeney answered, and he laughed. "Every year a century."

VI

They Still Have Talcum in the States

THERE WAS a room reserved in another building for accredited correspondents. A number of men and a few women were there, all in the usual khaki uniform of the Pacific, slouching over their typewriters or reading newspapers, looking tired and bored and physically unfit. They did not bother to suck in their stomachs or to hold up their heads, and they were not worried about rank because they had none. When Bob entered and they saw he was an officer, they looked at him resentfully. In spite of his civilian past, Bob also felt a twinge of resentment. He had the impression of walking into enlisted men's quarters, and he wondered almost instinctively why some sergeant did not bring them to attention.

"Is Mr. Ouerbach here?" Lieutenant Sweeney called, but there was no need to ask, because Milton Ouerbach was already hurrying toward them.

The last time Bob Tasmin had seen Milton Ouerbach, Milton had been wearing a double-breasted suit designed for him by one of those New York tailors who supplied copies of *Punch* and the *London Sphere* for waiting patrons. This custom-made product with adequate padding for the shoulders had given Milton's figure a svelte athletic grace; but now that Milton was in khaki, his body looked more like a pear and less like an hourglass. His shoulders were somewhat rounded, and his belt made a groove around his middle. His nose was peeling and his horn-rimmed spectacles must have been uncomfortable. Nevertheless, his face was about as Bob had remembered it, a slightly cadaverous face that photographed well, particularly from a three-quarters view when the wind was blowing.

They always photographed Milton in the wind, gazing out toward new vistas and new horizons.

"Well, well, well," Milton said, and he held out both hands. It was not overdone. It was a genial, graceful gesture, implying that Milton never forgot an old friend, but somehow it was not exactly right for Guam.

"Hi, Milt," Bob said, and his own greeting also sounded out of place. He felt for a moment like a clergyman who had turned his collar around and was trying to be one of the boys.

"Well, well, well," Milton said. "How did you ever get into anything like this?"

It was that inevitable question, and Tasmin began to laugh.

"Fancy your being here, Milt," he said. "It's a small world, isn't it?"

They were both trying to pick up old threads and trying to remember where they had left off, but it was very hard at Guam.

"How long have you been here?" Milton asked.

"Since just this morning."

"Oh, since just this morning. I came here yesterday," Milton said.

"How did you find I was here?" Bob asked him. Milton drew a handkerchief from his pocket. The handkerchief had a purple border and Milton mopped his forehead.

"I have a lad taking me around," Milton said, "a Lieutenant McKay from the Secretary's office, and I just gave him a list made up in Washington of people I might run into. He's a very bright lad. He's out now buying me some talcum powder."

"What do you want talcum powder for?" Bob asked.

"Because I have prickly heat. You'll have prickly heat when you've been here for a day."

"But you wouldn't miss it for anything, would you?" Bob asked.

"When you're asked to do a thing like this," Milton said, "it's almost a directive. I'm going to do a little broadcasting from here, that's all."

" 'Good evening, everybody,' " Bob said. " 'My talk tonight comes to you from Guam. I wish we could all be here together.' "

69

"Let's get out of here," Milton said, "or I may start getting funny too."

Milton Ouerbach's tone implied weary rebuke, and Bob Tasmin did not blame him much, for he imagined that people were always saying trite things to Milton, and that Milton spent a good part of his working hours making replies. When they had first met in an English Composition course in college, Milton Ouerbach had been a very shy boy who had written poetry without any capitals or punctuation. Milton had worn nickel-rimmed spectacles then and pastel ties, and he used to blush when his works were read aloud.

Bob could remember a line even now.

oh pillow me on the buoyant breasts of spring . . .

Of course, everyone in those days did a good deal of writing, as they still doubtless did, about breasts, but he could never think of spring, which was a season, as being so equipped. He could remember the gentle titter when the line was read. He could even recollect that Milton had been wearing a light green tie, and that Milton's face, which was thinner then, with heavy half-parted lips, had also looked slightly green.

"Milton," Bob said. "Do you remember that poem of yours — 'oh pillow me on the buoyant breasts of spring . . .' ?"

Milton Ouerbach's head jerked sideways.

"What?" he asked. "What's that?"

"You heard it," Bob said. " 'oh pillow . . .' "

Bob Tasmin looked in front of him. Before the Bachelor Officers' Quarters the ground fell away sharply, and the road wound past groups of Quonset huts and tents, past a gorge filled with lush, strange vegetation.

"I was a very callow little fellow once, Robert," Milton said, "and naturally I've written a great deal that I'm ashamed of, but never, never, so help me, did I ever write anything like that. In the first place I was never that sort of person."

"Well, you wrote it," Bob said. "I remember it very well, Milton."

"I remember you very well, too," Milton said, "now that I put my mind on it, and God knows how you ever got out here."

"Everyone gets hysterical in a war. That's why I'm here," Bob said.

"I can't imagine you getting on with generals," Milton said. "*I* can, but I can't imagine *you*. Will you be with General Bogart at the admiral's dinner tonight?"

"It's a funny thing about generals," Bob answered. "They usually seem to be able to do their eating without me. They only want me when they're puzzled. They're never puzzled when they're eating."

"Well, I've been asked," Milton said.

"'oh pillow me on the buoyant breasts of Spring . . .'" said Bob.

"Can't you think of something pleasant about me?" Milton asked.

A sentry presented arms, and Bob Tasmin saluted. They were a long way from adolescence and spring, a long way from anywhere, but Milton was like a guest in a hotel with all the customer's privileges and capacity for complaint, while Tasmin was like a doorman in gold braid, or a house detective.

Milton had a room to himself at the Bachelor Officers' Quarters, which proved that he was a visiting celebrity. The roof of the Quonset hut curved over one side, and just below the curve there was a line of open screening, like the windows in a chicken house. The room was bare except for a washbasin with a faucet and two beds, two bureaus and a wardrobe, a chair, a table and a typewriter. It was clear that Milton had been given extra baggage allowance since there were two large canvas bags and a typewriter case on the floor by one of the beds. He had probably asked one of the clerks in a sporting goods establishment that outfitted officers what one should bring on such a journey, for he had a trench coat and a visored cap and too many trousers and shirts and too many shoes. Judging from the bottles on his bureau, Milton must have also consulted a physician about tropical disease, for he was obviously ready for any contingency. There were large bottles of paregoric, and sulfa tablets, and Eno's fruit salts, and bismuth, codeine, sleeping tablets, aspirin, iodine, gauze bandages, adhesive tape, and sunburn cream.

71

"It's much more comfortable than I thought it would be," Milton said, "except for the chlorine in the water. Would you rather sit on the chair or the bed? I have some Scotch."

Bob sat down on the bed.

"Thanks, but I'd better not take any this noon. I'm working," he answered.

Milton pulled out the chair from behind the table and sat down and sighed.

"I never thought of you as being a soldier," Milton said. "You make me very ill at ease, Robert. You look unapproachable. We're fighting for democracy, and nothing's democratic."

"That's right," Bob said. "Nothing's democratic."

Milton raised his hands and let them fall limply on his knees. "I had thought that I could get the feel of things out here," Milton said, "that there would be an interchange of aspirations and ideas, that there would be some great concentration of spirit, some social give-and-take such as exists in the Russian Army."

"What do you know about the Russian Army?" Bob asked.

"It isn't what I know," Milton said. "Everyone says there is the spirit of the new world in the Russian Army, and out here is — anachronism. Out here" — Milton raised his hands and let them fall on his knees again — "it's like the National Association of Manufacturers, only worse. The men who are directing this war are living in a social vacuum. Am I right, or am I wrong?"

"You don't know anything about the Army, Milton," he said. Milton would never know the necessity for the chain of command because he would never have a part in it.

"Of course I don't know," Milton said, "and that's what I'm here to find out. I want to interpret what fighting men think, and everyone is completely inexpressive. What do you want the world to be like? How do you handle the Negro problem for one thing? No one seems to be giving it any serious thought. That is the sort of question I want answered, and I meet with a blank wall of platitudes. Of course, I've only been out here for a day."

"Why don't you take it the way you find it?" Bob Tasmin asked. "It would be easier and you'd get somewhere, Milton."

"No one talks freely," Milton said. "That's why I wanted to see you, Robert. You used to talk intelligently once, and now you act as though you were afraid to cope with an idea." Milton took off his glasses and began to polish them. "You are all like eunuchs in a harem."

"That's very interesting," Bob said. "I never heard it put quite that way before, but I wouldn't try to say it on the air."

But Milton made no direct reply.

"Now coming out on the plane," Milton said, "I tried to start a little discussion with some of the young boys — and mind you, they knew who I was, Robert. I thought they would be interested to hear about the home effort. I thought they would ask questions. They were naturally polite, but no one asked questions."

"You mean they didn't care about collective bargaining?" Bob asked.

But Milton paid no attention.

"Do you know what one young fellow asked me? And he seemed like a fully integrated boy."

Bob did not know what the fully integrated boy had asked Milton.

"He wanted to know," Milton said, "whether they still have Coca-Cola in the States."

A knock on the door interrupted them. It was a young, blond naval officer, Lieutenant McKay, that nice boy who was detailed to show Milton around.

"Here's your talcum powder, sir," Lieutenant McKay said, "and you'd better get squared away for lunch, sir."

Milton took the package of talcum powder and shook it.

"Is it true," Bob asked, "that they still have Mennen's in the States?"

But Milton paid no attention to the question.

"Thanks ever so much, Lieutenant," he said. "I don't know what I'd do without you. Have I got time to sprinkle some of this on?"

"Yes, sir," the lieutenant said. "I'll go ahead and keep a table for you and the colonel if you like, sir."

"Thanks. We'll be right along," Milton said, and he began to take off his shirt as the lieutenant closed the door. "That's an awfully

73

nice boy, McKay, but he doesn't tell me anything either." Milton was rubbing himself with talcum powder. "That's better," he said. "That's fine. Robert, I forgot to ask you. How's Mildred?"

If you flew to Kwajalein and then to Pearl and then to San Francisco and across the continent you would come to Mildred, but she was farther away than that.

"Mildred's fine," Bob said. "At least she was when I saw her last. We're in Washington. We have an apartment off Scott Circle."

Milton pulled the zipper on one of his bags and drew out a clean shirt. He was wriggling into it, thrusting out his arms in helpless, flapping motions, and then his head emerged.

"My!" he said. "That's better. I must remember to ask McKay what they do about laundry here."

"Did you know that Burton Fulton's dead?" Bob Tasmin asked. Milton had finished buttoning his shirt.

"Oh, yes," he said. "It was very sudden, but maybe it was just as well."

"How do you mean 'just as well'?" Bob asked, and his tone made Milton turn around.

"I'm sorry," Milton said. "I didn't intend to put it exactly like that, Robert. I was only thinking in a most impersonal way of fixed ideas. If you have a reactionary ideology, a mode of living that is out of step with what's coming, maybe it's just as well not to be disappointed. That's all I meant. Now you take Burt Fulton. Naturally he was a man of good will . . . but then you were more mixed up with them than I ever was." He stopped and looked at Bob. "Of course, when Polly met Tom, we all used to play around together, but you and Polly were in a different world." He stopped again, but Bob Tasmin did not answer.

"I mean," Milton spoke more slowly, "the idea of inheritance and possession, and all that sort of static continuity, has pretty well gone out the window. I don't mean to say Mr. Fulton was fascist. I don't want you to think that I use that term loosely, but Polly would know what I mean because it used to bother her."

"Go ahead," Bob said. "Just what do you mean?"

74

Milton moved his hands slowly back and forth in front of him, as though he were smoothing a table of sand.

"It's a little hard to give it any definition," he said. "I suppose I'm speaking of privilege and the *rentier* class. I suppose I'm thinking of the Veblen theory of the leisure class, but not exactly. I'm certainly not thinking of Marx because I'm an absolute believer in free enterprise." He stopped again.

Bob Tasmin felt uncomfortable. "Go ahead," he said. "Never mind the social significance."

"I wish you'd be a little more sympathetic, Robert," Milton said, and he sighed. "You know what I'm trying to say as well as I do, although you can't move far enough from your class to accept the meaning. It may be that I use ugly, unliterary terms. All I mean is that vaguely, but at the same time rather definitely, Burton Fulton represented a way of life and a mechanism of belief that is completely gone." Milton Ouerbach paused and looked at the floor in front of him, and Bob Tasmin waited.

"It's gone," he said again, "and I don't know when it went, and what's more, I can't entirely remember what it was, although we all lived in it. We're like fish being moved from one aquarium to another."

It was what Bob Tasmin was afraid he was going to say, except about the fish.

"We were in one body of water, and now we're in another, but everything is moving so fast I can't remember what it used to be like. Can you remember?"

Bob Tasmin sat silent. Milton had said it very badly, and yet he had expressed something which must have been in the back of Bob's own mind since he had heard about the death of Burton Fulton.

"No," he said. "No, I can't remember."

Someone was knocking on the thin panels of the door, and Tasmin was jolted back again to the Bachelor Officers' Quarters, a grim, transient place, devoid of personality or permanence.

"Come in," he heard Milton call, and the door opened. It was a tall master sergeant, an able, rangy-looking noncom. From the way

75

he clicked his heels together and saluted, he evidently took his position seriously.

"Colonel Tasmin, sir?"

"Yes, I'm Colonel Tasmin." Bob noticed that his own voice had changed. It had become alert, formal and precise. He examined the sergeant approvingly, thinking of him not as a person but as a valuable, though expendable, piece of military mechanism.

"What is it, Sergeant?"

"General Bogart's compliments to Colonel Tasmin." The sergeant knew his lines. "Colonel Tasmin is to report to the general immediately."

"Very well," Bob said. "Have you got a car, Sergeant?"

"Yes, sir," the sergeant answered.

"I'll have to see you later, Milton," Bob said.

When the Old Man wanted you, you dropped what you were doing and forgot what you were thinking and snapped right into it. The sergeant stepped aside and followed Bob into the hall.

"The car's right out in front, sir," he said. They both were walking quickly. That was an interesting remark of Milton Ouerbach's about moving from one body of water to another.

VII

Just Because He Sold the Factory . . .

As FAR AS Bob Tasmin could remember, the Fultons had bought the old Holcombe place at Gray's Point the year his father had given him a Quackenbush air rifle. Bob's mother had been afraid that he would put Will's eye out with one of the darts it shot — Will was always getting something in his eye — but George Tasmin had said that boys had to learn to handle firearms. Bob could start with a good air rifle, and then when he got to be fourteen, he could have a .22. That meant that Bob must have been almost twelve years old, because he could remember thinking it would be two years before he got that .22.

The Holcombe place — it was always called the Holcombe *place* instead of the Holcombe *house,* perhaps because of its gray, Gothic stable and its stone gateposts — stood near that restricted real estate development already known, in 1916, as Maple Ledge. The Holcombe place seemed quite a distance from the Tasmins' house. First you had to cross the Tasmins' own vegetable garden, that was tended by Joe who lived with the other Italians near the New York, New Haven and Hartford tracks. Next you climbed a board fence and crossed a field, always watching for the Lansings' German police dogs, and entered the woods by Prout's Brook, where you used to find skunk cabbages and later cowslips in the spring. You followed the path through Prout's Woods until you reached a rustic footbridge and then you turned off the path to the right near a large oak tree, which usually had a gray squirrel's nest in it, and walked until you encountered some gray granite boulders with hemlocks growing above them. Beyond the boulders was a low wall of dressed stone which was the boundary of the Holcombe place and beyond the wall was a field with a blue gravel drive running through it, and then came the lawn and a rustic summerhouse, and then the Holcombe house itself.

The house was one of those monstrous, the-public-be-damned efforts that sprang from the mixture of architectural taste and Victorian ideas that was fashionable in the '90's and indigenous to the suburbs — a style which had not come from Europe or from anywhere else. The walls were of bulging fieldstone, and so were the chimneys. It had, in those days, two wings and gambrel roofs with dormers and a terrace and a garden surrounded by a somber hemlock hedge. It had not been occupied for years, and even in Bob Tasmin's boyhood it had an indestructible, archaic look.

The grounds had usually been deserted, except for the old and disagreeable caretaker who lived over the stable, and if you edged around the rhododendron bushes by the drive, you could get to the house without his chasing you away. Bob had always been attracted by the sense of solitude and the feeling of vanished people which surrounded the empty house, but one morning in September that solitude was gone. He had climbed over the stone wall, holding his air rifle as though it were a real firearm, and when he moved nearer, he saw a large, red van beneath the *porte-cochère*. Then a team from the Gray's Point nursery drove up, and laborers got out and began walking toward the garden. He stood for a while watching, with a feeling of resentment, sure that the Holcombe house would never again be fit for games of the imagination. He would never again be able to crouch in the shadows of the garden hedge watching the caretaker trim back the shrubbery. He would never again be able to re-create the people who had lived there, of whom he had heard his parents speak.

Mr. Holcombe, who had built the house, had lost his money in the panic of 1907, and afterwards the Holcombes had stayed on desperately for a few years with everything growing weedier and shabbier, and then they had gone . . . no one seemed to know exactly where.

"Holcombe was very overextended," Bob had heard his father say once. "He could not put it up when he was called."

Bob used to piece the whole thing together, when he visited the Holcombe place, and make it into a story. He could see Mr. Holcombe coming home broken, after he had been overextended, and he used to imagine Mrs. Holcombe crying because there was no money. Now a moving van and a few men with lawn mowers and shears were already driving out the shadowy imprint of those people — ruthlessly, contemptuously. Now the song of the September crickets and the smell of musty dampness in the rhododendron thicket would no longer be lonely. He was facing his first experience with the end of an era, a trivial experience, but somehow it set a standard of behavior for the end of greater eras. Why was it that, although a child's life was always fluid, he desired everything to be static and clung stubbornly to old habits and conventions?

Bob remembered his relief, when he got back to his own place, at finding that everything was the way he had left it. His brother Will was in his father's den, pasting in his new Panama-Pacific stamps. Katie the waitress was setting the table for luncheon with the usual blue-and-white plates, and there was a centerpiece of marigolds as there always was in September. His mother was on the side porch snipping nasturtiums from the window boxes with her small garden scissors and laying them neatly in her garden basket.

"Mother," he said. "Someone's moving into the Holcombe place."

"Yes, dear," his mother said. "Don't point that thing at me. Please take it up to your room."

He was not pointing the rifle at her. He explained that he was holding it exactly as his father had shown him, in the crook of his left arm with his hand over the trigger guard.

"You might forget and point it," his mother said. "You mustn't play with it in the house."

It was an insult to the Quackenbush, because you never played with such a serious and beautiful object — with a Daisy air rifle, perhaps, but not with a Quackenbush.

"I'm not playing with it, Mother," he said. "I took it out to use it in Prout's Woods. Someone is moving into the Holcombe place."

"Yes," his mother said, "it's some people called Fulton, dear."

79

"Who are they?"

"I don't know who they are, dear, his mother answered, "because we haven't met them. Now run upstairs with that thing, and see if you can pull up your stockings."

The subject of the Fultons came up again that night when the Tasmins were at dinner.

On summer evenings Bob's father customarily arrived from New York on the six-five, and Carlson would drive him to the Shadow Club, which had better tennis courts than the Mill River Club, and there he would play two sets of tennis before dinner. Now that he had reached forty, he complained that singles made him too tired after a hard day in the city, but he could always get up a quick doubles game at the Shadow Club, and Carlson would bring him down fresh clothes, so that he would be ready for dinner when he got back at seven.

That evening Bob was out on the front lawn, close by the yew bushes, raising his air rifle to his shoulder, sighting it, and lowering it again. The automobile drove up with a spattering sound of gravel, and his father stepped out quickly, holding the evening paper.

"All right, Carlson, that's all," he said. Carlson raised a finger to his visored cap. Then the gears ground noisily, and his father looked hard at the back of Carlson's neck, but he made no remark.

"You'll wear grooves in that gun if you fool with it so much," he said.

"I'm not fooling," Bob said. "I'm practising."

"Well, come in to dinner," his father said, and he slapped Bob on the back with his folded newspaper as they walked through the hall. "Put your shoulders back, or you'll never get in the Army."

Bob's father belonged to the military caste. George Tasmin could not sit still just because there was a Princeton, pacifist college professor in the White House, and because William Jennings Bryan had said not to worry, that a million men could spring to arms overnight. He had gone that summer to the businessmen's training camp at Plattsburg.

"How's the war going, Dad?" Bob asked.

"They're active along the Somme," his father said. "That's the place to watch. We'll fix the map after dinner."

They were in the dining room and the candles were lighted.

"Will hasn't washed," Bob said.

Will looked at him unblinkingly.

"I did, but you smeared up the towel," he answered.

"Pull out your mother's chair, Will," his father said.

His father's chair faced the portrait, very carefully varnished, of a sallow, unpleasant-looking man, in black with a white stock. It was Courtney Tasmin, Bob's great-grandfather, who in 1830 had served a term in Congress from New York. But Bob thought very little of him because he had not been in the Army.

"George," his mother said. "Do you think Carlson looks tired?"

"I didn't notice," his father said.

"You know what Carlson does when he gets tired, dear."

"I've told him what would happen if he did it again. I told him the last time," his father said. "Did you boys go swimming today?"

Will told him that they had gone swimming at the Yacht Club.

"When I was your age," his father said, "we used to swim right off the beach at Mamaroneck. Well, what is there that's new?"

That was when Bob told him that someone was moving into the Holcombe place. His father set his glass of water carefully back on the table.

"They're not wasting any time," he said. "They only bought it last week. Do you remember what their name is, Ruthie?"

"Fulton," she answered.

"Like the Hudson River Boat," George Tasmin said. "Are these our own beets, Ruthie?" His mother said that they were their own beets.

"Well," George Tasmin said, "it's about time we got something out of the garden."

"When we moved here," his mother said, "you were always talking about fresh vegetables, and how you were going to work in the garden every evening. Do you remember? As it is we really might just as well have stayed in New York and have gone to Easthampton in the summer."

"Come on, Ruthie," George Tasmin said, "this is better than Easthampton. There's a great crowd here, and the boys are in the country."

"I wonder what these Fultons are going to be like," Mrs. Tasmin said. "I wonder if they're going to fit in. They must have money if they're going to do anything with the Holcombe place."

George Tasmin took a sip of water.

"I don't care what they are, as long as they're not pro-German," he said, "or as long as they're not pacifists." Mrs. Tasmin sighed.

"I hope they're not just rich."

"How do you mean 'just rich'?"

"Just rich, and nothing else. There are so many of that type coming to Gray's Point, George, and I wish the boys could see something else."

"'Just rich,'" Mr. Tasmin said, "and you talk about Easthampton. Nobody earns his living in Easthampton."

"John Drew lives in Easthampton. Augustus Thomas lives in Easthampton."

"We've got some queer people here too," George Tasmin said. "We've got a brain surgeon, and somebody who writes for the *New Republic*."

"Darling," Mrs. Tasmin said, "don't take it so hard. I just meant I hope they'll contribute something. I hope they're not just uncultivated, self-made people like the Birches."

"Who are you talking about, Ruthie?" George Tasmin asked. "Who do you hope is not self-made?"

"These new people, dear . . . the Fultons," Mrs. Tasmin said. "These melons aren't from the garden. . . . I suppose we ought to call."

"Yes, of course, we ought to call," his father answered.

They were not greatly worried about the Fultons. People knew very little of the backgrounds and antecedents of newcomers at Gray's Point, because everyone who lived there had come from somewhere else, except people like the Hollisters who had been there for more than a generation. Of course, at Maple Ledge where the Tasmins lived everyone was all right because buyers were passed by the Committee. Yet this meant only that they conformed to certain standards of dress, manners, and financial stability. They met at the club, they played golf and bridge together. They even became great friends, but most of those friendships were based on surface values. There was always the probability that they would all move on someday when the children had grown up or when the place had become too crowded. Gray's Point relationships were much like those on shipboard, where all the passengers in First Class were thrown together congenially, where you knew someone very well, and then you parted. This was true of most suburban life, yet, pathetically enough, all the people at Gray's Point were striving to establish an environment in which to live always. They should have known that the environment was built on the shifting sands of circumstance.

Bob Tasmin first met Mr. Fulton one Sunday in October, and he knew who Mr. Fulton was right away, because, of course, everyone had been talking about the Fultons. On his return from school after his mother's bridge luncheons, Bob had often heard the ladies discussing them, describing the furniture and what they were doing to the house, telling about Mr. Fulton's car and the amount the Fultons had subscribed to the Boy Scouts and to the Community Fund. He had heard that the Fultons were nice in a way, and that they might fit in, given time, although they had rough edges, and he had heard his mother say that they were "small-town." Without knowing exactly what the phrase meant, he understood that it placed the Fultons with certain other people in Gray's Point whom no one saw very often.

Sunday was always a gay day at Gray's Point, even back in 1916, a day of expansive leisure when no one hurried to the train, when men put on tweed golf suits and went to the club, when families dropped in on each other in the afternoon. His father and mother had gone to the Mill River Club for the golf luncheon that Sunday after taking Bob and Will with them to the Episcopal Church. Will had stayed in the house with his stamp collection, but Bob had changed from his blue serge suit into a red jersey and corduroy trousers, and he had gone to Prout's Woods with his air rifle. He had just crossed the footbridge over the brook when he saw a man with sandy reddish hair standing by the boulders near the grove of hemlocks. At first Bob Tasmin thought he was someone's employee from the town out for a Sunday walk in the woods, but then Bob noticed that he was wearing sneakers and old flannel trousers and a flannel shirt without a tie, and anyone's employee from town would have been more elaborately dressed.

"Hello," the man said. He had a quiet, nasal voice, and Bob saw that his shirt must have been shrunk in the wash because the sleeves were too short.

"Hello," Bob answered.

It was more like meeting another boy than an older man. There was the same pause as they eyed each other, the same lack of social grace, and there were none of those easy jocular questions that people from older generations always asked — "Gun, where are you going with the boy?" or "Are you looking for Indians?" Instead the man only cleared his throat.

"It's a nice day, isn't it?" he asked. It was a clear October day, and the leaves, falling about them, made a golden mat near the hemlocks.

"You live over there, don't you?" the man asked, and he pointed through the woods. "I thought you did. I live over here," and he nodded toward the wall beyond the hemlocks. "How do you like Sundays?"

Bob told him that Saturdays were better, and the man nodded.

"Come on over, and I'll show you my place," he said.

"All right," Bob answered, and then he remembered that he had been corrected for saying "all right."

"My name's Fulton," the man said. "I've just bought this place."

They climbed over the stone wall together while he went on speaking. "I didn't realize it was going to be so big. It's even got a greenhouse, and there's a round house for pigeons by the stable. You don't know where I could buy some pigeons, do you?"

"I guess there must be places," Bob said. "They advertise pigeons in *Boy's Life*."

"Is that so?" Mr. Fulton said. "What I want are fantails."

Mr. Fulton was not drawing him out or trying to put him at his ease, and he did not tell what he used to do when he was a boy. It was just as though Mr. Fulton had not grown up but still had bought the Holcombe place.

"If you've got any ideas about how I ought to fix it up," Mr. Fulton said, "I wish you'd tell me. There's an awful lot to do, and I need help with it. I want part of the stable to be a garage, but I want to have a pony — and here's something I want to ask you. How would it be if I had a swimming pool?"

"I think it would be fine," Bob said; "then you wouldn't have to go to the Yacht Club."

"That's just what I've been thinking," Mr. Fulton said. "I like to go for a swim without getting all dressed up. Now you tell me — where do you suppose I ought to put the pool?"

"If I was doing it," Bob said, "I'd put it back of the flower garden."

"That's just what I was thinking," Mr. Fulton said, "and we'll have a little house there to get dressed in. I saw a pool like that on Long Island this summer, at Locust Valley. Have you ever been there? That's quite a place, Locust Valley."

Bob had never been to Locust Valley, but Mr. Fulton thought none the less of him.

"You ought to see it," Mr. Fulton said. "I went out there to spend the night with a friend of mine — well, not a friend, exactly . . . but he wanted me out there, because we were talking something over. He has quite a place — a swimming pool" — Mr. Fulton waved his hand — "a flower garden with a fountain, and a squash court." Mr. Fulton waved his hand again. "That was where I saw one of those round pigeon houses. Well, we've got to have this place along those lines. I don't know about the squash court, but certainly a swimming pool and a fountain. Now is there anything else you think I ought to have?"

"You might keep rabbits," Bob said.

"Now that's an idea," Mr. Fulton said. "I might keep rabbits, with lop ears. Do you know any place where you can get lop-eared rabbits?"

"I can look in *American Boy*."

"You look," Mr. Fulton told him. "Next time you come, bring around *American Boy*."

Bob was very pleased that he was being a help to Mr. Fulton.

"You ought to have a tennis court and clock golf," he said.

"All right," Mr. Fulton said. "All right. Do you know how to play clock golf?"

"Anyone can play clock golf."

"All right, we'll have it then," Mr. Fulton said, "as long as no one has to teach me."

"Don't you know how to play golf?"

"No," Mr. Fulton said. "Do you think I ought to learn?"

"Yes," Bob said, "I think perhaps you ought to."

He and Mr. Fulton were standing together on the threshold of an unknown, glittering future.

"Perhaps you ought to have a maze," Bob said.

"What's a maze?"

"It's made out of hedges," Bob told him. "You get lost in it; it's kind of a puzzle. Mr. Hollister has one."

"Oh, he has one, has he?" Mr. Fulton said. "Well, thanks, I'll ask about a maze. I'm a stranger here myself, Bob, but I want to do what everyone else does. Can you think of anything else?"

"Not right now," Bob said, "but maybe later."

"If you do, just let me know," Mr. Fulton said. "Come on inside, and let's find something to eat."

He opened the front door of the Holcombe house. It was a very large house inside. It smelled of fresh paint, and none of the furniture had been arranged and only half the curtains were up.

"The decorators stop on Sunday," Mr. Fulton said. "Don't look at anything, but here's the library."

Empty bookcases went right up to the ceiling. There was a Persian rug on the floor, and a new couch of green leather in front of the fireplace; and there were a number of great green leather chairs to match, and a flat-topped desk.

"Sloane's is going to do it all in green," Mr. Fulton said. "It's going to be quite a room, isn't it?"

"Are you going to have books?" Bob asked.

"Oh, yes," Mr. Fulton said. "Oh, yes, I've got someone getting books. There's an awful lot to do here, Bob."

"Gladys," Mr. Fulton called from the library doorway. "Oh, Gladys." And Bob heard a voice answer.

"Yes, what is it, Burt?"

"Come into the library," Mr. Fulton called, "and bring Poll and the baby, and see if Williams is in the kitchen, will you, Gladys?" He turned to Bob Tasmin again and smiled. "Everything is pretty mixed up right now," he said, "but we'll get Williams to get us something."

Bob Tasmin's impressions of everything had grown vague by then. A lady in a gingham apron had appeared in the doorway and he knew that she must be Mrs. Fulton. She had yellow hair, and she looked small and young.

"Polly," she said. "Come in, Polly, or else you'll get into trouble."

A little girl about six years old in a yellow smocked dress skipped into the room. That was the first time Bob Tasmin saw Polly Fulton.

"Gladys," Mr. Fulton said, "this is Bob Tasmin."

"I'm very glad to meet you, Robert," Mrs. Fulton said.

"Bob, here, has been a lot of help to me," Mr. Fulton said. "We've located the swimming pool and we're going to have rabbits."

"Now, Burt," Mrs. Fulton said. "I wish you wouldn't try to do everything at once, dear. Maybe we ought not to have a swimming pool, with all the decorations and everything. Maybe we won't have enough money."

"Now listen, Gladys," Mr. Fulton said. "Bob, here, agrees with me that we ought to have a swimming pool."

"Just because you sold the factory, it doesn't mean that everything will work. I wish you'd stop and catch your breath. People will think we're crazy, Burt."

"Oh, Williams," Mr. Fulton said. A tall, elderly man in a white coat had appeared in the doorway. "Williams, I'd like some root beer and pound cake. How about some root beer, Bob?"

"All right," Bob said. "Thank you very much." And then he was aware that he was still holding his air rifle.

"Put it down anywhere," Mr. Fulton said, "just throw it on the couch, Bob."

It was a very broadening experience, his visit to the Fultons.

That same evening at table Bob told his family about the library, and the root beer and the pound cake, and he must have told them also that Mr. Fulton was going to have a swimming pool, a tennis court, and lop-eared rabbits and a maze, for he remembered the expression of half-belief on his father's face, the effort to separate what was true from what was imagination.

"Did he really tell you all that?" his father asked.

The question made Bob Tasmin indignant, for it cast aspersions on a great man and on a great friendship.

"Of course he told me," he answered.

"Don't you see he was joking with you, Bob?" his father said.

But Bob Tasmin did not see. There was one thing he was very sure of. There might never be a swimming pool, or a maze or rabbits, but he knew as sure as he was alive that Mr. Fulton had meant all of it at the time. He believed in Mr. Fulton.

VIII

Portrait of an Industrialist

As BOB GREW older he used to hear people say that the Fultons were *arrivistes* and *nouveaux riches,* and that Mr. Fulton had no proper sense of proportion. He often wondered why this should bother anyone. He knew better than most the origins of Burton Fulton, because Mr. Fulton had given him a glimpse of the place from which he had come. Bob Tasmin had been too young to evaluate it fully, but it had left a deep impression on him.

It was during the summer that Bob Tasmin was sixteen, the summer he had completed his Fifth Form year at Groton, that Mr. Fulton asked him to take a four days' motor trip. Mr. Fulton asked him late one afternoon when he had gone to swim at the Fultons' pool. He still felt that the pool was somehow partially his own, and he still went there whenever he wanted without being invited. He still walked through the woods and climbed the wall, but now he crossed into a cutting garden and through a gate into a rose garden, then down a boxwood-bordered path with round pebbles on it and past a marble fountain. The men on the place all knew him, and now they called him "Master Robert." There were two diving boards by the pool, a high one and a low one, and he was practising from the high one when he saw Mr. Fulton. Mr. Fulton must have come on the six-five, and he looked pale and tired, as most Gray's Point commuters looked in the summer of 1920.

"Have they got too much chemical in the water?" Mr. Fulton asked, and he pulled a wicker chair up to the edge of the pool to watch Bob dive.

"I wish I'd learned to dive," Mr. Fulton said. "Harry's got to learn to dive."

"Aren't you coming in?" Bob asked. "The water's fine."

"No, not today. It's been pretty tough in town today," Mr. Fulton said. "Harry's got to learn how to dive and play tennis. We'll have to have the professional take him on next year. You can't learn these things when it's too late."

He sighed and looked at the row of cypress trees which lined the path from the fountain to the pool.

"I wonder if any of this will ever be real for Harry."

Bob Tasmin was growing old enough to understand that in some ways Mr. Fulton depended on him. "How do you mean — 'real'?" he asked.

"Don't let it trouble you," Mr. Fulton said. "Gray's Point isn't like the place I came from, but then, it's home to you, isn't it? I see it one way, and you see it another."

"I don't see why it isn't real," Bob said.

"Well, never mind," Mr. Fulton said, and then he smiled. "Listen, Bob, I'll tell you what we'll do. Let's get out of here for three or four days. We'll take the Duesenberg, and Rogers can drive us. What do you think of that?"

Bob thought it would be fine. He did not know what his father and mother would say, but he thought it would be fine.

"Eight o'clock in the morning," Mr. Fulton told him. "I'll call for you at eight."

He was a little surprised that both his father and his mother seemed to think it was a good idea, especially since they had suggested not so long ago that he go over to the Fultons' a little less frequently.

"I do think that's awfully kind of Mr. Fulton, dear," his mother said. "Are you sure he really wants you?"

"You know he's always liked Bob, Ruthie," his father said. "Now, Bob, I want you to listen to me. . . . Ruthie, have we any cash in the house?"

His mother had fifteen dollars in her purse upstairs, his father had twenty-five, and they borrowed forty-five dollars from Katie, and another twenty from the cook.

"Now listen to me, Bob," his father said. "When you stop at a hotel, I want you to offer to pay your own bill. I don't want Burt

Fulton to think we're taking advantage of him the way some people do around here. This is mighty nice of Burt Fulton. I'll just call him up to be sure everything's all right." And he hurried to the den.

"Yes, I'd like to speak to Mr. Fulton." Bob heard his father's voice through the half-open door. "I hope I haven't taken you away from dinner, Burt." Bob Tasmin was very much surprised. It was the first time he could remember that his father had called Mr. Fulton by his first name. "Bob says you've given him a mighty nice invitation. Are you sure you want him, Burt? . . . Well, that's fine . . . I wish I could get away myself. Things are pretty grim downtown, aren't they? . . . Well, that's the way I feel. Don't be a bear on the United States. . . . And Burt, when you get back, let's get together some night. Do you ever play poker? There's a little crowd that meets up at Mill River Saturdays. We all want you to join us sometime. Well, good-by, Burt."

His father walked out of the den with a quick, springing step.

"Let's go upstairs, Bob. I'll help you pack," he said. "It isn't everybody who can go on a trip with Burt Fulton these days."

Something had certainly happened somewhere.

They rode in the back seat of the Duesenberg touring car with the top down, and when they were on the Post Road headed for New Haven Mr. Fulton pulled his cloth cap over his eyes.

"I just came back from Detroit yesterday morning," he said. "We've got a factory there. I certainly keep moving around, don't I?"

Bob Tasmin always felt perfectly at home with Mr. Fulton, although he had not seen much of him since he had been going away to school. He sat there looking at the gasoline stations and watching the cars passing, and now and then he looked at Mr. Fulton's profile. The cap was pulled halfway over his nose, and he had gone sound asleep. His mouth, tight and alert when he was awake, was relaxed and drooping at the corners, but in spite of its droop, he seemed about to smile. He only awoke when they were halfway to Hartford.

"Oh," he said. "Hello, Bob. I missed New Haven, didn't I? What time is it, Rogers?" And Rogers told him it was half-past ten. "All right," he said. "We'll have lunch beside the road. We'll spend the night in Boston. I forgot to tell you where we were going, Bob."

It was true that he had never mentioned it.

"I sort of thought I'd like to take a look at home, and I don't like to go home alone" — but he never mentioned where home was, and Bob did not ask him. Then in the course of the afternoon Bob found that he was talking about himself and about his family, and he was flattered that Mr. Fulton should be interested.

"You see, I know a lot of people, Bob, but you're the only one who talks to me in just this way," Mr. Fulton said. "You're quite a help to me, Bob. You're giving me a picture of something I don't know much about."

Bob Tasmin said that his mother's family had a place near Rhinebeck on the Hudson, and that his grandmother was still living there.

"Rhinebeck," Mr. Fulton said. "I know Rhinebeck. What did they do there, Bob . . . I mean your mother's people?"

Bob did not know exactly what his mother's people did except that his grandfather had been a lawyer who had something to do with the railroads. Almost his only recollection of his grandfather was the time his mother had taken him at the age of five to visit there. They had been met at the station by a big carriage, and the place had seemed huge — a square, white house on the Hudson with a cupola on top — and the colored man had taken him out on the river in a rowboat.

"I like to think of that," Mr. Fulton said, "a big house on the Hudson — and I wonder what your grandfather did with those railroads in New York." But Bob Tasmin only knew about it vaguely.

He was better informed about his father's family. His father had been born in a brownstone house in New York City, somewhere near Sixteenth Street. His grandfather Tasmin was the senior partner of a banking firm, and when his father was quite young, his grandfather had built a summer place in Mamaroneck, and his father had gone to Yale.

"Yale," Mr. Fulton said. "I went to Williams. I worked most of my way through. What did he do when he got out of Yale?"

His father had been given a partnership in a firm on Wall Street, and after his marriage the young couple had lived for a while in New York, and then had moved to Gray's Point. They had built the house at Maple Ledge when Bob was very little. He must have told Mr. Fulton a great deal about himself and what he hoped to do. The year after next he would go to Yale.

"Yes," Mr. Fulton said. "You ought to go to Yale." They were driving through Worcester then. "They make very fine machine tools in Worcester. We almost bought a plant here last year. Yes, you ought to go to Yale, and then I suppose you ought to go to law school . . . the Harvard Law School, Bob. They turn out pretty slick lawyers."

In the country near Marlboro all the houses were small, compact, and old, without *porte-cochères,* or walls or gates, or ornamental shrubbery. The landscape reminded Bob Tasmin of his school, which was not far from there. Next year he would be in the Sixth Form and he would be a prefect.

"I suppose a prefect must be something like an officer in a high school class," Mr. Fulton said. "I never got elected to anything at high school."

It was difficult to explain to Mr. Fulton just what a prefect was or to compare one to anything in a high school because Bob had only a vague idea of what a high school was like. He did not want to say that he was going to a better place, and he did not want to exaggerate about being a prefect. Anyone who amounted to anything, he told Mr. Fulton, got to be one, if he did anything at all in school and if he behaved himself. He was not as good at his books as Will — Will was getting all the prizes that he never got — but he was on the Board of the Year Book. He might get his letter in football, Bob said, if everything turned out all right, but he did not think he would be good enough to try for Freshman football when he got to Yale. He would try for the crew, he thought, because his father said you had to go out for something.

"I see what you mean," Mr. Fulton said. "Now take Harry. Do you think he ought to go to a school like that?"

Bob thought that Harry certainly should, because it helped if you went to Yale or Harvard.

"Yes," Mr. Fulton said. "Yes, I see what you mean."

A change in Mr. Fulton's voice made Bob Tasmin feel that he might have been saying a lot of things which were not in good taste, as though he might have been boasting.

"I guess I've been talking an awful lot," he said, and Mr. Fulton smiled.

"Of course, you have," he said, "but why shouldn't you, when I made you? You mustn't think I'm laughing at you. You're telling me an awful lot that I don't know." Mr. Fulton was still smiling. "You see," Mr. Fulton said, "sometimes I wonder why I'm doing what I am. I don't suppose that's ever worried you."

He could not see exactly what Mr. Fulton meant since he was in no position to know what sort of things Mr. Fulton was doing.

"Well, it may sometime," Mr. Fulton said. "Maybe the main thing is to do something. There are a lot of people who don't do anything, that is, anything that's real. That's what troubles me, Bob. Nearly everyone gets far away from real things, and I don't know why they do."

They were near Boston then, and Mr. Fulton had pushed his cap back from his eyes.

"It's a great town, Boston," he said, "but in my experience it's hard to do business here. They don't act the way they do in Detroit." He leaned forward. "Go to the Copley Plaza, Rogers."

If Mr. Fulton had been a relative, Bob might have been worried about Mr. Fulton's rumpled blue flannel suit and his cloth cap, but he saw there was no need to worry. When they reached the Copley Plaza, the doorman greeted Mr. Fulton just as though they were old friends, and told him that he would get two boys for the bags; and someone who may have been the manager shook hands and said everything was ready, and that they were calling Mr. Fulton from New York.

"Thanks, Jimmy," Mr. Fulton said. "We'll have dinner upstairs. Tell Joseph to pick out what he thinks I'd like, and tell him to think up something Bob would like."

94

They had a big sitting room and two bedrooms on the third floor, and Mr. Fulton tossed his cap on a sofa, and sat down in an arm-chair.

"Well, Jimmy," Mr. Fulton said. "How's the family, Jimmy? And what are these boys' names? Come over here, boys, and tell me how you like the hotel business. You know one summer I was a bellhop. The Skyview House on Eagle Lake. That's near the Berkshires. Did you ever hear of the Skyview House?"

It would have embarrassed Bob Tasmin very much if it had been anyone except Mr. Fulton.

"There used to be quite a crowd at the Skyview House," Mr. Fulton said, "and there used to be an old party that the boys didn't like to wait on because he only tipped them a penny. But I'll tell you something, boys . . ." Mr. Fulton pointed his finger at them. "When the season was over, he called all those pennies back and changed every penny for a dollar. Now what I want is to have somebody go down and get me the evening papers, and Jimmy, you'd better get the girls to get me New York."

Almost his only memory of that evening was a picture of Mr. Fulton at the telephone.

"No, that isn't right," Mr. Fulton was saying. "You'd better handle it personally, and never mind about the inventories. . . . Well, ask the people at St. Louis, Paul, and if it doesn't work at St. Louis, try them at Toledo. . . . No, but I'll see you on Wednesday . . . and how is everything otherwise?"

Mr. Fulton clicked the receiver back on the hook.

"They seem to be a little mixed up in New York, don't they? There's a little trouble about scrap." The telephone rang again.

"Oh, hello, Gladys," Mr. Fulton said. "Yes, Bob and I are just sitting here. How's Poll . . . Yes, I want to speak to her. Hello, Poll . . . Yes, I know. I ordered those books. They don't look like much, but they're first editions. . . . Oh, it's come, has it? Well, don't have it uncrated until I'm there. . . . Yes, Bob and I are just sitting here, and we're having a grand time."

When Bob Tasmin awoke the next morning, Mr. Fulton had been

up for a long while working over piles of typewritten pages that he had kept pulling from a pigskin brief case. He tapped a page with a pencil when Bob came in and asked him to look it over. It was the first time Bob had ever seen a balance sheet.

"It doesn't look like much, does it, Bob?" Mr. Fulton said. "And those things don't even mean much to some people who've seen them all their lives. You've got to have an instinct and maybe I was born that way. It's funny — I can read these things in the evening before I go to sleep the way some people read about Sherlock Holmes. They teach you at school to be shy of figures and to be impressed by them, but you can learn to juggle them just like words and make them say exactly what you want. You've got to read them like a story, Bob."

Mr. Fulton must have said a good many things like that, but Mr. Fulton's mind moved from one thing to another so fast that he was hard to follow.

"Now when I was a little shaver in Oregon," he said — it was the first time Bob knew that Mr. Fulton had lived in Oregon — "before my father was run over, and before Mother sent me East, there used to be an old man by the Union Pacific yards in Portland. You ought to have seen him. He'd been to the Klondike and he couldn't read and write, but he certainly could figure, and do you know what he used to do? He never wrote down figures. He just drew little men, like the Egyptians, I suppose, or like the Indians. That's how I learned to read figures like a story."

Perhaps you never got to know anyone except by putting such vague, stray remarks together.

Later in the morning Mr. Fulton took him to the office of a dealer in old books, a soiled old man who wore a green eyeshade and sleeve protectors. He and Mr. Fulton sat by a dusty desk discussing Vinegar Bibles, and Mr. Fulton appeared to know more about them than the dealer.

"If you put your mind on anything," Mr. Fulton said, "why, it's funny how it all turns out to be very much like something else. Nothing's as tough as you think it is. You just want to get to the bottom of it. Maybe I ought to collect paintings. Maybe I will someday, but, I don't know . . . I rather like a library. I like to see the backs of books."

They did not leave Boston until after lunch. Then, as soon as they were in the Duesenberg again, Mr. Fulton went to sleep.

"I can always sleep anywhere," Bob Tasmin remembered Mr. Fulton's saying. "Gladys says what's the use in having Rogers drive me around if I just go to sleep?"

They were traveling through a part of the country which Bob had never seen before. The farmhouses were not well painted, and the land was hilly and rocky and partly overgrown with saplings. The road passed through a succession of small mill towns — little paper and textile mills — they never seemed to call them factories — that had been established because of water power, but now the power was not as important as it had been. Those little towns all looked as though they had been designed by the same person; they always lay in a valley beside a stream, and low, wooded hills always rose around them.

First, there would be the mill, built of stone or brick, with rows of mill workers' houses near it, small and white like the dwellings in a toy village, and then there would be the main street with a white church and perhaps a brick bank and a few stores, and finally, on lawns on a rising piece of ground, there would be the mill owner's larger house. Then the road would leave the town to wind through hills and pasture land. It was a lonely, forbidding country, with stooping, scrawny men dressed in workclothes, barns attached to houses with cordwood in the yards, and horses and battered buggies tied to hitching posts.

"Gladys is a funny girl," Mr. Fulton said when he woke up. "I guess women don't like moving around as much as men. They like to have everything all set just so. Gladys is the worrying kind. It's funny how people up around here always worry. Maybe it has something to do with the air. They're all tied up here until someone comes around to sell them oil stocks."

The familiar country had put Mr. Fulton in a reminiscent mood.

"Gladys can crochet anything," Mr. Fulton said. "Do you know what she made me once? A sort of a little hammock, with a piece

97

of an inner tube inside it, to keep things in. She used to sing in the choir. Her brother Herbert keeps the drugstore now. I got Gladys to give him a new fountain last Christmas."

It was getting on towards sundown, and Mr. Fulton was sitting up straighter.

"There's the Robbins place," he said, "and the one where the barn is falling in is the Hawkinses'. Every second farm around here belongs to a Hawkins. When I came here, it used to strike me as funny how small and mean the farms looked. They still look pretty mean, but it's a great place, America."

Bob Tasmin would often hear other people say that it was a great place, America. He would hear them say it when they were drunk or sober, and glad or sad, and sometimes he would feel the same way without saying it, but coming from Mr. Fulton, it had its own peculiar authority.

"It's a great place, America," Mr. Fulton said. "Any boy has a chance in America if he only sees the picture . . . if he only sees the picture."

There had been a faint chill of autumn in the air, and a cool, pink sunset behind the dark, wooded hills. When Bob was older and more cynical, the words often came back . . . if you only got the picture . . . if everyone could only have had the same picture . . . but the trouble was, everyone had a different one.

They were approaching another town.

"Slow down," Mr. Fulton said. "Slow down. There's my mill. American Paper owns it now."

It was a large brick mill, and the workers' houses were freshly painted. They were going down another of those main streets, and Mr. Fulton no longer seemed aware of the Duesenberg and the chauffeur. He was calling to acquaintances on the street.

"Hello, Arthur," he called. "Hi, there, Norman. Good evening, Mrs. Simmons. How's Mr. Simmons?"

Even then Bob Tasmin saw that Mr. Fulton was too gay and buoyant for the place. Mr. Fulton might have been brought up in Willett, New Hampshire. He might have been an American Boy. But he was not an American Boy from Willett.

"There's the drugstore," he said. "There's the hardware store. That's where I used to clerk for Uncle Walt."

The car drove into the yard of a small red house at the other end of the village, and Mr. Fulton said that here they were, and he told Rogers to get out their bags. An old woman in a gingham dress opened the kitchen door as soon as the car stopped. Her hair, done up in a hard knot, was almost white, and she wore steel-rimmed glasses. Mr. Fulton ran up the back steps and kissed her.

"I've been waiting for you, Burt," she said. "Supper's ready. You're twenty minutes late."

It was Mrs. Fallon, and she had been Mr. Fulton's uncle's housekeeper. The red house had been Mr. Fulton's uncle's house. He had bought it for Mrs. Fallon.

When Bob Tasmin started working for the firm of Barstow, Barstow and Bryce down on lower Broadway, just after he had graduated from law school, he encountered a good many "big" executives and captains of industry, individuals who kept coming from "outside" parts of the country to Barstow, Barstow and Bryce for legal advice on setting up Delaware and New Jersey corporations. Also Bob knew a number of them at Gray's Point, and he often wondered how these people had done it and what it was that made them successful. This was the period when magazine advertisements contained pictures of these individuals, staring out of the windows of skyscrapers and having visions, or using timesaving office gadgets, or doing fifteen minutes' simple exercises, or reading sets of the world's classics, but it seemed strange to him that none of the ones he had met exhibited any of the conventional attributes of greatness.

Most of them were crudely built with crude manners, and when Bob Tasmin took them out for an evening of relaxation in New York on an expense account — this was the duty of young men at Barstow, Barstow and Bryce, as neither old Mr. Bryce nor any of the other partners was able to stand the strain unless it was very important — they all ate and drank too much. It appeared that they all wanted to "play" when they got to New York. They used to have large hotel suites, and they all wanted the telephone numbers of bootleggers, and often between drinks just before they started doing what they called "playing" they were likely to become sentimental and introspective. That was when they all quoted something they had read somewhere about success, and they all said that success depended on the man. A real man started right from scratch, they used to say, and it was a great place, America. A real man ought to know how to handle other men, and he ought to have three attributes. He ought to be a thinker, a doer, and a getter, but in addition he ought to have vision and guts.

Sometimes up in those hotel suites, after their third or fourth drink of bootleg Scotch, they would look back over the rocky roads of their careers and would be a little awestruck when they considered where chance had taken them. They had all started out in ordinary jobs just like anybody else, and here they were. It was a great place, America. They had never had the privileges or the advantages that Bob Tasmin had (By God, he didn't know how lucky he was. He didn't have to sweat it out) but they wouldn't have missed a minute of the hard times, and here they were. It could only happen in America. There they were, but not one of them seemed able to explain how he got there. They had started as soda jerkers or shipping clerks or iron puddlers, and then something had happened — something. There was always a definite gap between mediocrity and distinction, a dusky, hazy hiatus. Once Bob thought they did not want to tell how they had achieved success, but later he began to believe that they simply did not know. Some dark impulse bursting inside them had blown them up to the top like corn in a corn-popper. Something had exploded and there they were.

Polly Fulton once told Bob that they did not know anything about it because they had no brains but only instincts. You ought to see the people B. F. brought home to dinner, Polly used to say. (She began calling her father "B. F." after she started going to Bryn Mawr.) They weren't clever, Polly said, and most of them weren't nice. She did not believe that any of them read a book a year, except B. F.; and all they did was to repeat the things they had been told. You ought to see the way they pinched under the dinner table, and the way they tried to play footie even when they were in their sixties. They lived in a tawdry world of cheap ideas and close harmony. They liked to sing "Bring the Wagon Home, John" after dinner, or "The Old Mill Stream," or about the Old Gray Mare not being what she used to be.

B. F. liked to have her around, Polly said, because B. F. said the boys liked to see someone who was young and cute, and she wished B. F. would not use that expression. B. F. said the boys had to play sometime, and he wanted them to feel at home when they came to his place, and they did. All they thought about, Polly said, was money and power and sex. They all liked to stick together because they were anachronisms, like dinosaurs or something else prehistoric. It was before they were called Rugged Individualists or Fascists or Tories. There was almost nothing, then, that Polly could call them.

Polly had once shown Bob a piece that had been written about her father in a very expensive-looking brochure called *Bulmaco Scrap.*

"Now, there you are, darling," Polly had said. "Do you know what *Bulmaco* means? I'll give you three guesses. It means Bulwer Machine Company. That's one of those companies that B. F. is playing around with now — I suppose he always has to play around with something — and I know he left this here because he knew I'd see it. I think he's really proud of it. I know you don't believe it, but he really is."

On the cover of *Bulmaco Scrap* was a heroic drawing of a work-man with a bare torso striding forward holding a cogwheel above his head. You could not tell what he was going to do with this piece of machinery, but it was obviously very heavy, for the muscles of his abdomen and shoulders bulged beneath its weight. Polly opened the booklet. The paper had deckled edges.

"There," she said. "Look at it yourself, darling. There's B. F."

There, sure enough, on the front page, was a photograph of Burton Fulton, which must have been taken at some outing or get-together of the Bulwer Machine Company. Mr. Fulton was in his shirt sleeves, holding a hamburger in one hand and a bottle of pop in the other. Beneath the picture was a caption: TAKE ANOTHER

The article about Burton Fulton was headed "Meet B. F. — the Man Who Hitched His Wagon to a Star."

It was incredible to recall that such things had been written once, and in the fairly recent past:—

Once upon a time in Oregon, a little barefoot farm tyke dug some worms behind the barn and went fishing in a creek. He was sitting there holding his sapling pole when a farmer chanced to encounter him.

"You're not getting many fish, bub," the farmer observed playfully.

Quick as a flash this little fellow turned and shook his tousled head, and looked up at the farmer with wide gray eyes.

"I'm not fishing for fish," he volunteered.

The farmer was nonplused.

"Then what are you fishing for, bub," he queried, "if it isn't fish?"

And the little lad came right back with, "Something better than fish. I'm fishing for ideas."

That little American farm boy by the stream, son of plain, hard-working American parents, was none other than Burton Fulton — just plain B. F. to you and me — now our chairman of the Board of Directors of Bulmaco. Maybe you've seen B. F. wandering around the plant, drifting dreamily through the shops, or poking around the yards, always friendly, with lots of time to "chew the rag" with the boys — a slender, sandy-haired chap with a congenial twinkle. That's B. F. Still just a kid at heart, still fishing for ideas and catching whales at Bulmaco . . . still with his wagon hitched to the star of quantity production. Yes, that's B. F., the dreamer and the thinker, but let him speak for himself in that voice of his, not Western, but with a Yankee twang that he picked up in the New Hampshire hills. "You get ideas if you see everything as a picture. Maybe it's a gift, but maybe it's just having lots of time."

And maybe it's just plain elbow grease. Let's take a look at that farm kid. When apple ranching failed, his father packed up and went to Portland where he was employed in the Union Pacific switchyards — the smell of grease and locomotives instead of new-mown hay, and running errands to the grocery store for Mom. Then tragedy struck at the little frame house by the railroad, the father being killed instantly by a switch engine. When the mother, Bessie Fulton, married again, she sent Burt East, where he lived with his Uncle Walter, a shrewd old Yankee bachelor and prominent hardware dealer of Willett, New Hampshire. So B. F. began following his star, dreaming out his dreams in Willett. At his uncle's death young Burt inherited the hardware store and married the beautiful Gladys Hawkins, daughter of Nathan Hawkins, proprietor of the local drug business. You may well imagine the surprise and consternation of his wife's folks when young Burt without a word sold the prosperous little hardware business, and with nothing but guts, elbow grease, and vision, purchased the Willett Paper Company, then in the hands of receivers, throwing the mere shoestring of his capital into it, and assuming a staggering bonded indebtedness. That took courage. It took more than courage. He had hitched his wagon to a star.

Willett being too small to hold him, and there being no more industrial worlds there to conquer, B. F., still fishing for ideas, moved with his wife and his two beautiful children (perhaps you saw Polly Fulton on a junket with B. F. at the Directors' Meeting last year. If you did, you would know we were right about those beautiful children) to his present home at Gray's Point, Connecticut. B. F. was on his way. . . .

Polly was sitting with Bob on the sofa in the Fulton library, and at this point she pulled the booklet out of his hands.

"You know he couldn't help it, Poll," Bob said. "They just write things like that."

"He needn't have left it around for us to see," Polly answered. "And you know what he told me? He said the sentiment was all he cared about. He said that old Lovelace wrote it himself."

"Who?" Bob asked. "Do you mean the poet?"

"That's very funny, isn't it?" Polly said. "I mean — old Homer J. Lovelace wrote it, the president of that damned company. He wrote it all himself, and it took him two days. They take it seriously, darling. They all keep writing things like that about each other."

The president of Bulmaco must have learned the details from Burton Fulton, but Bob was convinced that Mr. Fulton had never told the story about being a tousle-headed little boy fishing for ideas. . . .

* * *

When Bob Tasmin came back to Gray's Point after his trip with Mr. Fulton, and when everybody began to ask him what Mr. Fulton had done and what Mr. Fulton had said, he gave very few direct answers. It was Bob's idea that the trip had been confidential, and that Mr. Fulton had trusted in Bob's discretion when he had revealed those details of his background. Mr. Fulton was a friend of his not to be laughed at or discussed.

"Mr. Fulton's very nice," he told them. "We took long walks in the woods."

"Well, you must have talked about something when you were walking," George Tasmin said. "I hope he told you how to make money."

He said it in the tone so many people used then when they talked about the Fultons. He said it half jokingly, but still, it seemed to Bob that it was not said kindly.

"He didn't tell me," Bob answered. "He just said there wasn't anything to it. Mr. Fulton said any damn fool, if he wanted to, could make money in the next ten years."

"I hope he went into detail," George Tasmin said. "It may surprise you, Bob, that I've been giving a good deal of attention to that matter personally. A good many of our best minds are working on it."

George Tasmin should never have been a businessman, but perhaps he might have done well as a general. He loved order and action and authority. He might have been like General Bogart if he had gone to West Point.

"Mr. Fulton doesn't care about money," Bob answered, and he felt ashamed of his father's attitude. "He says it just comes naturally."

"That's an easy way of putting it." George Tasmin raised his eyebrows. "So it just comes naturally to him, does it?"

Bob felt superior to them all, because he was a friend of Mr. Fulton's.

"Mr. Fulton," Bob told the family, "says that any fool can make money if he sticks to a few facts. He says that any fool ought to know that everyone's going to have an automobile, and all he needs to do is buy General Motors. He says that any fool ought to know that everyone is drinking Coca-Cola and they're going to keep on drinking it. He says that any fool can buy a piece of the factory that makes Coca-Cola. He says that money doesn't matter."

Bob Tasmin never knew until long afterwards that he had divulged a useful piece of information. Perhaps if he had not spoken, they might not have kept on living at Gray's Point, and he might never have finished law school. In fact, when George Tasmin died, it turned out that the only part of the estate that was worth much, and fortunately the larger part of it, was the common stock of Coca-Cola and General Motors, purchased at the bottom of the market in 1920. Like a good general, when George Tasmin had received his information and had given it its due evaluation, he had not been afraid to take suitable action with suitable commitments, even though he had personally disliked very much the taste of Coca-Cola.

"I don't believe I can stand it much longer," Bob heard his father say once, "if I see any more of those pictures of that girl and that bottle."

It was all different now. The Coca-Cola pictures were on a global scale. Instead of pretty girls there were groups of soldiers, sailors and marines sharing their Cokes with fuzzy-headed Micronesians in G-strings, who were saying something like *Oom! Oom! Tallahassee,* which freely translated meant, "Thank you very much, pal. It's always good weather when good fellows get together." In some way those global advertisements had the ring of Burton Fulton and Burton Fulton's dreams.

IX

Dear Mildred . . .

IF THE decision were finally reached to embark on Operation Vanity, then there would be the delicate question of who should be put in charge, and Bob Tasmin imagined that this was already being debated between the theater commands and the Staff in Washington, with an appeal perhaps to even the highest levels. General Bogart had only come to the theater for consultation and discussion and was due to return and report to Washington, but there were rumors — you always heard rumors — that General Bogart had his lines out, and that he was not content to be simply with the planners. The Quonset hut assigned to the general and his staff for an office seemed to Bob Tasmin suspiciously active, and Lieutenant Colonel Gilkey, one of the general's aides, had dropped a hint that morning. Technical noncoms were already busy at their typewriters, and Gilkey was sitting at a table just outside the general's door sorting piles of papers.

"Hello, Gilkey," Tasmin said. "The Old Man sent for me."

Colonel Gilkey was a dark, trim officer who fell in the category known as a fine figure of a soldier. He had been to V. M. I., which he referred to playfully as "General Marshall's school," and he had worn the uniform so long that he appeared to have been born in it. It seemed to Bob, when he entered the Quonset hut, that Colonel Gilkey regarded him with a new sort of interest, as though he had just heard a piece of news which made Tasmin a little more worth knowing.

"The Old Man's busy as a bird dog," Gilkey said. "He really has his teeth right into everything."

Gilkey rose and stepped noiselessly to the general's door and knocked. A good aide always behaved like a palace chamberlain.

The general was seated behind a table staring at a map that was tacked on the opposite wall. He was also a fine figure of a soldier, and the service had given him the facial austerity that many generals had in common, and a spare, hard symmetry. His hair was steel-gray. His eyes were dark and deep-set. His mouth had deep wrinkles at the corners.

"Hello, Tasmin," he said. "Are they beginning to make you work?"

"Yes, sir," Bob answered. "We're starting."

A young, blond major from the Air Corps, a snub-nosed boy with pale blue eyes, who had been sitting on one of those collapsible chairs near the general's table, rose when Tasmin entered.

"This is Major Riley," the general said. When Tasmin and Major Riley shook hands, it seemed to Bob that the major also looked unnecessarily interested.

"Sit down, Tasmin; sit down, Riley," General Bogart said. "Will you have a cigarette? No, use my lighter. It's a damn good lighter, it always works."

They looked at General Bogart's lighter. It was made of silver.

"They're no good if they don't work, sir," the major said.

"It's called a Zippo lighter," the general said. "It was given me by Sandy Benton. Did you ever meet Sandy Benton?"

There was a silence which implied that neither Major Riley nor Bob Tasmin had met him. They both sat on the edges of their chairs watching General Bogart.

"He was three classes below me at the Point," General Bogart said.

"Yes, sir," Major Riley said.

The conversation seemed to lead nowhere, but it was clear that the general had something on his mind.

"Of course, I'm just an Army brat," he said, and he smiled. "Now, Colonel Tasmin here used to be a corporation lawyer, and I've never had much traffic with lawyers, but I guess they're good for the Intelligence. Tasmin has an excellent mind."

Bob was very much surprised at this outburst of General Bogart's because the general had hitherto concealed any such flattering opinion.

"Tasmin has only been with me a short time," the general went on, "but any time I've asked him for information, it's been what I've wanted. Tasmin's on my team."

"Yes, sir," the major said.

Tasmin could not understand why he was being highly recommended to a kid at least fifteen years younger than he. The general raised his hand and pointed to the map.

"Tasmin knows more about that damn place than the Japs do," the general went on. "I'd feel sorry if I lost him."

Major Riley nodded.

"Yes, sir," he said, and General Bogart smiled again and moved about in his chair so that he faced Bob Tasmin.

"You see, this is the situation, Bob," he said, and Tasmin was startled, because the general had never called him by his first name before. "I had something like a brainstorm this morning. The major is going out tomorrow to take some low photographs of Beach Blue."

General Bogart picked up his Zippo lighter.

"He's flying a B-24," he said. His eyes were on Tasmin's face. "Perhaps you've heard."

"Yes, sir," Tasmin answered, and his lips felt dry. "They spoke about it in Intelligence."

General Bogart set down his Zippo lighter.

"I don't want to go back to Washington without someone on our team's having seen the beach. There were the usual objections at the meeting about sending out officers with too much information, but I talked them out of it."

The general paused and stared at his lighter. Tasmin's lips felt very dry. He remembered what had happened to the P-38's from Area 300.

"The usual objections," the general went on — "about possible capture. I said my officer would take care of that. Besides, if you get it coming in low, that's about all there is, isn't it, Major?"

"Yes, sir," the major said, "and if we ditch at sea — " He shrugged his shoulders. "Mighty few people ever get out of a B-24. The water comes in the bomb bays, and the Martin turret usually falls and breaks the pilot's neck." The major smiled apologetically.

General Bogart laughed. "That's what I've always heard," he said. "No trouble about security."

Tasmin was surprised that his hand was steady when he lit another of the general's cigarettes.

"I want you to see it," the general said. "You will leave with Major Riley first thing tomorrow morning. You'll be at the briefing this afternoon. Riley will see about any extra clothing or equipment."

Tasmin knew he had to say something. He could only tell himself that he must go through with it properly.

"I would like to see that beach, sir," he said.

There might have been a sour, cynical note in his voice, but he hoped there was not. The last thing he wanted in the world was to see that beach. For a moment it was as if he were entirely alone in the room; he seemed to be dead already, and there was no past, no future.

"If you wish to withdraw, you can," the general said. "This is a volunteer mission. Have you got any reservations?"

Bob would only see the terrain for a few seconds but the general liked the idea because he had thought of it. Tasmin was going to risk his neck for nothing more than that thought, but he hoped his voice was all right.

"No reservations at all, sir," he said. "I want to see that beach."

Then that sense of being alone left him and he saw the general clearly as though a curtain had risen between them, and the general was smiling and friendly.

"Well, that's fine," he said. "You and Major Riley can go over the details."

"Yes, sir," Tasmin said.

He was on his feet walking toward the door when the general's voice stopped him.

"I'd like you to go to the admiral's dinner with me tonight. Gilkey will call for you at seven. See you at seven, Tasmin."

Then he and Major Riley were standing outside the Quonset hut.

"Have you ever been out on one of these things before?" the major asked.

"Why, no," Tasmin answered. "I've always sat at desks. I hope I didn't seem surprised."

"No, you didn't," Riley said, and he pushed his cap back from his forehead, "but sending you out to look at that beach — will you pardon my saying it's a damn fool idea?"

"Yes," Bob said, "I'll pardon you, Major." And then Major Riley laughed.

"Well, anyway," he said, "it's nice you're coming for the ride."

There was no use pretending in front of anyone like Major Riley.

"It isn't nice," Bob said. "I don't like being scared." And Major Riley laughed again.

You did not make a fool of yourself if you tried to take it lightly. Already Bob was weighing their chances of getting back alive, and the best thing was to be convinced that everything was finished. At the same time the photographic mission, though dangerous, was not necessarily fatal. Riley, for example, must have been doing such things for a long while, and the major was still alive and cheerful — but then the major's age carried with it a higher content of optimism. Bob recalled that when he was in his twenties he never had thought much about dying, or if he had, not in the same way one thought of death at forty. Death was more of an accident at twenty-five and not so much a matter of balancing the books. It seemed to Bob suddenly that everything he had done had led inevitably to this absurd, distorted moment.

"You'd better come out to the field this afternoon and meet the crew," Major Riley was saying. "I'll find you a place out there to sleep tonight. You see, we'll be starting early."

It was very hard to keep his mind on people and on the things they said. The flying field, the mess, and the boys' finding him a flying suit and gloves reminded him of the time he had been taken to the hospital as a child to have his tonsils and adenoids removed. He had gone to bed in the daytime, and everyone had been very kind and cheerful and efficient, in much the same way they were now. He heard himself asking intelligent questions about the technical details of photography and about turret and tail gunners, but at the briefing and all through the afternoon at the field he was convinced that he was leaving everything he had ever known and that all the things he had thought of doing when the war was over would never be done now.

The life he had led had never seemed so vivid or so satisfying. He thought of Mildred and he thought of his son. He thought of all the things in him which Mildred had been obliged to put up with, and Mildred had never seemed so kind, so generous or so beautiful.

Later in his room in the Bachelor Officers' Quarters he opened his valpack and took out a packet of letter paper which she had given him. He placed a sheet of it on a notebook, balanced the book on his knee and began to write her a letter. It was a quarter past six, and he knew that he must hurry.

"Dear Mildred," he wrote.

If you get this, it means I have gone out on a plane and not returned. I don't want you to take this too hard, and you know the same thing has been happening to lots of people nowadays. When we said good-by, I had no idea I should run into anything like this, but here it is. I've been thinking about you a lot this afternoon, but the trouble has been that I have been thinking about everything at once, and I suppose I'll go on doing it because there isn't any time to sort it out. I really love you in my introverted way. It may not have been very apparent always, but there it is. I've also been thinking how peculiarly everything turns out. Not a very original thought, is it? When I first met you at that dinner party at the Foxes' — you had on a black velvet dress — do you remember? — with a very wide skirt. Well, if we had known that night that we would be married — but maybe we did know that because we were both in the marrying mood — and that I should end up being bopped off by a Japanese somewhere off East Asia instead of dying peacefully of thrombosis or something, we would not have taken the idea seriously; but that's the way things are going nowadays, isn't it? Right in the barrel over Niagara Falls. We were all taught to expect something different — I don't know exactly what and I wish I did.

Who do you think I saw out here today? Milton Ouerbach. I'll see him again at dinner tonight. Bogart is taking me just as a treat because he thought of sending me out on this flying party. Don't you wish you could be at that dinner? You certainly would make the Waves and Wacs and other ladies out here look silly. Well anyway, Milton, if I see him, will talk about peace aims and the world of tomorrow — that saner, finer world, so much better than the one we used to know. Personally, I say "Nuts!" darling. I don't see how it's going to be much better with everyone run ragged by this war, and you wouldn't think so either if you could have a look at London. Personally, I think the world we used to live in, cockeyed though it was, was better. Right now, it seems to have been too good to last. Well, don't give up my ration card until you have to.

I don't know what they'll use for money in the brave world of tomorrow, but maybe Milton knows. In case he does, I'll get him to tell you. In case he doesn't, you have the keys to the safe deposit box and old man Willoughby has my will. I'd sell the country place if I were you. Don't keep living in the past the way I've done this afternoon. It takes your mind off your knitting. Give Ned a kiss for me, dear, and tell him to be a good boy, and make him feel that perhaps he will not be perfect simply by eating Wheaties. Also, if you can, see if he can grow up and not be a Peter Pan like so many friends of ours. Don't help him too much the way everyone was always helping me and try not to have him live in a little world of wonder the way so many of us did. Anyway, the Internal Revenue Bureau will take care of that. Milton Ouerbach is right. The income tax is the greatest social force in America, and oh, darling, maybe they haven't started with it yet.

I don't believe, until you get into a box like the one I'm in right now, you ever realize how much you have always taken for granted. First you accept day and night, and then the seasons, and then you accept a mode of existence and a whole assortment of theories and ideas. You accept them without paying too much attention exactly as you accept your friends. You fall into a groove. You only think about this when it's too late. I know now I've taken you for granted like everything else, and if I were to get out of here I probably would again, but right now I realize it and I'm awfully sorry. I'm awfully sorry too that I have such hazy ideas on religion, that I don't know very much about the hereafter, a question which has also troubled me this afternoon. I don't seem to know much about our war aims either, but I do know that I am glad I've seen this show. On the whole, I guess I'm pretty glad that I have lived, and I'm delighted that we met and got along reasonably well together. Well, you can see that I've been giving everything a great deal of thought.

Bob Tasmin stopped and his gaze traveled from the sheet of paper to the bare bulkhead of the Quonset hut. The wind was rising, and a gust of it blew a puff of coral dust through the screened aperture close to the floor, or the deck to you, if you were in the Navy. He had never dreamed that he could be capable of such an outpouring on a sheet of paper. It was like the Testament of François Villon, except that it was in colloquial, imperfect prose. He had never intended to say so much to Mildred, but now that he had started, he could not resist the impulse to go on with it. He rubbed his hand slowly on his khaki trousers and picked up the pencil again.

There's one thing that sets my mind a little at rest about you. Maybe this business of having taken each other for granted so long isn't as bad as it might have been. I know that this has been a damned frustrating time for you, and I've often wondered how women could stand it. . . . I hope you marry someone else eventually, if you find someone who'll be nice to Ned. This is no implication that you don't love me. It's just this damned war, darling.

Bob Tasmin stopped again and pulled a handkerchief from his pocket and mopped his forehead.

You might say good-by to Mother and let Will have the portrait if he wants it. And now this is about all, darling. I hear a car outside, and if I'm not mistaken, it is the Old Man's aide. He is going to pick me up and then we'll pick up the general, and then we will go to a brass-hat party which will be a page of history, consisting of a number of great characters in the area. Then off to an uncomfortable cot on the flying field, and then Tally-ho, if that is the proper way to put it. I'd better close now and brush my hair.

Love and kisses,

Bob

X

Goodbye Girls I'm Through

IT WAS a departure from any letter he had ever written. At any rate, there was nothing in it to make anyone feel too sad, but as a final document from someone supposedly intelligent it sounded futile. Nevertheless, it was the best he could do, and it was too late to try again because Lieutenant Colonel Gilkey had opened the door.

"All set?" Gilkey asked.

"Yes," Bob Tasmin answered. "I was afraid you were going to ask if I was squared away."

Gilkey laughed.

"We've got time for a quick one," he said, "if you've got any liquor."

Bob Tasmin opened his valpack and pulled out a bottle.

"Won't there be any where we're going?" he asked. There might very well not be any where he eventually might be going.

"The Old Man doesn't like it if you take more than one," Gilkey said.

"Then we'd better take two here," Bob Tasmin said. "There's a glass over by the water tap." He pointed to the glass and picked up an aluminum canteen cup.

"Thanks," Gilkey said. "They really do put chlorine in this water." He stood up straight and held up his glass. "Here's looking at you."

"Let's have another," Bob said, and then he remembered the letter. It was necessary to make some sort of speech, and anything he thought of sounded very bad. "In case of accident, would you mind

114

dropping over to Scott Circle when you get back to Washington and giving this letter to Mildred — that's my wife?"

Gilkey smiled and took the letter.

"Now don't get hunches," he said. "You don't look jumpy. You're not jumpy, are you?"

"Oh, no," Bob Tasmin answered, "not at all."

The general, when they called for him, was in a genial mood. He smiled at them as they saluted, so their manner toward him also became discreetly jocular, not unlike the relationship between a schoolmaster and two temporarily favored boys.

"I'll bet you two have been sneaking a couple of quick ones," the general said. "You don't want to tempt Gilkey that way, Tasmin. It isn't good for his figure."

Gilkey laughed happily.

"He didn't tempt me, General, sir," Gilkey said. "I tempted him, General."

"That reminds me of a story," the general said, as the driver closed the door of the car. "Can you stand an off-color story, Gilkey?"

"I'm right in there with you, sir," Gilkey said.

"Gilkey has to work out my stories on a slide rule," the general said. "You see if you can help him, Bob."

Again the general called him by his first name.

"It seems," the general said, "that there was a little boy who was behaving in a queer way and his parents brought him to a psychiatrist. The psychiatrist asked him what he liked to do most in the world, and little Willie said he liked to make slingshots and to chase little girls, and then the psychiatrist felt he was getting somewhere. Did you ever hear this one, Tasmin?"

"I don't think so, sir," Tasmin said. It was not his place to stop the general, and both he and Gilkey listened carefully and laughed.

"Oh, Tasmin," the general said, "one thing I forgot. When you go over there tomorrow" — Tasmin nodded — "see how much coral you can see. Coral and underwater obstacles never look right to me in pictures."

The admiral had taken over one of the Officers' Clubs for the dinner. There was a long table for the senior officers and smaller tables for the juniors. When they entered, an orchestra of four sailors was playing waltzes, and mess boys were passing cocktails and appetizers.

"You must meet the admiral," the general said, and they followed the general across the crowded room, and the admiral hoped they would enjoy themselves at Guam.

"I've got a story for you," the general said. "I wonder if you've heard this one." A captain and a rear admiral and two brigadier generals drew nearer.

"It's about a little boy who was having emotional troubles and went to a psychiatrist, and the psychiatrist said, 'Willie, what do you like to do best in the world?' Have you ever heard that one?" The group was growing larger.

"That's Bogart," Bob Tasmin heard someone murmur. "Yes, Bogart, talking to the admiral."

"I think I've heard it," a brigadier general said. "But it's worth telling a great many times."

"Yes," the admiral said. "Go ahead and tell it, Waldron, and don't let anybody stop you."

Bob Tasmin stepped backwards to where he belonged among a group of watchful aides and staff officers. They all stood there shyly while the sailors played "On the Banks of the Sas-kat-che-wan" from *The Pink Lady*. As the ancient music stopped the group around General Bogart burst into appreciative laughter, and a mess boy gave Bob Tasmin an Old-fashioned cocktail.

Tasmin's mouth felt parched as he tried to tell himself that this was a very remarkable scene, that there were figures present — figures whose names would go down in history with Farragut and Grant and Lee. They were the men who were commanding the combat groups in a bloody, ruthless war, enigmatic men, whose final judgment was the same as destiny, though they would have simply said, if asked, that they were the first team out in the West Pacific carrying the ball. They were having their chance, at last, to justify their existence. No one had ever heard of them a year or

116

two before, but now everyone was listening to them, searching for their human side and hanging on their jokes, which were not very good. They, too, would coin phrases which would appear in history — such things as "Damn the torpedoes!" "Fire when you are ready, Gridley," and "Don't give up the ship."

It was a page of Tolstoi, it was a painting of Nelson before Trafalgar, or Napoleon at Austerlitz. Bob Tasmin was trying to keep his mind on it when Milton Ouerbach appeared beside him.

"Is this an unusual function, or isn't it?" Milton asked.

"I wouldn't say it was unusual," Bob told him, "given the time and place. We all have to play sometime, Milton."

"Just the same, it discourages me," Milton said. "I don't seem able to translate it into common terms. I can't evaluate it."

Milton Ouerbach blinked nearsightedly at the room. "I know you won't quote me on this, Robert," he went on, "but this is a very undemocratic group."

"Don't repeat yourself," Bob Tasmin said. "You said all that this morning. Don't you know there's a war on?"

Milton Ouerbach sighed.

"Oversimplify it if you want to, but it's very disturbing to me, Robert. What are we fighting for? I don't believe anybody here is giving it any real thought."

"Maybe they've got too much else on their minds."

"What bothers me," Milton said, "is that they have so little on their minds. All today I've hardly heard a word of serious conversation. Now this afternoon I spent an hour with the admiral, and when I tried to lead him into a discussion of peace aims, what do you think he told me?"

"What?" Bob Tasmin asked.

Milton Ouerbach raised his left hand and let it fall limply to his side.

"He told me a story about a little boy and a psychiatrist."

"Oh," Bob said, "he told you that one, did he?"

"It's what I say . . ." Milton said, "there is something sinister about militarism. I wish I could see some of the little men in the

117

foxholes. I wish I could put my finger on the pulse of something human. There is nothing here but frustration . . . Why do you think that's funny?"

"All right," Bob Tasmin said — he had not known that he was laughing — "I'll tell you something human, Milton. I think I'm going to get killed tomorrow."

"My God," said Milton Ouerbach. "How?"

Bob Tasmin could not understand exactly why he was enjoying himself, but he was.

"I can't tell you how, Milton," he said, "because it's a military secret."

Milton stared through his glasses. He was shocked and concerned, but there was more to it than that. Milton was professionally aroused.

"This is really something for you, Milton," Bob Tasmin said, "and you might put it this way in a broadcast: 'Last night I was chatting with a friend and stumbled upon a little human drama, so common in this war. He explained to me that he thought he would be killed in the morning. I passed it off with a nervous laugh, and then sure enough, next day — well, I can never forget that gallant friend of mine on the threshold of the Great Adventure.' How's that, Milton?"

"It's not very funny," Milton said. "You're not serious, are you, Robert?"

Bob Tasmin was still enjoying himself.

"I'm going to a place tomorrow, Milton," he said, "that's got about all the antiaircraft in the Empire. I think the chances are about three to one against my coming back."

"My God," Milton said, "I thought you were with a general."

"That's what I thought, too." Bob smiled at Milton.

"This is terrible," Milton said, and he put his hand on Bob's arm and lowered his voice. "Suppose if I were to see the admiral . . . ?"

It was pleasant to have him so concerned, but Bob enjoyed telling him please to keep out of it.

"Robert," Milton said. "You act so calm."

"I'm not calm," Bob Tasmin said. "I'm scared."

"What do you think about?"

"That's the trouble," Bob said. "I'm thinking about everything at once." A Navy captain was walking toward them.

"You're Mr. Ouerbach, aren't you?" the captain said. "The admiral wants you at his table," and he took Milton Ouerbach by the arm. "The admiral hopes you'll say a few words after dinner."

If Milton had stayed, he would only have asked more questions, and as it was he had nearly succeeded in making Tasmin into a dramatic figure. Bob might have been pressed into saying something stuffy which Milton would have considered almost fascist. He might have quoted the late Justice Oliver Wendell Holmes on the Harvard graduates who had died in the Civil War, the few educated gentlemen who had made a gallant gesture that adorned the episode without in any way influencing the final result. This would have annoyed Milton, because Milton always gagged at the word "gentlemen," and coming from a liberal justice, Milton would not have known how to take it. Bob would have enjoyed pointing out that Milton and his whole intellectual class were just as pompous and supercilious, as careful of prerogative and protocol, just as arrogant and as much a privileged group as the military men whom Milton disliked. The truth was that all liberals were turning into self-righteous, complacent social snobs, and each faction was the only one that understood America.

Bob was just wishing that he might have another drink, when, a few yards away, he saw young Harry Fulton holding an Old-fashioned cocktail.

"You don't want that drink, do you, Harry?" Bob asked.

"Why, hello, Bob," Harry said. "I didn't know you'd be here."

"You didn't answer my question," Bob told him. "I said, 'You don't want that drink, do you?'"

"How do you know I don't?" Harry asked.

"Because you're young, and it might make you misbehave," Bob said. "Give it to me, Harry, and you'll feel better in the morning." Harry Fulton looked worried.

"I haven't been doing anything out of order, have I?" he asked.

"No, but you might," Bob said. "Give it to me, Harry."

Then Harry saw that it was all a joke and he began to laugh.

"It was awfully funny seeing you this morning," he said. "I've made a lot of friends in this man's army, but they're — " Harry paused, and he suddenly looked completely defenseless.

"They're what, Harry?" Bob asked him.

Harry moved closer to him and lowered his voice.

"Being a rich man's son, I mean. You can't be sure anybody likes you for what you are."

"Of course everybody likes you," Bob said. "You're a good kid, Harry."

"Now with you it's like someone in the family," Harry said. "Gosh, it's nice to see you, Bob. Father thought a lot of you, you know."

It was not the right time to be listening to Harry because it brought up all sorts of things about which it was too late to do anything.

"I'm sorry I didn't see more of him, Harry," Bob said. "I — " He spoke more slowly. "I thought a lot of him, too."

"He talked about you the last time I saw him," Harry said. "You know how he felt when Poll — "

"Yes," Bob said, "I know."

"You know he always hoped that you and Poll — "

"Yes, I know. It didn't work, that's all."

"Well, I wish it had," Harry said.

You could do nothing about things that did not work, and it was neither the time nor the place to talk about it, but then it might be the only time.

"Harry," Bob Tasmin asked, "will you do something for me?" He stopped, because the last thing he wanted was to sound melodramatic.

"When you see Poll again, I wish you'd tell her something." He looked at Harry and then down at his empty glass. There was even a maraschino cherry in the Old-fashioned cocktail. The Navy always thought of everything. "I wish you'd tell Poll that you and I were talking about her, and that I said she was absolutely right. Tell her I wouldn't have made her happy, will you? Because — "

"Because what?" Harry asked.

"Because I never could have been all the things she wanted," Bob Tasmin said.

"Well, neither has Tom," Harry said. "We've all been worried about Poll."

If you had loved anyone once, no matter how long ago, it was an experience that always remained a part of you. If Polly was unhappy there was nothing he could do about it now.

"I'm sorry," he said, "will you give her my love?"

The sailors' orchestra was playing another tune, a very old one, but one that had a quality of garish coincidence and it made Bob laugh.

"They certainly have dug up all the old, corny tunes," he said.

"What are they playing now?" Harry asked. "I've never heard it."

"You're too young," Bob said. "It's called 'Goodbye Girls I'm Through.'"

Bob was almost too young for it himself, but he remembered it at the summer dances at the Yacht Club when he stood outside in the dark with other little boys.

"How do the words go?" Harry asked. Bob had been humming in time with the orchestra.

"I've done with all flirtation, you've no more fascination. There's but one to whom I'm true. Goodbye, Girls, Goodbye Girls, Goodbye Girls, I'm through."

It would have been better if he had not taken those quick ones with Colonel Gilkey, for he had sung the chorus aloud, and a group had gathered around which included Captain Murphy and the general from the Intelligence Room and the British colonel. They all clapped when he stopped.

"Bravo!" Colonel Smythe Smythe Dawson called. "Bravo! Bis." And he saw Gilkey hurrying toward him.

"The general wants to know why you never said you could sing," Colonel Gilkey said.

"Because he never asked me," Bob answered.

"Well, come on over," Gilkey said. "The admiral wants you to do it again with the orchestra."

"Now, wait a minute," Bob began. "Wait a minute —" But no

one waited. The orchestra was already vamping the prelude of "Goodbye Girls I'm Through."

A jeep from the airfield called for him after dinner. Major Riley was finishing a rubber of bridge, and he said that a cot had been put up for Tasmin in his room, and as long as he was back early they might just as well turn in. Major Riley talked for a while about baseball, and he was willing to bet on the St. Louis Cardinals for the coming season — barring accidents to players.

"And don't worry about being waked up," Major Riley said. "They'll wake us up all right."

A few minutes after the light was out the major's even breathing revealed that he was asleep, but Tasmin could not sleep, and his conversation with Harry Fulton kept coming back and with it the words of "Goodbye Girls I'm Through." He thought of all the girls he had been through with. He did not believe he was particularly susceptible, but there were a number . . . for instance a girl named Betty whom he had met on a British ship. Everything had been organized into a solid round of games — boys and girls and games. Young people were always being thrown together, too much together, and without any proper oversight — including himself and Betty. He had met her in Paris later, and they had gone to the races at St. Cloud and to a number of night clubs. There was one thing about Betty. She had never cared about looking at the three-starred things in a Baedeker. That was before he fell in love with Polly Fulton, and in a way they had been as good as engaged, but Polly had seen her in New York when he and Betty had been dancing at the Silver Slipper — and Polly had said that Betty was just the sort of girl whose picture little boys like Harry pinned on the walls of their rooms.

"What you want to do is to stop getting in a rut, darling," Polly said. "Use your brain instead of being typical. You've got a brain if you don't fry it playing games."

He could see himself just as Polly must have seen him — a member of the well-stocked club group which was indigenous to the Eastern seaboard and which had a culture stemming from the

British upper middle class—a group with good manners and one which had trained itself in several generations of security.

"Darling," he heard her saying, "if you weren't so damned perfect—"

It did no good to tell her that there were a number of things wrong with him.

"That's exactly it. The things that are wrong with you aren't wrong," she said. "The things that are right with you are just too damned right."

She used to say that he danced too well and his tennis was too good. His clothes never looked rumpled and nothing ever seemed to sag. He behaved himself when he was tight, and he was wonderful with parlor tricks—those songs of his. He was even wonderful in the broad-minded, tolerant way he loved her.

"If you'd only chew tobacco and spit on the floor, darling," he heard her saying. "If you'd only walk on your hands or be unfaithful to me."

Every inflection of Polly's voice was clear. It was a slightly hoarse but musical voice. He had once said it was like cobwebs in moonlight, which for him was saying a great deal. That, of course, was when he loved her, and Polly had been pleased, but only for the moment.

"That's damned cute, darling," he could still hear her say. "It's what you would say. I could almost have said it for you. You're absolutely true to type."

Tasmin lay staring into the blank darkness. He had never felt so alive, too alive to sleep. Everything she had said about him had been partly justified, but then, most facts were compromised by half-truths. You lived in a narrow world from which you tried to escape in many tentative little ways, or else you burst out of it with a bang, but even if you did, you only got into another that had other limitations. At best, if you were a great man, you might put two or three of those worlds together. But then perhaps the main attribute of greatness was understanding limitations and accepting charitably what one did not know. There was only one thing you could take with you wherever you went, and that was a little knowledge.

He could not help wondering what Polly was doing now, and whether she still thought of him as often as he did of her. After all, he and Polly Fulton might have been married. In the last analysis it was his fault, not hers. At any time for more than a year Polly would have married him. If he had not waited until he had been made a junior partner, if he had not been so careful . . .

Finally, his muscles relaxed and his mind moved more slowly. He was calm and near to sleep, and he was thinking about God, the Maker of heaven and earth, in the resounding words of the Apostles' Creed. The Creed itself was a set of rules, a legal document, as definite as the rules of chess. You either moved on diagonals or one square at a time, depending on what you were, but you had to live by rules. He could hear voices reciting those solemn words. "I believe in God the Father Almighty, Maker of heaven and earth." Though he had recited the Creed often enough, he was not sure that he believed in all of it. That was the trouble with rules and creeds. Everyone kept interpreting them in slightly different ways, and if you did not believe in them you said they were symbolic. He had been confirmed as a boy in the Episcopal faith, and Polly once had said what else could you expect? It was just where he would be, with all the nice people, reciting that mumbo-jumbo, and listening to that fat-faced old nincompoop, Mr. Meel, in a white surplice, telling them how to be good, as though Mr. Meel knew anything about love and life. He did not even know, Polly said, that there was music in the words of the Book of Common Prayer. But still he could hear the voices. Outside on the strip a plane was warming up. First, there were a few coughs and then the motors were roaring, but he could still hear the voices.

"Oh, God," he was thinking. "Thanks for having let me live."

It might have been the time to promise to do better if he came back, but that seemed like a cheap attempt to strike a bargain with the Infinite, and he ended with a half-lost phrase from childhood.

"Bless everyone I love."

It all was as simple as that, so simple that he was embarrassed when he spoke the words in his thoughts, and he knew what Polly would have said — that it sounded exactly like him.

XI

It Was Very Bad Weather in Washington

AT JUST about this time Tom Brett had been called to Washington to "expert" a public announcement, and it was one of those things that had to be passed by a number of different agencies, and then all the conflicting suggestions reconciled. He had told Polly that he could do it in three days but he was always overoptimistic about his ability to get things done, and now it had already taken him two weeks. When Polly reached him at the number his office had given her Tom had said that everything was running him ragged and that he hated to leave her alone just a few weeks after her father's death, but after all, there was a war on.

This work he was doing, as far as she could gather — for he always talked very quickly over the telephone — was in some way concerned with a verbal directive which had been given the FEA, and no one could remember its exact limitations since it had been verbal. At the same time, it appeared that similar directives had been given to the Department of Agriculture and also to the State Department, though it was impossible for her to see how the State Department entered into it. In the meanwhile the Quartermaster General of the Army had issued a similar directive, and Tom explained that it was absolutely necessary to get the whole thing straightened out before it broke in the papers, and Tom had been unnecessarily vague over the telephone.

"Will you please not ask me any more questions?" he said. "I'm not where I can talk about it."

Polly heard the hum of voices over the telephone and the sound of a piano. "Where are you talking from?"

"What?" Tom asked.

"I said where are you talking from?"

"I'm talking from a meeting," Tom said.

"Well, what's the music for?"

"It's a cocktail party," Tom said, "but at the same time, it's a meeting."

"Oh," Polly said. "You mean you're run so ragged that you have to meet at a cocktail party."

"I mean nothing of the sort," Tom said, and his voice grew measured and edgy as it did when he was annoyed. "I mean I've come here to meet the Secretary and it's the only place where I could see him."

"Oh," Polly said. "What secretary, darling?"

"Never mind what secretary."

"Is he the one who is playing *The Chocolate Soldier?*"

"Poll," Tom said. "I wish you'd understand. I'm busy, and I'm very, very tired."

"You don't sound tired. You sound as though you'd had two drinks. I know the way you sound."

"That's because I'm tired, Poll. I can't help how I sound. Nobody can help how he sounds down here. He can just try, that's all."

"Oh, so you're just trying."

"Listen, Poll," Tom said, "what were we talking about before we started this? I wish you wouldn't go off on a tangent."

"I didn't. You're the only one who's on a tangent."

"Poll, I wish you'd stop. You can't run everything by remote control."

"What?"

"I said you can't run everything by remote control. I told you I can't possibly get home this week end. You let me run things down here, and don't you try to run them. It's too complicated already."

"Who's that playing the piano?"

"He's an awfully nice guy, if you want to know, who's working with me on this. He's a friend of Milton Ouerbach's."

"He may be a friend of Milton Ouerbach's, but he's a lousy piano player."

"I never said he was a good piano player."

"If you can't come home," Polly said, "I'll come down for the week end."

There was a pause and she could still hear the piano, and Tom spoke more quickly.

"Now listen, darling," he said. "You don't have to do that. It's useless travel, and there's a war on, darling; and on top of everything else, you don't have to mind about me."

"Don't you want me to come?" Polly asked. "I can leave on the two o'clock Saturday."

There was another pause, and the piano was still going.

"I didn't say I didn't want you to come, Poll," Tom said. "I'd love to have you come. I know you must be feeling lonely. How's your mother?"

"Oh, Mother's all right, considering."

"Well, I'd love to have you come, but I'm awfully busy, Poll."

Polly told him that she would come anyway, and she told him to get one of the suites on the fifth floor at the hotel if he could, and she said she could amuse herself if he was busy. Certainly she had distinctly told him when she would arrive, and he might at least have been waiting for her at the hotel if not at the station.

It was very bad weather in Washington, half snowing and half raining, and there were no porters, and her bag was heavy. It was a fitted alligator suitcase which her father had given her and it had a cloth covering to protect it. Polly was wearing her mink coat, and the bag and coat were both social errors. The concourse was filled with damp and dreary soldiers and sailors standing in front of the gates or seated on their barracks bags, or kissing their wives good-by in embarrassingly oblivious embraces. As she walked by a few of them whistled, and the sound made her feel younger and more cheerful, and halfway to the taxicab entrance a sailor, a red-haired boy in a pea jacket, offered to carry her suitcase.

"That's all right, ma'am," he told her when she thanked him. "I've got a sister myself back home."

It made Polly feel still younger.

"How old is she?" she asked.

"Quite a lot older than me," the sailor said. "She must be twenty-five."

She could think of herself telling the story later. . . . The sweetest sailor had carried her bag for her in the Union Station in Washington. He said she was like his sister, and how old do you think his sister was? There was one thing about Washington — there were lots of extra men.

There were lots of extra men in the taxicab, too, going to the hotel, whose sisters would never see twenty-five again. Two of them squeezed in with her on the back seat, and two sat beside the driver, who had a collection of little animals on the dashboard. The driver was smoking a cheap cigar and he turned on the radio. No one spoke except a man in the front seat who said it was good weather for ducks.

The brightly lighted hotel looked much as it always had, except that it was shabbier. The doorman standing beneath the glowing canopy looked shrunken in his horizon-blue uniform, and his eyes were red and tired. Even the old man standing by his heap of newspapers near the revolving door looked discouraged. The headlines said that we were blasting Düsseldorf as well as blasting specified islands in the Pacific, but Polly had read it all on the train. She had read without being able to understand what they were doing over there even when George Fielding Eliot or Hanson Baldwin tried to explain, and this, she supposed, was because war was a man's business. Women just sat on the edges of men's discussions, picking up bits of facts, distorting them and throwing them out again in conversation until their husbands laughed at them. Polly could not entirely blame the husbands either.

The lobby was jammed, as usual, with Army and Navy officers and their wives, with Wacs and Waves and with over-age civilians who were taking out other people's wives for cocktails. The sight of them milling about already in front of the cocktail room made Polly wonder where she and Tom would eat. Room Service was demoralized on Saturday, and unless they got down to the dining room by six o'clock, they would have to wait for ages. The alternative was to stand in line at Harvey's, or that other place across the street with raw meat in the window, where everyone practically sat in everyone else's lap. The more bizarre restaurants, the fish palaces by the river, or the Southern spots near Dupont Circle, or the one that tried to be like Paris, would also be jammed on Saturday night. The truth was that she was sick and tired of being a brave little woman, and of doing and saying the right and patriotic thing but at the same time not really feeling of any use.

A fat man, who she was perfectly sure had come from either Detroit or Toledo, was leaning against the marble counter, joking with the little blonde who handed out the letters. The clerk, who was a nice boy and who looked very tired, knew her right away.

"Yes, Mrs. Brett," he said, "Mr. Brett called up Mr. Morehouse, and we have something for you on the fifth floor."

Polly smiled at him and asked him to thank Mr. Morehouse, and she felt proud of Tom. Tom always knew the right person in Washington.

"Has Mr. Brett come in yet?" she asked. The clerk had not seen Mr. Brett, and there was no message.

From the way the women looked at her as she crossed the lobby, particularly the little Waves and Wacs, she felt that mink was beginning to have an immoral significance and that the coat, however old, might embarrass Tom. The elevator, like the lobby, was overstuffed. When she entered, all the men took off their hats, but they all shoved past her when they got out. Washington was no longer any place for a lady. Those people who believed in sex equality certainly ought to go to Washington.

The fifth floor, the nicest floor in the hotel, smelled of a violent antiseptic which the hotel had taken to using. It had been done over shortly before the war by a New York decorator, in a dashing, modernistic manner. The carpets were swirls of black and green, and the chairs and sofa by the elevator, done in white leather, looked like things she had seen in her solid geometry book at Bryn Mawr. The corridor was vibrating with the beginnings of Saturday night. As she followed the bellboy, she saw tables on wheels outside of doors, and she heard humming voices. The door next the suite that Tom had managed to get for them was open as she passed, giving her a glimpse of officers and girls, smoking, laughing and sitting around tables covered with ginger ale bottles. As she waited by the open door while the boy was working with the key, she had time to see that the officers were young, and she could see by their luggage that they must have come from overseas.

The suite on the fifth floor, which had obviously been intended to be very, very sophisticated, very, very amusing and oh, so gay, was already a prewar convention, fast falling into the category of the picture of the fur-lined teacup. The room was a place made for escape, and it was still so out of this world, as they were saying now, that it did not matter that it was growing nostalgic and soon would be *vieux jeu*. The little fireplace with its truncated fender and polished brass andirons had never been meant to work. It was simply a humorous, homelike confection to set off the print above it that represented a street scene or an abstraction — you had to study it quite hard to decide which.

A great many people had obviously been escaping in the suite during the last few years. All the jovial, modern chintzes which covered the chairs and sofas were thoroughly smudged. The cream-colored rug had stains on it. The white pickled shelves beside the couches, and the pickled drawers below them with wooden leaves for handles — you invariably left things there when you went away — all needed to be repickled. Still, it was warm, and so was the bedroom; but there were no flowers — and there had been a time when Tom or the management or someone had always been careful about flowers.

Polly gave the boy a dollar, a great deal too much. B. F. had taught her to be generous with tips, and she had never been able to get over it, though Tom always said that no one respected you if you threw money away. They simply took Polly, he said, for someone who didn't know her way around — but at least they all remembered her.

"And when you go down," Polly told him, "please go right away to the flower shop and tell them to send up some spring flowers." It was the end of February and nasty weather too, but it would be spring in some greenhouse or other.

She thought Tom would be coming at any moment, so she hurried in order to be done with her unpacking. She hung up all her dresses and put her underthings in the upper bureau drawer and her comb and brush and bottles, from the fitted suitcase, on the dressing table. It always gave her a sense of permanence to unpack everything in a hotel. She was in her dress with the peppermint candy stripes by the time the flowers came and her books which she always carried with her were near the couch by the telephone, the *Oxford Book of Verse* and Sumner Welles's *Time for Decision* and Ambassador Grew's *Ten Years in Japan,* and *Time* and the *New Yorker* and the *New Republic* and the *Nation.* The colored room-maid came in right behind the flowers to fix things in the bedroom.

"Hello," Polly said. "I've seen you before, haven't I?"

"Oh, yes, ma'am," the maid said. "I recollect you very well, ma'am."

She was young with bright eyes and white teeth and with a look full of a secret knowledge common to all hotel maids of white folks' carryings-on.

"What's your name?" Polly asked.

She had learned from B. F. how to get on with people, and it was very simple if you were kind.

"It's Opal, ma'am," the maid said.

"I've always liked opals," Polly said. "I don't know why people think they're unlucky. You look lucky, Opal."

"Oh, yes, ma'am," Opal said. "I'm lucky."

"Are you married?" Polly asked.

"Oh, yes, ma'am," Opal said, "but he's off somewheres."

"I don't know where my man is either," Polly said. "He ought to be here now, but he's off somewhere."

Opal giggled.

"It seems like women folks just do always have to set and wait for men folks," she said.

Perhaps she was being too familiar with Opal, but it never hurt, and you had to be friends with people if you wanted anything done these days. For instance, there was the matter of the bathtub.

"I know it isn't your fault, Opal," Polly said. "It must have been the girl who was here in the morning. She didn't clean the bathtub."

"My land, ma'am," Opal said. "She didn't clean the tub? I'll clean it."

The room was silent and devoid of personality when Opal had gone. It was half-past six and there was no sign of Tom. Polly began to think that there was no excuse, no excuse at all. The least he could have done was to have telephoned or to have left a note. It was all very well to say that Tom was vague, or that he was busy, or that there was a war on. . . . She sat down and began to read from one of the magazines, and it was as still as the reading room in a public library.

First she glanced through an article on Washington that dealt with the infiltration of businessmen and executives who were breaking down the social gains. She then read about a public school in which white children were persecuting the colored scholars, and the teacher had asked the white pupils if they had ever really known any Negroes. When it appeared they had not, she had started a study group whose duty it was to call on certain representative colored people in the community, and this ended the trouble.

It sounded just like Tom when he talked about labor. Tom was always saying that all anyone had to do was to talk it out across a table. As far as she could see, this was what tables were for in Washington. . . . There was no use saying that Tom was preoccupied or that he was not the sort of person who made small courteous gestures. The least he could have done was to have sent her a message, or if he was too busy, he could have left it to that secretary of his, Miss White at the Social Security Building, and she needn't worry about *her,* at any rate. Miss White was over forty if she was a day, and she squinted and needed dress shields. There was no reason at all why Tom should not have sent some message.

Next she picked up her copy of the *New Yorker*. Polly had always felt at home with the *New Yorker,* but now, perhaps because she was wondering where Tom was, it did not have its usual stimulating effect. There were the same funny pictures, the two convicts in a cell and the precocious little boy with the Tommy gun. The Letter from London and the Letter from the War Theaters seemed resurrected from lavender, and even her favorite Talk of the Town (she had often wished she knew that editor who wrote about "our helpmeet" and "our children's roller skates," and "our Siamese cat," and how "we" went to the place where a quaint old gaffer sold nothing but Victorian hair-receivers or horse nets, or something) sounded *précieuse* and a little flyblown. She had once said that she hoped she could die reading a Profile in the *New Yorker* and she had been outraged when Tom had said that the people who ran the *New Yorker* were all bright juveniles who were crowding fifty and old enough to know better. . . . Now that she was wondering what on earth Tom was doing, she did not give a damn about the Profile either.

Polly had been there for nearly an hour when there was a knock. It was just like Tom to forget to call at the desk for a key. Tom forgot his key in the same way he dropped his clothes anywhere and never washed out his shaving brush and never picked up papers. She was thinking of something really good to say to him, something better than Peter Arno at his highest point, but when she jerked the door open she caught her breath, and her thoughts broke into little pieces like parts of a jigsaw puzzle spread out on the table. It was not Tom. It was a young Army lieutenant, a flyer, but for just a second she was sure it was Bob Tasmin at the door. She had not thought of him since that night with Apples and the colonel, but the lieutenant had the fresh, bathed look that Bob used to have, the same perfect posture, the same quietness; it might have been Bob Tasmin as he used to be at Gray's Point, and she might have been Polly Fulton. The young Air Corps officer had Tasmin's chivalrous assurance and the slender build of someone who was good at games. He had Bob Tasmin's delicate features, his dark hair, and the same long fingers. It may have been the dim light that made the illusion so perfect. It was exactly as though Bob Tasmin had come from nowhere, unchanged, except that he was in uniform because there was a war on. It was exactly as though Bob Tasmin were calling for her as he used to, to take her to a Saturday night dance at the Mill River Club. The young officer smiled in the same way. She could almost hear Bob Tasmin's voice.

"Ready, Poll?" he would have said.

It was not what the first lieutenant said, but when he did speak his voice had Tasmin's enunciation.

"I hope you'll please forgive me," he said, and he paused, and Polly knew that of course the boy had been drinking. It affected him as it always had Bob Tasmin — it only made him more polite. "I hope you'll forgive me. I know this isn't just the right thing to do."

Bob Tasmin was always thinking of the right thing.

"I hope you'll write it off because I've been away for a long while. I just blew in this afternoon, and I happened to see you out in the hall."

The lieutenant was watching her, and she knew that if she had shown any displeasure he would have apologized and left.

"We were just talking it over, my friends and I, and I'm a sort of a committee" — he smiled — "the Entertainment Committee, and we just wondered whether you wouldn't be kind enough to join us, if you hadn't anything else to do."

It was just the way Bob Tasmin would have done it.

"Did you try this on a bet?" she asked.

The lieutenant looked embarrassed.

"Well, I wouldn't put it quite that way," he said. "The doctor put up a little money, but . . . Well, let's forget it. Please don't think I'm being rude."

"I suppose you mean," Polly said, "that everybody ought to do something for the boys?"

His face flushed slightly.

"No," he said, "I didn't mean that. Please believe I didn't."

"Well, when you come right down to it," Polly said, "I didn't mean it either. You startled me for a minute. I thought you were someone else."

"Oh," he began, "I'm awfully sorry."

Polly took a step away from the door.

"As a matter of fact," she said, smiling at him, "I'd like to come but I'm waiting for my husband." The lieutenant nodded. He was a nice boy. He did not show any disappointment that she was not alone.

"Well, we'd love to have him, too," he said. "It's right next door. Couldn't you leave a note or something?"

Polly smiled again. She was good and sick of waiting.

"I might," she said. "Suppose you come in for a minute and let's talk about it."

"That's awfully nice of you," the lieutenant said. "Thank you very much, and please forgive me, won't you?"

It was just as though Bob Tasmin were coming in after the dance at the Mill River Club. She would always ask him if he wouldn't come in for a minute, and then he would say it was too late, but he usually would come in, and then, like the lieutenant, he would thank her very much.

XII

Nobody Cares — If She's on a Yacht

POLLY sat down on the sofa by the telephone and leaned her head back. It was a relief to see the lieutenant. Tom and his friends were consciously casual. Tom and his friends felt that manners indicated a mental and personal vacuum. They took off their coats and ties in hot weather without ever asking her and they sprawled in chairs without getting up when she entered the room. They used a great many Anglo-Saxon monosyllables to express themselves, and flipped cigarette ashes on the rugs and put their highball glasses on the floor. They treated women just as they treated each other, and when they got excited they paced about the room and snatched wrappers from books on which to draw diagrams. When they were bored they yawned and stretched, or sulked in corners or fell asleep. There was always freedom of thought and freedom of speech and freedom from fear when Tom and his friends were around; but there was a restful quality in good manners, particularly when one was tired.

This boy stood waiting for her to sit down, and when she did, he still waited.

"Please sit down," Polly said, and she found herself speaking with a gracious, drawing-room manner.

"Thanks ever so much," he said, and he drew a cigarette case from his side pocket and opened it, took a quick step forward, and offered it to her. For just a moment she thought he might bow like one of the Free French, but he did not bow any more than Bob Tasmin did.

"Won't you have one?" he asked.

"No, thanks," Polly answered.

"Do you mind," he asked, "if I take one?"

"No, of course not," Polly said. "Won't you sit down? You make me nervous."

His hands and his head were very handsome, and he did not slump or slouch. His shoes, those shoes without laces, were beautifully polished, and the creases in his trousers were just as they should be.

"Where did you blow in from, Lieutenant?" Polly asked.

He snapped his cigarette case shut, put it back in his pocket and smoothed his coat. His wings shone in the light beside him, and his ribbons made inartistic, garish stripes of color. He had a red, white and blue ribbon, and a purple one and a yellow and red one with two little stars. They looked like the colors in a braided rug.

"From the China-Burma-India theater," he said, "mostly Burma. I picked up malaria. It's a funny thing, malaria."

"What's funny about it?" Polly asked.

"The way it hits you. One minute you're perfectly all right, and the next minute you're burning up and you're out of your head. It's embarrassing."

"Do you feel it coming on now?" Polly asked.

"Oh, no, I don't think so," he answered. "I think it's quieting down, but I'm afraid they're going to put me in the Walter Reed on Monday. I'm awfully sorry. I haven't introduced myself. My name is Meek — Will Meek."

"Well, 'Blessed are the meek,'" Polly said. "My name is Brett, Mrs. Thomas Brett. My first name's Polly, not that you know me well enough to use it."

"Brett," Lieutenant Meek said. "Polly Brett. Will you excuse me if I make a rather personal remark?"

"Make it and I'll see."

"Well, if I were Mr. Brett . . ." the lieutenant began.

"Well, you're not Mr. Brett," Polly said, "so don't try to be."

"Now, please," Lieutenant Meek said, "I'm not trying. I wasn't even thinking whether I wanted to be Mr. Brett or not."

"Well, you're a little too young for it, aren't you?" Polly asked.

"I wouldn't say that," Lieutenant Meek said. "I was only saying, if I were Mr. Brett, I wouldn't keep you here waiting."

"Have you ever been married?" Polly asked. Lieutenant Meek shook his head. "Then you're in no position to think anything."

"You have a very unusual voice," Lieutenant Meek said. "I heard it when you were speaking to the bellboy."

"Well," Polly said, "what's the matter with my voice?"

"There's nothing the matter with it," Lieutenant Meek said. "It sounds just the way you look. Do you remember what you said to the bellboy? You said, 'If you set down that bag, perhaps you can manage to unlock the door.' I wished that you'd said it to me."

"Well, I don't see why you have it on your mind."

Lieutenant Meek sat looking at her.

"It sounds the way you look. You look like Botticelli's 'Spring.'"

Polly laughed, and she almost said that at any rate she was not three months along like all of Botticelli's girls, but that would have spoiled it, and she did not want it spoiled.

"Someone used to tell me that," she said. "He said it once when I was learning how to dive. I must have come up with that breathless look."

"I wasn't claiming to be original," Lieutenant Meek said. "Anyone would say it."

"Not anyone," Polly said. "It's a certain type. You're like the one who used to say it."

"Was he in love with you?" Lieutenant Meek asked.

"Yes," Polly said, "he was."

"Was he Mr. Brett?"

"No," Polly said, "no, he wasn't Mr. Brett."

"Did he want to marry you?"

"Yes," Polly said, "of course he did."

"Why do you say 'of course'?"

"Because his intentions were honorable," Polly said.

Lieutenant Meek was silent for a moment.

"Are you sorry you didn't marry him?"

"What?" Polly asked.

"Let's skip it," the lieutenant said. "I had no business to ask you that."

She sighed and shook her head. "I haven't given it much thought lately." She looked at the clock. It was after seven, and she was grow-ing very angry with Tom. "But maybe, now that I do think of it, it wouldn't have been such a bad idea."

Lieutenant Meek stood up without heaving himself out of the chair the way Tom did.

"How would it be if we went into the other room," he said, "and had a drink?"

"I think it would be swell," Polly said, "if there's something to eat besides."

"That's all taped out," Lieutenant Meek said. "We're getting stuff to eat."

Polly stood up too.

"I'd better leave a note for Tom."

"Who's Tom?" the lieutenant asked.

"Oh, Tom," Polly said, and she laughed. "That's our old friend, Mr. Brett." The lieutenant picked up a memorandum pad near the telephone and handed her a pencil.

"Dear Tom," Polly wrote. "I'm in the next room with an Air Force lieutenant. Come and get me out if you're feeling in the mood. Poll."

"All right," she said. "Let's go."

Now that they were out in the hall the lieutenant assumed a grave, proprietary attitude. He made her feel that though the whole thing was unusual, she need not be worried about anything simply because he was there. She felt that she ought to give a little scream if she were to see a spider. She was a Jane Austen heroine in spite of her-self because it was expected of her. She was as good as she was beautiful, and her glove was something to be worn on a knight's helmet on the field of honor. She was Jane Eyre and Lieutenant Meek was Rochester. Once upon a time that sort of thing would have made her very nervous, but now it was pleasant for a change. Polly felt happy and gay.

"You know, I really can't believe it," Lieutenant Meek was say-ing, "that you're here and I'm here."

It was just the sort of remark that Tom and his friends would have referred to vulgarly as corn.

"Well, you can pinch yourself just to be sure you're not dreaming," Polly said.

"I only meant," the lieutenant said, "that it's hard to believe anything after countries and continents go rolling under you like railroad ties. Sometimes it's hard to believe that I'm alive. . . . It's very confusing."

"Do I confuse you?" Polly said.

"Only because you're so beautiful," the lieutenant said.

"I'm not as good as all that," Polly said. "Don't have it on your mind."

"Of course it bores you," the lieutenant said, "but please don't be bored for just a minute."

"I'm not bored," Polly said. "I'm glad to be popular again. It's quite a change."

Lieutenant Meek was opening the door.

". . . And there we are, just like that," she heard a voice saying, "and they come out of the sun, period; and then down goes the –47, period, paragraph. It's the top-drawer kids. It's the real college team, period."

She used to be afraid to go to dances. She used to feel sick to her stomach up in the dressing-room with all the girls giving her hard, bright looks, and with the sound of the music outside. She used to be scared to death unless Bob Tasmin was waiting to take her in. Her shoulders might be bony, and her hair too frizzy, and her dress too frilly and her nose too long and her mouth too big and her eyes too narrow, but Bob Tasmin would be sure that everything was absolutely right. She could lean upon that assurance as she leaned upon his arm, and now her old feeling of well-being came back because, thank God, someone else thought she was all right, and unlike that colonel in New York, he was not in Air Force Public Relations.

There was a sharp silence when she appeared in the doorway. The room had another stage fireplace and another indecipherable picture. A fat, red-haired Army lieutenant was standing in front of the fireplace holding a glass; he must have been the one who was speaking. A Navy lieutenant junior grade was seated on the sofa with his arm around an Army nurse. A Medical Corps captain, who was growing bald, sat on the other sofa beside a petulant-looking brunette. They were all motionless for an instant, and then they all stood up.

"Oh, please don't get up," Polly said. There was a pile of canvas luggage in the corner, and two leather flying jackets with American flags stitched on the backs of them. The owners' names were inked above the flags in rough block letters — MEEK and BRODIE — so she assumed that the boy by the fireplace would be named Brodie. The nurse's name was Carlson, and the other girl was Miss Driver, an employee from the American Airlines, Lieutenant Meek was saying, who was kind enough to come up with them from the airport.

"And you want to get this straight," the fat, redheaded lieutenant said. "It's Driver, not Ryder, or am I off the beam again? Is it Ryder, Miss Driver?" Judging from Miss Driver's expression the joke had been going on for quite a while. Women had a way of looking at each other, Polly often thought, particularly when there were men around, as though they guessed things about each other which men could not perceive and that was just the way the airlines girl looked at her, and Polly looked right back.

They had picked up Nurse Carlson at Karachi, and she was their private nurse, the boys said, and they called her Stuffy.

"She helps us with our combat fatigue," Lieutenant Meek said, "don't you, Stuffy darling? And she's brought back a shawl for her mother." The naval lieutenant, junior grade, was named Wilkins, and they had picked him up at Acra, and the doctor, whose name Polly could not catch, was a flight surgeon from the C.B.I., and Lieutenant Meek said he was their personal physician.

"It's really nice of you to join us, ma'am," the doctor said. "God bless America."

"Where's the champagne, Doc?" Lieutenant Meek asked.

"It's gone," the doctor said. "There's nothing but rye left."

"Well, somebody get Room Service," Lieutenant Meek said. "Mrs. Brett wants champagne."

"Don't bother," Polly said. "I'd just as soon have rye."

"Oh, no you wouldn't really," Lieutenant Meek said.

"She wants rye, period," Lieutenant Brodie said. "Look at her striped dress. She's an American girl. Give her some rye, and I'm dreaming of a White Christmas."

The doctor handed her a glass of rye and ginger ale. She stood beside Lieutenant Brodie while Lieutenant Meek began talking to Room Service.

"They say it's on the way," he said. "Everything's on the way."

"Away," Lieutenant Brodie said. "Bombs away, and I'll take a Bronze Star."

"You Joes always keep getting Bronze Stars, don't you?" Lieutenant Wilkins said.

"Yes, sir," Lieutenant Brodie said. "They hand them out automatically. Where was it I left off?"

"You never leave off, you red-top," the Army nurse said.

"Show us the shawl you bought for your mother," Lieutenant Meek said. "It's beautiful, Stuffy."

"Why do you always ask me to yank out that shawl, Meek?" Nurse Carlson asked.

"Because it's beautiful," Lieutenant Meek told her. "It has camels on it. It's a beautiful piece of native handcraft, made by people to whom time means nothing."

"I remember where I was," Lieutenant Brodie said.

"Suppose you do," the captain said. "Don't we all remember where we were?"

"He was on my tail," Lieutenant Brodie said.

"Listen, Red," Lieutenant Meek said, "they always are."

"He was on my tail, period," Lieutenant Brodie said, "and Meekie is over there. It's a deflection problem, period, and Meekie gets him, period."

Lieutenant Meek found Polly a chair and sat beside her on the edge of the table. She was afraid he was beginning to feel that it had been a mistake to have asked her, and this was annoying because she really did know how to get along with people. With the exception of the airlines girl they had all just arrived from places with preposterous names which she had hardly heard since she had studied geography. They were back, and yet they were not really back, for distance clung to them like mud on shoes, and they could not accept Washington.

She imagined that the boy beside her understood all this, vaguely. He said that she must not mind that kid Brodie, that he was a good kid, and he felt responsible for him because they had been out there together for quite a while. If you spent two years of your life talking about flying and living it, it was hard to get it off your mind, or to get back to what you had been before. Of course, he was only discussing what Tom would have called the problem of rehabilitating combat personnel, but it was simpler the way Lieutenant Meek put it. When she asked him what a combat pilot's life was like, he said, if she did not mind, he would tell her sometime when he knew how to describe it, but now it would not work.

"Perhaps it's silly," he said, "but there's one thing that bothers me. I'm afraid I'll never quite get back to understanding things as they used to be."

"I don't think that's silly at all," Polly said. "It's true with everyone. You asked me whether I wished I'd married someone else. Well, that's exactly the same thing." They could talk that way because they did not know each other. He said it would have been easier for him if things had not moved so fast. He could have gotten them straightened out if he had come back by ship instead of by air. Five days ago he had been on his last mission over Burma, and here he was in the hotel, and after the hospital check-up, he would see his family in the suburbs outside New York.

"That's where I used to come from," Polly said. "Do you know Gray's Point?"

It was discouraging to see how he brightened up. Of course, he was just the sort who would be familiar with Gray's Point, and he recited names of people he knew there, asking her if she knew them.

"Never mind it," Polly said. "I've spent a lot of time trying to pretend I wasn't brought up there."

"Why?" the lieutenant asked. "Didn't you have a good time?"

"No," Polly said, "not very."

She could not understand why the boy was interested when

there was so much else to talk about. Room Service had come at last and two waiters were setting the table, and there was more champagne, but all the while Lieutenant Meek kept reverting to her not having liked Gray's Point.

"You must have been awfully popular," he said. She supposed he meant that everyone had danced with her, and perhaps she had been popular, but she had never belonged there.

"We weren't like the other people," Polly said. "At any rate, my father wasn't, or I didn't think he was. I was always trying to escape from it, I was always a sour note."

"I wish I'd been there," Lieutenant Meek said.

She knew all about him by that time, his class at Princeton, his club, and about his older brother and his sister who were both married.

"You wouldn't have been any help," Polly said. "You'd have been too young, darling." She was on her third glass of champagne.

"I'm not so young now, and I still don't see why you disliked it," he said. "There are a lot of swell people at Gray's Point. Let's see, did you ever know the Fultons?"

At first she thought she had not heard him correctly because everybody in the room was getting noisy.

"Who?" Polly asked.

"The Fultons," Lieutenant Meek said. "There was Harry Fulton. You must have heard of him. I stayed there once with Harry."

It was something which had never happened to Polly before. It was almost like being invisible.

"Let's see," she said, "the Fultons. They had that big stone house, didn't they? They were the ones who were so awfully rich." Though it was not fair she was not able to resist it, for there had never been a time before when anyone who knew the family did not know her too.

"So you've been there, have you?" Lieutenant Meek asked. "Well, I know what you mean. It was all a little overpowering, but I thought they were swell. Do you know Harry?"

"Oh, yes," Polly said. "I've seen him around quite often. Of course, he was younger."

"Well, I always thought he was a very nice guy," Lieutenant Meek said. "Some people used to say he was a little snotty, but I think he was just shy."

"That's the usual excuse, isn't it?" Polly said.

"It was only his manner," Lieutenant Meek replied. "When you got beyond his manner Harry was a darn good Joe. He was just afraid that people would take advantage of him."

"Who else was there at the Fultons'?" Polly asked.

"No one, just Harry and me, and then Mr. and Mrs. Fulton. Harry asked me out for the week end. You see, we'd been playing squash at the Racquet Club and it was Saturday. He always used to hang around by himself at the Racquet Club."

"I suppose he did," Polly said.

They had pushed their chairs away from the table, but there was still no sign of Tom. She did not want to ask what time it was, and besides she was not bored.

"You must have known Harry's sister," Lieutenant Meek said.

"Yes," Polly said, "I used to know her."

"Judging from what Harry said she was on the unconventional side."

"She used to want to get the hell out of Gray's Point, darling," Polly said. "That's what we had in common. I don't think she ever fitted there. She had braces on her teeth until she was fifteen. How did you like B. F.?"

"I thought he was swell."

"Did you? I thought so too in certain ways," Polly said, and she looked away quickly. "Did you know he was dead?"

"Why no, I hadn't heard," the lieutenant said. "I'm awfully sorry. I liked him a lot. He talked to Harry and me as though we were all just the same age. Mrs. Fulton kept trying to shush him up, but he didn't mind. He just went barging ahead. He had a lot of ideas."

"Yes," Polly said. "He always did."

But now the thing had gone too far. She could see them all in the dining room at Sunday lunch, and afterwards B. F. would have taken the boys into the library, and he would have shown them the first editions, and opened the safe and got out the early American silver, or else he would have gone on about the New Deal or the budget or Chamberlain in Munich or sending scrap iron to Japan. It made her want to cry. Or he might have talked about raising vegetables in water with chemicals, or about new alloys in some new steel. It made her want to cry, but she did not have to go on with it because there was a knock and the captain had opened the door. Tom had come at last and it was about time.

"Oh, there he is," she said.

Tom's entrance created a jarring note. He acted like an adult looking oversolicitously at little children. He had the adult's condescending smile, and exaggerated desire to understand. He must have left his overcoat in the other room, but he was still wearing his stained felt hat, pushed back from his forehead in the way she did not like. His herringbone suit, the one that she had made him buy, had not been pressed for days. His soft collar was not pinned and his tie had drifted to one side. She was very sure that he had deliberately not had his suit pressed, and that the whole getup was at least partly intentional, done partly out of revolt, she supposed, and partly because he wanted to show that he could afford to look that way. Also, he was smoking a cigarette and allowing the smoke to curl into his eyes.

"Well, well," Tom said. "Don't mind me. Don't let me break this up."

When Polly introduced him, Tom looked about him quickly, putting each face in its place. Then he took a glass of champagne. She saw that he was trying to make an impression as he always did when he was not entirely at ease. There was no reason, Polly thought, why he should have tried to be a Grover Whalen welcoming committee, or have tried to show that he understood all about G. I.'s and their gripes.

"Only this afternoon," he said, "I happened to run into a general just back from Kunming. He was telling some pretty hot stuff, pretty strictly off the record. He says you lads have been having a rugged time."

Polly was embarrassed listening to him, but she was impressed by what Tom knew, without ever having been there, about Kunming and Ramgarh and Assam. She wished he would not show off and intimate that he knew so many little secrets, and that he would not refer to General Stilwell as "poor old Uncle Joe," but he was well posted on his subject. He seemed to have the whole map of the subcontinent and of Africa right in his mind. He was asking about places of which she had never heard, and then he was giving a quick free lecture on the Nationalist Movement in India, and the problems of Lord Mountbatten.

"Now the whole question," he said, "is the gesture we're making in the C. B. I. I suppose you boys are pretty sore because you feel we haven't backed you up. You've got to know our future operations to understand it. You'll see what I mean before long, and it's going to come out all right. That supply job is magnificent, and the Air Force job is something out of this world. Don't you boys think for a minute we don't appreciate it over here."

Recently, Tom had been assuming the manner of an official representative of the War Department and of the O.W.I. and of everything else. Now having given a refresher course on the present situation in the China-Burma-India theater he was getting down to cases, giving the two flyers his particular, sympathetic attention because he understood a lot about the Air Force.

"It's going to be a little tough for you boys adjusting yourselves," Tom said. "The main thing is to enjoy yourselves and take it easy. You'll have a lot of free advice, but if you get snarled up with anything, I might be able to help you. I'm not in the Service. My chief wouldn't let me get into it, but at the same time . . ."

Polly wished he had skipped the explanation about his chief, and she was afraid that he would go on with it in detail, but he refrained.

"If there's anything that bothers you, just let me know. We'll be right next door all week end. I might be able to tell you who to go and see. Just knock on the door any time." Tom rose and put his empty glass on the table. "Well, I guess I'd better be turning in now, but you don't need to, Poll. Stay and talk to the boys. Learn about the war."

"Oh, no," Polly said. "It's getting late." Then she was shaking hands.

"Good-by, Mr. Meek," she said, "it's been awfully nice."

"Drop in tomorrow at cocktail time," Tom said, "if you haven't got anything better to do. We'll be having some friends in. Well, it's been swell seeing you. Good night."

It was very quiet back in the other room. Tom threw his hat on the sofa, took off his coat and dropped it on the floor, unbuttoned his vest and lighted another cigarette.

"Those kids back from the theaters never seem to talk," he said.

"How could they?" Polly asked. "You held them simply spell-bound."

Tom dropped into a chair and the smoke of his cigarette curled into his eyes.

"So, I talked too much," he said. "But somebody had to say something."

"Well, you were superb," Polly said. "You put everybody at ease."

The corners of his mouth drew up in a way which had always annoyed her, for it was never quite a smile. It was a habit which he fell into when he was tired or nervous, and now it made his face look haggard.

"It's too bad I'm not a U. S. O. hostess," he said. "Well, how's everything back home?"

Polly looked at her traveling clock. It was a quarter before eleven and she did not answer.

"How's your mother?"

"Mother?" Polly said. "She's all right."

It was not kind of him to be so perfunctory and she wished the room were not so quiet. He sat there listlessly like anybody sitting across the aisle in a Pullman, glancing absently at the ceiling, playing with the Phi Beta Kappa key on his waistcoat.

"Well, that's fine," he said. "I'm glad she's making some sort of an adjustment." She might have known that he would sum it up with a trite psychological term.

"Oh, my God," he said, and his eyes were on her. "Oh, my God, what is it now?"

When you tried not to do what she was doing now, you always

did it. She had been fighting against it for the last three minutes, and now she was beginning to cry. It was utterly humiliating.

"None of your damned business," she said. "If you're so bored, why don't you go to bed?"

Tom stood up, hunched his shoulders forward, and stuck out his chin.

"Oh, my God," he said. "The end of a perfect day."

"Oh, shut up," Polly said. "Won't you get out of here and go to bed?"

"You know damned well what'll happen if I go to bed," Tom told her. "It'll only make you madder."

They were both silent for a second. They knew each other so well that they must each have known what the other was going to do. Tom took a step nearer.

"Listen, Poll," he said. "I'm just not up to a scene. I should have met you at the train with orchids, and so what? My God, you know me well enough." He pulled his right hand from his pocket and rubbed the back of his head. She even knew what he would say next. "My God, Poll, I didn't ask you to come down here."

She turned her head away from him.

"All right," she said. "That's about enough." And she stood up. What he had implied was perfectly true. She had pursued him down to Washington.

"Oh, my God," Tom said. "Don't be mad, Poll. I said I didn't ask you. I didn't say I didn't want you."

"Don't be so damned smooth," she sobbed. "You don't want me."

It was as completely conventional as the structure of a Greek tragedy. Tom was beginning to pace about the room, picking up ash trays and books and setting them down again, and at the same time reaching the inevitable stage of being very, very tired.

"I certainly don't want you," Tom said, "if it's necessary for you to go into one of these emotional, compensative tailspins. I should just like to point out to you, if you'll give me a minute without implying that I'm a heel, Poll . . . For God's sake, *will* you stop crying?"

149

"Never mind me," Polly heard herself saying. "Go ahead and point it out."

"All right," Tom said. "Go ahead and keep on bawling then, if it gives you any emotional release. It's too much to ask you to see yourself logically. Oh, my God."

"Go ahead," Polly said, "go ahead. I'm listening."

Tom drew a deep, patient breath.

"Of course, I should have met you," he went on, and his voice was very patient, elaborately controlled. "I should have dropped everything. I should have made my mind a perfect blank. I should not have expected you to understand, and, by God, I won't again, that all life is not a duel between the sexes. It just happens that there's a damn tough situation here, and I'm right in the middle of it. I can't tell you what's been going on. I can't tell you who's trying to upset the apple cart. There were some meetings this afternoon that just happened to be scheduled before you decided to come down. There was a call from the White House at three o'clock."

"Oh, you've been at the White House, have you?" Polly said.

"No, no, no," Tom answered. "I wish you'd try to keep your mind on what I'm saying. I said there was a call from the White House. The chief had to go, and I had to get all his papers together and write a memorandum and refresh his mind. I had to stand by. They're always losing papers."

"Well, why couldn't you stand by here?" Polly asked. "There's a telephone right here. Were you standing by in your office?"

"Oh, my God," Tom said. "It's something that we just can't discuss. There were a lot of us who had to stand by and wait."

"Well, what happened?"

Tom drew another patient breath.

"I'm trying to tell you if you'll only listen. Nothing happened. I said the chief went to the White House."

"I know you did," Polly said.

"I said the *chief* went to the White House." Tom paused and then he spoke more patiently. "It happens that a great many other people go to the White House too. General Marshall goes, and so does Admiral King, and Senator Barkley."

"How about Winston Churchill?" Polly asked.

"What?" Tom asked. "What has Winston Churchill got to do with it?"

"I don't know," Polly said. "I just brought him in."

Tom looked startled.

"Did anybody tell you that Churchill was over here?"

"No," Polly said. "I just happened to mention him."

"Well, don't talk about things you don't know about," Tom said. "Nothing happened. There wasn't any decision, but the chief went to the White House."

"Why did he go if nothing happened?"

"Never mind," Tom said. "Never mind all that, Poll." And he began weaving back and forth about the room.

She knew that Tom could have explained the whole thing if he had wanted. She knew that he was not explaining because he was annoyed.

"Well, where were you all afternoon and evening?" Polly asked. "Or is that a secret?"

"I was in Georgetown," Tom said. "Does that answer your question?"

"Georgetown?"

"A number of people live there," Tom said. "I had to go up there to get this settled."

"What was it," Polly asked, "a cocktail party?"

"I supposed that was coming," Tom said. "All right, it was a cocktail party. I went there for the chief. He had to be at the White House."

"Oh," Polly said. "That makes it perfectly all right, and then you stayed to dinner."

"We were all waiting," Tom said. "We were waiting for the chief."

"It must have been very hard on you, darling," Polly said. "I suppose you were too busy to telephone, was that it?"

"Now look here," Tom said. "I should have telephoned and I didn't, and so what? I had other things on my mind."

"Yes," Polly said. "I know. I suppose it would have broken the balance of everything if you had telephoned. I suppose that would have lost the war for us."

Tom sat down and played with his Phi Beta Kappa key. He did not answer.

"Who did you go to see in Georgetown?"

Tom did not answer.

"Was she animal, vegetable or mineral?"

Tom's lips twitched. It was all ending in an anticlimax. He was not even angry. He was completely, wearily indifferent.

"Never mind," he said. "Let's skip it, Poll. I guess I'll go to bed."

"That's what I told you to do," she answered, but he sat there without making any reply.

"Tom," she began, "isn't there anything . . ." and then she stopped. The truth was that there was not. Everything was entirely empty, entirely futile, and everything that had been seemed to have gone. Tom stirred uneasily.

"What's that?" he asked.

"Isn't there anything I can do," Polly asked, "about anything?"

Tom looked worn out. She was almost frightened as she watched him sitting there considering her question.

"Not at the moment, Poll," he said. "I'm awfully tired."

"But, Tom," she asked, "what are we going to do?"

Tom did not answer immediately, and the worst of it was that though they were unexpectedly on the edge of something terrible and important, her question did not appear to disturb him.

"Poll," he said, "I'm damned tired, and I simply can't go over everything. Let's skip it. I'm going to bed."

Tom rose. Then he bent over her and kissed her.

"All right," she said, "let's skip it, darling."

"Have you heard anything from Harry?" he asked.

"No," she said, "not since his last letter."

"Then don't worry about him," Tom said. "He's all right. You see . . ." He began pulling off his tie, and his mood had changed, and everything seemed a little better. "You see, this damned war mixes everybody up."

152

"That's a very interesting thought," Polly said. "It ought to be in an anthology."

"Those kids in the other room —" Tom said, "nobody makes sense. You and I don't. Let's blame it on the war."

"As long as you don't blame it on me," Polly said.

"That kid" — Tom was pulling off his waistcoat — "that lieutenant in the other room — I suppose you noticed he was crazy about you, didn't you? Poor kid."

"Why do you say 'poor kid'?" she asked.

Tom began to smile.

"Just the effect you have on people. He looked like Tasmin — just the way he used to look. Oh, my God, I'm sorry."

"What are you sorry about?"

"Don't," Tom said, "please, Poll, don't begin to cry again."

"I'm not," she said.

"Well, that's swell," Tom said. "I'm going to bed."

"It seems to me you've said that before."

"Well, I mean it this time," he told her. "You'd better turn in, too, and maybe the situation will look better in the morning."

"I'm going to read for a while," Polly said.

She could hear him moving about in the bedroom, and he was even whistling. He was whistling with relief as though he had been let out of school. It was almost as though she were sharing the hotel suite with a stranger. There was something unbearable in the idea of undressing in the bedroom and of crawling into that other twin bed, because too much had happened, and yet nothing at all had, actually — nothing, at any rate, that affected him in any way. He was still whistling, and she recalled the tune. It had been written especially for the election last autumn.

> Don't Change Horses in the middle of a stream,
> If you want to keep your britches dry . . .
> Don't change sweeties in the middle of a dream
> Or you're gonna be a sorry guy . . .

You always understood, at odd moments, the things you should have known for a long while, and they usually became clear for no apparent reason. You would cling to illusions and reservations and make allowances as long as possible, and then suddenly the magic would be gone, and you would be awake, looking at all those things in the cold north light. She had wondered at other times why she had ever married Tom, but she had never wondered in just this way — now that she heard him whistling. All at once enthusiasms and loyalty and beliefs became very tiresome. The intelligentsia, the bright planners, working on those streamlined blueprints for the brave new world, were always repeating themselves. She had heard enough of the coined jargon that was all mixed up with cheap synonyms. It made no sense. There was something mechanical about Tom and all those boys with minds like steel traps, minds equipped with dogmatic lucidity. There was some basic lack of understanding in spite of all their aptitudes. They had convictions, but they still seemed to be working out just what the war was all about. They stood for freedom of speech, except for disloyal fascist columnists, freedom from fear, except that Tom was going to put the fear of God into certain industrialists who still lived in the Dark Ages, and freedom from want, except for the obstructionists who could not see the light. Or you could turn to the other side, to the ones who said the country would be ruined by inflation, and that it was being run by crackpots and Communists. It made her sick to death to hear those people talk, too, because they also had their own jargon and their own intellectual foibles. There was no common understanding any longer, no patience or tolerance — nobody even wanted to understand.

"Tom," she called.

"Yes," Tom called back, "what is it?"

"I wish you'd please stop whistling."

Tom came to the door of the bedroom in a suit of silk pajamas.

"All right," he said. "I've stopped." And everything had stopped. "Anything else on your mind?"

"Yes," Polly said. "How's the C.I.O.?"

"The C.I.O. is swell," Tom said. "I thought you wanted to read."

"I thought I did," she said. "How's industry?"

"Listen," Tom said. "What's all this about?"

"Nothing," Polly said. "I'm just thinking about the world."

"Which world?"

"I thought it was all one world," Polly answered.

"All right, it's one world, and so what?"

"I don't know what," Polly said. "It ought to be one world, but it isn't. There are lots of little worlds like soap bubbles."

"I don't know what, either," Tom said, "but in my opinion this is getting a little corny, Poll."

"It sounds about like everything else."

"You go ahead and read," Tom told her.

"I can't read," Polly said, "I'm thinking about all the worlds. Who's going to write the directive that puts them all together?"

"My God," Tom said. "I wish you'd read. I'm tired. I want to go to sleep." He yawned, and rubbed the back of his hand across his forehead. "All right, maybe you've got something. Maybe there are too damned many worlds. Maybe we've been through too many of them, but I can't help it personally. You stay in your world until tomorrow morning and let me stay in mine."

"To hell with your world," Polly said.

"O.K.," Tom said. "To hell with yours too. Good night, Poll. We'll co-ordinate them in the morning." And he closed the bedroom door.

The room was filled with the echoes of their words. Loose thoughts began to move languidly about, running through her mind and out into the room again. She was wondering why she went on with it, but it did no good to try to find the reason for anything. She had married him to get away, and now where was she? Where was she, and just why?

Polly was already telling herself it was only a mood, and that if she were back in New York she could have skipped it. There she would have to be worrying about the Russian War Relief or the inheritance taxes, maids who gave your sugar stamps to their relatives, or the meat and clothing shortages. But here in this synthetic hotel room there seemed to be no demands upon her, nothing she could give any longer. It was dreadful, she was thinking, for a woman to be empty, without the power to give. Men could handle

155

the problem better. At least, she knew a great number of useless men who seemed to be happy and adjusted, but it was terrible for a woman. It was terrible to sit and add things up and to have the net result before you equal zero.

Tomorrow she knew that she would think of something, of some new way to amuse Tom, of some new design. If Tom liked Georgetown, they could close up New York and get a house there, one of those old houses with a walled garden, and she could plant it with two-hundred-year-old boxwood, and she could fix a writing room for Tom. There would be the usual discussion about having things simple, but actually he liked good food and elaborate parties.

She might make another suggestion tomorrow. They could go away somewhere for a while to Mexico or Arizona or somewhere. Tom would go into the usual routine about being a gigolo, but he would like it when he got there. There had been a time when the same sort of restlessness would come over them at the same moment, and all you had to do was to ask that man who worked for Raymond Whitcomb to come around, or Tom would know someone who knew something about the Amazon or Haiti. Or they would get out the books on Egypt or Persia. All you had to do was to buy a ticket in order to get away. They had gone somewhere every year before the war, and Tom had loved it.

They had been able to make fun of the same things and the same people once, and they had loved to stay in queer and uncomfortable places, and make queer friends. It all answered his intellectual curiosity, and it was something she had been able to do for him; and, indirectly, she had taught him a good deal too. Once they had been restless in exactly the same way but now there was nothing left but restlessness.

"Say, Poll." It was Tom's voice calling from the other room.

"Yes," she called back, "what is it?"

"Are you going to sit there all night? Why don't you come to bed?"

"Why?" she asked. "I'm not keeping you awake."

"It gives me the heebie-jeebies. Can't you be normal and go to sleep?"

She rose and walked into the darkened bedroom, and she could see the glow of his cigarette. That habit of his of smoking before he went to sleep was something that she had never been able to break. No matter how many stories she had told him of people who had died from falling asleep with a cigarette, it made no difference. Tom was propped up against the pillows, smoking.

"Just as a personal favor," he said, "can't you try to go to sleep?"

"Tom," she said.

And he sat up suddenly in bed.

"Oh, my God, Poll," he said. "What is it now?"

"Tom, can't we go away somewhere?"

"Oh, my God," Tom said. "We're here, aren't we?"

"Away somewhere," Polly said, "where there isn't anything else."

"Now, listen, Poll," Tom said. "Let's not have a travel talk."

"And let's not have you tell me there's a war on," Polly said. "There's always Florida."

"Florida," Tom said, and he made an uncomplimentary sound. "Have you tried lately to get into a train to Florida?"

"We could find someone," Polly said, "who could get us something. Tom, can't we go away somewhere?"

She waited in the silence, and then his voice sounded gentle and completely final.

"You and I can't get away from anything by going anywhere," he said, "unless we go to sleep."

Other women she knew had their troubles, and spilled them all over the place like leaky pots and pans. They were brave little women, all coping with ogres who had undergone some complete change due to certain characteristics concealed before marriage. All those husbands sounded about the way Tom sounded now. If she were to confide in anyone, she would be saying that Tom was not even agreeable any more, that somehow they never did anything together, that nothing she did about the house amused or interested him, that he just came home and read a book and did not want to be interrupted, that she could not get a single thing out of him about himself, that something must be worrying him, and she did not know what. There were a lot of friends with whom she could have talked about Tom, and she even felt that some of them were waiting to have her begin. She had also suspected that some of those psychiatrists and analysts whom you were always meeting at dinner parties, and who knew all the rules of happy marriage, though often they could not practise them themselves, were looking at her in a hopeful, professional way. Even her mother, who seldom noticed anything, was aware that things weren't right, but Polly was damned if she would say anything to anyone alive, even if it were true. There were only two people to whom she had ever talked much about herself. Bob Tasmin had been very kind and had tried to understand without ever being able to, and Tom had understood perhaps, but he had not been kind.

"And then the limousine called," Tom used to say, "and I suppose Meadows and the second man were waiting at the door. Just get this through your head, Poll. Nobody cares what happens to a girl if she's on a yacht."

XIII

There Was a Little Girl . . .

THERE ONCE was a brief time when Polly Fulton had been very happy. Her happiness made a sort of reference point to which she often returned, and she did so again that night in Washington. Her mother had taken her on the only long visit they ever made to Willett, New Hampshire. She was about ten and Harry had been left behind with his nurse. It must have been the year that B. F. had bought that old English country house and had arranged to have it sent over in crates and cases to Gray's Point, because the architect and her father had been going over blueprints at breakfast. B. F. had said that Rogers could take them up in the limousine, and she remembered gripping the edge of the dining table because a long trip in the closed car always made her sick.

"No," her mother said. "Polly and I can manage on the train. It won't be anything, Burt, and you know how it was when we went up there with Rogers."

Her father said he thought it was pretty good going up with Rogers, and that a car was meant to take you places and that Rogers was meant to drive it.

"But you know, Burt," her mother said, "I don't want them to think we're . . . you know what I mean, Burt."

From New York to Keene they sat in one of those old-fashioned parlor cars with little fine-mesh screens in the windows which did not keep out the cinders, and several times her mother moistened the corner of her handkerchief to remove smudges from Polly's face, a mortifying procedure.

"Smudges look queer with freckles," her mother said. "You have freckles like your Uncle Herbert."

She had been thinking that Willett would be like a place in the Alps, and that after Uncle Herbert met them at the station in a Democrat, they would have goats' milk for supper and she might sleep in a hayloft. She had acquired this idea from reading *Heidi* and because her mother had told her that Uncle Herbert and Aunt Martha did not have as much money as her father. The house, though, when they got to Willett, was not like a chalet. It had a round tower and a porch with gingerbread trimmings, and a bathroom with a stained glass window and a zinc tub, and Polly slept in a small hall room beside her mother's. Her Aunt Martha wore an apron, but she was not a maid. Instead of having any, they did their own cooking and washed their dishes right on the dining room table.

She had been happy even though she was always being introduced to strange people who said well, well, so this was Burt's little girl, and she certainly did take after him, and time would tell whether she was as smart as Burt. She was allowed to help behind the soda fountain at the drugstore, and she could have a soda any time she wanted, and she could give one to her friends. She was allowed to play croquet on the lawn with her mother and Aunt Martha after supper and her Uncle Herbert brought her mother's old dollhouse from the barn for her to play with in the parlor.

Everything was perfectly all right at Willett from the time she awoke in the morning and helped light the kitchen stove to the time she said her prayers and went to sleep. It was the only place she could ever remember where she was like everyone else. When she walked down the main street everyone on the narrow sidewalks knew her, even the people in the paper mill, and she could go anywhere in Willett and talk to anyone. At heart she must have been like her mother — small-town.

Those two weeks at Willett of bringing kindling from the woodshed, of making her own cot bed, of sweeping out the kitchen and drying the dishes, formed the only occasion in her childhood when she was useful to other people, or even an essential part of anything. It was surprising that her parents, though they had been brought up in just this way, could have completely overlooked that aspect of a child's development.

She spoke to B. F. about it one of those last Sunday mornings when he was an invalid at home. It pleased her very much, she felt warm and happy, because B. F. preferred seeing her to anyone else. In a way, it was like forming a new friendship, for neither of them had ever realized how much they were alike. Polly was very proud of the way B. F. took his illness, for she was sure that he knew it was only a pause before the end of everything. He had never looked so handsome and rested as when he sat in the easy chair in his bedroom, all beautifully turned out and dressed by a Swedish male attendant whom he called Nursie.

Nursie had started as a professional pugilist with a cauliflower ear and two broken knuckles to show for it, and B. F. had found out all about him, as he always did about everyone. Nursie had catered to tired businessmen and dypsomaniacs at a Health Farm and he had handled violent gentlemen at a Nut House, and now he was in what he called Private Work, which consisted in seeing a number of rich and invalided gentlemen through their last days in their Palm Beach villas, or their apartments in New York. Nursie was called in just one jump ahead of the undertaker, B. F. said, but he was a broad-gauged man with a lot of human contacts, and it was a pleasure to have him on call day and night.

Polly met Nursie in the hall that morning. He was carrying up a freshly pressed suit from the lower floor, and he said what do you know. The Big Boy has ordered six new silk dressing gowns, all colors.

The silk dressing gowns, all very loud, all from Sulka's, were spread out on B. F.'s four-post, Elizabethan oak bed, and he was wearing the loudest of them, purple with yellow stripes. He was seated by the east window with his antique kidney-shaped table in front of him, looking across the rain-drenched roofs to the misty East River.

"Hello, Cutie," he said, "what's new?" Polly sat beside him and held his hand for a little while, but finally he drew his hand away.

"Cutie," he said, "I wish you'd light a cigarette and let me smell it. I guess I've always lived in smoke-filled rooms."

Polly lit a cigarette, and his words made a lump rise in her throat.

"It's a mean day, isn't it?" he said. "All the planes are grounded —just like me."

"What did you do last night?" Polly asked.

"Last night?" he said. "Let's see. I didn't sleep much last night. I kept on the radio. There's something big going to happen in the Pacific, and I wondered how Harry was . . ." He leaned forward in his chair. ". . . and then I played gin rummy with Nursie. I took twenty-seven dollars off him, and then he tucked me in and I began thinking."

"What did you think about?" Polly asked.

"About you, Cutie. I gave you my full attention for about an hour. I was thinking about when you were a little kid, and how I always wanted you to have a good time, and I'm afraid you never did. I don't know what the answer was. Do you know?"

That was when she told him about Willett, and about the only time she had ever felt useful. It appeared to surprise him.

"You know, I never thought of that, and I should have. Of course, you're dead right, but you're being mighty useful now. Ring the bell and ask for a Scotch and soda, will you?"

"It's too early," Polly said.

"Well, tell them to bring it anyway. I want to see someone take a drink. Cutie, you were happy sometimes, weren't you?" B. F. said. "Go on, tell me, please."

That was when she told him about all the things that had bothered her when she was a little girl.

"But let's forget it," Polly said. "You see, no one cares what happens to a girl if she's on a yacht."

"Who told you that?" he asked. "Tom?" Then he began to laugh.

"What are you laughing about?" Polly asked.

"About the yacht," he said. "I care, Cutie. I care because, you see, I built you that damned yacht."

* * *

162

There was surely nothing worse than being different, particularly in childhood when your main desire was to conform. Once at Miss Eldridge's School at Gray's Point, Susy Hollister and some of the other girls had organized one of those children's societies with passwords and secret meetings, and Polly had asked Susy if she could not join it too, which showed how very dumb and innocent Polly used to be. For years afterward she would be awakened in the middle of the night by dreams of the awful time when she had asked something of anyone like Susy Hollister.

"We don't want you," Susy had said, "because you're just rich, rich, rich."

It would have been less painful if Susy had told her she was too dumb or not attractive enough. It would have been much better if she had refrained from arguing, but instead she had asked Susy why, since Susy was pretty rich herself.

"But we're not *nouveau*," Susy said, and she raised her eyebrows in a precocious manner, "not *nouveau*."

Polly understood the allusion, because she too had a French governess, and it left her speechless. She could see that her mother's voice was flat and high and nervous, and that she referred to her Personal Maid, that she was always being too generous, sending too many vegetables and flowers to people who did not want them, and that though she had friends, a good many of them seemed to be ladies in the antique business. Her father was more perplexing when she was a little girl, for when she was with him everything seemed all right, but she frequently wished he would not be so sure that everyone would like him, and that he would not talk to everyone, no matter who.

There was one terrible thing that she could never forget one summer at Gray's Point. Rogers had taken her to the Yacht Club for her swimming lesson, and her father was going to meet her there when he came back from New York. She waited for a long while by herself on the verandah, rocking and looking at the Sound, and finally an old man spoke to her. It was Mr. Hollister.

"What are you sitting all alone for, Polly?" Mr. Hollister said.

"Why aren't you out on the beach with Susy and the other girls?" Mr. Hollister's ruddy tanned face and his closely clipped mustache swam dizzily before her eyes. She could not tell him that she was not on the beach with Susy and the other girls because she was *nouveau riche*. Her mouth felt like flannel and her words were thin and distant.

"Because I'm waiting for Father," she said.

"Well, I saw him a while ago," Mr. Hollister said. "Let's go and find him."

Polly wanted to tell him not to bother, but instead she found herself walking beside him through the big room, around the other verandah, waiting while he looked inside the bar — and the worst of it was that he made a joke of it.

"Burt Fulton's left his daughter flat," Mr. Hollister kept saying. "She's a damsel in distress."

They finally came to the parking space where all the chauffeurs were waiting with their cars, and there she saw her father. She could never forget the smell of tar and oil and of leather upholstery in the sun. The hood of a touring car was open, and her father was standing by it in his shirt sleeves, with a circle of chauffeurs around him. He was holding a wrench and a screwdriver, and he looked up when he saw them.

"Hello," he said, "I'm just helping Carlson here with the Tasmins' distributor. I've told those boys in Detroit again and again . . . Well, there's the way it goes, Carlson." And he began wiping his hands on a piece of cotton waste.

When her father was by the car it seemed perfectly all right. It was only later that she was aware how dreadful it all was to have Mr. Hollister discover him in the parking place with the chauffeurs. Once she had found him pitching horseshoes with the Italians in the garden, and that had seemed all right, too, until she had thought of it later. Then she realized that her father could not help it. He was different from those other people just as she was, and they all were vulgar, all of them *nouveau riche*.

"Don't those children like the swimming pool?" she heard her father ask one time.

"She doesn't seem to want to have them come," her mother answered. "I don't know what it is, Burt. She seems to act ashamed."

Sometimes later when Polly was ill with the grippe, or in the midst of a tiresome train journey, she would imagine herself as a little girl again, walking through the place at Gray's Point. Even in her memory it was like one of those eighteenth-century French engravings which you could see without believing. It had no more relationship to its surroundings than the Petit Trianon of Marie Antoinette out in that lonely corner of the grounds near the Palace of Versailles, and it had been built in just about the same arbitrary way.

She could see the walks of white gravel, the borders of box, and the espaliered trees along the walls of the formal garden, laid out by J. Howland Makepiece, the great landscape architect. She could remember B. F. and Mr. Makepiece watching huge trees being moved and grouped on the lawns. B. F. had always been moving trees like pieces on a chessboard in a game of his own that was never entirely finished. She could see again, through a child's eyes, the terraces, and the cutting garden and the greenhouses, and the sub-terranean dugouts where the great bay trees were stored in the winter. She would dream of the children's wing, her schoolroom, Harry's nursery, Harry's nurse's and Miss Prentiss's rooms, the elevator for the firewood and the breakfast trays, the library for the first editions, the music room, the conservatory, the servants' dining room, the great cellars with their huge steam boilers.

Sometimes she would dream of the Tudor wing, furnished by the experts in just the spirit of the period, heavy, dark oak with tapestries and suits of armor, and choir stalls and wooden statues of saints. B. F. always had the best people to help him, strange little professors, and pixie-like museum curators, one of whom had to be carried there in a wheelchair. B. F.'s business friends were the ones who really enjoyed it. Quite a layout, she used to hear them say, and sometimes even quite a little layout.

The first time she had taken Tom to Gray's Point she had been afraid that he would never look at her again after he had seen the place. They had walked down to the walled garden after lunch and through the maze and everywhere. Tom had been cautiously silent, as you sometimes were when wandering through a picture gallery, but when Polly turned on the sprinkler system, and all at once little fountains sprang up out of the turf, he had whistled.

"Well, Poll," he said. "It's like something in the old Hippodrome." She could vaguely remember the stage where the girls sank in the water singing. "I keep thinking that it may all be put on flatcars tonight, and that it won't be here tomorrow."

What would happen to all that stuff, Tom used to say, the Early American and Georgian silver, the first editions and the Chippendale? Why, they would all end up someday in the Parke-Bernet Gallery to be purchased by a lot of refugees who feared inflation. What would happen, he used to ask, to that mausoleum at Gray's Point? It would either be torn down or made into an overprivileged lunatic asylum; and her old man must have known it, because he had a mind when he wanted to use it, in spite of his conditioned reflexes. Then why did he keep doing it, Tom used to ask?

It was something that belonged only to one person and certainly not to Polly. It belonged only to B. F. It was a magnificent projection of his imagination, and somehow it was not pretentious or ludicrous when he was there. If it had been suddenly destroyed, she often thought that B. F. would have let it go as an artist might dispose of a canvas. She could almost hear him saying: —

"Well, it was all just a little idea of mine — something I dashed off in my spare time."

It was all right when B. F. was there, but he was fortunate. He never had to live in that idea of his for any great length of time. He was away all day in the city, or off for a week or so on business trips. He never had to cope with it like Polly's mother. He was not brought up like Polly or Harry, in the midst of his idea.

One day, when she had heard that he was planning a three weeks' trip, Polly ran away. This must have been the first of her later efforts to get away from things. Afterwards a number of people asked her all sorts of questions, all of which circled around the final question: What was it that had made her do it? It was impossible to answer, since she did not know, herself.

A strange lady named Mrs. Featherstone appeared in the house for what Mama said was a little visit. Judging from the way her mother and B. F. acted, Mrs. Featherstone was not a friend of theirs. In fact, Polly was sure that Mrs. Featherstone annoyed B. F., because finally B. F. began whistling through his teeth whenever he saw her. When Polly asked Mama whether Mrs. Featherstone was a doctor, her mother asked her what ever gave her that idea? Mrs. Featherstone was just a friend making a little visit, and Mrs. Featherstone was terribly fond of children. So Polly must be nice and play with Mrs. Featherstone, and so must Harry.

Mrs. Featherstone kept poking her nose into everything very rudely, looking at all the books that Polly read, asking her what she dreamed and whether she loved Harry; and once she went so far as to ask whether Polly loved her father and if so how much did she love him? Polly had been taught that such talk was rude and impertinent; so, because it was none of Mrs. Featherstone's business, Polly did her best to make it clear that she loved everything. She loved her pretty room and all those lovely dresses; she loved everyone she played with, particularly Susan Hollister; and yes, she was completely happy.

Then one day Mrs. Featherstone became very confidential. It seemed that once Mrs. Featherstone had been very unhappy as a little girl because people neglected her, and her father used long, hard words and her mother was busy with the housekeeping. It seemed that Mrs. Featherstone's mind got tired keeping up with all of this — and what do you think? Mrs. Featherstone too had run away. So she and Polly had a great deal in common, and Polly could tell Mrs. Featherstone everything, because Mrs. Featherstone had gone through it all.

So why was it that Polly left home, without telling anyone, or without making any scene? Was it because she was jealous that Daddy loved Mama more than Daddy loved her? Or was it because she wasn't in that club with the Hollister girl? (Polly could never understand how Mrs. Featherstone had learned about that club, except that she was very nosy.) Or was it because she felt that Mama loved Harry too much? Or had any of the men on the place done anything — well, anything to frighten her? Or was it because Polly was worried about how babies came? Mrs. Featherstone knew that these things sometimes worried girls of Polly's age, because they had worried Mrs. Featherstone, and Mrs. Featherstone wanted Polly to know all about it, since what you knew never worried you. Then Mrs. Featherstone told Polly a lot of things which seemed to her vulgar and none of Mrs. Featherstone's business. Then she asked Polly whether she had ever seen anything like that. Then she asked Polly to call her by her first name; her first name was Maisie. Just tell Maisie why it was she ran away.

Polly only knew that she could not have done anything else.

One Saturday morning in October her mother told her that she had a big surprise, that Mrs. Damon had just called up and had asked Polly over there for lunch with little Gertrude, and you could see that Mama was quite excited. It was the first time that Polly had been asked there, but then Daddy had been playing poker with Mr. Damon, and they were beginning to know how nice Daddy was. So Polly must go over and play with little Gertrude, and Rogers would take her over at half-past twelve.

After Miss Prentiss had dressed her and put on her new blue coat, Polly found a hammer in the tool chest that B. F. kept in his dressing room, smashed in the door of her iron bank and took out fifteen dollars. She did not know why she did it, except that she did not want to have lunch with Gertrude Damon. She sat in the back of the limousine with her hands folded while Rogers drove along the twisting road lined with maples, past Miss Eldridge's school and up the drive to the white house where the Damons lived. When she pretended to ring the bell, Rogers drove away and she waited, looking at the neatly clipped bushes and the design on the Damons' brass knocker, until he was out of sight.

Suddenly, she felt as though she were a leaf blowing in the sky. She walked, she did not run, down the Damons' drive. She turned into Lawrence Street, holding her purse very tight, crossed the main road, and walked by Holtz's grocery store, the bakery, the

Jumble Shop and the Gray's Point garage, to the railroad station, and bought a ticket for New York. She knew her way well enough around Grand Central Station, for she had often been to the doctor and the dentist and sometimes to the opera. She bought a copy of *Collier's* magazine at the newsstand, and took the three o'clock train to Keene, but she never thought of eating lunch or supper. She simply sat in the day coach very straight as Miss Prentiss had told her, with her hands folded, never looking at anyone, never smiling. She was just a neatly dressed, unpromising little girl to whom no one spoke.

Polly was not even hungry when the train reached Keene at about nine o'clock on a cold, clear night. She knew how to change for the Willett train, and it must have been eleven by the time she got there. It was half a mile from the station to the Hawkins house, but Polly knew the way. It never occurred to her until she saw how dark the houses were that everyone would be in bed. It was much colder than Gray's Point, so that she shivered in her party dress, as she rang and rang the bell. When her Uncle Herbert in his old dressing gown and slippers unlocked the door and looked out on the porch, he did not know who she was.

"What are you doing here, little girl?" he asked. Then the light of the candle he was holding fell on her face — they still did not have electric light. "Martha," he called, "come down here. It's Poll."

The house had the same musty smell that houses had in Willett. Her Aunt Martha was kissing her. She looked very queer in her flannel wrapper with her hair in papers.

"Why Polly Fulton," Aunt Martha was saying. "Where's everybody else?" But there wasn't anybody else. She was just there herself, Polly Fulton.

They went into the kitchen where it was warm and Uncle Herbert was shaking down the fire.

"How did you get here, dear?" they were asking. Then for some reason she was clinging to her Aunt Martha's flannel wrapper, choking with hard sobs.

"I just came," she said.

She had done it by herself without anyone's having told her how. There was one beautiful thing about it all which she never forgot, and that was the way B. F. felt. She had never thought that he would be sorry, or dreamed that he would be hurt. He came up in the car the next day with Rogers driving and burst into the kitchen where Polly was learning how to make a cake and snatched her up in his arms although her hands were covered with dough. His face was rough because he had not shaved, and when Polly saw him she began to cry again, and he did something which she had never seen him do before or since. B. F. began to cry.

"Poll," he said. "Why did you do it?"

That was the first of all those questions, and she could not explain why. She only knew that she had never been so glad to see anyone as B. F., and she would never do such a thing again as long as he was so hurt.

"Poll," he said. "Go ahead and make your cake. I want to see you make it." And he sat there by the kitchen table, watching her and reading from the cookbook.

"Now you put it in the oven," he said. "It's got to be a good hot oven. You're restless like me, Poll, but don't run out on me again, unless you take me too."

Quite often after that he took her with him to Pittsburgh, Cleveland and Detroit, and it must have been hard for him, dragging around a little girl. That was why, of course, she was sent away to school. Things were never quite the same after that trip to Willett.

Sometimes later at dinners in New York she could get people into stitches by telling about Heatherbloom Hall. Whenever Tom was bored by the company, he would ask her to tell how she had been elected to make the pansy chaplet or about the singing contests when the Heathers under one apple tree sang against the Blooms under another. Tom was never tired of hearing Polly tell of Heatherbloom's Head Mistress, Miss Agatha Ralston, and her addresses to the school on spirit, honor, resignation, and on cigarette smoking versus motherhood; but Polly always felt a sneaking disloyalty when she made fun of Heatherbloom, for she had loved it once.

Heatherbloom Hall [the catalogue read] while nestling on a country hillside, and while affording peaceful vistas of sheer beauty, offers the advantages of a harmonious and cultured home combined with the discipline of thought and manner in which girls can learn to be ladies. Rambling rooms of an old homestead afford ample space for living, thinking and learning, while the large grounds of Heatherbloom offer the facilities of nature and the healthy out-of-doors.

Obviously Miss Ralston had written it herself — because Miss Ralston was always partial to "while" in compositions. "The Quiet Evening Hour" was the title of one of the illustrations; it showed the girls of the Upper School in their apron uniform (there was no nonsense about dress at Heatherbloom) all lying and lounging about in Miss Ralston's parlor, while hot chocolate and sponge cake stood on the table and Miss Ralston sat reading from Shakespeare. Then there was a picture of the Heather and the Bloom dramatic club ("While Being a Garden Spot, the Lawns of Heatherbloom Are, Too, a Stage"), doing Aristophanes' *Frogs,* with all the girls in sandals and white draperies which they made themselves at the Craft Shop. Polly was a Heather, and after she had been there for a term she would gladly have died for the Heathers — she had played the Third Frog.

Each new girl was assigned an "advisor" (Polly's advisor was Apples Sandler) who taught her the Heatherbloom song, the first line of which was "Oh, girls of Heatherbloom, loyal and true." She was sure that Miss Ralston must have written that song, because Miss Ralston could do anything, and she must also have written the Heatherbloom creed which they used to recite by the light of the fire with all other lights extinguished: —

I believe in being worthy of Heatherbloom. To be worthy I am on my honor. I must love and respect every teacher and girl at Heatherbloom. I must do my best in work and play.

Those were the things that Tom loved to hear about, but if B. F. thought they were funny too, he had never even smiled when she told him about them in the vacations when she could think of nothing else but Heatherbloom. He said he did not know what it was that Miss Ralston had, but she certainly had something. He said that Miss Ralston certainly put on quite a show, and later he gave Heatherbloom a gymnasium and an indoor stage.

No one appeared to notice Polly's freckles or the bands on her teeth. Instead, they all thought she was quite a girl, and she was all at once the brightest girl in her class, and a whiz at algebra. When she came home for Christmases, she was no longer unhappy at the parties at Gray's Point, and she was able to smile at Susy Hollister and Gertrude Damon charitably because they were not Heatherbloom girls.

Heatherbloom had turned Polly into a perfect corker. She had only to look at her photograph later in the Heatherbloom Hall Yearbook to be sure. She might have looked pretty then if she had not tried to look soulful, if she had not done her hair in a sort of Civil War braid like Miss Aggie. At any rate, it was at the end of that year that Bob Tasmin first thought she looked pretty. She had been president of the Junior Class, and she had come back from Prize Day the winner of the All Around Prize, and the holder of the Miss Ralston Pennant, and for the first time they had a long talk alone.

The heat of that June day and all the chatter and the standing around in the sun, together with the chicken salad and the pineapple juice punch, had made Mama feel a little sick during the two-hour ride home after the exercises, so Mama had gone right upstairs to lie down after they reached Gray's Point. Harry was away somewhere, and B. F., who had not been able to attend the exercises because of a directors' meeting, was not back from New York yet. Timmons carried Polly's bags and books up to her room, and after going to the kitchen to speak to all the servants, who said that she was growing to be a big young lady, she went out to see the garden.

It was after four, the hour when all the flowers were especially bright and still, and all the birds were singing. The rose garden was in full bloom and so were the peonies, and she told Harrod, who was squaring the borders, that everything looked beautiful. She told him so, sweetly and graciously, because she had been president of her class, and Harrod answered that he was very glad she liked it and that Miss Polly was getting to be a fine young lady, but America was no place for roses or for turf. Then she walked over to the maze and then down to the swimming pool, and she was not surprised to find Bob Tasmin there, for as long as she could remember Bob Tasmin had been coming over to the swimming pool from the Tasmin house. He must have just arrived, for he was standing at the edge of the pool, bareheaded, dressed in white flannels, holding his coat on his arm.

"Why, hello, Poll," he said, and he looked at her almost as though he did not recognize her. "I didn't know you were back."

She told him that today had been Prize Day and that school was over.

"Well, it looks as though it agreed with you there," Bob Tasmin said. "You're getting to be a pretty big girl."

A year or so ago such a remark would have made her self-conscious, but not now when she was the Best All Around Girl at Heatherbloom.

"Yes," Polly said. "I've been putting on weight, but none of it is fat."

"That's so," he said. "You look pretty well set up."

"They give girls a pretty good workout at Heatherbloom," Polly told him.

Bob Tasmin stood by the edge of the pool with the sunlight on his dark hair, smiling, and Polly smiled back at him as she might have at an older girl at Heatherbloom. He was tall and handsome, but, after all, she had been a class president, and she was not sure that Bob Tasmin had been.

"What do they do?" he asked. "Run you around the track?"

"It's field hockey, mostly," Polly said, "but we do track too. I won the broad jump."

He took her arm gently and gave it a little pinch.

"That's right, all muscle," he said. "What do you do besides jumping?"

"Well, besides math and English and history, and biology," she said, "there's Student Government. As a matter of fact" — she laughed and shrugged her shoulders, because she did not want him to think she was boasting — "I'll be President of the Student Council next year."

"No," Bob Tasmin said, "not really." And then he saw that it was important. "Why, Poll, you must be pretty proud."

"Oh," Polly said, "those things sort of come by accident, don't they? You must have gone out for lots of things in school and college."

"Oh, yes," Bob Tasmin said; "but now it's only law school, only books, Poll."

There was something in the way he spoke that made her feel sorry for him. He was too old to be young again.

"Well, studies are all that really count," Polly said.

"That's all that counts at law school," Bob Tasmin answered.

You had to read and read, Bob Tasmin said, and it was pretty much up to you whether you did well or not.

"But I bet you're good at it," Polly said.

"Well, it's a little new to me," he answered, "but maybe I'm not so bad. I just feel I've been pushed around a lot. I just want to sit in the sun and think."

"I know what you mean," Polly said. "Now on the biology exam this year, I sat up all night. I wasn't supposed to. You know what I did?"

It was almost as though they were the same age for just a little while.

"No. What did you do?" Bob Tasmin asked.

He relaxed and lay on the grass, looking at her as she sat beside him describing the examination blow by blow and giving him a little lecture on the elemental principles of biology. Then she saw that he had closed his eyes.

"Are you listening?" she asked. "Or have you gone to sleep?"

Bob Tasmin began to laugh, just as though they were old friends.

"Poll," he said. "You're a nice kid, and I want to tell you something."

"What?" she asked.

"You're going to be pretty someday, Poll."

She remembered the sun and the blue color of the swimming pool, and the shadows of the plane trees across the lawn. She remembered her incredulity and how she caught her breath.

"Don't be so wet," she said. "I'm all over freckles."

It was a coarse piece of slang which she had heard Apples Sandler use, and she had never meant to say such a thing to an older man.

"They're going," he said, "and you've got gray-green eyes."

That was all he said, because B. F. was walking toward them from the garden, just back from town, and she ran to meet him.

"Hello, Poll," B. F. said. "How's the All Around Girl?" And he put his arm around her. "Isn't she quite a girl?"

"She certainly is," Bob Tasmin said.

That night, for the first time in her life, Polly took two kinds of lotion from her mother's bathroom and began working on her freckles.

XIV

She Had Everything Once

IT APPEARED to Polly that summer that everyone at Gray's Point was kinder, even Susy Hollister. There were new boys back from boarding school, there were picnics and luncheons, and that was the year the Country Club allowed her age group to go to the dances. This was the first year, too, that Bob Tasmin ever danced with her.

It was after the dinner that the Heaths had given for Nancy Heath, who was just about Polly's age. She would never have dreamed of going, except to please her mother and B. F., but when she got there it had not been so bad because she found that Nancy Heath was just as frightened as she was. Nancy told her in the dressing room that the party was going to be awful. All those older people at the other tables would be laughing at them just as though they were kids in a nursery. Her mother made her do it, Nancy said, and she wished she could go somewhere and hide.

There were ten of them by themselves at a round table. The boys, in white trousers and blue coats, were at that awkward age when they were too old to be tripping each other up, and too young to make much sense. Polly sat next to the Williams boy from Pleasant Street, Hughie Williams, whom she had always known at dancing school, and who was suffering from acne. On her other side was Norman Bell, a pale boy with horn-rimmed glasses. Norman Bell knew a number of riddles which she could not guess, and some jokes from the latest shows which she had not heard. Norman had been visiting recently at Watch Hill, and he was very tired and very bored. He told her that this was certainly a hick party, and that no one who amounted to anything stayed in Gray's Point all summer. What he wanted, Norman said, was a party with horns and whistles, such as they had at sophisticated places in New York. He had been to New York with some friends last New Year's Eve, and that was where you saw sophisticated people. Hughie Williams could not think of anything to say except to ask her if she had been swimming lately, and what was the school she went to and how long would they give her for Christmas vacation. Nevertheless, you had to look happy.

Susy Hollister across the table looked extremely happy sitting next to a very smooth boy named Roland Scott who could imitate a saxophone. But to Polly nothing was worse than those parties when you were fifteen — having to pretend it was fun with all those gawky boys. The college men in dinner coats at the other tables did not fidget in their chairs or scratch themselves, and the debutantes and older women knew how to sit quietly without wriggling. They had little bags out of which they could take lipsticks and mirrors, and some of them knew how to smoke. Though Polly knew it was bad for them if any of them wanted to be mothers, at least it gave girls something to do. The young married set had all come from cocktail parties and were not worried about anything at all. Their troubles seemed to be over, Polly thought, since they were safely married, all in houses of their own.

She could see Bob Tasmin from where she sat, talking to a girl in a beautiful organdy dress. He must have said something that was very funny because the girl laughed and laid her hand on his arm for a moment. Then when the music started those two stood up, and the girl leaned toward him still laughing. Her lips were red, and Polly was sure it was lipstick. She remembered that Miss Ralston had said that no one with real beauty of soul ever used such things because it was not necessary. Yet, the girl in the purple organdy would not have looked nearly so well without it, and Bob Tasmin did not seem to object.

"What are you looking at?" Norman Bell asked.

"Oh," Polly said. "Just at the people. I'm always amused by people."

It was a line, of course. She was not amused by people.

"What's so funny about them?" Norman asked.

"I didn't say they were funny," Polly said. "I merely said I was amused."

"Well, it doesn't take much to give you fun," Norman said. "These are very boring people."

Polly did not answer. Bob Tasmin and the girl in organdy were moving to the dance floor.

"Say," Norman said again. "What are you looking at?"

"I just recognized a friend of mine," Polly said.

"How about dancing?" Norman asked. "I suppose we've got to."

"I should love to," Polly said. Norman was right. Dancing was expected of them. Polly had gone for years to dancing school, and she was able to follow Norman though he was off the beat. She was even able to follow some of his fancy steps, but when these grew a little sophisticated for Gray's Point, she saw Bob Tasmin walking toward them. It had never occurred to her that he would cut in until he touched Norman's shoulder. . . .

"May I have some of this?" he asked, or something like that. He held her close to him, and for the first time that evening everything was in time with the music.

"You shouldn't have done that," Polly said. "Now you'll get stuck." It was what she dreaded most, and it had happened often enough in dancing school.

"Why, that would be wonderful," Bob Tasmin said. He always said exactly the right thing.

"Well, if it gets too bad," Polly said, "you can hold out a dollar bill and I'll pay you back."

It was wonderful because she was the only girl at their table who had been asked to dance that night by an older man.

The unwritten conventions of Gray's Point made Polly know her place, just as they must have made Bob Tasmin aware of his. It helped a girl, of course, to be noticed casually by an older man, but it would have been awkward had it gone too far, for it might have seemed that there was something wrong with both of them. If she had been on any sort of familiar terms with all those golf players and horse jumpers who had their own lockers in the men's bar, it would have been ridiculous. Bob Tasmin could never have taken her anywhere without everyone's laughing at him and without

178

her being embarrassed herself, but he did see her often at the house that summer.

Polly was not sure, but she thought that he used the swimming pool more than he ever had in the past, and that he generally came over by himself without bringing some of his own crowd with him as he had once. She came to count on finding him sunning himself on the flagstones at about five o'clock almost any afternoon. Though there were all sorts of things that she had started doing ever since the other girls at Gray's Point had become so much more friendly, Polly began finding herself at the lower part of the garden by five — not making a point of it in the least, just being there. So much of life for a girl, particularly when you were young, was a matter of chance, of drifting somewhere without knowing it. Then a time came when she used to feel a definite surprise and disappointment on a day when Bob Tasmin was not there, a sense of something having gone wrong with routine and order; and once when she had gone on a party that Gertrude gave on the Damons' thirty-footer, Bob Tasmin spoke of it the next afternoon.

"Where were you yesterday?" he asked. "I missed you."

That was all either of them ever said.

It was very wonderful that she should have anything to say that would be amusing and interesting to an older man and she used to think at odd moments of things that would make him laugh. She told him about Mademoiselle and Miss Prentiss. She told him about how Susy Hollister and Gertrude Damon, and all that group, used to snoot her, and how when she was nine or ten she used to feel sick when she went alone to their parties.

She told Bob Tasmin how only two years before she had secretly drunk a glass of mustard and water so that she could throw up and thus get out of going to the Christmas cotillion. He was always interested, and the best part of it was that he seemed sorry. Sometimes he was almost like a student advisor at Heatherbloom, although he was an older man. He told her that he could see she must have been awfully lonely, but she said this was not so, that she was always happy alone, thinking and imagining. It was a great relief to have him listen, for somehow it put all of that into the discard.

Those girls at Gray's Point, she said, were awful goops, all except Nancy Heath. Those girls all got the sillies whenever they saw a boy, and how anybody could go crazy over pimply boys like Hughie Williams or Norman Bell was more than she could imagine — and Roland Scott, that New York friend of Susy Hollister's, wasn't any better. That little lizard put grease on his hair. Frankly they were all goons and goops and did not know anything, none of them.

"Well, you mustn't be serious all the time, Poll," Bob Tasmin said.

She wasn't, but they just bored her, bored her, bored her.

"Now, Poll," Bob Tasmin said. "You mustn't be afraid of them."

This made her angry, because she was not afraid of such goons and goops. They amused her. They were simply ludicrous. . . .

They had nothing to offer now that she knew an older man. She sometimes thought later that if it had not been for Bob Tasmin, she might have fitted in at Gray's Point a little better, but she was not sure. Her own environment, probably, was so specialized and peculiar that she was already seeing and learning more than those simpler boys and girls.

It was August of this same summer — August 1926 — that B. F. took her abroad for just three weeks. He made up his mind to go so suddenly that there was no time to arrange for her mother and Harry to go too, or at least her mother could not adjust herself to it.

"Gladys," he said, "those Frenchmen we're in with are mixed up with Citröen, and they aren't playing ball right. I'll just catch the *Aquitania* Monday and hop right back, and I guess I'll take Poll along."

Her mother said that Polly ought to have a chaperon.

"It won't look right," Mrs. Fulton said. "When young girls go to Europe they need an older woman, particularly in Paris, Burt."

"Well, if it's necessary, we'll pick someone up in London," B. F. said. "It's just full of women who do that sort of thing." Then he said this would not look well, because if Polly had a chaperon traveling with them, why he would need a chaperon.

That trip, so long before the war, was a memory from the

Never-Never Land. Polly did not know now whether the *Aquitania* was still afloat, but she sailed that summer at midnight, her deck lights blazing, and the most wonderful thing in the world was to hear her warning blast and to walk up the gangway with the crowd that eddied and swirled through the passageway, and along the decks. Polly remembered the peaceful humming sound of the steam, and all those correct stewards in their white monkey jackets, hurrying with the bags, and B. F.'s suite, and all the friends who were there to see him off. Mr. Royall was there from the bank, looking out of place as New York bankers sometimes did with the rest of B. F.'s friends. He had brought B. F. a case of champagne, and Mr. Murcheson had obtained two pounds of caviar, and someone else had hired a man with an accordion. They all gathered around B. F., telling him to watch those Frogs and not to take any wooden money, and a purser was there with a director of the line as well as some strange people who got in by mistake.

They sat at the captain's table and the captain had them on the bridge and the engineer took her down to see the engines. An older man, not as old as Bob Tasmin, but a Harvard man, kept dancing with her and he tried to kiss her on the boat deck while they watched for the Lizard Light, and she thought she was in love with him and that they certainly would be married — until they reached Cherbourg.

When Polly returned that autumn Bob Tasmin seemed closer to her own age, and she was awfully glad to see him.

She had brought him three beautiful Dunhill straight-grain pipes all set in an alligator-skin case as though they were pieces of jewelry. She was doubtful of the propriety of giving an older man such a present until she handed him those pipes, and it was a great relief that he did not appear to think it extraordinary, nor did he pretend to be pleased as older people always had when she gave them presents she had made herself.

"Now it's worth having you go away," Bob Tasmin said, "if you come back with pipes like that."

It was the sort of remark that might have meant nothing or a great deal depending on the way you thought of it. He had missed her, three pipes' worth at any rate, but then the man in that store on Regent Street had said they were the three best pieces of briar in London, and Bob probably realized it since he knew so much about everything.

"I thought of getting you a shotgun," she said, "but I was afraid it might have looked like too much."

"Yes," Bob Tasmin said, "that would have been a great deal too much. Everyone would have started talking."

Later she was worried at the indelicate manner in which she had brought the subject up, but he seemed to have understood the way she meant it.

That September, just before she went back to school, she had a big, almost a grownup party, on her birthday. Her mother had insisted that she have a party whether she liked the idea or not in order to repay people for all the nice things they had been doing for her. Polly wished B. F. had been busier at the time because he suddenly took up the whole idea himself. He said it was about time that everyone realized Poll was growing up, and that they would have a dance for her in the Tudor wing with an orchestra and caterers from New York and entertainers and champagne, and even a detective.

Two days later a plump, middle-aged lady arrived who told dear Mrs. Fulton that she would attend to everything, if Mrs. Fulton would help her check the lists. It seemed that B. F. wanted to have three hundred people.

"It's all right," Polly told him, "if you ask very old people, but they won't understand it if you ask middle-aged people like Bob Tasmin."

She could not very well tell Bob Tasmin it was her father's fault that engraved cards from Tiffany's were being sent to him and to his friends. It was something she had to accept no matter how gauche and unpleasant, if only because she could not let the family down. She hoped the other middle-aged people would refuse, and that Bob Tasmin would not feel he had to come, out of any sort of loyalty. The most distressing part was that B. F. was so convinced that she was going to have a wonderful time that she had to pretend, and keep walking about the house with him, looking at the decorations, saying they were lovely. Harry was the only person in whom she could confide, and Harry, being so young, was not much good; but Harry understood because he was going to be downstairs himself.

"Well, anyway," Harry said, "maybe no one will notice us."

That was all very well for Harry. He could play sardines upstairs with those rough boys and that littlest Hollister girl, but everyone had to notice her in her new white satin dress from Lanvin. Moreover, without asking her, B. F. had arranged to have some of her friends from Heatherbloom, Apples Sandler and one or two others, come and stay at the house, so it was going to get all over school.

Polly rubbed her cheeks with a nailbrush and drank some aromatic spirits of ammonia which Apples Sandler had given her. It may have been because she knew she could blame the whole thing on B. F. or it may have been the dress from Lanvin, but when she came downstairs she did not care, and that was the way to go to a party. Before she knew what was happening, she was actually enjoying it. It was all very well to realize that everyone had to dance with her because it was her party, but it was not necessary for them to dance as often as they did, particularly for the men Bob Tasmin's age. Even Bud Hollister danced with her three times, and Bob Tasmin much more than that, until she was afraid he felt responsible.

"You don't have to worry about me," Polly told him. "I'm getting along all right."

"But it isn't any work," Bob Tasmin said. "You won't have much time for me after this. You might as well face the facts, Poll. You've got everything."

"That isn't fair," she said. "I can't help it if we're rich."

"Now, Poll," he said, "you ought to know me well enough to know that isn't what I mean."

Once, she did have everything. She could see herself accepting it, at one time, without questioning where it came from; but no one ever had everything for long, and after you had it for a while it did not seem like much. You did not want it when you had it. She did have everything once, and she could have had Bob Tasmin too.

XV

Have You Seen the Fultons Lately?

IT WAS eleven o'clock on a Saturday in the spring of 1930 when Bob Tasmin's father called him up and asked if he could be uptown in time for lunch.

The offices of Barstow, Barstow and Bryce, the firm that had employed Bob Tasmin after his graduation from law school, occupied a major part of the fourteenth floor of a building off lower Broadway. The elevator took you up to a large waiting room with comfortable leather chairs, from which anxious clients could get a glimpse of the library when the door was open. Then came a broad passageway flanked by the partners' offices. First was the corner office of the former senior partner, Mr. Barstow, now deceased, currently occupied by Mr. Bryce, the sole surviving partner of the original firm. Bob Tasmin often thought that Mr. Bryce rattled slightly in the mid-Victorian furniture of the late Mr. Barstow. Then came the room of Mr. Harris, the trial lawyer, from which you got a fine view of the Battery. Next came the office of Mr. Willoughby who handled divorces and family disputes, a gayer, more modernistic room than the others, reflecting Mr. Willoughby's bland disposition. The junior partners' offices farther down the passage each grew smaller depending on seniority, and the partners' row reached an end at the partners' toilet with its private key.

Beyond this line the offices of Barstow, Barstow and Bryce degenerated into a grim series of stuffy rooms, furnished with golden oak and green filing cabinets, and occupied by the secretaries and clerks. Finally came the rooms where those bright boys worked who had been selected according to their grades from the leading law schools.

There was a transient atmosphere at this end of the office, since most of its occupants were tacitly there on trial, and only a limited number survived annually, for Barstow, Barstow and Bryce believed as a matter of principle in sweating their young employees right to the verge of a nervous breakdown. If they could not develop a capacity for work in their first year, if they weren't willing to sit up nights and Sundays, there was no future for them. Bob Tasmin had contrived to adjust himself to this environment because he had an orderly mind and a capacity for detail. He did not allow piles of work to drive him into a panic, and he had a good constitution. For about a year and a half he had been where he had first been placed, in a cubbyhole overlooking an air shaft, and recently Mr. Bryce had nodded to him twice in the hall.

Bob Tasmin was doing a special piece of work for Mr. Willoughby that morning on the contested will of a former client. The residuary legatee of Mr. Simms's last will and testament was a lady of whose existence none of the immediate family had known until the will was opened. The idea was to avoid the embarrassment of publicity, and Bob Tasmin was going through a large amount of confidential correspondence dealing with Mr. Simms's more recent exploits and putting it in the digest for Mr. Willoughby. It seemed that their client had been a very enterprising as well as a very rich old gentleman.

Bob had asked his friends never to call him at the office as he had no extension of his own and had to take his calls at the desk of a Mr. Bowles who had no future but a long past in the firm. When Mr. Bowles opened his cubbyhole door and said that Bob's father was on the wire, Tasmin said he was sorry.

"It's all right," Mr. Bowles said, "but I'm not a goddam switchboard."

Bob Tasmin said again he was sorry, and Mr. Bowles pushed back his eyeshade and sat grimly waiting for him to finish. George Tasmin always spoke very loudly over the telephone, and it did not help to realize that Mr. Bowles without much effort could hear both sides of the conversation.

"Are you busy, Bob?" George Tasmin asked. "I want you to come uptown to the club for lunch."

From the corner of his eye he could see Mr. Bowles drumming noiselessly on the desk.

"I can't very well," he said.

"Of course you can," George Tasmin said, "it's Saturday."

Finally he understood that his father seriously wanted to see him. He did not like to go to Mr. Willoughby, because it was just the sort of thing that might be held against you, but it would have been worse to walk out without asking. So he went up the hall and asked Mr. Willoughby's secretary, a gray-haired, motherly lady, whether he might see Mr. Willoughby for a minute. When she opened the door there were sounds of a radio in Mr. Willoughby's office, but this was turned off by the time he entered.

"Well, well," Mr. Willoughby said. "So we want time off for lunch? Have I ever interfered with your eating habits, Tasmin?"

"No, sir," Bob said, "not usually."

"Well then, for God's sake," Mr. Willoughby said, "go and eat."

"Well, I don't want you to think, sir — " Bob Tasmin began.

"That's just it," Mr. Willoughby said, "no one here wants me to use my mental processes. Don't come back till Monday morning, and if you're going to your father's club, I'll take you up myself."

Mr. Willoughby carried a lacquer cane and he used it to push the button for the elevator, and they chatted together on the corner of Broadway while they waited for a taxicab painted to fit Mr. Willoughby's mood, a green and white with a kindly driver.

"It's a great town, New York," Mr. Willoughby said when they entered the taxicab. "You meet so many charming people. They keep running through the office, a little *distrait*, but oh God, so charming. It's queer that they never seem able to charm each other for more than a limited time . . . But when the magic's gone, there's another client!"

Bob Tasmin wished his life so far had not been a series of initiations. He always seemed to be a new schoolboy undergoing a process of chivvying, hazing and hardship. Good character training was what educators and older boys called it. He had hoped that this sort of thing would be over when he stepped into the world to earn his living, but here was Mr. Willoughby of the Sixth Form at Barstow,

Barstow and Bryce being kind to a new boy. Experience had taught Bob Tasmin to know his place exactly, and it was now necessary to laugh with Mr. Willoughby in a measured, sympathetic way.

"I think they like rudeness and realism," Mr. Willoughby said, "if it is dished out to them pleasantly, but perhaps you've noticed this already."

"No," Bob Tasmin answered. "I've never had a chance to be rude to clients."

Mr. Willoughby beamed at the sunlight on lower Broadway, at the bootblacks by City Hall park, at the news venders by the subways.

"But you will have, Tasmin," Mr. Willoughby said. "I think you're going to develop the technique in time."

"That will carry me through Sunday if you really think so, sir," Bob said, and he laughed again.

"They all want to be loved," Mr. Willoughby said. "Please, please don't think for a moment that I'm being bitter or weary, Tasmin. . . . Now take our dear late Mr. S. on whose letters you were working, and that senile adventure of his, that groping for love and understanding."

"You must have seen a lot of that sort of thing," Bob Tasmin said.

"An amazing amount," said Mr. Willoughby. "That's why I'm so young for my age and so romantic in the spring. Sometimes, of course, I wonder whether infatuation is worth a million or more dollars — but that's only the whim of a moment. Love has bought me my little place at Manhasset — you must come and see it some time, Tasmin — and three saddle horses, and a fair wine cellar, and some good examples of Matisse and Picasso . . . all from misplaced love."

The taxi had already turned into lower Sixth Avenue, and they skirted Washington Square, where the trees were budding and the grass was beginning to look green.

"Their lives all fall into a pattern," Mr. Willoughby said. "These poor charming meal-tickets of ours are bored with their God-damned establishments, and with their servants, and their dull wives or husbands, as the case may be, with their lace tablecloths and their silver pheasants full of bonbons, and with all their friends' silver pheasants. So what can they do?"

"They fall in love," Bob Tasmin said.

"Yes," said Mr. Willoughby, "mad, delightful love — and what love objects do they select? The cigarette girl at the night club. The lifeguard on the beach. The riding instructor with the Continental background. Sometimes I don't know whether I can stand it another moment, but someone has to, Tasmin. Do I discourage you?"

"Yes, sir, you do rather," Bob Tasmin said.

"Well, don't let me," said Mr. Willoughby. "No, no, no. We must stand shoulder to shoulder and help, Tasmin. And think of the balance and beauty of those separation agreements. There's nothing more fascinating than a good negotiation with angry, love-sick people who can pay for it. Well, here we are at your father's club, and mine too, God help me, and please, please don't thank me, Tasmin. I am grateful for all your bright ideas."

The taxi had stopped on the corner. There was a warm smell of asphalt from Fifth Avenue. His father's club across the street looked gray and solemn in the sun, an imitation of an Italian *palazzo,* done by an architect who had also loved unwisely and too well. He was able to appreciate Mr. Willoughby's cynicism without being completely involved in it. It was spring, and for once, except for making notes on a few decisions, he had nothing to do until Monday.

His father had wanted Bob's name entered for the club, but Bob had always hesitated, saying that the Yale Club did well enough. The club seemed to him a very stodgy place where older men gathered to play backgammon or bridge or to doze in the alcoves of the big library upstairs. Yet that day even the club had the atmosphere of rest and anticipation that came at the end of the week.

The doorman told him that his father was in the large room which overlooked Fifth Avenue, the one with the Hudson River landscapes, and when he entered there he glanced about. The older members looked like the portraits in directors' rooms and the younger members lurked in corners, awed by the room's majestic proportions.

188

George Tasmin in a blue suit with pin stripes was seated at one of the windows, looking out at the stream of traffic on the Avenue, and when Bob spoke to him, the bright, rather harsh light from outside struck him full in the face. For a moment Bob thought that his father looked tired and not well but the impression left him as soon as George Tasmin spoke.

"Hello, there, Bob," he said. "You're early. Well, let's order lunch."

He stretched out his hand to a bell on the table and struck it sharply.

"Mr. Willoughby gave me a lift uptown," Bob said.

"Who?" George Tasmin asked. "Nat Willoughby? Quite a sense of humor, Nat. Now put your mind on what we're going to have. Oysters? It's still April, and maybe as long as it's Saturday we might have a cocktail. I have something in my suitcase. They mix it at the bar."

There was a secretive, rebellious atmosphere in the bar. The members there seemed to feel that they were a minority in the club and to hell with it. His father gave a bottle of gin to the bartender and told him to mix it with orange juice.

"They still threaten to close the bar," he said. "If Al Smith had got in we wouldn't have to do this. Well, how've you been, Bob? Working hard?"

"Yes," Bob told him, "pretty hard."

"We miss you," his father said. "How about coming out to the country tomorrow?"

"I can't," Bob Tasmin said. "I have to go to my apartment and catch up on some legal reading, but tell Mother I'll come out next week."

His father nodded slowly, and Bob Tasmin felt a twinge of remorse. He had been so busy that he had not seen much of the family in the last months.

"All right," his father said. "Will's coming back next week. Perhaps we can all get together and have a long talk." He lifted his glass and stared disgustedly at the gin and orange drink. It seemed to Bob that for years his father had spoken of a long talk sometime and that the moment for it had never arrived. The truth was, he was thinking, that he had never greatly amused or interested his father. They could never talk of anything except the stock market and personalities on the floor of the exchange. That and some friends in Gray's Point apparently made up nearly all there was to his father's life. Yet, Bob was thinking that he should feel more gratitude, because George Tasmin had given him an education, and he had seen that his son had done the right things and had met the right people. He had gone to great pains, too, to teach him tennis and trapshooting, bridge and poker, and an appreciation for a few Victorian novels.

"You still get your clothes at Brooks, don't you?" his father asked.

"Yes," Bob said, "I'm pretty used to Brooks."

"The materials might be better if you had them made up in London. That little tailor in Albemarle Street is sending over a representative. You ought to get some measurements and give him an order. I know it's a gamble, and the whole thing plus duty brings a suit to more than Brooks, but it might be worth trying."

"All right, I'll try it," Bob said. "You're looking a little tired."

"Oh, I'm all right," his father answered, "except I haven't been sleeping so well lately. It's quite a responsibility, all our customers' accounts. A lot of things we've learned don't seem to be working right. Of course, I realize it's temporary."

"Security prices were obviously too high," Bob said. "I've often heard you say so."

"Yes, I know," his father answered. "If I had to follow my own convictions, I'd go short on the market."

"Well, I hope you don't monkey with anything like that," Bob Tasmin said.

His father squared his shoulders and smiled.

"Don't talk like a Methodist minister," he answered. "I've been downtown before you were born. I've seen it when I was a kid in 1907, and I've seen it in '21. Well, I guess lunch is ready upstairs. Will you have another before we go?"

"No thanks," Bob Tasmin said.

The dining room was beautifully proportioned, and so large that there was no clatter of dishes, and the voices of the members were muted.

"Well, I hope you're keeping up with your friends," his father said. "It doesn't pay to get out of touch. The Norths said you were there at dinner last week."

"Yes," Bob Tasmin answered, "but I don't get much chance to go anywhere."

"They're getting very sloppy in the kitchen here," his father said. "This chop is like shoe leather. I'm going to call the waiter."

"Oh, don't do that."

"You never like to have me make a scene, do you?" George Tasmin asked. "Well, all right, but you ought to keep in touch. If you're not seen in this town, people forget you're alive."

They were maneuvering conversationally like strangers. It was obvious that his father wanted to see him about something, but he appeared reluctant to get to the point. Bob was sure his father had not asked him there simply to tell him that he should be more in touch with people.

"By the way, Bob," his father said, "have you seen the Fultons lately?"

His father had clearly intended the question to be casual, but Bob remembered his mother's having said that his father always put his foot in it when he tried to be devious.

"No," Bob Tasmin said. "Not for quite a while. Why?"

"No reason at all," his father answered. "I was just thinking you used to be around there a lot. Don't they ever ask you to anything?"

"No," Bob Tasmin answered. "They haven't for quite a while. Of course there was Polly's coming-out party."

"That was the year before last," his father said. "You ought not to get out of touch. Someone like Burt Fulton is worth knowing, Bob."

"I wish you wouldn't bother about my being out of touch, Father," Bob said. "Why should I see Mr. Fulton? He's busy. Why should I see Polly? She's just a kid with her own friends. She's busy too. She's away at college."

His father lighted his cigar deliberately.

191

"Funny people the Fultons. They never quite fitted in, did they?"

"I don't know," Bob said. "Poll had a fine time when she came out. She's a very popular girl."

"I thought you liked popular girls," his father said. "You used to."

"Now listen," Bob Tasmin told him. "Poll's six years younger than I am. She's just a kid."

The waiter brought an ash tray and poured the coffee. George Tasmin unwrapped the paper from a lump of sugar.

"Don't you think that sounds juvenile?" he asked. "You're old enough so that six years don't make much difference. Your mother's four years younger than I am."

"All right," Bob Tasmin said. "I guess I'm out of touch."

His father looked out of the window, and then Bob saw his glance move slowly about the dining room. He smiled and nodded to someone at a table in the distance.

"That's old Clint Butterworth," he said. "I thought he was at Sea Island. . . . If it hadn't been for your mother, Polly wouldn't ever have got into the Manhattan dances."

"I never heard about it," Bob said.

"Your mother took her to the tea, and she did very well."

"Who," Bob asked, "Mother or Poll?"

His father was not amused.

"There was a time when we made quite an effort about the Fultons. Of course, your mother always said that Mrs. Fulton was a twittery, small-town little thing and I think our ways may have confused her, but I've always rather liked her. She's appealing, like a lady who's lost in the subway with her arms full of bundles, trying to follow the green line."

"Yes, I know what you mean," Bob said.

"Now, Burt Fulton . . ." George Tasmin flicked the ash from his cigar. "I used to try to take him around at Gray's Point. I got him into our poker game, but he never seemed to want to mix with the crowd."

"Maybe you confused him, too," Bob Tasmin said. His father glanced at him quickly. He seemed about to say something and then to change his mind.

"There's a company that Burt Fulton's interested in, the Bulwer Machine Company, up around Pittsburgh. Did you ever hear him mention it?"

"No," Bob said, "Mr. Fulton's in a lot of companies."

His father rested his elbows on the table. He suddenly looked tense.

"Bulmaco they call it. It makes me tired — that silly way of shuffling names together. They're having a directors' meeting Wednesday."

"Bulmaco," Bob repeated. "It didn't take much imagination to think that one up."

The conversation was making him uneasy.

"I'd give a lot to know whether they're going to pass their dividend next week," his father said.

Bob Tasmin sat motionless.

"They don't tell things like that, do they?"

"No," his father said. "That's why it pays to keep in touch with directors."

"Well," Bob said, "why don't you see Mr. Fulton?" He had the impression again that his father looked strained and tired. If Bob did not like the conversation, he was sure that his father enjoyed it less.

"I couldn't naturally," he said. "How do you think it would look if I did a thing like that?"

"Of course you can't," Bob said. "Well — " And he half pushed back his chair, but George Tasmin did not move.

"I don't like this any more than you do, Bob," his father said. "I don't recall that I've ever asked anything of you . . . have I?" He leaned a little nearer. "I'm not asking now. I wouldn't even bring this up unless — "

He stopped, and there was nothing to do but sit and listen.

"Well," George Tasmin said and cleared his throat, "things are a little tight downtown, but there may be something new on Monday."

Bob felt deeply shocked for a moment, but it would have been intrusive to ask explicit questions. He simply sat there listening.

"If you were just to drop in at the Fultons' this afternoon," his father said. "I don't even ask you to bring the matter up — but if you could only get some general impression, some estimate, some hint . . . or do you think I'm asking too much?"

It was very bad. Bob Tasmin wished he did not feel ashamed, and he only hoped he did not show it. There was something indecent about his father having to say such things.

"Why didn't you tell us?" Bob asked.

He did not want to look at his father but he could not keep his eyes from his face. George Tasmin stared at the white tablecloth and knocked another ash from his cigar.

"What do you mean? Why didn't I tell you what?"

It was very hard to give a blunt answer. There was the emotional relationship, the difference of age and point of view.

"Why didn't you tell us," Bob asked, "that you've been having a tough time? I should think it would've been easier for you."

Suddenly he felt deeply compassionate. He could see his father pulling himself together, thinking of appearances.

"Look here, Bob," George Tasmin said, "you're making this ridiculous. You're jumping at conclusions. It was merely an idea that crossed my mind. I'm not good at making things sound right."

"If there's anything I can do," Bob said, "anything but — "

George Tasmin stood up.

"Let's go downstairs," he said. "We might play a game of billiards."

"Billiards?" Bob repeated.

As they walked out of the dining room his father took his arm.

"I'm sorry I brought that up," he said. "I hadn't any right to ask — "

"Now wait," Bob said. "You didn't ask anything."

"That's right, I didn't, did I?" George Tasmin answered. "Well, I'm glad I didn't."

"I can go home with you," Bob said, "if there's anything I can help you with." He thought that his father looked better.

"Before you could help me," he said, "you'd have to help the whole damned United States. Don't worry, Bob. It isn't as bad as that."

Bob Tasmin had never given much thought to money or how

it was made or the injustices it produced until that Saturday afternoon in April, 1930. The catch phrases for these matters were coined later — "forgotten men," "one-third of a nation," "the New Deal." No one had yet spoken of rebuilding the station while the trains were running. He had never even realized that much was the matter with the station.

As he walked uptown around four o'clock, past all those great apartment buildings on Park Avenue, he felt for the first time in his life that nothing was as permanent as he had thought it. He knew that all those apartments were built on mortgages and contractual agreements, for he had examined a great many of the documents at Barstow, Barstow and Bryce, but it had never occurred to him until that afternoon that all this foundation of carefully balanced legal paper work might not be entirely secure. It had never occurred to him until he thought of his father's face at lunch and of the Board Room in his father's office, of the tickers, and the board boys in their shirt sleeves changing the quotations, of the comfortable chairs where the customers sat, and the customers' man chatting with the clients. He thought of his father's own private office with its telephones. His father had worked hard and conscientiously; but it was a superficial, parasitical way of living which made no basic contribution to society, when one thought of it. It was trading on other people's work, and a large part of his world was living in just that way.

Bob was sharply aware that he was partially supported on money that he had not earned, and he did not entirely like it. Even his own simple apartment, a two-room walkup between Third and Lexington Avenues in the sixties, suddenly appeared like an undeserved extravagance. His father had told him that there was no reason why he should live on less than five thousand dollars a year, and he had never thought before that it could become necessary to live on less. His own salary was twenty-five hundred, and certainly it would be possible to get along on it if he rented a single room and gave up his car. It would be possible, but it would be embarrassing. If he were to start economizing now, his father would take it personally. He would know that it had something to do with that luncheon. Neither of them would ever forget that luncheon.

XVI

We've Got to Stick Together

It was a beautiful afternoon with a clear sky and warm sunlight and a soft westerly breeze and the Avenue stretched ahead of him, rising to the low hill at the seventies. He found himself walking faster because he had always loved to walk, and the exercise made his mind run more smoothly. He was just nearing the corner of Sixty-third Street — he remembered he had passed the brick church with the white columns — when a girl called to him.

"Bob," she called. "Hello, darling."

A very pretty girl had stopped in front of him. She had on a light gray spring coat, and a gray felt hat with a feather on the side. Her dark, reddish-yellow hair came out from under it in little curls. Her hands looked very small in tight gray gloves, and she was carrying the sort of gray purse that already was known as an "accessory." It was Polly Fulton all grown up, with beautiful legs, calling him "darling" as girls did then, but with the same eyes and the trace of freckles on her nose and the voice he remembered at Gray's Point.

"Why, hello, Poll," he said. "How's everything?"

"It's funny," she said. "I was just thinking about you and there you were."

"Well," he said, "you've got a great mind, Poll."

"I was just thinking I never see you any more," she said. "Where are you going? What are you doing now?"

As he stood there with her on Park Avenue, he remembered his father's voice asking him just to drop in on the Fultons.

"As a matter of fact," he said, "I live near here between Lexington and Third."

"I don't see why you never told us," she said. "Why haven't you ever come to see us?"

If you got out of the habit of seeing people in New York, you simply did not see them, and it did not mean that you did not like them.

"You know how it is," he said.

"You haven't got anything to do now, have you?" she asked. "You don't act that way."

He often thought of them standing there in the April sunlight in an undefined region between two eras. Everything about her looked fresh and new like the spring. She might so easily have been busy and have said it was swell to see him, and that he must come around just as soon as he could, and now, good-by.

"Why, no, nothing in particular, Poll," he said.

"Then I'll tell you what we'll do," she told him. "We'll go up and see this place where you live, and then you can take me home. I'm going to one of those damned parties tonight, but there's lots of time."

There was a colored maid who picked up his apartment each day, but even so he could not be sure how it would look.

"This is very sudden, Poll," he said.

"Just get used to it," she answered. "I won't compromise you, darling."

"Well, come on, Poll," he said. "I'm sure it will be a great experience for you, and I can stand it if you can."

"You mean you'll face the consequences like a gentleman?" Polly asked.

"Yes," Bob Tasmin said. "We'll face them fearlessly. If necessary I can always marry you to clear your name."

"Oh," Polly said, "please hurry. I can't wait."

It did not sound as Polly had once, but then girls grew up faster than they used to.

"You're getting to be a big girl, now," he said.

"Yes, I am," Polly said. "I'm getting too big for my pants, I guess."

"Oh, now, Poll," Bob Tasmin said. "That's a major problem."

"It's a coarse expression, isn't it?" Polly said. "Excuse me. Girls get to using the most awful words in college."

He had never been in his apartment for very long at a time. He had treated it like those other rooms he had occupied at New Haven and Cambridge which one avoided as much as possible. Its furnishings were mostly odds and ends which his mother had sent him from Gray's Point, a worn Persian carpet, a mission bookcase, three faded upholstered chairs and an old sofa. Besides there were some things which he had accumulated in the phases through which he had lived, a portable typewriter, a traveling clock that he had won at tennis, a set of Balzac that he had bought on the Left Bank, a Chippendale desk from London, one of his photographs of that society at Yale, where all the members were grouped on the front steps as though they had been squeezed out the door like tooth paste from a tube, and a picture of the second crew by the boat-house.

"I haven't given it much thought," he said, "but it's a gracious room, isn't it?"

"No," Polly said. "It's a nice room. I was afraid it was going to *be* something. It's nice to be somewhere that *isn't* anything. You don't know, but I do."

She pulled off her felt hat and tossed it on a chair. Then she began to take off her coat.

"Wait," Bob Tasmin said, "let me help you." And she smiled at him over her shoulder.

"Oh," she said, "thanks. It slips right off."

Her dress was a light blue and gray silk print that matched the lining of her coat. It had a full pleated skirt that billowed and tossed above her knees as she sat down on the sofa. She opened her bag and pulled out her compact and stared at herself in the little mirror.

"Those damned freckles," she said and she rubbed her nose hard. "You've never had to live in as many period rooms as I have. Come on, give me a cigarette."

Bob Tasmin handed her a silver box.

"What's written on the top of it?" she asked, and then she began to read, " 'Robert Tasmin, Winner of Men's Singles, Mill River Club, August, 1926.' I remember."

That was the summer when he had spent hours watching Tilden, when he had felt that tennis was very important and that all his personal problems would be solved if he could only cultivate a proper backhand stroke.

"Listen," Polly Fulton said. "Let's tell each other about everything."

What she really meant, of course, was that she wanted to talk about herself. As she sat in the corner of the sofa with her feet curled under her, she told him that college was a fine place because you met girls there who didn't know who you were and cared less. It wasn't like New York where so many people in hotels and speakeasies, and even salesgirls in department stores, recognized her. She could never tell whether people liked her or not, that is, for herself. She didn't want to be just a picture in the rotogravures. She wanted to *do* something, and she didn't mean just doing something for the Junior League. Oh God, those girls in the Junior League, with their lectures and their tea parties and their piddling little ideas of social service . . . When she got through college, how would it be if she got an apartment in Greenwich Village where she could meet all sorts of queer, different people?

"It wouldn't do any good," he said, "because you wouldn't belong there, Poll."

"I don't belong anywhere," she said, "but I've got to have some sort of life."

"You mean a life of your own?" he asked.

"Don't be so nasty," she said.

She rolled her gloves into a little ball and threw them on the floor. Then they sat for a while without speaking.

"Poor little rich girl," he said.

"That isn't original," she said. "Don't be so dull. Do you know you're awfully dull?"

"Do you know you're awfully pretty?"

"There you go." She shrugged her shoulders. "Don't bring sex into it."

"I just said that to cheer you up."

"Darling," Polly said, "I never thought you'd be like this."

"I never thought you'd be like this either," Bob said.

"Well," Polly said, "I suppose you know I always used to be attracted to you, don't you?"

"I didn't know," Bob Tasmin said. "I'd never thought of it particularly."

Polly sighed. "Well, you might think of it now."

"All right," he said. "I'm thinking of it. Listen, Poll. Nearly all the girls I know want to get apartments and want to express themselves, but after all who doesn't. I do. Maybe if we had the courage, we could be emancipated, but I haven't got what it takes and I don't believe you have either. Perhaps it isn't courage. Perhaps we'd better get along with what we've got."

Bob Tasmin was trying to say something that had been on his mind all afternoon, but he had not succeeded.

"For example," he said. "All week I've been reading an old man's love letters because his family are trying to break his will. I don't like it. I could chuck the whole thing and go out to the South Sea islands and raise coconuts and spear fish, but I won't do it because I might not like it there either."

"Why, darling," Polly said, and she was smiling. "I never knew you thought of things like that. You've always seemed so contented. Aren't you happy?"

"No," Bob Tasmin said, "not particularly."

"Oh, Bob," Polly said. "I'm awfully glad." And she danced across the room toward him, and perched on the arm of his chair.

"What are you glad about?" he asked.

"I'm so awfully glad you're not happy."

"Well, thanks," Bob Tasmin said.

"Darling?" She touched his head very softly, and he felt it would be better if she should move somewhere else.

"Yes," he said. "I'm right here. What is it, Poll?"

"If you do go to that island, I'll go with you."

It was the old desert island *motif,* and his common sense told him it was dreadful but it was not bad at all at the time. He wished she were not sitting on the arm of his chair. He knew that he could reach and take Polly Fulton in his arms, and it was a struggle not to do it.

"That's fine. We'll get a schooner, Poll," he said. "There must be a lot of good ones going cheap now."

"Please . . ." Polly said, "don't spoil it. . . . I mean it. I'll go if you will."

"Well, that settles it," Bob Tasmin said. "We'll just drop everything and start tonight if you can throw a few clothes together."

Then he heard her sigh and she stood up. The desert island was gone. He had behaved like a stuffed shirt, and it was gone.

"Well," Polly said, and she sighed again. "I guess you'd better take me home."

"Yes," he said. "I suppose so. Poll, do you know what you look like?"

"Something dim, I guess," she said, "everything considered."

"No," he answered. "You look like Botticelli's 'Spring.' "

"Gosh," Polly said. "Is that a pleasant reaction?"

"Yes," he answered. "Pretty pleasant."

"Well," she said, "I'm awfully glad."

The sky ahead of them was red from the sunset as they walked back to Park Avenue, and he told her quite a lot about Barstow, Barstow and Bryce. He told her that he was taking a beating in that place, and that he was tired of being pushed around. Yet, if he left there, he would have to go through the same thing in some other office. Apparently it did her good to realize that he had troubles of his own.

"Bob," she said. "I wish you'd tell me something."

"All right," he answered. "What is it?"

"It's personal, but I wish you'd tell me."

"Well, all right," he said, "if it's only personal."

"Well, it's something I can't ask. . . . Never mind, I like it better the way it is."

He was not entirely sure what she had been about to ask, but he was almost sure, because he had been asking himself the same question.

"I'm just a shy boy. I guess I'm naturally backward, Poll," he said.

"Darling," she said, and she linked her arm through his.

He had been to the Fultons' apartment the year Polly had come out. It was an enormous duplex apartment and he remembered the portraits in the hall — the British officer by Lawrence, in a red coat with his left hand resting on his sword hilt, and a portion of a cannon near his feet, and the lady by Gainsborough, very tightly laced, holding a small Griffon lapdog. Mr. Fulton had bought the pictures, and the Chippendale dining table with a set of twenty-four matched chairs, and the Waterford chandelier and the flat silver, all at one time, out of a house in Ireland — at exactly the right time, too, for the place had been burned down by the Irish six months later. The living room in the apartment was Louis Quinze. He had bought the paneling and everything from a French château.

"And I'll tell you what all the bedrooms upstairs are some other time," Polly said as they came in. "Every one of them came out of something. B. F. keeps switching them. I never know whether I'll be Mary Queen of Scots or Nefertiti the next time I get back from college."

The Fultons' apartment was very large, but then so were a great many others. If Burton Fulton was interested in antique furniture, so were a great many other people. Yet, Bob Tasmin was thinking, if you owned Chippendale and Gainsboroughs and all those other things, they never belonged to you entirely; a part of them always belonged to the people who owned them first. That Irish dining room, the Lawrence, the Gainsborough, and the Louis Quinze living room had never been made for Burton Fulton. They had come to him as the result of a breakdown in some order and they were not meant for transition and haste, but for permanence and serenity.

"Where is everyone, Timmons?" Polly asked, when the butler took Bob's hat.

Timmons said that Mrs. Fulton was having tea, and that Mr. Harry, who was then in the middle of a school vacation, had gone to the cinema.

"I suppose he's looking at Garbo again," Polly said. "He's in love with Garbo. . . . All right, we'll go and have tea with Mother. Mr. Tasmin will have a Scotch and soda. Timmons, is Father back yet?"

Timmons said that Mr. Fulton was not back, but was expected.

Mrs. Fulton was alone in the Louis Quinze room. The tea table was on an Aubusson carpet in front of a marble mantel.

"Look who I caught," Polly said. "Bob Tasmin!"

Mrs. Fulton looked a little like one of Mr. Fulton's pigeons in that dovecote at Gray's Point. Her beige velvet tea gown had a feathery sheen, and her string of amber beads looked well with her gray hair, but she was not a part of the room at all, not a Marquise de Rambouillet.

"Oh, Bob," she said. "What a nice surprise. Burt — Mr. Fulton, that is — will be so pleased. Now sit down and be comfortable. Not in that chair. The other one. I told Timmons that I wouldn't have tea upstairs. We ought to use this big room as long as we have it, but I don't feel it approves of me and I don't like to crochet in it."

Bob Tasmin could see what she meant. The brocade curtains, the old gold lines on the woodwork, the mirrors, the screens with shepherds and shepherdesses, were like wine which did not travel well.

"I always feel as though I ought to be very witty in this room," Mrs. Fulton said, "and you know I'm not. When I first saw it in France — you remember when Father took us to that château, don't you, Polly? — I said to Mr. Fulton, 'Now, Burt, don't do it. I don't like shepherds and fauns, Burt.' I thought we ought to have a homey room that young people would like to sit in, but Mr. Fulton did it. You know how he is."

"Where do you think I've been, Mama?" Polly asked.

"I'm sure I don't know where you've been, dear," Mrs. Fulton said, "but I wish you'd sit down, and pull down your skirt a little."

"I've been to Bob's apartment," Polly said.

"Oh," said Mrs. Fulton. "How nice. Was Mrs. Tasmin there?"

"No, Mother," Polly said. "Just Bob and me."

"Well, if Bob thought it was all right, dear," Mrs. Fulton said, "I suppose it was. I hope you gave her some good advice, Bob."

Bob Tasmin nodded.

"Polly wants to go with me to the South Seas," he said.

Mrs. Fulton sighed.

"Polly wants to do anything but stay at home. Now, when I was a girl, I used to love home, but Polly says no young people want to be there any more. It's New York, isn't it? So many things to do."

Bob Tasmin saw that Polly was watching him uneasily, afraid he might be bored, and he thought it was unkind of her. It was pleasant to sit there listening without trying to make bright conversation. The Louis Quinze room was formidable but Mrs. Fulton was managing to make it like a front parlor in Willett.

"And now I'll tell you where *I've* been," Mrs. Fulton said. "I've been to the Yearly Club."

"Oh gosh," Polly said, "an afternoon with a trained seal . . . helping a lot of ladies in gold chairs digest their lunch."

"Well, I think Bob would be interested if you aren't, dear," Mrs. Fulton said. "It was about the man who wrote Shakespeare's plays for him."

"I know there's been a good deal of debate about it," Bob Tasmin said. "Just because Shakespeare had bad handwriting, everyone keeps picking on him."

"Timmons," Polly said. "Mr. Tasmin will have his whisky now."

"I've always thought it wasn't fair to Shakespeare myself," Mrs. Fulton said. "I've always loved Shakespeare. Once in high school we did a scene from *The Tempest.* I was Titania, and Burt, Mr. Fulton, was in it too. He was Bottom."

"*Midsummer Night's Dream,* Mother," Polly said. . . . "No, give him more than that, Timmons."

"Oh, yes," Mrs. Fulton said, "but they're very much the same thing. Don't you think they are, Bob?"

"Yes," Bob Tasmin answered. "Anything with wizards and fairies always is."

"I never knew B. F. was Bottom," Polly said. "You never told me that."

"He's ashamed of it, dear," Mrs. Fulton said, and she laughed.

"He's ashamed of the queerest things, but to get back to who wrote the plays — did anyone ever show you the cipher in the second folio?" She stopped at the sound of a distant door closing. "That must be Mr. Fulton now" — and she left the tea table and hurried to the door.

"Burt," she called. "Is that you, Burt?"

"Thanks," Polly whispered, "for being so sweet to Mother."

You could always look at someone else's parents tolerantly, but not your own.

"Don't take it so hard, Poll," Bob said. "Everybody's mother goes to lectures."

"I don't mind you," Polly began, "but *whenever* I bring a man here . . ." She stopped. Mr. Fulton entered the drawing room with his arm around Mrs. Fulton's waist.

"Poll," he said, "give us a kiss. . . . Why, hello, Bob."

Mr. Fulton crossed the room quickly and shook his hand, seizing his elbow at the same time. His sandy hair looked rumpled as it always had. His clothes looked as though he had put them on in a great hurry.

"Where have you been keeping yourself?" he asked. "How's the law? How's that concern, that firm of yours?"

"I wouldn't say it was mine, sir," Bob Tasmin said.

"Don't call me 'sir,'" Mr. Fulton answered. "You're Bob and I'm B. F. Now wait, don't tell me, and I'll remember the name of that concern."

"Wouldn't it be easier if he told you?" Polly asked.

"Don't tell me," Mr. Fulton said. "Wait. Don't be so impatient, Poll. I've got it. It's Barstow, Barstow and Weiss."

"Bryce," Bob Tasmin said.

"Yes, I know," Mr. Fulton said. "I just said it to see Poll jump. Poll's always afraid that Glad and I are going to say the wrong thing. Poll's a Bryn Mawr girl. She's always right."

"Father," Polly said. "Who let you out in that tie? Come here and let me fix it."

"No," Mr. Fulton said. "Bob and I are going to leave you girls. I want to have a little talk with Bob."

"Don't take him away," Polly said. "What are you going to do —
ask him his intentions?"

Mr. Fulton took Bob Tasmin by the arm.

"Come on, Bob," he said.

Bob could not imagine as they walked together into the hall what
Mr. Fulton had to say to him that could not be said anywhere.

"I was thinking about you the other day," Mr. Fulton said.
"You've been sort of on my mind."

Mr. Fulton opened the door of a small room down the hall. It
obviously belonged to Mr. Fulton and to no one else. In it were
letter files, a desk with a typewriter, a bare table with two telephones, an architect's elevation of a factory, some brown leather
armchairs, and an ash receptacle.

"I might have taken you into the library," Mr. Fulton said, "or
somewhere upstairs, but I can always think in here. I don't keep
moving furniture around in my head, or wondering where it came
from, or why the owners had to sell it. I've had my mind on that
quite a good deal lately. Well, sit down, and don't mind me. I like
to move around. How's your father, Bob?"

"Father?" he asked. "Why, Father's pretty well."

Mr. Fulton put his hands in his pockets and drew them out again.

"I saw him a few days ago. He dropped in to see me. I hadn't
seen George for quite a while."

He stopped as though he expected Bob to speak, but Bob Tasmin
could only look at Mr. Fulton blankly. He thought at least his father
might have told him.

"You know," Mr. Fulton said, "the way people are. We see each
other, and then we get busy and we don't see each other — like you
and me, Bob. When I saw George, I began to think of you. Well,
that's about all except — " Mr. Fulton put his hands back in his
pockets. "Well, I'm glad everything's all right."

"Oh, yes," Bob said. "Everything's fine. Mother's well, and Will's
looking for some sort of job in a publishing house."

Mr. Fulton nodded. "I don't know much about the publishing
game," he said, "but it's always struck me that they ought to be

206

able to print and bind books in one machine — just put in the paper at one end and have the books come out the other. Well, I always get mixed up with ideas like that. There's a company I work with up near Pittsburgh. Bulwer, Bulwer Machine. George was talking about it. It's on the big board."

He stopped and Bob Tasmin did not speak. Mr. Fulton jingled some money in his pocket and looked at the floor. "I gather your father's been playing around with Bulwer, Bob. Personally, I don't know much about that sort of thing. The boys keep me too busy thinking of ways to keep the plants going."

Mr. Fulton stopped again, and Bob Tasmin finally knew that he had to say something.

"That must take all your time," he said.

Mr. Fulton nodded.

"We're going to have a little meeting at Bulwer on Wednesday. Now, Bob, this isn't strictly ethics, but I've just been thinking if you were to hear somewhere, not from me particularly, but just from somewhere that Bulwer's earnings are holding up, and that they'll declare the dividend, well, I have an idea, Bob, that your father might like to know."

Mr. Fulton stopped again. His eyes moved up from the carpet, and he and Bob glanced at each other. His eyes looked gray and cool, and he was smiling faintly, very faintly. It must have been the way he looked when he did business with strangers.

"We've got to stick together these days, Bob," Mr. Fulton said. "I'm trusting you to do it right. I think your father would like to know."

Bob Tasmin moved uneasily in his chair. There were all sorts of imponderables in that room, queer questions of ethics and loyalty. He had never had business dealings with a man of Mr. Fulton's caliber. It reminded him of the time he had boxed with a professional at Yale, just in a friendly way. Mr. Fulton had the same smoothness, the lack of lost motion. He wished he were not sitting down with Mr. Fulton standing in front of him, but it would be awkward if he stood up.

"You're being very kind," he said. "That's a lot for you to do."

Mr. Fulton looked down at the floor again and clasped his hands behind him.

"Well, Bob," he said. "It doesn't cost me anything."

"No," he said, "but it's a lot for you to do."

All at once his mouth felt dry and his voice was hoarse.

"I don't want to tell him that, Mr. Fulton," he said. "I can't."

He wished he might have had the poise of Mr. Willoughby. Mr. Fulton did not look surprised, but his voice had changed.

"Why can't you, Bob?" he asked.

He would have to tell Mr. Fulton . . . there was no way out. It was better to tell it quickly, and bluntly.

"Well, you see," he began, "this noon . . ." He wanted to make it very clear that his father had not actually asked him, that he had seen how it would have looked. ". . . and then I just happened to meet Poll," he heard himself saying. "I didn't know he had been to see you. The main thing is, I don't want you to think I came here on purpose. I don't want him to think so either. He wouldn't like it, afterwards."

"Why, that's all right, Bob," Mr. Fulton said. "That's all right."

"You *did* think so, didn't you?" Bob Tasmin asked.

"Well," Mr. Fulton said, "I've got a mean sort of mind, Bob. I won't say it did occur to me, and I won't say it didn't. You don't know who your friends are always."

"Well," Bob Tasmin said, "as long as you don't think so now."

"All right," Mr. Fulton said, and he rattled the change in his pocket. "I'll take care of this myself, Bob. I was thinking a little of going out to Gray's Point tomorrow. I guess I'll go and look up George."

It was a play in human relationship that one could go over endlessly in one's thoughts, considering how it all might have been said differently. The memory was acutely embarrassing to Bob as at times the episode had made him feel disloyal to his family, and at other times it had a sort of honor-of-the-school aspect with a priggish aftertaste. Yet that old desire of his to make it emphatic that he did not want anything from the Fultons, and that he was not to be used in that way, usually made him end by believing he had done the best he could.

Mr. Fulton had handled the situation without appearing to handle it at all.

"I guess you'd better stay here and have dinner, Bob," he said.

"Oh, no," Bob Tasmin answered, "but thanks just as much."

"I wouldn't leave now," Mr. Fulton said. "We won't be friends if you do that."

That was all he had to say. There was nothing harder to deal with than obligation or gratitude, and Mr. Fulton must have been forced into that position often. At any rate, he had arranged it somehow so that Bob Tasmin never did feel particularly grateful. He only felt that Mr. Fulton liked him.

Once Polly asked Bob Tasmin about it, at a time when he never minded telling her anything.

"I always wondered what he wanted to talk to you about," Polly said. "Darling, that must have been terrible for you. You do have a lot of guts. I don't know why I keep forgetting it."

Then she shook her head and laughed.

"I don't see what's so funny," Bob Tasmin said.

"I wasn't laughing at you exactly," she told him. "I was just thinking of you in there with B. F. I was just thinking it was all so exactly like you — reliable, like a clock."

He was never sure whether she approved or whether it annoyed her.

"B. F. is so damned surprising," she said. "Look at the way he manages people. I wish he'd realize how good he is — as a person, I mean — but he never has the time."

Sooner or later her mind always got back to her father. She said she knew it was an obsession with her. She did not want to be dominated by B. F., but she could see it coming on.

"I don't want him to, but someone's got to," Polly said. "You've got to dominate me before he does, darling. Damn it, please go ahead and dominate."

XVII

It Was Bound to Happen Sometime

Bob Tasmin did not know when it was that he fell in love with Polly Fulton. You could never set a date on such a thing. It might have been sometime while she still had braces on her teeth and was going to Heatherbloom Hall or it might have been the night when she had been sitting at that table with all those other adolescents. He had left Babs Weatherby flat to dance with her, and Babs was quite a number, too, in or out of a rumble seat. Yet his common sense told him that none of this was true. They had started quietly liking to be with each other, and seeing more of each other, sometime in 1930. It must have been that take-it-or-leave-it phase that his mother's generation called being "interested in each other," not that there was much opportunity to be interested. Polly was usually away at college, and he was often working late. Besides, there were a lot of men around, all sorts of them, who were always taking Polly out. The hell of it, she used to say, was that she couldn't tell whether they liked her or the idea of living on B. F.

When the Fultons moved out to Gray's Point that next spring, he saw more of Polly than he had for a long while, and that autumn, in the beginning of her last year at Bryn Mawr, they began writing each other, so that he always knew when she was in town. Polly began to talk to him frankly about her "young men" as Mrs. Fulton called them, the way Harry Fulton did about the stars in the motion picture magazines, and Bob was able to take a lofty academic interest in them though he was certainly not anxious to be identified with any of that crowd. They were just the sort who would hang around people like the Fultons.

The girls who went to dances were selected with meticulous care, but the main requirements for the men they met seemed to be dancing ability and passable evening clothes. Those friends of Polly's all came from the stag line or were friends of friends in college, and most of them represented what Bob Tasmin considered borderline types — not solid, self-respecting boys, because most of these did not want to make themselves conspicuous by running after a wealthy girl. However, some very rich, neurotic boys gave Polly quite a rush.

There was Ira Drackling, for instance, whose father owned the Drackling Drug chain and a racing stable. Ira used to take Polly around to speak-easies, and for a while Polly felt he was romantic, but Ira was always being followed about by friends who, Polly said, were lousy, and when he had too much to drink, he was always getting into fights. Polly would not have minded so much, she said, if Ira were any good at fighting, but someone was always knocking out his teeth, or knocking him cold, and there you were.

Then there was a friend of a friend of Apples Sandler named Simeon Something, and Bob Tasmin was told that Simeon was going to be a playwright. He was one of those boys who referred to the Lunts as "Alfred" and "Lynn," and to Gertrude Lawrence as "Gertie." He had always just been or was just going to some party with Alfred and Lynn, and he was always just about to read something or other to Gertie. It was quite clear to Polly that Simeon did not really know anyone, but she said it was sweet of him to want to know people like that. There was also an English boy who had been in some sort of scrape at Oxford, and so had come to America because he loved America. His family gave him a little something on which to live while he was looking for a good post in some bank or manufacturing business. Polly said he had his limitations, but she had learned a lot about life from Cyril; he had beautiful manners and he was someone you could take out anywhere.

There was only one boy that winter whom she could really go for, she told Bob Tasmin, and he was a divinity student named Waldo Goldsborough, and you needn't think it was such a funny name either. Waldo had played football at Colgate, and she didn't care whether Bob Tasmin called him a muscular Christian or not, because that was exactly what he was. He coached basketball teams at an East

Side Boys' Club, and he gave Polly a Book of Common Prayer, and to Mr. Fulton, Bruce Barton's life of Christ, *The Man Nobody Knows.* Mr. Fulton once said that he was sorry when Polly got tired of Waldo Goldsborough because he was the only one in all that crowd who didn't think life was a trick out of which you could get something for nothing.

"I can't get it through my head," he said, "all these friends of Poll's aren't like anything I've ever seen. I guess Poll likes unemployables. She's that age."

Polly said this was not true at all. She said there must be something about her that attracted them, but at any rate, they weren't dull. All the dull, serious boys always said the same things, and they were afraid of anyone who had a mind. At least she didn't go to sleep talking to her friends. All she wanted was to know interesting people, but how could anyone be interesting unless he had *lived?* She wanted to meet polar explorers, lone eagles, or anthropologists.

"All right," she said to Bob, "you make fun of Simeon, but at least he's been around where those people are, and that's more than you have."

"Well, suppose he has," Bob said.

"Well, do you know Alexander Woollcott?" she asked.

"No," he said. "Good heavens, no. Why should I?"

"I don't know why you shouldn't," Polly said. "Do you know F. Scott Fitzgerald?"

He had never met F. Scott Fitzgerald, and he had never met Hemingway or Franklin P. Adams, and he did not know Walter Lippmann either, and he knew no one on the stage.

"I just don't see those people, Poll," he said.

"Well, who do you know?" she asked. "You must know someone."

When he stopped to think of it he had a good many friends, but not one of them was in this category. Some were married, working downtown and involved with apartments and diaper services; others who were still unmarried were worried about keeping their jobs. Tasmin had to admit that most of them did not have much lightness of touch or originality. He also knew some former college athletes, some good golfers and some excellent tennis players, but they could only discuss their specialties. Frankly, his particular crowd in Yale and New York had been a pretty wild crowd once, along the pattern of what was already being called the Jazz Age, but now they had settled down, and those who had not settled had gone somewhere else.

"I don't see how you can go around with no one but lawyers and stockbrokers," Polly said. "Don't you know anyone else?"

That must have been the point at which he thought of Milton Ouerbach. He had first known Milton at Yale in a friendly, casual way, for he had been taught that it was a good thing to have a speaking acquaintance with everyone in the class. He and Milton had once heeled for the *News* together and had both been dropped, and then they had met again in that course in English Composition. Since then he had seen Milton occasionally at the Yale Club, but Bob had always been just about to play squash, and Milton never played anything.

"Well, I know a newspaper man," he said.

"Why didn't you ever tell me?" Polly asked. "I've always wanted to meet newspaper men. Is he like something in *The Front Page?*"

"He's peculiar enough," he told her. "He used to write free verse in college, and he never takes any exercise. He's on the *Herald Tribune* and he lives in Washington Square."

"If I gave a party, would you ask him here?"

"I can't just pick someone up cold and ask him somewhere," he told her, "and I don't know whether you'd like him, Poll."

She said, of course, she would like him. He must have been partly in love with her by then, or he never would have considered seriously brushing up his acquaintance with Milton. He must have wanted her to see that he was not in a rut, and perhaps he was secretly afraid that he might be in one. At any rate he called Milton at the *Tribune* and a few days after that he and Milton had dinner at Sardi's, and Milton introduced him to a book reviewer and a police reporter and an actor who was a friend of Dudley Digges. Then he went one night with Milton to an Italian place in the Village, and afterwards to a party at someone's apartment where he met a great many people who were against capital and the profit motive and who knew all the fine points of difference between Stalinists and Trotskyites. When he awoke the next morning, Bob realized that he had been to one of those parties of long-haired men and short-haired women, except that all the men had haircuts. He had sat there arguing and drinking red wine from a gallon jug, and it had not been such bad fun either, because they all had passionate convictions and no great power of reasoning, and he had tied all of them into knots. Yet they must have liked him in spite of the names they called him, because the next week Milton asked him to a party at his apartment and asked him to bring a girl. This was an opportunity for Polly, he thought.

"If you want to see different people," he said, "you might come with me to Milton Ouerbach's tomorrow night. They all sit on the floor and they never stop talking, and they have a lot of unusual ideas."

It was the first time that he had ever taken Polly Fulton to anyone's house, and it was a very queer way to start. Yet, if it had not been for Polly, Bob might never have been so useful in the office when all the New Deal legislation started. He might never have become interested in other points of view. He might never have been able to cope with all the Frankfurter crowd, and he would never have been taken down to Washington with Mr. Bryce to help him examine precedents.

Bob Tasmin went back to Washington Square one Sunday in the autumn of 1941 when he was sure that the country was going to get into the war, and when he had just returned from talking with a general in Washington who was a friend of Mr. Willoughby's. He had a great deal on his mind that Sunday. Mildred had said they hadn't been to church for a long while, and she thought they ought to go if he was going to drop everything and join the Army, but he had told her that the two things did not necessarily go together, and that he had promised to take Neddie to look at the animals in the Park. Then Mildred had said she would go to church alone, and she put on Neddie's best coat and gloves, and told Bob to be sure to bring him back by half-past twelve. Things were serious by that Sunday, and he remembered that he wanted very much to be alone for a few hours with his little boy, and the visit to the Park seemed unreasonably important.

The victorias were lined up opposite the Plaza, and the men with the balloons and pinwheels were out by the Fifty-ninth Street entrance. The wooden animal houses that Tasmin remembered as a child were gone. Now they were brick and there was a pond for sea lions.

"Neddie," he said, "when I was a little boy, my father used to take me here to see the animals."

But, of course, Neddie was not interested. It was exasperating that children never cared about your childhood. All that Neddie wanted was the balloon on a string which a balloon man was inflating near the sea lion pool. Bob tied the string to one of Neddie's buttons so he would not lose the balloon, and then he lifted Neddie up to see the sea lions.

"They didn't have these," he said, "when I was a little boy." But Neddie was not even interested in the sea lions. He was pointing to an exhibit under glass of some marbles, buttons, and bottle caps.

"What are those there for?" Neddie asked.

"Because they came out of a sea lion's stomach," Bob Tasmin told him. "They made him sick."

"Why did he eat them if they made him sick?"

"Because he didn't know any better."

"How did they get them out of his stomach?" Neddie asked. "Did he throw them up?"

Then they walked to the pond where children sailed the toy boats but Neddie did not want to watch the boats. He wanted to ride on the top of a Fifth Avenue bus; so they rode to Washington Square. The streets of lower Fifth Avenue were deserted as they always were on Sunday, but the Square itself was crowded and noisy. He thought as they waited for another bus to take them back uptown that Mildred would not have liked to have Neddie playing in that dirty place.

"It's time to go home now," he said, but Neddie did not want to go home. Getting Neddie back to the bus was a little like trying to coax a drunken friend. Then all at once, while his son was trotting across the Square, he saw the building to the south where Milton Ouerbach had once lived. He remembered how one used to look from the front windows at night straight up the lighted ribbon of Fifth Avenue, and for a few minutes the Square and all his surroundings formed a sort of borderland between that era and the present. It did not seem so long ago, but here he was again, this time playing nurse to a five-year-old child, his child. It did not seem so long ago that he had walked with Polly Fulton through the dark just where he was walking now.

"Neddie," he said, "Neddie, don't make me speak to you again. You can play with your balloon when we get home."

He had said almost the same thing to Polly Fulton in a different way. He had told her that it was two in the morning. He had told her that they could come back again.

When the taxicab stopped that night at Washington Square South, he began to doubt the wisdom of bringing Polly Fulton to such a place, and he wondered why he had not told her that she was dressed as though the whole thing were an uptown dinner party. She was wearing an evening gown of pastel blue chiffon, and its deceptive simplicity showed that it was very expensive. A darker blue satin cloak hung from her shoulders, and as she stood bareheaded on the sidewalk, with the street lights shining on her, she looked much too chic. Tasmin was wearing a dinner coat himself, and he was sure that this also was too much. They were like the uptown tourists who come to Greenwich Village after the theater, condescending and supercilious.

The vestibule of the apartment house had a dim, musty odor. It was hard to see the names on the letterboxes.

"Isn't it exciting?" Polly said.

Polly actually had a sense of anticipation about the little bells and electric latches. She was tired of doormen and elevators.

"If you don't like it," Tasmin told her as they began to climb the stairs, "just let me know. We don't have to stay."

"Why, I'm going to like it," Polly said. They could already hear the chatter of voices from the open door of Milton Ouerbach's apartment on the third floor. "It's wonderful."

The narrow hall was filled with hats and coats draped over two chairs and lying on the floor. Even the hall was thick with tobacco smoke, and the congestion made Bob Tasmin wonder why people wanted to gather in such a small space. Milton Ouerbach was wearing a velvet smoking jacket; he met them at the top of the stairway.

"You mustn't mind if it's a little on the *rive gauche* side here tonight," Milton said, "just candles, smoke, and talk." He lowered his voice. "W. J. White is here tonight. He just dropped in."

"Oh," said Bob Tasmin, "did he?"

"W. J., not E. G. White," Milton said. "Be sure not to get them mixed up. It makes him very angry to be confused with E. G. White."

"All right," Bob Tasmin answered. "I won't confuse them, Milton."

"He just dropped in with two models," Milton said, "out of the blue."

"Who is he?" Polly asked. "I know I ought to know."

"What?" Milton said. "You don't know W. J. White? W. J. White — the photographer. He just dropped in, and Wilfred Harrison's here too. He just dropped in from the theater. Don't you know Wilfred?"

Bob Tasmin did not know Wilfred, but he did not want to be impolite.

"The dramatic critic, Bob," Milton said gently. "Now you know, don't you? And Jack Fulheim's here too. You know — the painter." Everyone seemed to be The Something — standing in individual splendor.

"And then there's Emily Mickleworth."

"What's she?" Bob Tasmin asked.

"You don't mean to tell me seriously," Milton said, "that you don't know Emily. She's the one who gives parties. Emily knows everybody."

"Well, it's awfully nice of you to have us, Milton," Bob Tasmin said.

"Not at all," Milton answered. "I just wanted to get you oriented. It's easier when you know who people are."

The divan was covered with people. People stood in corners, and sat on the floor. They were all talking loudly, but there was a sharp, astonished pause as Bob and Polly entered.

"Winston," Milton Ouerbach was saying, "I want you particularly to meet Miss Fulton . . . Burton Fulton's daughter, you know. She just dropped in . . . and this is my old college friend, Robert Tasmin — the lawyer."

For a second Bob Tasmin did not know who Winston was, but then he assumed he must be W. J. White — the photographer. Mr. White was a dumpy, pale man with dandruff on the shoulders of his blue coat.

"My God," he said, "don't sue me."

"And this is Mr. Harrison," Milton went on.

"Oh," Mr. Harrison said. "Oh, dear God, who is that lovely creature? Stand there for just a moment, sweetheart. Don't move. Just let me look at you. Who are you, sweetheart?"

"She's Miss Fulton," Milton said. "You know, Burton Fulton's daughter — the industrialist."

Of course, they were all very much younger then, particularly Milton, and later Milton used to speak of it as his "salad days" or his "Greenwich Village phase."

"I wince when I think of that evening," he told Bob Tasmin a long time afterwards. "I don't know why I used to be impressed by so many second-rate people. Now take Harrison. Who is Harrison? Dear me, I was callow. Don't say I wasn't."

Bob Tasmin was very anxious not to look conspicuous but when he had taken two tumblers of some sort of sticky Marsala wine, he stopped caring. Polly was sitting on the floor beside Mr. Harrison, and they were talking about Proust. Then he found himself on the floor, leaning his back against the wall, conversing with a strange brunette who might have been one of the models.

"What the hell are you doing here, sweetheart?" she asked. "Hasn't the depression hit you?"

It was not so hard to go on from there after he had finished a third tumbler of wine. He found himself asking her where she had been all his life. He found himself telling her that she was just what he had been waiting for. Then about fifteen minutes later he began to know everyone very well. Milton had started playing records, and sometimes Bob was dancing and sometimes he was talking and quite a while afterwards he found himself dancing with Polly.

"Aren't they nice?" Polly asked. "Aren't they darling people?"

After a while they all left Milton's apartment and walked around the block to somebody else's place. Then they went somewhere else to get coffee, and then it was time to go home. They had all reached a first-name basis and they were all promising that they would see each other soon. As he walked with Polly across the Square looking for a taxi he began to wonder again whether he should have taken her, but Polly Fulton did not wonder.

"They were having such a good time," she said. "I did all right, didn't I?"

"Why, yes," he said, "of course, you did."

"And you weren't nervous about me?"

"No," he said, "of course I wasn't." And he waved to a taxicab.

"I'm awfully happy," Polly said.

Polly Fulton's intense desire to succeed in that environment was both amusing and pathetic, but he could sympathize with it because he had enjoyed parts of the evening himself. There had been a welcome freedom from restraint, a comfortable feeling that it had not mattered what he did. Actually they had all been posing so intensely as carefree, enlightened people that they had finally begun to believe they were, and Bob Tasmin began to feel that way about himself. He had never said so many unconsidered things as he had that evening, and yet some of them had sounded rather well. The whole thing had been off-the-record, as though he and Polly had run away together, and it was the first time that he had ever thought seriously of making Polly Fulton happy.

"Bob," she said, "thanks. Thanks so much."

"Thanks for what?" he asked.

"Oh," she said, "for everything. For every single thing you've ever done for me."

"Why, I've never done much, Poll," he said.

"Oh, yes, you have. You weren't bored, were you?"

"Bored?" he answered. "Why no. I hope I didn't act that way."

"Oh, no," she said. "You're too polite. That was why I asked, and you aren't bored with me, are you?"

"What makes you worry about things like that?" he asked.

"Oh, I was just thinking about everything," she said. "I always seem to have you on my mind."

"Well, you're on my mind sometimes too," he answered.

"You mean I bother you?"

"No, I don't mean that at all," he said. "Why should you?"

"Well, as long as I don't bother you, that's swell," she said, "because . . ."

They were sitting in the dark taxicab hurrying up Fifth Avenue. There were very few lights left in the buildings, but he could see her face as they passed the street lights.

"Because what?" he asked her.

"Well, never mind," she said, "but maybe I would like to have you bothered. You see, I think it would be awfully nice . . ." She stopped and stared straight ahead of her. "I don't know why I always think of the darnedest things to say to you, and then I never say them."

"Well, go ahead," he said. "Don't mind me, Poll."

"You'd be shocked," Polly Fulton said. "It would spoil your picture of me, and it would sound like something in eugenics."

"Now, Poll," he told her. "No one can get shocked by eugenics."

"All right," she said, "but you'll be shocked just the same because it isn't the right thing for me to say. You'll think it's an indecent proposal."

"Why, Poll," he said. "I love indecent proposals."

"No, you don't," she said, "and I don't believe anyone ever made one to you."

"Go ahead," Bob Tasmin said. "Don't keep me waiting, Poll."

"All right, I think it would be a good idea if we tried to fall in love."

Bob Tasmin laughed.

"This is very sudden, Poll," he said, and he wished that he did not sound so old and formal.

"Oh, dear, I knew you'd say something like that," Polly said. "Well, go ahead and pull yourself together."

"All right," Bob Tasmin said. "I'm gathering my wits. If you want my immediate offhand reaction, I don't think it's such a bad idea."

"Well, go ahead and think," Polly said. "Give yourself time. What is your considered opinion?"

"This is quite a funny scene."

"Yes," she said, "it is. I knew you'd make it that way."

"Well, when do we start?" Bob Tasmin asked her.

"What would be a convenient time for you?" Polly asked. "Could we make it at half-past five in the afternoon, or will you be busy at the office? Or perhaps we could start next week so we could get a perspective on it. How about next week?"

"I don't know," Bob Tasmin said. "I'm going to be pretty busy next week."

For a second or so he had a feeling that he was taking advantage of Polly Fulton, but then he kissed her.

"You'd better do it again," Polly said, "or else you may forget you ever did it."

"You don't need to ask me," he told her. "I've always been in love with you, Poll."

"You have not," she said, "but maybe you'll get to be. I hope you will."

When he sat there with his arm around her and her head resting on his shoulder, he did not know that there would be nothing for him but Polly Fulton for days and months and years.

"Call me up in the morning," she said, "won't you?"

"Yes," he said, "and Poll — come on downtown for lunch."

"All right," she said. "Darling, I hope you don't mind this. I don't think it's all such a bad idea."

"I can stand it if you can, Poll."

"It's all so reasonable, isn't it?" she said.

When he saw Polly the next day, she made no allusion for a while to that passage in the taxicab. He thought perhaps she wanted to forget it, but it turned out that she thought he was the one who wanted to forget.

"But let's not get the impression that we're committed to anything," Polly said. She said it as they sat in a booth at a smoky steak-and-chop house on Cedar Street. "It would only make everything shopworn."

Bob Tasmin was not exactly relieved, but he was a little more comfortable in his mind.

"I wouldn't say that we'd gone too far, Poll," he said.

"I wouldn't either," Polly answered. "You can't very well in a taxicab."

She was smiling, but her smile was more in her greenish eyes than on her lips.

"I heard a girl say once," Bob Tasmin told her, "that nothing matters that happens in a rumble seat."

"Darling, give me a cigarette," Polly said, and she put her hand over his as he leaned across the table to light it for her. "I don't mind about how far in that sense. I wouldn't mind a companionate marriage if we could get away with it, but I would mind getting involved too soon."

The corners of her eyes wrinkled and he knew that she was laughing at him.

"Wouldn't you call that being involved?" he asked.

"Don't argue," Polly said. "Don't balance all the pros and cons. It was just an idea. Of course, you wouldn't fit into anything like that."

He felt a slight spasm of annoyance.

"You wouldn't either, Poll," he said.

"Oh, darling," Polly said, and then she was really laughing. "Of course, I wouldn't. I was only treating you like another Bryn Mawr girl. They talk about sex in college."

That husky, musical ring in Polly's voice always made what she said sound confiding and important. He was reminded of a play by Philip Barry called *Holiday,* which was a perfect picture of that time,

222

although its situation and the way the characters spoke and behaved seemed improbable a few years later. Polly was like the restless heroine who wanted to break away from industry and security. The bizarre and whimsical couple from the Riviera, who had become her friends, and who shocked all the stodgy people, might have been the sort of companions that Polly wanted then, and perhaps she had always wanted him to be like that young lawyer in the play who threw the girl's family into confusion because he wanted to take a year's holiday for no good reason.

"Darling," she asked, "what are you thinking about?"

"About that play," he said, "*Holiday.*"

"Did you think of that, too?" she asked. "Just the other day it reminded me of you and me. Of course, I haven't got a poisonous sister, but maybe Harry's going to make up for it. B. F. isn't exactly like that old millionaire papa, either, but there's a lot in that play."

"They certainly all got in a lather," Bob Tasmin said, "but they always do in the theater."

The smoke from her cigarette curled upward toward her eyes, and she blinked.

"Darling," she said. "I do wish we could get away from all the Gainsboroughs and crowned leopards, from all this gilt-edged stuffy security. You'll take me away sometime, won't you?"

She was so pretty when she said it. She must have been counting on him, and at the time it was not an impossibility.

"Any time at all," he said, "when we find out where to go."

"It isn't where," she said. "What I really mean is that we mustn't let this get sticky. It's too serious, and it can all be wonderful."

It was wonderful, even in that businessman's chophouse, where you had to be careful not to overeat at noon.

"We've got to learn so much about each other first," she said. "You've got to know B. F. and Mother, and everything else, and you can't do it if it all gets sticky."

He left her by the steps of the Subtreasury, a good solid place to leave a girl, she said, and George Washington would look out for her. When he crossed the street, he looked back, and saw her standing on the sidewalk against a background of hurrying people. He saw her take off her glove and wave a kiss.

He always kept that memory of the lonely figure of Polly Fulton, standing for an instant apart from everyone. He was beginning to think, as one always did on such occasions, that her problems were simple, that he knew the causes for her discomfort, and that he could surely give her what she wanted. What she needed, he was thinking, was security and continuity, devotion and understanding. As so many girls did, she wanted a home and a life of her own. Girls, when they got married, always settled down.

He could not ask her to marry him then because he was not earning enough to support her, but he was beginning to think from certain reactions in the office that he had a good chance of being taken in as a junior partner, perhaps not that January, but a year from January when such events occurred in law firms. It was something he could almost count on in spite of the depression. She wanted to get away, and he could take her away to a little house with a little land around it, where they could have a garden, not too far from the Country Club. He would see that she learned golf well enough to go around the course with him. He imagined Polly Fulton's meeting him at the station in the afternoon, and sitting with him in the evening by an open fire in a little house that was perfectly equipped but not elaborate, because she hated ostentation, and so did he. You could never tell what friends you would make when you got married, but Polly could pick them out. They would go for walks on a Sunday with the dogs. They would have to have two dogs, one for her and one for him, but they would be gentle dogs that would not bite babies. What she wanted was peace, and something that they could build on, which would grow better year by year. She was tired, as he was, of not having any object in life, of not working or living for someone else. That was what she needed.

In the marble hallway, near the cigar and newspaper stand and the elevator which would take him upstairs to the office, he ran into Mr. Willoughby.

"I hesitated to interrupt you until now," Mr. Willoughby said.

"You appeared to be lost in thought, and, God knows, I never break into thought."

"I was just out to lunch, sir," Tasmin said, and he realized it was late for him to be coming back. "I usually just eat at some cafeteria."

"Oh, dear, it must be nice to have a cast-iron stomach," Mr. Willoughby said. "I ruined mine long ago. I've been having tripe at the Lawyers' Club. A cow's stomach is full of pepsin. Tasmin, who is that beautiful girl?"

"Which one?" Bob Tasmin asked. He thought Mr. Willoughby must be referring to one of the girls in the building.

"The beautiful one with the Titian hair, the one who made that gesture toward you by the Subtreasury."

Though the question annoyed Bob Tasmin, he could not take exception to it considering who Mr. Willoughby was.

"Oh, that was Miss Fulton," he said.

"Fulton?" Mr. Willoughby repeated. "Any relative of Burton Fulton?"

"Yes," Bob answered, "his daughter." It was pleasant to be able to explain Polly, and he realized that the information did not hurt him.

"Well, I wish all girls were as easy to look at," said Mr. Willoughby. "By the way, Tasmin, there's going to be a partners' dinner, rather dull, just a few of us getting together, a week from next Thursday. Perhaps you'd care to come, if you have nothing better on."

It was evident that Mr. Willoughby and the rest wanted to look him over. It was like joining another club. They always wanted to look you over.

"Let's see," Bob Tasmin said, "a week from Thursday. That's very kind of you, sir."

It was always an open question whether Mr. Willoughby would have asked him if he had not noticed that Polly Fulton had come all the way downtown to meet him and had blown a kiss to him across Wall Street.

XVIII

God Bless You, Joe

THE SNOW of the previous evening had turned into rain when
Polly Brett awoke that next Sunday morning in Washington. When
she closed the bedroom window, she could see the back yard of
the hotel piled high with cases of empty soda bottles soaking
drearily in the downpour. They represented now a dismal escapist
effort, a modern version of "Tenting Tonight on the Old Camp
Ground, Waiting for the War to Cease," and they meant that hundreds of reasonably intelligent people must have hoped last night
that you could turn the clock back, or stop history, by calling for
Room Service. It was not consoling to recall that she had done the
same thing herself.

Tom's clothes had been aimed at a bedroom chair, but most of
them had missed. He always threw things, never hung up his coat
or trousers, and that was why his clothes looked as they did. His
suitcase was open on the floor, showing that he must have been
burrowing for something through a maze of dirty shirts just before
he went to sleep. She saw with relief that his evening clothes were
in the suitcase, and at any rate she could get those pressed, but there
was no use trying to have his other suit sent out, because he would
be sure to wake up and want it just after she had given it to the
valet.

The heaviness of Tom's slumber showed that he had taken one of
those barbiturates again, the ones that, according to a popular magazine, formed a habit and destroyed the nerve ends and the kidneys.
She had told Tom again and again not to take them, and he had told
her that he had been familiar with his kidneys ever since he was
three, and he would take a chance on them rather than tossing

around all night. Something else was bound to kill him, he had told her, either a Roosevelt-hater or a taxicab, before he got Bright's disease — and besides he had to relax sometime. He couldn't face anything without sleep, and there was always some damn new thing in that town cropping up in the morning, including Sunday.

Room Service was slow, but Polly was able to get the *Washington Post* and the *Times-Herald* while she waited for her breakfast. The news was about bombings both to the East and West, and already they were arguing about what to do with Germany, as though the whole war had been settled. The room was warm and stuffy, and still seemed to re-echo everything that had been said the night before. She had just drunk her orange juice from a glass perched on one of those ridiculous ice bowls, decorated by a strange rubberlike leaf, and she had poured her coffee and was examining her dry toast when she heard the thump of Tom's feet on the floor of the bedroom. Even when he was full of sedatives Tom awoke as though he had received an electric shock, and he always bounced galvanically on the floor.

"Poll," he called, "are you out there? What time is it?"

"What's the matter with your watch?" she asked.

"The goddam thing stopped again," he called. "It isn't four o'clock, is it?"

It was that self-winding watch of his that kept itself going by ordinary arm motions. Tom insisted on using it and it always stopped. They said at Cartier's where she had sent him to buy it that Mr. Brett must lead a very sedentary life. This had made Tom so angry that he had gone to Cartier's himself and had explained to Mr. Jeroboam, who had sold him the watch and consequently seemed to be permanently connected with him, that he was always moving around and always waving his arms. Then they had called the watch man, who had said that perhaps Mr. Brett gesticulated too much. There could be such a thing.

"Don't send me anywhere to get another watch," Tom called to Polly. "Let's cut out that routine. What time is it?"

As she listened to him from the other room, he sounded like

B. F., and it made her wonder why they had never got on with each other when they were alike in so many ways.

"It's a quarter of eleven. What of it?" she said.

"My God," Tom called. "Where's the radio?"

"What radio?" she asked, as Tom paused in the doorway. His eyes were dull, and his hair, now that it was rumpled, appeared unusually thin on top, and both he and his pajamas looked as though they had gone through a wringer.

"I've got to get a radio," Tom said. "Didn't you order me any breakfast?"

"How could I?" Polly answered. "You were asleep."

"Well, let me have some of your coffee, will you, Poll?"

"I've told you again and again," Polly said, "that I don't want you drinking my coffee."

"Don't be so sore," Tom said. "I thought you came here so we could have a happy Sunday."

"Oh, all right," Polly said. "First you take sleeping pills and then you take coffee."

"That's right," Tom answered. "First I go to sleep and then I wake up. They cancel each other out."

"Everything cancels out, doesn't it," Polly said. "You and me. Everything."

"Listen. Let's not get going on personal relations," Tom said. "I'm trying to concentrate." He held his cup of coffee in one hand, and picked up the telephone in the other. "What are those operators doing?" he asked. "Having a manicure? Poll, hold the paper up in front of me. Not the *Times-Herald*. You did that just to make me mad, didn't you?" . . . Tom's voice changed. He was the delightful and genial friend of all the world. "Is Mr. Armstrong at his desk yet? Get me Mr. Armstrong . . . Albert. This is Tom Brett. How is everything, Albert? Listen Al, I overslept."

"Tell him to send you up some benzedrine," Polly said.

Tom scowled at her.

"Listen, Al, I'm in a hell of a hurry. Help out an old customer, will you, and I'll see you get a reduction on your income tax. Listen, Al, I need a radio quick. There's an eleven o'clock broadcast

I've got to hear. Get a boy up, will you, Al, and I'll do the same thing for you." Then he began jiggling at the telephone for Room Service. He was asking if there was any bacon, and there wasn't any.

"Well, kippered herring, then," Tom said. "I know there's a war on, but you must have something in the kitchen. All right, scrambled eggs and hotcakes, and a double order of coffee and a triple orange juice." There was one thing about Tom — his posture was terrible, but he never put on weight. "What time is it now, Poll?"

"What are you going to do?" Polly asked him. "Go over the top?"

Tom stood before the artificial fireplace and yawned.

"You heard me," he said, and his voice became slow and patient. "There's a broadcast at eleven o'clock. One of my ideas. Occasionally I do have an idea."

"Yes, occasionally," Polly said, "but don't tell it to me until I brace myself. Aren't you going to put something on?"

"Put what on?"

"Something over you, and some slippers."

"I've got these pajamas over me," Tom said, "and I don't want slippers. Where's a cigarette?" Polly tossed him a package.

"What is this idea?" she asked. "What is this broadcast?"

"It's Ouerbach," Tom said. "'A Quarter Hour with Ouerbach.' I've got to see if he puts his foot in his mouth."

"Couldn't you think up anyone better than Milton?" Polly asked.

"It isn't a question of personal entertainment," Tom said. "I've got to hear this, because I'm handling him. He's one of those VIP's we sent out there."

"Don't talk in initials," Polly said. "What's a VIP?"

"Very Important Personage," Tom said. "We sent a lot of VIP's out there to help in the news roundups. They didn't want Milton much. All those uniformed fascists tried to stop him, but we put it over."

"Well, if you don't hear Milton from one place," Polly said, "you hear him from another."

"That's what I told them," Tom said. "They send out Lowell Thomas, why not Milton? What time is it?"

There was a knock on the door. It was the boy with the radio.

"Plug it right in there," Tom said. "Have you got a quarter, Poll?"

"No," Polly said, "not here." He had taken her coffee and her cigarettes. He could go into the bedroom and get his own quarter.

The radio was already making static sounds.

Tom flicked his cigarette ash on the floor before he began turning the knobs. He was not good with gadgets, and they always made him angry.

"God damn it," he said. "Where is that program?" There were snatches of jazz, the song of a choir and a voice in prayer.

"I don't know," Polly said. "Where is Milton Ouerbach?"

"In the Pacific," Tom said, "and I hope he's getting a workout. Where is it? It starts with internal sluggishness. Oh, here it is."

Polly folded her newspaper on her lap and listened.

"And now before we bring you to the key spots of the world," a voice was saying, "I'm going to ask you all a personal question. How do you feel this morning? Bright and gay? Everything inside all in tune? Or do you feel headachy and discouraged?"

"Where's Room Service?" Tom asked. "Where's that coffee?"

"Can't you turn it off," Polly asked, "until Milton comes in?"

"I don't know where he comes in," Tom said.

There was another knock on the door. Room Service was wheeling in a table with three ice bowls of orange juice, two carafes of coffee, and dishes with shiny covers.

"That's it. Push it over there," Tom was saying. He certainly should have put something on. He looked very unappetizing beside the breakfast table. "Here, give me the check. Have you got a pencil, Poll?"

"No," said Polly.

The waiter had a pencil.

"It's a nasty morning, sir," the waiter said. "They say there's going to be a flood."

"Just stir it in water," the radio was saying, "and watch the happy

230

sparkle and savor the peppermint aroma. Remember, it's all vege-table. Not a drug, but a food. And now . . ."

Tom drew up a chair and lighted a cigarette from the one he was holding, and threw the first toward the fireplace. It missed.

"Pick it up," Polly said, "or you'll burn the house down."

"You pick it up, Poll," Tom said. "I've got to listen."

"Damn it," Polly said. "You pick up your own cigarette butts."

She found herself growing angry, what with the rain and Tom in his bare feet and internal sluggishness. It was all a slow, farcical projection of the night before, and Tom apparently had forgotten that there had been a night before. He did not even bother to look at her when he picked up the cigarette.

"We take you now to Paris," the radio was saying.

She wished somebody would take her to Paris, but not Tom. That boy last night, that flyer who looked like Bob Tasmin, would be better.

"And now to the Pacific," the radio was saying, "and Milton Ouerbach."

There was no reason for Milton's being in the Pacific. This busi-ness of trying to bring the war home by having bits of it seen through the eyes of people like Milton was never rewarding because of censorship. The result was always a dash of sickly local color enlivened by a few cloying anecdotes, but there was one good thing about Milton. He always started right in without saying "Good morning, friends" and his voice was clear and cultured and resonant.

"I'm witnessing a pageant here," Milton said, "a free people and a free way of life on the march. You too are in a part of this proces-sion, you buyers of War Bonds and Stamps, you housewives."

"Saving tin foil and bottle caps," Polly said.

Tom frowned and waved both hands at her.

"Farmers, workers. We're all in the Big Parade."

Polly smiled sweetly at Tom.

"It's a parade," she said. "You'd better find your slippers and come along."

"Out here at the front is the spearhead of a way of life, and don't

231

think the boys I have talked to here don't know it, not merely the brass, if you want to call the leaders that, but the plain GI's and gobs — your boys and mine who are going to run this country when they come home. They're doing a lot of pretty serious thinking about it up here at the Front, and they know that you won't let them down."

"Where's the front?" Polly asked. "Where's he talking from?"

"Guam," Tom said. "I know it's terrible, but people like it, Poll."

"Who?" she asked, and she could not imagine anyone's liking it. Milton and his colleagues always moralized, whether they were in Guam or C.B.S. in New York. She sometimes thought they did not want the war won at all, unless it were won in just their way.

"Coming out on the plane," Milton said, "I had quite a talk with a group of the lads in the great democracy of the Armed Services. These lads know what the score is out here. They know that they're fighting for a better way of life. They feel it simply and intuitively. You'd have been pretty proud if you could have seen them in the plane, and have heard their questions — not about trivia, but about the basic things that are distressing us all. Everyone's a good Joe at the front. He has to be."

Milton's voice reverberated through the sitting room. He might have been sitting there opposite her on the modernistic sofa, in his blue double-breasted suit, delivering that discourse. For some reason everyone she had seen lately wanted to give a little talk about something. You sat up nights hearing about the place where you could still get steaks if you knew the headwaiter, or about the little clerk at the corner drugstore who could get you cigarettes. Or there was the problem of servants' wages. Perhaps it was better to do the work yourself and be done with it. There was always someone who said it was fun to do the cooking; housework was great exercise. Or there was the gas rationing — if you were offered a B book, was it ethical to take it if you could get along with an A? If you got away from the home front, someone could give a Round Table Introduction to the Labor Front, or an editorial on giving air priorities to dogs. If you went farther afield, someone could hold the room spellbound by telling just what ought to have been done with General

Patton after he slapped that soldier, or by explaining how Russia was really a democracy. Everyone had his troubles, everyone always knew someone who had just heard something, and everyone wanted to give a picture of the whole situation without being interrupted.

Polly thought, as she listened, of the last time Milton had come to call. He had just been through Iowa on one of his lecture tours and had been so deeply impressed by the agricultural activities of the state that he had written a very earthy radio drama in blank verse dealing principally with corn and the feel of the soil. It had never seemed to occur, either to Milton or to Tom, who had been impressed by the effort, that Milton had never spent more than an hour on any farm except a health farm on the Hudson. Details never seemed to matter to Milton or Tom.

"You learn a lot out here," Milton was saying. "You learn lessons in patience, fortitude and courage. You learn to respect people you never did respect. There is greatness in everyone out here, regardless of race or color or creed."

Polly winced. Milton had said it, but at least he had twisted it — he had not said "race, creed, or color."

"The men here at the front come from all walks of life — rich and poor, underprivileged, overprivileged, but few of those distinctions which vex us (and so very rightly, too) at home amount to much here in the great crucible of war. There is a brotherhood between officer and man, a new and kindly tolerance that will last into tomorrow. It gives me, and it would you too, new faith to see it. Out here is a vision of the new America. It makes me proud, and also just a little humble."

"Now he's going to rededicate himself, isn't he?" Polly said.

"Shut up," Tom shouted. "Will you please!"

Milton's voice was going on inexorably. You could never talk down the radio, and its wave lengths never reacted to insults.

"My time is growing short, but I can't leave you without touching on a bit of human drama I encountered out here inadvertently — the story of a man whom I misunderstood."

"He must be losing his mind," Polly said. "He couldn't misunderstand."

Tom groaned, but he did not tell her to shut up.

"I met him here, a college friend — I'll call him Joe, though that is not his name — a college friend who had always seemed to me stiff, aloof, not able to get along outside his narrow little set. I used to know Joe as a club man, a child of privilege, a corporation lawyer whose life was spent in defending vested interests, not a bad fellow, clever, rather charming, but, I thought, shallow. Well, yesterday I ran into Joe again, as ever the polite, adroit aristocrat. He was not the type I had traveled to see, but we chatted a while together. The same old Joe he seemed to me, untouched by war, and personal influence had given him a respectable, cushy staff berth. I'm afraid I shrugged my shoulders mentally when that same evening at a dinner attended only by officers (*brass* is the GI term) I encountered Joe again, dark, handsome, a man of measured merriment, his eye upon his superiors, doing the right thing. Someone asked him to sing. I was not surprised, for Joe always had a fine baritone. I can see him now, standing in that officers' clubroom in his tailored 'pinks' as the GI's call them. And what was he singing? 'Goodbye Girls I'm Through.' I thought to myself that playboys must be playboys and it made me sad. I did not know, I never suspected, the high courage that lurked behind this polished façade. Later, he bade me good night, suavely, charmingly, and, I'm afraid I thought, with a little condescension. I remember his words, so slick, so smooth. I'll repeat them to you simply to round out the picture. 'Good-by, Milt,' he said, 'take care of the little people, won't you? I'm afraid I can't.' It left a bad taste in my mouth. I felt there was a sneer in his voice, an undertone of class against class, but I knew later that I had been wrong. When I looked for him next morning, Joe was gone. Where had he gone? Off for enemy territory, off with all the chances against him. There is nothing unusual about this out here, and Joe would be the last to have me mention it. The only reason I tell you now is that he knew last night where he was going and yet he left us as gaily as he might have gone to breakfast, a brave man, a gentleman unafraid, but don't let me say gentleman — rather, another brave American. Bravery does not belong to privilege. I'm only saying this because I want to apologize to my friend's memory for anything I may have thought. Where is he now? As I speak a message has been handed to me. Joe's plane — the censor says I can tell you that it went on low reconnaissance — is now overdue. Well, God bless you, Joe. This is Milton Ouerbach speaking from the Pacific."

Tom switched off the radio, and for a second the room had that dead stillness that a shut-off radio always brought. When Polly started to speak, her voice was choked.

"Tom," she said.

"What is it now?" Tom answered. "Didn't you want me to turn it off?"

"Tom, did you know who it was?"

Tom frowned. The broadcast was over and he was eating his hotcakes.

"Who it *was?*"

"The *other* one," Polly said. "The one who sang."

"Nobody sang. Or am I going crazy? Come on and get your coffee."

"I don't want any coffee," Polly said.

"Well," Tom said, "nobody sang."

"The gentleman unafraid," Polly said. "Don't you know who it was?"

Tom finished his hotcakes — he always ate too fast — and began pouring out coffee.

"You don't want your sugar, do you?" he asked. "Is it my imagination, or is it getting cold in here?"

"I told you to put something on," Polly said. "Didn't you know who it was?"

"Certainly," Tom said, and he smiled sourly. "It was a pure figment of Milt's imagination, and a pretty corny figment too. Everyone we send out there gets corny."

"No, it wasn't," Polly said.

Tom pushed back his chair, lighted a cigarette and began to pace about the room. "Listen, Poll," he said. "If you're trying to pick a fight, don't do it now. I've got to get organized. I've got to get dressed. I've got to be up and out."

235

"It wasn't any figment," Polly said. "It was Bob Tasmin."

Tom flicked his cigarette ash on the floor, then put his cigarette carefully in the corner of his mouth.

"What's that again?"

"It was Bob Tasmin."

"Oh, my God," Tom said. "That kid last night was like Tasmin, and now Tasmin's on the radio."

"It couldn't have been anyone else," Polly said. "They went to college together. He sang. He's a corporation lawyer."

"And a big stuffed shirt," Tom said. "Listen, Poll, the Army's full of Tasmins. They crawl around all the cocktail parties. Go out to the Pentagon sometime. . . . What should Tasmin be doing in Guam?" Tom gave a mirthless laugh and threw his cigarette at the fireplace, and missed. "All right," he said. "I'm going to pick it up."

"Well, if he isn't there, where is he?" Polly asked.

Tom hunched his shoulders forward. He should have put something on. It was just the way he caught cold, but she did not care, now, whether he did or not.

"I know a lot," Tom said, "but oddly enough I don't know where Tasmin is. You know how I react to that guy, and if he can't help it, it doesn't make it any better. It's guys like Tasmin that we're fighting this war about. I don't know where he is, except that he's in a good safe place because the Tasmins know how to look out for themselves. He's probably playing squash right now at Chevy Chase, or he's hooked a pool car and gone to Warrenton on a military mission. That's where he is, inspecting the fox-hunting setup. You needn't worry about Tasmin."

"Well, I wish you'd find out where he is," Polly said.

"All right," Tom said. "As long as we don't have to have him around."

She sat there looking at him.

"You're not being very nice," she said. Tom was never kind about people. He was simply brilliant, simply mechanical.

"My God," Tom said. "Are you falling in love with that guy all over again?"

"You're not being kind," Polly said. "He may be dead."

Tom stood up and whistled "Taps."

"Stop it," Polly said.

"A gentleman unafraid," Tom said. He was a very good mimic. His voice sounded exactly like Milton's. "God bless you, Joe."

"Don't do that," Polly said. She found herself reaching toward her empty glass of orange juice. She was filled with an intense desire to throw it at him, but instead she grew icily calm.

"This doesn't sound very well coming from you, does it?" she asked. "Don't forget you're a civilian, darling."

He had been growing sensitive about this lately, and she was glad that it could hurt him.

"I know you whooped it up to get us into the war, dear," she said. "You did a lot more than he did, but he's in the Army."

"Yes," Tom said. "I know. He would be."

"I'm only saying that it doesn't sound very well, does it, darling, to be so awfully funny?" Polly said. "Of course, I know how crazy you were to enlist, and I know that what you're doing is much more important. I know you're nearly forty, too, without any military background. I know how hard you've been working mobilizing public opinion and helping with speeches and directives, and I know how beautifully you speak too. Don't think I'm being critical. You don't, do you, darling?"

"Is that about all?" Tom asked her.

"That's about all," Polly said, and she was wondering how he would have looked to her in those pajamas if she were meeting him for the first time, "but if you make fun again of anyone who's fighting this war for you, I'll go in the bathroom and be sick."

"Is that all?" Tom asked.

"Yes," Polly said. "That's all."

"Well, go ahead and be sick," Tom said, "as long as you let me go in first. I've got to shave."

It was worse than last night. It was the ugliest passage that had ever arisen between them. She had thrown words at him at other times as she might have thrown that glass, but it took her breath away to think she could have gone so far, and it was not fair. She knew he would never have been able to get by the doctors, but still, he might have tried, and now he looked sick, too, as he walked into the bedroom.

"Tom," she called.

If he had answered she would have told him she was sorry. She had spoken that way because she had wanted to make him angry. If he had only been violently angry at her, everything would have been all right again.

"Tom," she called. He did not answer. She had faced that desolation before when she had quarreled with him, but behind it there had always been a certainty of ultimate reconciliation, and now she had no such confidence. She sat there waiting because there was nothing left but to wait.

She could hear him dressing in the other room, and from the faint sounds she could tell just what he was doing. Now he was pulling on his shirt, now his trousers. Now he was stamping into his low shoes. Now he was putting on his tie, twisting it into one of those knots that always drifted sideways. Now he was getting out his hairbrush, one of the gold-backed pair she had given him. He never carried two. Now he was putting on his coat, and now he was back in the sitting room.

"Where are you going?" she asked.

"Just out," he answered. "I should have told you. I've got to go out to lunch."

"Can't I go too?" she asked.

"No," he answered. "It's some more about that directive. I guess I'd better tell you something, Poll."

Her heart missed a beat while she waited without answering.

"You're right, you know, Poll. I'm a heel in many ways."

"Tom," she said. "You made me so angry."

"Oh, that's all right," he said. "Let's skip it, Poll. You're right. I haven't got any guts any more. They're all gone somewhere. Where are they gone?"

He frowned at her just as he always did when he asked what had happened to his shirt studs, and she tried to smile. She wanted to bring back something, anything.

"Maybe they're under the bed," she said.

He smiled in a sickly way, just as though he were about to say that he had looked under the bed.

"No, I'm soft. It isn't your fault, Poll," he said before she could go on. "It's like living in the tropics, or too much candy." His face grew brighter. "God, but you and I have had a lot of candy."

"Tom," she asked him, "are you talking about the money again?"

"It isn't your fault, Poll," he said. "It's like miscegenation."

"What's like miscegenation?" Polly asked. "You and me?"

"Not a happy simile," he said. "Well, no, maybe not as bad as that."

"If it's the money," Polly said, "I've told you — how many times have I told you — that if you didn't want us to live — "

"I know," Tom said. "It isn't your fault, Poll. I get habits."

"Tom," she said. "Please stay and talk. You're going out because you're mad."

"I was," he said, "but I'm not mad now. I've really got to go."

"Where are you going?" she asked.

"I told you, Poll," Tom said, "that I've got to do some work down at the office and around, but I'll be back at five. I'm bringing some of our friends in at five. They've been asking for you."

"Well, don't forget the dinner party," Polly said.

"What?" Tom stood up straighter. "What dinner party?"

"I wired you," she said. "The Smedleys."

She supposed he would refuse to go, but instead he looked brighter.

"Well, well," he said. "The Smedleys. All right. I'll meet you here at five."

A few minutes after he had gone the telephone rang. She was in the bedroom by then, at the dressing table.

"Hello," Polly said.

It was a woman's voice, a high contralto.

"Hello, is Mr. Brett there?"

239

"He's just gone," Polly said. "This is Mrs. Brett, if you want to leave a message."

Instead of an answer there was a faint click. Whoever it was had hung up the telephone very carefully.

Polly stood very still. So it was not all the money. She wished that Bob Tasmin were there or B. F. or even Harry, but all of them were gone.

It wasn't as though she did not know all about this sort of thing. You ran into it among your friends after a few years of marriage in New York or anywhere else. There was never anything you could do about it except to take sides. You could only think how terrible it must be, and thank goodness, it would never happen to you, for you and your husband understood each other. Granted there might be quarrels, these were of a humorous nature that you could laugh at later; nothing bitter, nothing harsh — the way Tom would never have his clothes pressed, the way she wanted all the windows in the bedroom wide open — all differences that you could joke about. You could look at those other wives with pity and compassion as you used to look at girls who were expelled from school. It could happen to anybody else, but not to you, never to you.

And now it was only a question of time before everyone would be talking about Tom and her. All sorts of eccentricities in Tom's behavior were now as clear as daylight, and it was entirely possible that her closest friends had guessed already. Already they might be saying that Polly did not know, poor thing. Or if they had not guessed already, it was only a question of time. There were some things you could take and some you couldn't, and it was not fair after all she had done for Tom.

She sat down at the dressing table and picked up her lipstick. When she saw that her hand was shaking she put it down, waited for a while, composing herself very deliberately, and picked it up again. Then she smeared it over her lips, hard but accurately. It always made her feel more competent when she put on lipstick. The darker hue of her mouth made her eyes darker. She never looked foolish or felt foolish when she put on lipstick right.

240

In the mirror Polly's face stared back at her insolently, with an expression that it had taken years to cultivate. She must surely be as good-looking as that other one, as young, and as intelligent . . . but it was only a question of time.

"My dear," they would be saying. "Have you heard about the Bretts? You never really can tell where lightning will strike next, can you? She's off to Reno, poor thing."

And that was something she would *not* do. She would be damned if she went out to Reno, and hung around at one of those dude ranches with other distracted people. He could go to Reno and see how he liked it, and whoever she was, he could take her with him. *"Hello, is Mr. Brett there?"*

"He's very selfish," they would be saying. . . . "You know, that egotistical, intellectual type. Of course, she spoiled him. . . . It wasn't all his fault. She romanticized him, and made herself a perfect doormat, and you know what it does to a man, being romanticized. She spoiled him, but then, that's what happens, doesn't it, when a rich girl marries a poor man? It never does seem to work out. Don't ask me why, my dear, but it really doesn't. It must be very hard on the man, you know. There must be a continual sense of inadequacy, and no man can be inadequate. He literally didn't have a cent, you know . . . and then all those trips to Japan and China, and then that preposterous study she built for him in the Berkshires. She literally gave him everything except a quill pen. . . . And those parties she built around him. He was what I said, my dear, a perfect abstraction in her mind, and a man simply does not like it. Of course, if there had been children — but he was the one who did not want them. . . . Well, thank goodness, there aren't any."

Polly was putting on her black wool dress and she yanked its gold belt savagely through the buckle. Then she unlocked her jewel box and put on her topaz clips.

"Of course, I'm sure I don't know what she saw in him," they would be saying. "He was brilliant, very New Dealish, and some of those New Dealers are so emotional, without mentioning any names. Sooner or later they all end up in somebody's gossip column,

241

don't they? I don't know what ever possessed her. It must have simply been revolt. If she had only settled down, but then perhaps rich girls can't, or if she had married into motors or machine tools. Sometimes those marriages work. I saw the nicest young couple from Detroit at Santa Barbara. Or if she had married some nice, quiet young man who *could* have been pushed around. I'm sure I don't know what they'll do now, but they're saying . . ."

Polly snapped her jewel box shut and locked it, and put it in her suitcase and locked the suitcase. She was not going to leave things around to tempt that poor colored chambermaid. Then the telephone rang again and she stood listening while it rang twice. Then she picked up the receiver, standing very straight.

"Hello," she said, and her voice was soft and husky — cobwebs in the moonlight, that was what Bob Tasmin used to say — and she made a face, but not of pleasure.

"Why, Sylvia, darling. How did you ever track me down here? Lonely?" She laughed. "We're never lonely when we're reading the Sunday papers. . . . Why, yes, he's right in the sitting room. Do you want to say hello to him, darling? I'd call him in to speak to you, but you know how Tom is when he's taken away from the newspapers. . . . I know, dear, but he has to relax sometime. . . . That's sweet of you. I wish I could, but he would be perfectly furious if I left him. I promised to check over some things with him. You know, those government papers. Wait, I'll call him. . . . Tom, it's Sylvia calling up to say hello. . . . He says give you his love and kisses, darling. He says keep checking on us, whatever he means by that. Oh, darling, I *will* see you before I go. . . . Yes, I'll write the number down. Dupont. . . . Yes, I have it. . . . Oh, darling, wait. . . . Now that you've called, there is something I want to ask you. Do you know where Bob Tasmin is? . . . No, I don't need any extra men, but if an old beau should be in town, there are amenities. . . . He is? I don't see how you have time to know everything about everybody. Well, all right, good-by, darling."

Polly set the telephone down carefully. She knew they were talking about Tom already.

"Good-by, you little bitch," she whispered. It was five minutes past twelve, very early for lunch, but she was going downstairs. She could not stay in that room any longer. If she did, she would think about Bob Tasmin's plane.

Polly wondered if the elevator would ever stop at her floor. It was exasperating to stand and look at those dials above the doors, each with a hand that moved as eccentrically as the needles of a compass. She would watch an elevator go up to the ninth or the tenth floor, according to the dial, and there it would stay and stay until she began to wonder what the operator was doing. Was he waiting up there to be annoying, or to show his authority, or was he reading the Sunday comics or making love to the chambermaid? Then the elevator would come down very fast. The indicator would move to eight, seven and six. She would get ready for the doors to open, but the elevator would rush past the floor, and she would jab the signal again. Though this could not have happened more than twice, and she could not have waited more than three minutes at the longest, the effect of the wait was exaggerated out of all proportion.

It had the lagging frustration of a sequence in an unpleasant dream. It was silly to be annoyed and tap your foot and pace about in front of an elevator. After all, there was a war on, and she did not know how lucky she was, but she was tired of being told that she did not know how lucky she was. You might as well slap on the lipstick, if you could get any that was the proper shade, and put on the Chanel, if you could get that, and take it. But just exactly what was it that you were going to take?

When the elevator stopped, the occupants made room for her politely. There were a naval lieutenant and a frowsy girl who must have been his wife, a superannuated colonel with bifocal glasses, and two middle-aged businessmen, the durable, traveling type with Army-Navy E Award pins in their buttonholes. In spite of the awards, they had a prewar look. Polly smiled sweetly at the bald-headed elevator boy in a blue uniform that did not fit him.

"Thanks ever so much for stopping," she said. There was no answer. They all looked at her disapprovingly. She did not know there was a war on.

XIX

Not You, All Women

In contrast to the night before, the hotel lobby had the weary, tranquil atmosphere of Sunday noon. There was no pretty girl behind a War Bond table. The pile of bags by the reception desk had dwindled. The usual luncheon-hour crowd had not yet gathered, and the bar and the cocktail room were closed. Nevertheless, a few people were already seated in the gigantic upholstered chairs and sofas, waiting for their friends and trying to read the Sunday papers beneath dim lights which discouraged reading. The revolving doors to the street kept pushing in newcomers, wet from the rain outside. It was better than being upstairs, but not much better. She turned and began to walk down the broad corridor to the dining room, and as she did so, Milton Ouerbach's voice came back to her. *. . . Few of those distinctions which vex us (and so very rightly, too) at home amount to much here in the great crucible of war. . . . And what was he singing? "Goodbye Girls I'm Through." . . . Where had he gone? . . . Where is he now? . . .*

She was just going down the steps past the place where you checked your hat when she heard her name called so loudly that she could not miss hearing it, and, at the same time, whoever had called her seized her by the shoulders.

"Baby," the voice bellowed right in her ear. "Yes sir, she's my baby."

Polly whirled on her heels. She did not want to be anybody's baby, particularly Sunday at noon in front of the main dining-room headwaiter, but when she saw who it was, she felt relieved, though she also felt a little like one of those girls in an *Esquire* cartoon. It was Mr. Homer J. Lovelace, the president of the Bulwer

Machine Company, and ever since she was ten he had called her "Baby."

"Why, Mr. Lovelace," she said. She was no longer Polly Brett. She was Burton Fulton's little girl again.

"H. J. to you," Mr. Lovelace said, "and how about a little kiss?"

She had always found it very difficult to kiss Mr. Lovelace gracefully and at the same time to play the part of a nice little girl being sweet to an old friend of the family. Mr. Lovelace always pawed and he always said "Hmm-mm". . . and now the hat-check girl was watching them.

"Hmm-mm, Baby," Mr. Lovelace said. "What are you doing all alone? Didn't anyone tell you that old H. J. was here?"

No one had told her, though everyone like H. J. was always in Washington at some time or other. Besides, if she had known, she could have done nothing about it. Tom always said that it never helped being seen around with those people. They might be all right in their place, which was in their factories turning out war materials, but when they were down in Washington pulling wires, you might be misunderstood if you were too friendly with them — but at the moment, Polly did not mind. There was something solid and very reassuring just then about H. J.

"Why didn't you call up the suite?" H. J. asked.

"What suite?" Polly asked him.

He was a square, chunky man with a smooth, florid face and bushy eyebrows, and he smelled of Bourbon and bay rum when she kissed him. In all the years she had known him he always seemed to be in the same very carefully pressed gray suit, in the same gray tie, with the same carnation in his coat lapel, but now besides the flower he was also wearing one of those Army-Navy E buttons.

About three years previously the award had been given to the Bulwer Machine Company, and B. F. had especially asked her to go up with him for the presentation ceremony. Mr. Lovelace had stood on a platform of red, white, and blue bunting in front of the main office building. The yard had been filled with workers, men and women in jumpers, and Mr. Lovelace had read a speech prepared for him by the Public Relations office.

"We, the management and workers of the Bulwer Machine Company," H. J. Lovelace had read, "are one and all deeply conscious of this honor. We each and every one, standing shoulder to shoulder in the production line for the Arsenal of Democracy, hereby rededicate ourselves anew."

It was only one of a series of set speeches, horribly phrased, but the painful ineptness in itself made the occasion solemn and moving. A general made the award, and he must have done the same thing again and again at hundreds of other factories until he could not have helped but be very bored; but his set phrases, too, rose above their rhetoric, judging by the faces of the people listening.

"This is a military decoration," he had said, "awarded for work well done by the combat team of industry."

It had been as close as Polly would ever get to the war, out there at the Bulwer Machine Company on a sweltering August day, but Tom had not been nice when she had told him about it afterwards. Those people, he said, always used the awards for advertising and made them occasions for a big party which they could write off as business expense, and why sound off about those flags and pins when everyone was getting them? That might have all been true, but there had been something more—they had all been a part of something. She still remembered how everyone had cheered when they ran up the flag with the Army-Navy E.

"What suite? Why the company suite, Baby," H. J. said. "We have to keep some of the boys here to see that no one pulls anything fast on us. We're having a buffet lunch right now. Come on, and don't say you've got something else to do. Come on up and look us over." And he put his arm around her on the way to the elevator.

"And we'll ask that boy you married, too," H. J. said. "We're not particular. He can eat on industry too, and we can stand it if he can." Polly laughed nervously.

"Oh, Tom," she said. "I know he'd love to . . ."

"The hell he would." H. J. laughed loudly.

"Well, we won't have to find out," Polly said. "Tom's off somewhere working on a directive."

H. J. gave her a gentle squeeze.

"I'm mighty glad to see you, Poll," he said. "You're like old B. F."

Though she had known Mr. Lovelace always, as someone several years older than her father, she could not escape the feeling that she was embarking on a slightly illicit adventure. She had been conditioned too long by Tom's ideas, even though she told herself that she did not care in the least, under the circumstances, what he might think if he knew. Tom was convinced that anyone even remotely resembling Mr. Lovelace represented a subversive force. It was even dangerous to admit that some of them were what Tom called Men of Good Will. In the end that good will was the smile of a crocodile. In the end they were antisocial and antilabor, and antidemocracy — and they were particularly dangerous when they talked about good housing and company unions. You had to watch them, Tom said, or else they were bound to fool you. He did not want anyone to think for a minute that he was one of those tamed liberals like some people he could mention. You had to be very careful not to fraternize with Business.

Polly hoped Mr. Lovelace would not say anything that was antilabor, but she knew he probably would. She hoped he would not tell any of those jokes about the President, but she knew he probably would. People like Mr. Lovelace never had the remotest conception that they were backward or that their ideas amounted to very little.

"I'm right behind everybody who's winning this war," Mr. Lovelace said. "We're all trying to win this war. Are we, or aren't we?"

"Yes," Polly said, "of course we are."

"And if anybody tells me I'm not trying to win this war," Mr. Lovelace said, "he can take off his coat and fight. That's what I said down there yesterday."

He did not explain where down there was, because he seemed to take it for granted that Polly knew.

"That's what I said down there yesterday," Mr. Lovelace repeated. "I said, 'Gentlemen — '" They were out of the elevator on the third floor, and Mr. Lovelace had stopped in front of her. Right there by the elevators on the third floor, he was telling what he had told them down there yesterday. "I said, 'Gentlemen, one more sly insinuation, one more innuendo that I or my associates or every man and woman at Bulwer is not trying to win this war, and we'll break off this conference.' I said, 'Gentlemen, just get off our necks, and damn the social gains.'"

"Did you really say that?" Polly asked.

"Of course I really said that," Mr. Lovelace answered.

"But who did you say it to?" Polly asked.

Mr. Lovelace waved his hand vaguely toward a winaow.

"I said it to them down there. 'Gentlemen,' I said . . ." He was going to go right on saying it, and Polly wished he would not say it by the elevator. "'Gentlemen, we'll make those fuses without one cent of profit, but let us do it by ourselves. We can do it better than you can, period. Which one of you gentlemen has ever sweated out a payroll?'"

Mr. Lovelace paused and shook his finger at her, but he did not move. Polly could put the details together, and she could guess what they had thought of him down there.

"'Gentlemen,' I said, 'my son, Major Walter Lovelace, is in France, and one more insinuation about the Bulwer Machine Company, and we'll go higher up. Let's fish or cut bait. Let's give those boys their fuses, Type A–27, Special Project II. Let's get the machines set. Bulwer can do it for you, if you keep your fingers out of it.'"

Mr. Lovelace stopped again.

"What did they say down there?" Polly asked.

"What?" Mr. Lovelace said.

"What did they say down there?" Polly asked again.

Mr. Lovelace shook his head.

"It doesn't matter what they say, Baby. They're all on our necks. It's what we all have to go through to turn out anything. I'd like to tell the columnists some of the things I know. I'd like to tell Westbrook Pegler."

Polly hated to think what Tom would have said.

"Oh, no," she said, "not Pegler."

"Pegler is a great American," Mr. Lovelace said, "and don't let anybody fool you, Baby — but I'm getting emotional. Let's go and get a drink. B. F. used to say I'm too emotional." And he took Polly's arm and patted her hand. "You do look like B. F., Baby. You've got his eyes, and I want to tell you something."

Polly guessed he was going to tell her again what he had told her at the funeral, but there was never any way of stopping Mr. Lovelace.

"B. F. was a war casualty," Mr. Lovelace said. "Don't you ever forget that B. F. died for his country."

Everything Mr. Lovelace said about B. F. was so common-place that she could not understand why she was very close to crying.

"I just want to tell you," Mr. Lovelace said, "before we go in and meet the crowd. He's gone, but I'm here, Baby, and any time anything's wrong and everything isn't all right, you come around to me."

"Why, that's awfully sweet of you," Polly said, "but everything's all right."

He looked kindly, reserved and watchful, as B. F. used to look when he knew more than he said.

"If you ever want to talk to anyone, I'm here, Baby . . . You know, I've got two girls of my own."

When you thought that they were dull, they were not dull at all.

The rooms on the third floor of the hotel looked as though they had been prepared for the reception of great national figures, or foreign potentates who traveled with what used to be called an *entourage*. There were small hallways and all sorts of adjoining rooms, soft carpets, chandeliers, sconces, mirrors, French prints of shepherdesses, brocade curtains, silk-upholstered Empire furniture. The main room of the suite, which had been rented by the Bulwer Machine Company for its visiting executives and for the entertainment of business associates, was stuffy and sumptuous. Its walls still echoed with the political reverberations of the '20's. Polly could almost hear the voices of the lobbyists. She could picture members of the Harding cabinet dropping in there for a discreet chat with someone. She could think of Herbert Hoover as sitting in one of the chairs. It was all a part of those *Only Yesterday* books; but the people who were gathered there that Sunday had brought it up to date. She knew now why it was so hard to get Room Service; all the available Room Service appeared to be in the Bulwer Machine Company's suite.

Waiters were working over chafing dishes of crab flakes and creamed chicken. Other waiters were passing appetizers. At the end of the room a bartender was mixing drinks behind a long table. Upon its white cloth were rows of glasses and an elaborate assortment of bottles. On the wall behind the barkeeper someone had pinned a red banner, on which was inscribed in white letters the word "Bulmaco." When they entered Mr. Lovelace paused to look over at the guests, who might all have been lifted bodily from any part of the lobby downstairs. Polly saw a general talking to a feeble old gentleman with spots on his vest, and some very pretty girls talking to Army and Navy officers and middle-aged businessmen. Their voices all rose cheerfully, and you could see that they were having a wonderful time disposing of the entertainment offered by the Bulwer Machine Company. It was one of the industrial scenes of which she had often heard but which she had very seldom witnessed.

The moment Mr. Lovelace appeared a youngish man in a double-breasted blue serge suit hurried toward him. His necktie was blue, with geometrical designs, and his handkerchief stuck from his pocket, in intricate folds like a dinner napkin.

"Well, Eddie," Mr. Lovelace said. "How are you making out?"

"Not so badly," Eddie said. "They certainly go for that crab, and we may go short on Bourbon. No Martinis, no champagne cocktails, they only want Bourbon."

"Well, you ought to know," Mr. Lovelace said, "that Washington's a Bourbon city."

"Yet, if you only give them Bourbon," Eddie answered, "they always ask for something else."

Mr. Lovelace still lingered by the door.

"Anybody here you don't know?" he asked.

"Nobody, except that couple over there," Eddie said, and he

250

nodded toward the chafing dishes. "I think they think this is a public dining room."

"Well, maybe," Mr. Lovelace said. "Eddie, I want you to shake hands with Mrs. Brett, Burt Fulton's daughter, and I want you to make her feel at home."

"He doesn't have to make me," Polly said. "I feel at home."

"Well, shake hands with Eddie Howland, Poll," Mr. Lovelace said. "Ed's one of our contact men. Ed can do anything."

"Can you do card tricks?" Polly asked him.

"Eddie's used to it here," Mr. Lovelace said. "Eddie can do anything. Who's the general, Eddie?"

"Major General Paisley," Eddie said. "You remember, you saw him yesterday at the Pentagon."

"Oh, yes," Mr. Lovelace said, "and there's the senator. Now I'm getting the picture straight, and there's the W. P. B. No newspaper boys, are there?"

"No, sir," Eddie said.

"Anyone from the Department of Justice?"

"Yes," said Eddie, "over there. They still keep coming in."

"All right," Mr. Lovelace said. "That's fine. Now you take Poll here and give her a drink. I'll just walk around."

The Bulwer Machine Company contact man gave Polly a cocktail and a dish of creamed chicken. Polly felt that she looked very well in her dress with the gold belt and her clips, and she could see the general and other people looking at her approvingly.

"Is there anyone you'd like to meet?" Eddie asked.

"Well," Polly said, "no, not particularly."

"That's right," he told her, "nobody wants to meet anybody. They just come here to eat."

"Well, it's wonderful food," Polly said.

"It has to be," Eddie answered, "or they wouldn't come."

"Why, Mr. Howland," Polly said, "don't make it sound so grim."

"It isn't grim," he answered, "it's just business. We all miss your father, Mrs. Brett. He always looked as though he were having a good time at these parties. I don't know how he ever did it."

"Oh, Father," Polly said. "Father always had a good time." But she did not want to think about him then. "Would you get me another cocktail?" she asked.

A pale lieutenant commander, who wore a Pacific ribbon with three stars, had been looking at her uncertainly, and now he edged his way toward her across the room.

"Hello," he said. "Do you remember me?"

There was no reason why you had to remember everyone you had ever known, but if you did not, it was always embarrassing. His face looked like a dozen other faces. His nose looked too long and his mouth too wide. His forehead was high because he was losing his hair, and the corners of his lips kept twitching.

"Why, not at the moment," Polly said. "Should I remember you?"

"Yes, you should," he answered. "Try to think."

"I don't want to try to think," Polly said.

"Well, if you don't want to try," he said, "I'm Norman Bell. Does that mean anything?"

"Norman Bell," Polly repeated.

"We were at a dinner dance at Gray's Point once. We were younger then. That is, I was younger, but you still look all right."

It was that first dinner dance at the Mill River Club. It was Nancy Heath's party with all those adolescent children, and he was Norman Bell, the sophisticated boy who had sat next to her.

"Norman Bell," she said. "Yes, I remember now. What are you doing here?"

He did not look sophisticated any longer but he still seemed very bored.

"What is anybody doing anywhere?" he asked. "Let's sit down and talk."

There were two chairs beneath a mirror and she sat down. She only hoped that he would not ask about Susy Hollister and Nancy Heath, and all the rest of them.

"I've improved since then," he said. "Have you improved?"

"No," Polly answered, "not particularly." It had been the first time she had ever danced with Bob Tasmin, and she did not want to think about Bob Tasmin either. She only wanted to be quiet in that alien room, looking at those strangers.

"Where have you been all this time?" she asked.

He was holding a very stiff drink of whisky, and she noticed that his hand shook. "That's just what I was wondering," he said. The answer made so little sense that Polly thought he was drunk at first, and then she saw that it was nerves. "Where have any of us been since then?"

She remembered that Norman Bell was always telling jokes, and she supposed it had grown on him.

"Don't be so indirect," she said. "It isn't funny."

"I don't mean to be," he answered. "I'm just out of Bethesda for the day. I'm going back tonight."

Polly had often seen the white tower of the Naval Hospital in Bethesda, Maryland, and there was no doubt that something had happened to Norman Bell.

"Oh, I'm sorry," she said.

"There's nothing to be sorry about," he answered. "I'm doing all right. I go before the Board next week."

Polly was sure he should not be drinking.

"But Norman," she said, "how did you get here?"

He nodded toward a naval captain across the room.

"The doc," he said. "He brought me. We're just in for the day."

"You're back from the Pacific, aren't you?" Polly asked.

"Yes," Norman said. "I knew what I was doing there."

Polly hoped the doctor would come over.

"Norman," she said, "are you sure you ought to be drinking?"

"Don't bother me," Norman said. "I was just thinking of your question. Where have we been? The war's all clear, but where were we before the war? What were we all doing? That's what I mean. Nothing we did made sense."

Then she saw the captain striding toward them, a heavy, bald-headed man who looked like General Eisenhower.

"That's your last drink, Norm," the captain said, and he put his hand on Norman's shoulder.

"This girl is Polly Fulton," Norman said. "You know the Fultons, Doc. I used to know the Fultons before the war, and nothing that Polly Fulton and I used to do made sense."

253

"Well, come on, shipmate," the captain said, and he exchanged a glance with Polly as Norman stood up. "He's been through quite a lot, but he's all right."

"Well, good-by, Polly," Norman said. "You know, I've improved since then — and just remember, nothing before the war makes any difference. That's what I mean. It's out — Bell to Fulton — unshackle. But you're not Fulton any more, are you?"

"No," Polly answered, "not any more."

"Well, it doesn't make any difference," Norman Bell said, "who you married before the war. That's all out, too. Unshackle — "

He held out his hand to her, and she tried to smile.

"Norman," she said. "Perhaps you've got something there. Maybe it *is* all out."

"Come on, Norm," the captain said.

There was no continuity any longer in the way people materialized.

All the time the room was filling with new guests, and she could see Mr. Eddie Howland telling jokes, and shaking hands and moving from group to group.

"Did you hear about the lady in the Pentagon?" she heard him saying.

A lady had told the guard that she had to go to the hospital right away because she was going to have a baby, and the guard told her that she should not have come to the Pentagon when she was in that condition, and she had told the guard that she was not in that condition when she had come to the Pentagon Building.

It was another of those Washington stories, but they all laughed.

Mr. Lovelace and the general joined the group. The general was wearing the Army Service Forces insignia, the one they called a star of hope in a dense fog, surrounded by red tape.

"General," Mr. Lovelace said, "I want you especially to meet Burt Fulton's daughter. You remember Burt Fulton in Project 20. Well, this is his daughter."

The general blinked at her.

"And a very pretty daughter," General Paisley said. "What are you doing? Telling stories?"

"Yes," Polly said. "They're telling Pentagon stories."

A large group had gathered by then around Mr. Lovelace and the general. There was an involuntary respect for the uniform, just as there used to be for the clergy. Everyone was smiling and waiting for General Paisley to say something else.

"I know a Pentagon story," the general said.

"Well, don't keep it to yourself," Mr. Lovelace said. "The general knows a Pentagon story."

"It's about a Western Union messenger," the general said. "He went to deliver a telegram and he was lost in there for three months. When he came out he was a lieutenant colonel."

The story was three years old, but everybody laughed.

"I suppose you've all heard this one," Mr. Lovelace said. "Stop me if you've heard it."

But Polly knew that no one would stop him. It was the one about the colonel who was brought to the Pentagon to do some very secret work.

"And a general gave him a desk in a special private office," Mr. Lovelace said. "That's the way it goes, isn't it, General?"

"Go ahead," General Paisley said. "I've heard it. It's a fine story."

"It's a little off-color," Mr. Lovelace said. "Are you sure you can take it, Poll?"

People like Mr. Lovelace were always much more proper than Tom and all his friends.

"Well," Mr. Lovelace said. "It seems that about three weeks later the general dropped in to see how the colonel was getting on. Eddie, get them to bring the general a drink. Everybody wants a drink. Well, the colonel had gone, and his desk was gone too. Everything was gone. The office was empty."

"Where had he gone?" Polly asked.

She knew where he had gone because Tom had told her the story months and months before. Your mind had to move in those days from one thing to another so quickly that nothing was clear. Tom, Bob Tasmin, her father, the Bulwer Machine Company and Norman Bell, and now the colonel and the Pentagon.

"Listen to that, General," Mr. Lovelace said. "Polly's never heard it. Well, that's just the point. Where had he gone? Well, this general looked and looked. He went up and down the escalators, and he looked through Corridor B, and Corridor C, and at last he looked in the Men's Room. There was the colonel with his desk and all his papers right in the Men's Room."

"Oh," Polly said, "was he?"

"Yes, he was," Mr. Lovelace said, "and the general asked him how he had got in there with his desk, and do you know what the colonel said?"

"No," Polly answered.

"He said he was working in there because it was the only place he could find in the Pentagon where anyone knew what he was doing."

You could not tell who had heard it or who had not. You could not tell anything about anybody any more. One of the pretty girls who had been talking with the naval officers was talking to her now, asking how she liked Washington and saying that her husband was in the South Pacific, and she supposed that Polly's husband was doing something or other, and then her whole face brightened.

"Oh," she said, "is he Tom Brett? Why, I never knew Tom had a wife."

"Oh, you know him, do you?" Polly asked.

"Know him?" she answered, and she laughed. "Why, everyone knows Tom. He really gets around."

"Yes," Polly said, "Tom never stays anywhere long."

They had to speak loudly to compete with all the voices. She was a bright little thing, younger than Polly, a naval officer's wife living in Washington, and Polly thought from the girl's sudden, almost avid, interest that she must know something about Tom's activities. Polly smiled her coolest smile.

"It's all so confidential here, isn't it?" she said. "No one really knows what anyone is doing. Even Tom can't tell me everything."

The girl's glance wavered slightly.

"Of course, he can't," she said quickly, "and you mustn't ask. I never ask what Charlie does."

Polly looked at her serenely. The words had come too quickly, too warmly; without a doubt she knew who it was that Tom was seeing.

"I know," Polly said. "It's a man's war, isn't it? Now, I wouldn't dream of asking Tom what the directive is that he's working on today in Georgetown." Polly smiled at her again very brightly.

She thought that she had done it rather well, and it would have been stupid to have gone further with it. "That lieutenant commander," she went on, "who was here with the medical captain, Norman Bell. Do you know him?"

Those Navy wives always knew everyone in the Navy.

"Oh," the girl said, and she looked relieved that they were talking about something else. "Poor Norman."

"What happened to poor Norman?" Polly asked.

"Poor Norman was on the —" The girl stopped. "I'm not supposed to know. It isn't out yet."

"Did the *It-Isn't-Out-Yet* go down?" Polly asked.

"Well, I'm not supposed to know," the girl answered, "but poor Norman was in the water three days."

"Well, he said something very sensible," Polly told her. "He said it doesn't matter whom you married before the war. Everything before the war is out." She hoped it would get back to Georgetown.

Everything that had been a constant quantity was lost. All those long-term plans and solid friendships, all the things that she had been meaning to do when the war was over and when life became less hectic, the places she wanted to see, that course in Spanish conversation that she was going to take and that Columbia Extension course on Russia, the new border she was going to plant in the garden at Pyefield, the new window seats for Tom's study — she could not think why they had ever interested her. It was like a poem she had once read on termites boring into sills and rafters. Externally everything had looked strong and square, and then suddenly the whole house collapsed in dust. She had never thought of human relationships as so fragile or so susceptible.

"It's the war," she was saying to herself, "this damned war."

She had plenty of nothing. She remembered that song in *Porgy and Bess*. She could see herself in the theater in New York with Tom. They had invited twelve for dinner, a number which Tom had never liked because it was too large for general conversation, but she had told Tom that they could pay off more people that way, and besides, they were going to the theater. She recalled, when they had asked the Tasmins, that Tom had said why the Tasmins, and she had said they hadn't done anything about the Tasmins for two years. She had not sat next to Bob Tasmin at dinner or the theater, and she had hardly said a word to Mildred, but still they had asked them, and it was a great weight off her mind. An operetta was just the sort of thing Bob Tasmin liked best. She remembered the words of the song and all the colored cast on the stage: "I've got plenty of nothing, and nothing's plenty for me."

She had plenty of nothing, plenty of complete nothing. It did no good to tell herself that other people must be going through what she was, or that lots of men got mixed up with what was known as "some other woman." There was only one thing of which she was sure. She was not going to stand it much longer, pretending she didn't know. If it was dished out to her, she could take it; and she was not going around talking about it — even when it came out she was not going to talk about it — but she would certainly like to see who it was in Georgetown. She would like to see what that little number had that she hadn't.

It must have been something like drowning, or at least what they always said about people drowning. Her mind was all cluttered with extraneous details — how Tom had looked when she had first seen him, what they had said to each other. It was not her fault — she had always done everything for him. She had bet everything on him. She had followed all his interests. She had wanted something intelligent, civilized and gracious, something that Tom could give her that was not in the least like her home, and she had tried, dear God, how she had tried. She had tried to do it all without ostentation. The thing to do was to skip it and try not to think about it. They had once had a perfectly swell time, and it wasn't money. She would have done all the housework if he had wanted. He need never say that she had ever pushed him into anything either, and yet he probably would say it. She had always seen that he was not tied down.

He was the one who had not wanted children and now perhaps if there had been children, if they had been more like other people — but he was the one who had not wanted them. They were always going to have them some day when everything was set. At least, she would have had something now, and it was not too late at thirty-four, but then it was too late. The thing to do was not to think about it.

That afternoon when Tom brought some men up from the office and a lot of their other friends came up, she could almost believe that he had really been working on a directive. They were Mr. and Mrs. Brett again, entertaining a few friends, each helping the other to make general, intelligent conversation. They were talking about books and plays, *Guadalcanal Diary, A Bell for Adano, Thirty Seconds over Tokyo, The Doughgirls, The Voice of the Turtle,* and Tom was telling something he had heard about the Battle of the Bulge. Most of their guests were prewar friends — Tom's writing crowd, Polly had always labeled them — newspaper men, critics, editors and executives from publishing companies; and mingled with them were instructors and professors from Tom's teaching days. They had been swept from all sorts of peacetime pursuits into the O.W.I. or the State Department or psychological warfare or the W.P.B. Once they had all been blatant individualists, but now the war had conditioned them as it had conditioned Tom. Now they were all working on identical streamlined ideas. They all held the same beliefs about France and Russia. They were all in accord on the dismemberment of Germany, and they all had the same feeling that the public must not be told too much, that the public might be upset if it knew as much as they did. They all seemed to drink more than they used to, and they gave Polly one curious impression — that they were all a little afraid of each other.

Still everything had been alive that afternoon over cocktails. She and Tom had always been able to have interesting people around, and they were both good at making them talk. She and Tom were a part of everything again, Mr. and Mrs. Brett who knew everyone. It was only when the last of them had gone, and it must have been around seven o'clock, that everything seemed dead.

The tables were covered with empty glasses, and the ash trays were heaped with smoldering cigarettes. The air was stale and smoky, but when the window was opened the room was chilly.

"Well," Tom said. "That was quite a party."

He was making another of his non-stop tours about the room with his hands in his pockets. Polly shrugged her shoulders. She wished that someone would come and clean away the glasses and tidy the place up. She wanted to do it herself, but there was no time. She only hoped that someone would do it later while they were out at dinner.

"Yes," she said, "I suppose so."

"You suppose so," Tom said. "You're always wanting to see some of our old friends, and I got them all around, didn't I? I had to telephone my head off to get them, and then you just say you *suppose* it was quite a party."

"Yes," Polly answered, "that's what I said — I suppose."

"All right," Tom said. "Don't say I didn't do the best I could. It isn't everyone who could get that crowd all in a room at once. They're all busy, they're all overworked. It's quite a tribute to you and me that any of them came."

"I suppose so," Polly said, "but none of them said anything — anything new, anything different, I mean. No one seems to say anything any more."

Tom was still wandering about the room, touching things, picking up matches and putting them down again. He never could keep his fingers still when he was in a certain mood.

"Except you, baby," he said. "You say plenty."

"Did you have a nice time in Georgetown?" Polly asked.

Tom stopped walking.

"Listen, Poll," he said. "I wish you'd try to get it through your head that there's a war on. Nobody's having a good time. Everybody's run ragged. I'm doing the best I can, Poll, but there's a war on."

"All right," Polly said, "I guess you're right. No one has a good time when there's a war on."

"Now we're getting somewhere," Tom said. "That's just the point I'm trying to make."

"What point?" Polly asked.

It did no good to talk. She was growing impertinent and disagreeable again.

"Now you come down here," Tom said, "just all of a sudden out of the blue, and you expect to be specially entertained. It isn't fair, Poll, and God knows, I'm doing the best I can. I've set aside this whole afternoon and evening. I got everybody around" — Tom waved at the empty glasses — "but you can't expect people to be balls of fire. They haven't got time to try. They all want to relax, they're tired. Look at me, I'm tired."

"Then why don't you relax too?" Polly said. "I wish you'd sit down."

Tom sighed. He did look very tired.

"There isn't time," he said. "We've got to go out to that damn dinner."

"If you're too tired to go, I'll call up," Polly said. "We don't have to go."

She had often said the same thing before, and she knew what he would answer.

"No, no," he said. "We can't do that. Besides, you'll like it, Poll. It's a good idea for you to go out and I'm not complaining at all. I want you to be amused."

"Do you?" Polly asked.

"Of course I do," Tom said. "I know this isn't fun for you with everything you've been going through. I'm only saying I'm trying to do the best I can, but please don't expect too much. What time is dinner?"

"At eight," Polly said.

Tom was brisk and efficient.

"Well, I'd better start moving and getting out my clothes," he said, and he started moving toward the bedroom. "There aren't many taxis, and they don't like it around here when you're late."

Just when he reached the bedroom door, just as he was taking off his coat, she called to him.

"Tom."

He turned around, holding his wrinkled gray coat in one hand.

"Listen, Poll," he said. "We've got to get moving. We haven't any time to talk."

"Do you really think I expect too much?" she asked.

"Now, listen, Poll," he said; his voice was almost pleading. "All women expect too much of men these days, but let's not get personal. We've got to get out of here. I just said *all* women, not you, all women."

"I don't want to be all women," Polly said.

"I know you don't," Tom answered, "but you can't help it sometimes. You can break your neck trying, but you can't always be an individual."

"I know," Polly said. "No one seems to be an individual any more."

"Listen, Poll," Tom said, "let's not go off the deep end with long, long thoughts. It's late."

"Tom," she said, but he was in the bedroom. She could hear him rustling through his shirts in the suitcase.

"Where's my dinner coat?" he called.

"It's hanging in the closet," she called back. "I had it pressed. Tom."

"Yes," he called back. "Here it is. My God, they took off the suspenders. Where are the suspenders?"

It was undignified, farcical. They were in a hurry and she had unbuckled her gold belt. She was twining her arms behind her head, reaching for the zipper on her dress. They were in a hurry and she would have to find his suspenders. He would have to look well, and he usually did in evening clothes. It was no time to bring up anything new because they were in a hurry, but still she brought it up.

"Tom," she called. "Just when you left this morning someone called you up."

"All right," he called back. "Who was it?"

"She didn't say. When I told her who I was, she hung up."

"Oh," Tom said. "Oh, yes. That. Listen, Poll, won't you help me? I've got to find my suspenders."

He was opening and shutting bureau drawers and slamming the doors of closets. His suitcase was open, and his shirts and socks were on the floor. If he kept on, he would lose his studs and tie looking for those suspenders.

"All right," he said. "If I can't find the damn things, I can't go. Aren't you going to help me, Poll?"

"Stand still," she said. "Don't get into everything."

The suspenders were just where she thought they were, hanging on a hook in the closet.

"My God," Tom said. "I looked in there." He snatched them from her and picked up his trousers.

"Tom," she said.

"Listen, Poll," he said, "we've got to hurry. They'll have ambassadors."

They did have to hurry, and the zipper in her black velvet dress was apt to stick.

"Have you got your black pearl studs, Tom?" she asked.

"I can't wear those," Tom said. "Everybody looks at them."

"But I gave them to you," Polly said.

"Yes," Tom said, "but I don't want everybody looking at pearl studs. Don't you know there's a war on, Poll?"

Tom jerked up the collar of his tweed overcoat and pulled down the brim of his felt hat as they waited for a taxicab. He had not worn his pearl studs, and she wished that she had not brought her mink coat. She saw him looking at it and then he laughed.

"What are you laughing at?" she asked.

"Have you heard," he said, "that if this war goes on another year there won't be a live mink left in the world?"

"You ought to write those gems down," Polly said, "so you won't forget them when you start on your autobiography." But Tom had taken her arm. He had seen a taxi. He was always very good about taxicabs.

"Taxi," he was calling. "Connecticut Avenue. Come on, Poll, let's go."

263

XX

It's So Easy to Exaggerate

ONE SPRING when Tom was recovering from the flu, he and Polly had been at Sea Island in Georgia, and there they had met the Arthur Bryant Smedleys, their hosts for dinner that evening. The Smedleys prided themselves on knowing everyone worth while, and though it was several years before the war, Tom was already worth knowing. His book on *The Communists of Brook Farm* had just been published.

It was the period when composers were writing symphonies about Puritans and covered wagons and prairies, and all those artists began cropping up — the Grant Woods, the Bentons, and the Burchfields, with their red barns, their swayback mules and their small-town streets. It was very exciting to discover that a basic sort of American culture had been developing right under everyone's nose with hardly anyone's having recognized it. The only drawback was that so many ingenious people had discovered it simultaneously. It seemed to Polly that book after book began appearing on Herman Melville, Thoreau, the Alcotts and Walt Whitman. Later they were going to find out that Henry James knew how to write rather well too, and in time it would doubtless be discovered that William Dean Howells, though stuffy, had in the back of his head certain acceptable social ideas. At any rate, Tom had finally done something about the underlying forces behind American life and thought.

Polly had to admit that the book was rough in places, and that Tom had involved himself in a good many difficult and unprovable abstractions, but still it was a book. It was a great relief to her to have it appear, because for years everyone had been asking when Tom was ever going to write that book he was always talking about. Tom often said later that he never should have published the damn thing, that she had pushed him into it, and that he had made a fool of himself. Nevertheless, it had been seriously discussed, and she had all the reviews pasted in one of her scrapbooks. She used to say that it was almost as if she and Tom had had a baby, and Tom had told her that she acted just that way. She had told him that it was better to write something than nothing, and she had given a publication party in New York without telling Tom until the last moment, because she knew Tom.

When he came down with the flu, he was not so difficult as he generally was when he was sick. He had only objected mildly when she suggested that they go to that hotel at Sea Island. As always, he had said that he loathed those places filled with rich old men with heart trouble and arthritis, trying to play golf, or bridge or bingo, and with pampered little brats imported for their Easter vacations. He had said, as always, that she had better give up trying to make him into a gigolo; but once he was there, as always, he got used to it quickly and began complaining about the service. He even bought some yellow neckties, a canary-colored sweater and a pair of doeskin trousers at the store in the hotel. Whenever she could get him to one of those places, he always got used to it.

That was where they met the Smedleys — down from Washington for a little sun — and Mrs. Smedley had asked Tom if he was really the Mr. Brett who had written that intriguing book. The next day they found out who Polly's father was, and finally they all became great friends although the Smedleys were a good many years older, particularly Mr. Smedley. Tom used to say that he was sorry for that poor old guy married to that rich wife. He said that poor old guy was a preview of himself ten years hence, completely dominated, completely beaten down, and he used to tell Polly she could get a lot of good ideas from Mrs. Smedley — but this was all in fun and the Smedleys were pleasant company.

They were violently New Deal, and they could explain why the Roosevelt revolution had saved us from a much worse one, and they knew everyone, literally everyone in Washington. When they heard that Tom was there quite often, and that he was a New Dealer too, they wanted Tom and Polly to come for dinner the very next time they were in town. A few days later Mrs. Smedley asked Polly to call her "Irene," and Tom began calling Mr. Smedley "Arthur," though Tom said it was inappropriate and gave him pains in his knee joints. The Smedleys, Tom said, typified a group that lived in Washington for the sole purpose of knowing everybody.

The Smedley house off Connecticut Avenue, built of marble and granite, had a conservatory and a *porte-cochère* and magnolia trees on the lawn. Everyone went there to dinner, the Cabinet and the Supreme Court, all the diplomatic corps that mattered — particularly the British and now lately the Russians — and even outstanding legislators. Mrs. Smedley used to say that there was no place like Washington, and that everyone came there eventually. Of course, you had to be constantly on the alert, you had to know the latest news and all the latest little jealousies, and Mrs. Smedley used to say that she felt like a Rip Van Winkle, white from worrying about protocol and all the little secrets that everyone had told her. Once one of those Polish ministers, or was it someone from one of the Cabinets, had told her that she was the little grandmother of Washington. This had pleased Irene Smedley very much.

She wished everyone could know Washington as she did. She had come there as a girl, just married to Arthur, whom she had met when she was traveling with Papa on the Continent. Arthur had been Third Secretary to the Embassy in Rome. It had been love at first sight and Arthur had proposed to her in the Borghese gardens, and it was just as well he had because they should not have been walking there without a chaperon. Then when Papa had not wanted her to live indefinitely in Europe, Arthur was given home duty at the Department, and when Arthur was through with the Department, they stayed right on in Washington. First they had lived near Lafayette Square, and then when poor Papa had died, they had built the house off Connecticut Avenue so that they could have a *pied à terre* large enough to turn around in.

266

Sometimes Tom would speculate on the love life of the Smedleys, and just what Old Man Smedley had ever done after he had come back to Washington. He also wondered how they could keep right on giving those dinners. The story was that Irene Smedley was nobody's fool. She had put her money into tax-exempt securities long ago, and that, some people said, was why she was for the New Deal — because she could view it all from the right perspective and without emotion. But then, people were always saying such unkind things about everybody and there was nothing like a dinner at the Smedleys'.

The taxicab smelled of stale cigar smoke, and Polly thought the driver might have taken time to sweep out the cigarette butts on the floor.

"Can't you open a window, Tom?" she asked.

"It makes a draft," Tom said. "We like it warm in here, don't we, son?"

"Yes, sir," the taxi driver said. "This bus really has a good heater."

"We're going to the Smedleys', son," Tom said, "the Arthur Bryant Smedleys. Do you know where?"

Yes, sir, the tax driver knew where.

"You see," Tom said, "everybody knows the Smedleys."

Polly wished Tom would not always try to be a Great Commoner.

"Tom," she said, "everyone will have white ties."

"No they won't," Tom said. "Don't you know there's a war on?"

"I don't have to remember," Polly said, "because you know."

"All right," Tom said, "dish it out and I can take it, Poll."

"Then don't keep reminding me," Polly said, "period. Did you do what I asked you?"

"Probably not," Tom said. "What was it?"

"Did you find out where Bob Tasmin is?"

"Not yet," he answered. "Maybe I'll see someone tonight."

Neither of them spoke for a while. The streets and the sidewalks around Dupont Circle were dark and shining from the rain. The houses there looked pretentious and impractical. They spoke mutely of an expansive past when no one gave much thought to inequities. The glowing windows and the lights by the *porte-cochère* of the Smedley house made the leaves of the big magnolia trees shine defiantly. There was a war on, but the Smedleys were seeing it through. The taxi was in a line of limousines moving toward the front door. Tom was craning his neck to read the diplomatic plates in front of them. Tom always liked big parties once he got to them.

"I hope your face is on straight," he said. "Don't keep me waiting in the hall." It was what Tom always said before any large gathering.

They had gone to a good many dinners with a semiofficial tinge during the war because Tom had been called down to Washington for consultation more and more, and lately on high levels. He had been engaged in so many behind-the-scenes improvisations that no one knew just where he fitted in the picture, and he said sometimes that he did not know himself — but it gave him a position. He was used to those dinners, but nevertheless, he was always fidgety. He said if Polly kept him waiting too long with the butlers and coats and hats, people always began to think he was a detective.

"Now, I'm doing this for you," Tom said. "You like rat races. I don't. Now, don't keep me standing in that hall."

The hall had a black and white marble floor, and a baroque marble staircase, the ladies' coatroom to the left, the gentlemen's to the right. From the preparations Polly decided that there would be about twenty-four for dinner. Several men were standing beside a table which held a little silver bowl filled with envelopes, waiting just as Tom would wait, and there were several other men in the hall who did not look like guests.

In the dressing room an elderly lady in sequins was staring at herself in the mirror, and a faded blond lady was having trouble with her shoulder straps. No one spoke except the blond lady who asked with a British accent for a pin. There was nothing, Polly thought, as forbidding as a dressing room before one of those dinners, and at the same time no place as intimately revealing.

"Thank you so much," the blond lady said to the maid, "a little higher on the shoulder. There, it does keep slipping."

Polly sat down at the dressing table and took out her little gold

268

box with her compact and lipstick. She was going to look as well as possible whether Tom had to wait or not. The lipstick helped and all her hair needed was a touch here and there. She looked very well considering everything. She never needed jewelry with that black velvet. Jewelry took away the effect of her reddish-blond hair and spoiled an impression of simplicity that she particularly liked to create. She might not have learned much since she had married Tom, but she had learned what she could wear.

Tom was fidgeting by the staircase, holding his little card.

"It's nice of you to remember to come out of there," he said, and they walked together up the marble stairs.

"Who's here?" she whispered.

"British, Free French, and brass," Tom said, "and the Vice President."

"Oh," Polly said. "Is he here?"

"He was right here when you came in," Tom said. "The one with glasses. He called me Tom, and then there's a Chinese. His wife is in one of those gowns."

"What did he call you?" Polly whispered.

"You don't have to whisper," Tom said. "This isn't a wake."

He looked very neat except for his tie.

"Tom, your tie is crooked," she said. "Who did you draw for dinner?"

"A lady," Tom said. "It says she's a lady. Lady Stagness."

"Oh," Polly whispered, "why that's —"

"Yes," Tom said, "that's who she is. For God's sake, don't whisper."

Then the man at the door was saying "Mr. and Mrs. Brett." Irene Smedley looked ecstatic as she always did, and Mr. Smedley's white mustache was carefully waxed.

"Oh, darling," Mrs. Smedley said. "How perfect."

Polly hoped Mrs. Smedley meant that she looked perfect.

"And there's your more and more essential husband," Mrs. Smedley said.

"Is he essential?" Polly asked. "I wouldn't know."

"I know what he's doing if you don't," Mrs. Smedley said.

"Well, I'm dying to hear," Polly said. "I only know that he's doing most of it in Georgetown."

Mrs. Smedley's smile was unchanged, but her eyes had narrowed as their glances met. Irene Smedley did not have to speak to make it very clear that she knew all about Georgetown, too.

"It used to be such a poky little place, didn't it?" she said, "but they're making over all the old houses now. You can't rent anything there for love or money."

Tom was talking to Mr. Smedley, and it was time for them to move on, to mingle with the others who filled the large room, to take a glass from the waiters, to talk, to laugh.

"I didn't know about money," Polly said, "but I always thought that love . . ." She let it go at that. At any rate, she knew where to find out about Georgetown. She was going to find out before they left, and she would rather hear it from Irene Smedley than from most people.

"I'm afraid I'm a little out of touch with things here," she added.

"Darling," Mrs. Smedley answered, "one always is, unless one stays here all the time like me — but I haven't told you who's taking you in to dinner."

"Who?" Polly asked.

"Dr. Straight. You know who Dr. Straight is, darling, don't you? You'll be fascinated by him. He's the gray-haired man by the fireplace talking to the admiral and the Vice President."

"Oh, yes," Polly said. "I see him."

"It's perfectly all right to ask him about Russia, if you don't ask him what he was doing there. Of course, you know everybody, and there's another friend of yours — Mildred Tasmin. Bob Tasmin's away, you know. He vanished all of a sudden, the way they do . . . and now, Arthur. Tell Polly our secret, Arthur."

Mr. Smedley held her hand and patted it.

"We're having roast beef for dinner," he said, "from our own steer off the farm. So don't worry about the points."

"Come on, Poll," Tom said. "Poll always stops and talks."

It was a top-drawer dinner, and everyone there had done something or was something. The long room was lighted by sconces and chandeliers, and its heavy chairs and tables and the French land-scapes on the walls, and the tapestries near the Italian marble fire-place, made a good background for the women's gowns and the American and British uniforms. It all was like a steel engraving of a President's reception, of Franklin at the French court, one of those engravings that had a key under it telling all the names. If people there would only speak you could have found out how long the war would last, about Yalta, what would happen in the Pacific next, whether the President was well or ill, but instead they would discuss noncontroversial subjects; they would talk pleasantly and easily, they would move in to dinner according to precedence, they would move out and talk again, and then they would all leave to-gether, following the most distinguished guest.

Yet, no matter how they dissembled, there was sometimes a com-mon mood at those dinners of preoccupation which could not be entirely hidden. Faces told whether things were going well or not. It was Sunday, but the guards would still be patrolling the White House grounds. The Pentagon Building across the river, the State Department, the guarded buildings along Constitution Avenue, would still be open. It was Sunday, but the teletypes would be tap-ping, and clerical forces would be producing Top Secret dispatches, and at any moment someone, the florid-faced admiral sipping his sherry, or the tall, elderly general standing by the fireplace, might receive a message and then make a polite excuse and leave. They had to fold away and hide all their anxieties, and she could not see why they wanted to appear at those dinners at all unless it were to prove that everything was going well, or from some compelling desire to escape into artificial normality.

"I can never understand about women and thermostats," the tall general was saying. "They always turn them up to eighty-five."

"But there's no use arguing with them," the admiral said.

"No use at all," the general answered, "but Dr. Straight knows all about these mechanical gadgets. Where should you set a thermo-stat for an oil burner, Dr. Straight, to get the maximum efficiency?"

"It all depends upon the number of coupons you have," said Dr. Straight.

Everyone laughed in a gentle, measured way, and the general looked thoughtful. He may have been thinking that he had said too much. He had intimated that Dr. Straight was not a doctor of medicine, but one of those scientists, and that could place him somewhere in the Office of Research and Development where they were inventing secret weapons. Since the general had revealed that Dr. Straight knew all about oil burners it might very well mean that the doctor was working on flame throwers. You could put those bits of conversation together and guess.

"How did you think George looked yesterday?" the admiral asked.

"His knee still hurts him," the general said.

"He ought to bake it regularly," the admiral said. "He could have an infra-red lamp up there."

"George never does take care of himself," the general said.

You could not be sure who George was, but you could guess. It might very well be General Marshall. That was the way stories and rumors started. General George Marshall was having trouble with his knee. General Marshall was suffering from arthritis. General Marshall was not well. They had to be very careful of everything they said, but still they had to say something. Dr. Straight had turned toward her. He looked like a retired professor from a small town, and perhaps he had been before he had been called to Washington.

"I hope you're Mrs. Brett," he said.

"I'm glad you hope so, because I am," she told him.

"I was afraid you wouldn't be," Dr. Straight said. "I'm lucky. I'm taking you in to dinner."

"Aren't you usually lucky?" Polly asked.

"Very seldom with women," Dr. Straight said. "I don't understand women."

"Well," Polly said, "I can tell you all about them. All they want is attention, Doctor. They don't want to be understood."

She thought of Bob Tasmin again. He had always tried to understand her.

The men were already searching for their dinner partners, and the doors to the dining room were open. The general had given Mildred Tasmin his arm. She was dressed in green, and she looked tall and beautiful as she always did, never a fold out of place, just enough wave in her smooth brown hair. She seemed very tranquil and Polly remembered what everyone said about the Tasmins. What a happy couple! She wondered whether they had invariably been happy and if so, why, and whether Bob had tried to understand Mildred. Mildred showed no sign of anxiety as she walked with the general to the dining room, but then, there was no reason why she should have heard Milton Ouerbach's broadcast.

"Of course, I know your husband," Dr. Straight was saying.

"I suppose so," Polly said. "Everyone knows Tom."

"I saw quite a little of him about a month ago. They lent him to us."

"I hope you turned him back in good condition," Polly said.

"We wouldn't have dared not to," Dr. Straight said, "not with his secretary. Of course, you know the one I mean."

"Oh, yes," Polly said, "of course."

"I don't know why they never give me pretty secretaries," Dr. Straight said. "Now that girl of Tom's. Just tell him any time he doesn't want her, I do."

"You mean the one who lives in Georgetown?"

"That's the one," Dr. Straight said. "That's an awfully pretty house she has in Georgetown."

"It's wonderful what they've done with those old houses lately, isn't it?" Polly said, and then she took his arm. They were moving toward the dining room. She saw Tom ahead of them. He was taking in the bony, faded blond lady. It would be Lady Stagness.

"When the history of this war comes to be written," Dr. Straight said, "there ought to be a chapter on confidential secretaries. They're amazing women. They get to know everything about you. They can't help it."

It was a beautiful dinner table, Sèvres place plates, Chinese Chippendale chairs and Georgian silver. Dr. Straight had put on a pair of horn-rimmed spectacles, and he was looking for their place cards.

"Oh, here we are," he said.

She had been given a very good place between Dr. Straight and the general.

"It's strange how you move from group to group here, isn't it?" she said. "Particularly if you're not down here all the time. We live in New York, but of course Tom is always coming back and forth. . . . I've seen so many people this week end. Now, last night there were some flyers from Burma, and this noon there was industry and the W.P.B., and this afternoon there was the O.W.I. and then tonight there's this. It's hard to fit them all together, and don't tell me there's a war on."

"But they all do fit," the doctor said. "Not very well, but they fit."

"Now this noon," Polly said, "a boy I used to know said that nothing that happened before this war matters any more."

"Anyone who stays in this show long enough forgets," Dr. Straight said. "I don't know what home is like. My boy's in the Army, but I can't remember what he looks like. All I can remember is my room in the Wardman Park."

"It's because there isn't anything to hold on to," Polly said.

"My dear," the doctor said, "I'll tell you something. The same thing is going on in London and Paris and Moscow, and God help them in Berlin. You mustn't let it upset you. Now, even Mr. Stalin doesn't know what's going on. He thinks he does, but he doesn't. Don't let it upset you."

"It doesn't," Polly said. "But how is it going to end? How are we going to live afterwards?"

"We'll live," the doctor said. "If you're unhappy, just think of everyone else."

"What makes you think I'm unhappy?"

"Because everybody is," the doctor said. "How can anyone be happy? I wouldn't try if I were you."

"I'm not trying."

"I'm afraid you are," Dr. Straight said. "It's attractive, but I wouldn't try too hard."

It was absurd to suspect something behind what everyone was saying. She was losing all sense of proportion. She was talking to a stranger, and yet she believed he was implying something.

"How do you know I'm trying?" she asked.

"That shows you are," the doctor said.

"Why?" she asked.

"Because you asked me."

"You scientists are awfully quick, aren't you?" she said.

"Only in a specialized way," he said. "By this time everyone's life is twisted somehow. Even Hitler's. Now there's someone who tried too hard to be happy. I saw him try once until half-past five in the morning."

But the table was turning, inexorably. The general was smiling at her, and the doctor had turned away.

"Dr. Straight says that Hitler tries to be happy," Polly said.

"Well, if Straight says so, it must be true," the general said, "but if he wants to be happy in the next few months, he'd better try damned hard." Then the general looked uneasy, as though he had said too much. "But I don't have to try to be happy, not tonight, sitting between the two prettiest girls in the room."

"I used to know Mildred Tasmin's husband," Polly said. "Do you know him?"

"No, I don't," the general said, "but I know he's a very lucky man. I know your husband, though, Mrs. Brett."

"It's wonderful," Polly said, "how everybody knows Tom."

"We had quite a time once," the general said, "at a meeting with O.W.I. and Public Relations, when General Clark said he'd lost his pants in North Africa. The idea seemed to be that Clark never should have said that — it was undignified. Mothers might not like their boys led by generals saying things like that."

"I hope my husband made it all right," Polly said.

It seemed to her that everyone knew more about Tom than she did. He was living a vivid, fascinating life while she sat wondering what he was doing. She had no chance to be interesting to Tom against such competition. It would have been different if she had been living in Washington, and often in the last few years she had suggested moving down, but Tom would never hear of it. He always said that his work in Washington might close down at any time, and he wanted her in New York.

"It was out of my line," the general said. "I just happened to be called in. We had to build up Clark."

"Do they build you up, too?" Polly asked.

"My dear," he said — she always liked it when they called her "my dear" — "there's a demand for heroes now. We have to do the best we can. It would be better if they had given a course in it at the War College."

Then he began talking about dogs. It seemed that the general, who lived at Fort Myer, had a terrier he had found somewhere over in England (and he hoped Polly would not tell anyone that he had brought the terrier back in the plane) and that the terrier's name was Ike. He had named him that without giving a thought to Eisenhower . . .

The chairs were being pushed back. The men were going to smoke in the library, and the women moved into the long room.

"Hello, Brett," she heard the general saying. "I didn't know your wife liked dogs." And she heard Tom laugh.

"Poll?" she heard Tom saying. "Did Poll tell you she liked dogs?"

Then Mildred Tasmin called to her. . . .

"Well, Polly Brett! I can't remember when I saw you last. It seems like ages."

It was easily as long ago as that. Suddenly Mildred looked kinder than anyone in the room and when Polly thought of the tragedy that might be hanging over Mildred she was able for the first time that day to forget about herself.

"I remember now," Mildred Tasmin was saying. "It was when we went to *Porgy and Bess*. I wish you'd come to see us, Polly. We have an apartment on Scott Circle."

"I'd love to come," Polly said.

"You can see Neddie," Mildred said. "Neddie goes to a school in Georgetown."

"Georgetown?" Polly repeated after her. "Is there a school in Georgetown?"

"They have everything in Georgetown," Mildred said. "Do come tomorrow afternoon. I wish Bob were here."

"I wish he were too," Polly said. "I just heard he's away."

It was obvious that Mildred could have had no news to disturb her.

"Yes," Mildred said. "He went about a month ago into the blue the way he does sometimes. He said it was perfectly safe because he was on a Staff. They say his party should be back any time now, and Bob's always on time, isn't he?"

"Yes," Polly said, "he always is."

"Couldn't you come for tea tomorrow," Mildred asked, "sometime around five o'clock? Just you and me. We'll have so much to talk about. Polly, I was so sorry — "

She could not think for a second why Mildred should be sorry.

"About your father, dear. Bob was always so fond of him."

"He was talking about Bob," Polly said, "one of the last days I saw him."

The coffee and liqueurs were coming in, and everyone was sitting down. They each took a small coffee cup of Japanese lacquer, though Mrs. Smedley said she called it "Chinese" lacquer now, and a spoonful of granulated sugar because lump sugar was so hard to find. When Mildred sat down with her little cup, she had an exasperating composure. If Bob had been *her* husband, Polly would at least have realized that any trip to the Pacific was dangerous. If any husband of hers had given her any such sense of fulfillment, she would at least have worried about him. There was something almost indecent in that serenity of Mildred Tasmin's. Without intending it, women in the midst of a successful marriage always conveyed a sort of rebuke to other people, implying that if they could do it why couldn't everyone else. Besides, contentment made women so blind. Polly wondered how much Bob Tasmin had ever told Mildred about her. Admitted that Mildred was really just the right person for Bob, and that Polly was really very glad of it, still it was a little ludicrous that Mildred so completely ignored the past.

"You were just the right person for Bob," Polly said.

It was even irritating to have Mildred tacitly admit it.

"And you were just the right person for Tom," Mildred said. "It's nice when things work out."

There was no insinuation, nothing between the lines. Contented women were always so colorless.

"It must be more comfortable being married to Bob," Polly said. "I mean Bob must always get home when he says he will and keep the checkbooks balanced, and pack things the right way in the automobile. Now Tom, well, Tom . . ."

She stopped. She was not going to discuss Tom, and Mildred laughed.

"You can't ever have a dull moment with Tom."

"That's what people always say," Polly answered, and she laughed too. "It's trying, but never dull."

"Of course, Bob and I are both on the dull side," Mildred said. "Perhaps that's why we get on. Bob's awfully easy to live with."

"It's nice to think of a marriage being easy," Polly said.

"I know," Mildred answered. "When I read all those books and marriage manuals, I feel guilty sometimes, as though Bob and I were missing something. We never have those troubles you read about, not even as many as Mr. and Mrs. have in the Sunday paper."

"What paper is that?" Polly asked.

"You know, in the *Tribune*," Mildred said.

"Oh," Polly answered. "I haven't seen the *Tribune* for ages."

"Bob doesn't like the *Post* or *PM*," Mildred said. "Sometimes I wonder whether there's anything wrong with us."

"I wouldn't let it bother you too much, dear," Polly answered, "not enough to let it keep you awake."

Mildred put down her coffee cup on a little table. She looked like a Sargent portrait. The men were coming back, and it was time for them to move away from each other as women should when the men appeared.

"If you haven't got a car," Mildred said, "I can drive you home."

"Oh, no thanks," Polly told her. "The Smedleys want us to stay for a few minutes afterwards."

"Irene Smedley's such a dear, isn't she?" Mildred said. "It was so sweet of her to ask me here without Bob."

It was not strictly true that the Smedleys had asked them to stay

278

afterwards, but Polly was going to find out about Georgetown before she went home that night.

Of course, Irene Smedley said, she would never have dreamed of saying a word if Polly had not asked her, but she loved Polly. She always had. Polly was almost like her daughter. She would never have dreamed of saying a word, and perhaps she should not now. She was very fond of Tom too, and everything of this sort was always grotesquely exaggerated. Yet at the same time, frankly, there was talk. So many men were at loose ends in Washington, so many men under strain. It probably meant nothing and Mrs. Smedley did not want to say anything.

"Go ahead," Polly said. "He's tired of me. Why don't you say it?"

But Mrs. Smedley did not want to say it. It was a time to be understanding and very patient, she said, and everything would turn out all right. If Polly were older, she would realize how often such things happened, and how many women had to bear them. Mrs. Smedley had seen the girl and she was a pretty little thing.

"You say you saw her?" Polly asked.

Irene Smedley had only seen her once across a room. You could never tell what it was that might attract a man. She was pretty with a trig sort of prettiness, and she had that high rating Civil Service look that all girls acquired after a few years of working for the government, particularly during the war. It was a look and a manner that must have come from having been thrown all the time with so many busy, intelligent men, and from having those men so dependent on them.

"You don't mind my being curious?" Polly said. "I can't help being."

"Of course not, dear," Irene answered. "I'm ever so glad that you've come to me."

They were sitting in the little room where Irene Smedley had her desk and her telephone and address books, and the *Social Register* and both the British and American *Who's Who* and *Burke's Peerage*. Tom and Mr. Smedley were having a highball in the library, and Polly could hear the footsteps of the servants in the dining room.

She asked Irene Smedley to be absolutely frank, but she was not sure Irene would be.

"But who is she?" Polly asked.

"My dear, I don't know who she is," Irene Smedley answered. "No one knows any more with everyone coming down here like air filling a vacuum."

"But everyone comes from some place originally," Polly said.

"Yes, but their antecedents leave them in the queerest way," Irene answered. "They develop a veneer after they've rattled around here for a year or two, particularly those 'government gals.'"

The word "gals" sounded like an artificial effort to make that conversation unspectacular.

"I think the Navy brought her in," Irene Smedley was saying, "Naval officers collect more different gals from different places than any other group. One of them, the dearest little commander, called the other day with a wife from Pago Pago."

"I suppose they travel more," Polly said.

"They have more varied tastes than the Army," Irene said. "Have you noticed they're a great deal more susceptible? Even the admiral tonight. The poor things are always away at sea."

"Let's not worry about the poor things," Polly said. "Please go on about *her*."

"I'm afraid I'm underlining it and making it more than it really is," Irene said. "It's so easy to exaggerate. And in the end, what happens? You'll hold it against me, and we won't be friends."

"Is she married?" Polly asked.

Irene Smedley sighed and arranged some papers on her desk. It was not late because those dinners always ended early, but it seemed late. It reminded Polly of what they used to say early in the war, "later than you think," "too little and too late."

"They say she was," Irene said. "He's off somewhere. Navy, I think."

"Do you know her name?" Polly asked.

"Why do you want to know, dear?"

Though Irene Smedley was older, there was no reason why she should be so diplomatic and so careful, and besides, Tom would be

280

growing fidgety in the library. He would be sure to ask what they were talking about if they stayed much longer.

"Because I want to see her," Polly said. "I'm not going to be in the dark when everyone —" Irene Smedley leaned forward and took her hand.

"Oh, dear," she said, "it isn't the thing to do, it simply isn't. Just let it pass." She took her hand away and sat looking at Polly. "Everything breaks so easily, dear."

Polly shook her head and clasped her vanity bag tightly on her lap.

"Then let it break," she said. "If you think . . ."

She stopped because she knew that she must not let herself go.

"It's so much better to be patient," Irene Smedley said, "so much better to try to understand. My dear, I could tell you — I know how it sounds — but you must give yourself time."

"How can I understand if I don't see her?" Polly asked. Though she wanted to be reasonable, she knew that she was being unattractive. "If you don't tell me, you know that I'll find out, Irene."

Irene told her. The name was James, she thought, Winifred James.

"What can you possibly say to her, dear," Irene asked, "that won't make a scene? If you love Tom — and you do love Tom, don't you? — it will be all right in the end. You mustn't let everything break, dear, just because momentarily he's lost his head."

"Damn his head," Polly said.

"Hush, dear," Irene said. "They're coming. Please see me tomorrow before you do anything. Please, tomorrow."

Polly could hear footsteps and Tom's voice.

"If we don't break it up, Poll will be in there all night," Tom was saying.

Polly glanced quickly at Irene Smedley, and Irene shook her head.

"Pierre will drive you back in the car," she said. "Now, Polly, please —"

There was no reason why anyone should think that she was going to do anything that was silly or extreme. Actually, she felt better than she had all day, completely cool and competent. Mr. Smedley was twisting his mustache, as men always do who have waxed mustaches. After all, no one knew the gal, as Irene called her, but if Tom was stepping out, he might at least have paid her the compliment of selecting someone who amounted to something.

"I hope we're not interrupting, dear," Mr. Smedley said. "Is the post-mortem nearly over?"

The word had a jarring sound. Tom was looking at her curiously, and she wondered whether her face showed anything.

"In case you don't know it," Tom said, "there's a war on. I've got to be at the office tomorrow at eight, Poll."

"Yes," Polly said, "there's a war on."

"What have you two been talking about?" Tom asked.

"Post-mortems, darling," Polly said. "You're sure it isn't too much to ask Pierre to drive us, Irene? Tom can run out and find a taxicab. He's wonderful with taxis now that there's a war on."

As they sat in the Smedleys' limousine, and goodness knows where the Smedleys got the gas to drive it unless they took it from the tractors on their farm, Tom did not appear to have the least suspicion that anything was wrong; he leaned back with his hat over his eyes. He was always making fun of limousines, but she knew no one who could make himself more comfortable once he got inside one. He pulled the monogrammed fur rug over his knees and yawned.

Polly sat grimly thinking of herself and Tom in terms of the stock characters in those sophisticated, triangular, drawing-room comedies, which were usually vehicles for an actress like Katharine Cornell. They were the plays that the critics called a refreshing breeze in a turgid Broadway season, plays in which the husband, talented and whimsical, would become foolishly enamored of Another Woman, and Katharine Cornell as the wife would view this aberration with sweet, tolerant, restrained amusement — merely the prank of a little boy. Those husbands, though very scintillating, were always little boys at heart, and the wives were invariably — adult.

In the second act the wife and the Other Woman would confront each other. In some sequences of adroit and laughable repartee, the wife would point out that she merely wanted to do what was best for Charles, and of course the Other Woman, a blind, selfish little thing, did not know what was best. Then Charles would see the tinsel and the sham, and in the third act Katharine Cornell would give him an aspirin, and the hallucination would be over. Polly wanted to be like Katharine Cornell, but she found it very hard to hold on to herself with Tom beside her dozing. It was a help to think that she and Tom were in a play. If you kept it like a play, it was much more adult, but still she could not help wondering how it had ever happened and what she had done to make it happen.

When a married person became involved with someone else, everyone always said that the marriage had not worked, and that it was both their faults equally, but when Polly tried to think over the ways in which she might have failed she found herself growing furiously angry, and she could not keep anything straight. Of course, he did not love her. That was what was clearest in her mind, and she was sure that she did not love him any longer, or almost sure. She wished that she did not keep hearing Mildred Tasmin's voice, so nicely modulated, one of those New York girls'-school voices.

Of course, Bob and I are on the dull side. . . . When I read all those books . . . I feel guilty sometimes, as though Bob and I were missing something. We never seem to have those troubles you read about . . . And once she used to feel just that way about Tom.

She would like to see Mildred Tasmin coping with this, because at least it would make her more human. She could not understand how Bob Tasmin stood her complacence, but if Bob had ever gone off the deep end, he would not have done it with his secretary. He would have known it was not good taste, because he was a gentleman, and Tom was not a gentleman. He wasn't anything at all. Once this had been a blessed relief, but still Tom could have done with some instincts along those lines.

"Tom," she said, and she nudged him with her elbow.

"What is it?" he asked. "Are we there?"

"Almost. Have you got something to give Pierre?"

Tom wriggled and began thrusting his hands in his pockets and pulled out a bill.

"Have you got a dollar?" he asked. "I've only got five dollars."

"No, I haven't," Polly said. "Give it to him."

"Good God," Tom said. "I'm not the Rockefeller Foundation."

Tom delivered his customary editorial on losing the respect of people if you gave them too much.

"Perhaps he doesn't respect you anyway," Polly said.

"Well, the Smedleys pay him, don't they?" Tom said. "Look at his neck. He's overweight. He ought to be in a defense job."

"Oh, be quiet," Polly said. "Don't try to run the world."

"I was quiet," Tom said. "Why did you wake me up to face a problem?"

"Darling," Polly said, "it's about time you faced something."

Certain aspects of the situation were almost amusing. She was going to make him face it as soon as she was ready and not before. The car had stopped in front of the marquee of the hotel and Tom was holding the five dollars in the secretive way you did when you tipped other people's chauffeurs. He was being gracious about it because he was a democrat and all men were brothers.

"Thanks ever so much, Pierre," he said. "I'm sorry we kept you up so late." And then Polly heard him mutter as they entered the revolving doors. "Damned old capon." Tom always hated chauffeurs.

The hotel was beginning to grow brisk and businesslike now that Sunday was nearly over. The lights looked brighter and vacuum cleaners were buzzing in the lobby making it clean for another wartime week. If only she and Tom had been going home, back among all their possessions, it would have been much easier, but instead they were returning to that modernistic sitting room which would still smell of alcohol, antiseptic and tobacco, and the thought of it made her almost ill. For a moment she thought of going to the desk and asking for a room of her own, but she pulled herself together.

"Good evening, Mr. Brett," the night clerk said. "It's nice to have

Mrs. Brett with us. Are you keeping the suite through tomorrow?"

Polly smiled her brightest smile.

"Yes, through tomorrow and the next day, I think," she said. "There's so much going on in Washington." When she glanced at Tom his face looked very blank.

At least someone had hoed out the sitting room. It was all as neat as though they had never been there, as impersonal as that tent in *The Rubáiyát* prepared for another guest. It was like a clean page in one of those New Year diaries which she used to buy when she was younger, in which she always grew tired of writing after January tenth.

"Don't you have to be home by tomorrow?" Tom asked her. "That's what you said."

"Why, darling," she answered. "You don't mind my staying for a while, do you? There's no real reason for me to get back."

She hung her mink coat in the closet because she did not want to look at him.

"But I thought you said — " she heard him saying. "I thought the lawyers needed you to sign those papers."

She did not want to look at him.

"You don't mind my staying, do you?" she asked again.

"Why, of course I don't," he said. "It's swell, Poll, but I'm all tied up next week."

"I thought you were planning to come home on Tuesday afternoon," she said. "That was your last plan."

"I know, but I'm all tied up, Poll," he said. "It's swell you're going to stay, but you mustn't feel hurt if I'm not around. You mustn't expect too much of me."

"I don't," she answered. "I don't expect anything at all. Just do whatever you were going to do."

It sounded rather well when she said it, and she turned quickly from the closet, but Tom was not aware of any hidden meaning. He was taking off his dinner coat. She did wish he would not always take his coat off the moment he came into the sitting room, and he would not have done it in New York.

"Well," Tom said. "Every day is like another down here, isn't it?

285

I don't know why you like it. Personalities, personalities. I've got to turn in. I've got to be down there at eight tomorrow. What did you think of Straight?"

"Who?" Polly asked.

"The one who took you in to dinner, Hugo Straight. He knows Hitler. It's funny how few people around here have ever talked to Hitler."

"Oh, yes, Dr. Straight," Polly answered. "He said he knew you, too. He was telling about your secretary."

"Oh," Tom said, "was he?"

It was interesting if you could keep your emotions out of it, and at the moment nothing that either of them said could alter what was surely going to happen. Polly was beyond any sensation of pain, and she could see herself and Tom almost as though she were a third person. She was sitting calmly in the corner of the sofa, very straight with her hands in her lap, as she had been taught to sit at Heatherbloom Hall by Miss Elkins the posture teacher, and Tom had laid his dinner coat on the other sofa, first turning up the sleeves as one was taught to fold a coat in those diagrams from Brooks Brothers. She wondered why he was doing it instead of putting it back on a hanger, and she could hear her own voice, sounding like a stranger's. The things they were saying were like careful, set, formal speeches that had all been prepared a long while before, just as though this crisis between them had been bound to arrive eventually. She wanted to tell him to stop folding that coat. She wanted to take his hand and beg him to carry her from that confusion as he had once carried her away from Gray's Point and Park Avenue — but time was marching on and there was no way out of it.

"It's queer you never mentioned her," she said.

"Who?" Tom asked. Of course, he knew who, but still they had to go on speaking.

"The secretary he was talking about," she said. "She sounded so pretty, so intelligent."

"I don't know which one he meant," Tom said. "The office is full of girls. Everything's in triplicate."

286

"So they come in triplicate?"

Tom sat down beside his folded coat and rested his hands on his knees.

"What's all this about?" he asked.

She wanted to tell him everything she thought, and to find out whether it was true or not, but it was like one of those dreams in which you could only move in a certain way.

"Why should this be about anything?" she asked.

Tom leaned farther forward.

"Look here, Poll," he said. "Has anybody been telling you any thing?"

"Why, what should anyone be telling me?" Polly asked.

Tom relaxed and leaned back, and folded his hands behind his head.

"This place is like a sewing circle," he said. "Everybody has to talk about something that's safe. I guess he must have seen the one called James. She's the best-looking one — Winifred James. I don't know why I should have mentioned her to you particularly. She's a darned nice girl, not your type, Poll. Her father was a Congregational minister like mine."

"Oh," Polly said.

Tom leaned forward again and put his hands on his knees.

"Why do you say 'Oh' in that prissy way?" he asked. "It isn't 'Oh' anything. I don't see why we have to drag in Winifred James. The office is full of personalities. I'll see you meet everybody down there if it's bothering you."

"It isn't bothering me," Polly said.

"Well, something is," Tom answered. "I wish you'd try to relax, Poll. Relax, and smoke a cigarette. Here, have a cigarette. D'you know who you look like?"

"Who?" Polly asked.

"You look like Hayes or Cornell. For God's sake, relax."

"How can anyone relax," Polly asked, "when everyone's so secretive?"

"Now we're getting somewhere," Tom said. "Who is?"

287

"You are."

"Me, secretive?" Tom began to laugh. "So you've noticed that, have you? Well, that's what we're down here for."

"Propaganda isn't secret," Polly said, "and neither is twisting facts, and I wish you would stop acting as though you were winning the war. I don't know what you're doing here or who you see or anything. It's all so — "

"So what?"

"So unnatural. You're so unnatural."

"My God, Poll," Tom said, "so are you. Everyone's unnatural. Don't you know there's a — "

"Stop it," Polly said. "Don't say that again."

"Well, it makes everyone abnormal," Tom said. "You included. You ought to see that, Poll."

"You used to tell me all sorts of things you did," Polly said, "little things that didn't matter, and now you don't. I find them all out from somebody else. You never told me you helped the general with General Clark's trousers."

"Clark's trousers?" Tom's face looked blank. "What about them?"

"His losing them in North Africa."

"Did the general tell you that?" Tom asked. "He shouldn't have. That's the way those things start. You'll tell about that at a cocktail party and then he'll lose them all over again." Tom's face had cleared and he was smiling. "Listen, Poll, let's skip it. Let's hear the news. How's the apartment?"

"What apartment?" Polly asked.

"Ours, for God's sake," Tom said. "New York."

"Why don't you find out for yourself?" Polly asked. "When are you coming back?"

"Just as soon as I can. Just as soon as we straighten out this directive. How's your mother, Poll?"

"You asked about her yesterday."

"Well, I'm asking about her again," Tom said. "Let's put our minds on your mother, Poll. She must be awfully lonely in New York without Harry or anybody."

"Miss Finch is with her," Polly said.

"You ought not to leave her alone with a theosophist. She might start a colony or something, Poll."

"I don't see why you're going so soft about Mother," Polly said.

"I've always liked your mother," Tom went on. "I like the way she's always tried to clutch at straws, and the way she's always been running, trying to catch the bus."

"That was Chamberlain, not Mother," Polly said.

"She and Chamberlain both," Tom went on. "I've always been fond of your mother, Poll. We have a lot in common, and sometimes when she puts her mind on it, I think she knows what I've been up against."

"Well, be specific," Polly said. "What have you ever been up against?"

"The same thing as she," Tom said, "but never mind about it now. No one worries about a boy who's on a yacht. Don't you think you ought to go back and be with your mother, Poll?"

"I'll be back," Polly said. "She's perfectly happy with Miss Finch."

"I was just suggesting it, that's all," Tom said, "not that it does much good to suggest."

"Well, I'm going to stay here for a while," Polly said, "even if you'd be happier without me."

"Now, why should you imply that?" Tom asked. "I think it's swell you're here. I was only being thoughtful."

He stopped and looked at his wrist watch.

"Well," he began, and stopped again, and Polly cleared her throat.

"Tom," she said, "isn't there anything left?"

She thought he looked as though he had expected it.

"Anything left where?"

"Anything left between you and me. Anything we used to have."

He stood up and walked to where she was sitting and looked down at her.

"I'll tell you what I'll do," Tom said, "I'll give you two sleeping pills. You'll see things differently in the morning, Poll."

"All right," Polly said, "if you don't want to answer. I didn't know you were a coward."

"Now, Poll," Tom said. "There's nothing like a sedative."

He went into the bedroom and came back with two white tablets and a glass of water.

"Here," he said. "They never were so popular. The factory's working overtime. Just relax, and make your mind a blank, Poll. I've got to turn in now, I've got to get some sleep."

"Then close the door," Polly said. "I'm not coming to bed just yet."

"You're not going to sit up," he asked, "the way you did last night?"

"Not so long," Polly said. "Just close the door and I won't wake you up."

He stood looking down at her without speaking for a moment.

"I can't help thinking," Polly said, "even if it doesn't matter if a girl is on a yacht."

"Or a boy," Tom answered. "Don't forget the cabin boy. Good night, Poll."

Then he bent over her and kissed her. She did not move a muscle.

"Happy dreams," she said.

It was a horrid expression, "Happy dreams." He closed the door carefully without slamming it as he generally did. She was going to cry, and she did not want him to hear her crying. She was not going to go to bed until she was over it. She lay with her head buried in the sofa cushions, and between her sobs she could still hear Mildred Tasmin's voice.

Rather on the dull side . . . as though Bob and I were missing something. We never seem to have those troubles.

XXI

Nothing Keeps unless You're Careful

Bob Tasmin was rather on the dull side, as far as his interests went, but Burton Fulton maintained that he had a fine legal mind. B. F. should have known because he had a lot of lawyers around all through the financial uncertainty of the thirties. He was always sitting with them in that queer, half-furnished office of his down the hall, and the telephones were always ringing, and Mr. Royall and Mr. Lovelace kept dropping in. B. F. was preoccupied that winter, but Polly could not recall that he was very concerned. He said that depressions came logically after any war. They were a part of what he called the business cycle, and anyone should have seen this one coming years before and should have watched his inventories and his markets. Everything would come out all right if they didn't get too excited down in Washington, but if the government started monkeying you couldn't tell where it would end. You could not legislate economic forces. You might as well try to stop water coming into a leaky cellar. The answer, B. F. said, was equality of opportunity. When Polly told B. F. that he had started with more opportunity than most people because he had inherited a hardware business, B. F. was not impressed.

"I could have started anywhere," he said. "It might have taken a little more time, but this is a free country. I'd have ended about here."

The demand for "know-how," B. F. said, was vastly greater than the supply. You could try men out by the dozens in executive positions, and all of them would fall down at a certain point. The few up at the top had no competition. If he were to start right now as a laborer he would be in the front office inside of two years because in America everyone had a chance.

"What about little people?" Polly asked.

"Little people?" B. F. said. "There aren't any little people in America. Everybody's as good as everybody else. We haven't got any classes in America."

She was never sure whether he believed it or whether he wanted to believe it, but he always stuck to it.

"It's going to be all right here," he always said, "if everyone has an equal chance. They don't have it anywhere else. Name me any other place — England, Russia, anywhere."

That was about all there was to B. F.'s political and economic creed. Tom often said later that B. F. was socially in the Stone Age, but then, perhaps you could not be everything. He was somewhat like Bob Tasmin, naïve when he stepped out from his own field, but when he said that Bob Tasmin had a good legal mind, Polly was very much gratified.

Polly had reached the stage by then of feeling that Bob belonged to her, and she was delighted when anyone recognized his abilities as B. F. did. She kept wishing she could share more in his interests, but she was sure, given time, that she would understand all about the things that occupied him. There was never any sense of pressure in those days, only a conviction that it would turn out all right in the end, that they would reach an inevitable point at which they would marry and live happily ever after.

There was none of the emotional upset that plagued some people when they were engaged, because as far as that went they were not engaged. There was nothing at first but an understanding that they would be someday when Bob became a partner in his firm. There was none of that tiresome convention of always being asked everywhere together. There were so many divorces and misunderstandings that they both agreed they wanted to be sure. For one thing, Polly wanted to be sure she was old enough so that her whole point of view and attitude would not change after marriage, and then Bob was against being married and living partially on her allowance, because he said it was too much like playing house.

The day after that lunch of theirs downtown he had asked her to tea at the Plaza. He was waiting for her when she got there, because he was always religiously punctual, and she remembered how delighted he looked when she arrived.

"Hello," she said. "How are you, darling?"

"I can't believe any of it, Poll," he said.

"I can't either," she said.

They walked without speaking to one of those little tables in the big room by the fountain.

"Let's try to keep it this way," he said.

"It's always going to keep," Polly said.

"Nothing keeps unless you're careful," he said. "You know what I want for us, don't you? I hope you want it too."

There was no need for her to answer. The way he looked at her told her everything.

"Oh, Bob," she whispered. "Darling."

She could not recall whether there were canary birds in the Plaza or not, or whether there was an orchestra, but the air was full of music.

"I guess I've always been crazy about you, Poll," he said, "subconsciously."

"Well," she said, "I've always been crazy about you, not subconsciously."

"I've been thinking about you all night," he said. "I'd like to ask you to marry me, Poll."

She had not expected it to come up that afternoon at tea, and she felt a little frightened but at the same time exultant.

"Are you asking me now?" she asked.

When he shook his head she could not tell whether she was relieved or whether she was hurt.

"No," he said, "not now. I haven't any right."

"You have more than anyone," Polly said. "I don't want anyone else to have the right."

She felt closer to him than she ever had, more sure than ever that he belonged to her.

"It wouldn't work, Poll, right now," he said. "You see, you're a pretty rich girl, and you're pretty young. I wouldn't want you or anyone else to think — you might resent it sometime, Poll. You might say I never gave you the chance to make up your mind."

"Well. Why are you bothered by money, darling?" Polly asked.

"I love you too much," Bob said. "I don't want anyone to think that's why I want to marry you."

"I wish you wouldn't talk that way," she said. "It sounds so cheap."

"Yes," he said, "I know. It sounds that way, but I haven't any right to ask you until I can support you, Poll. That's all I mean." There was never anything irresolute about him. "Now, if the depression will ever ease up and I get this junior partnership, we'll take this up again," he said. "You wouldn't like it if you had to support me, Poll." He leaned across the table. "Would you?"

"You mean if I weren't rich — " she began.

"You've got to believe me," he said. "I love you too much, Poll."

"Well, as long as you love me that's something," Polly said. "That ought to be enough."

Perhaps it was her fault that she was always wanting something more, and at the same time not wanting it. She was always wanting him to carry her away to some sophisticated Land of Oz, and he was always keeping both feet on the ground. It must have been because he had a good legal mind.

It must have been hard for him to say those things drinking orange pekoe tea.

"Just as long as you understand me, Poll. I have honorable intentions."

"Just as long as you're not always too honorable," Polly said.

Bob laughed, and everything was just as it always had been.

"Do you know what you look like?" he asked.

Polly shook her head.

"You'd look like Botticelli's 'Spring' if you didn't have on that hat. I wish you'd take it off."

Polly laughed and took off her hat.

"I'm not pregnant like those Botticelli girls."

He laughed at her. He was never shocked by anything she said.

"Do you know what your voice sounds like?" he asked. "It sounds like cobwebs in moonlight."

"Darling," Polly said. "That's a very pathetic fallacy."

"It isn't so bad this way, is it, Poll?" he asked her. "Let's keep it this way."

It was not bad at all. It was like having your cake and eating it too. It was being engaged and yet not being. It was having somebody love you without any strings attached, and that was the way Bob kept it — because he did the right thing always. She always knew that the time would come someday when they would marry and live happily ever after.

The time element in that era when she was so wrapt up in Bob Tasmin seemed brief, although it really was not. Perhaps her mind slurred over the details as a mind does with something that is slightly embarrassing, not that she and Bob Tasmin were not always the best of friends afterwards. Still, it was sometimes hard to realize that he had been on her mind continuously for nearly two years. She was growing up in those two years. Her character was constantly developing, and she was very lucky to have had someone interested in her who was as patient as Bob. Only long afterwards did it occur to her that her self-absorption might have distressed him. Yet, if it did, she could not recall that he ever showed it. Even toward the end, when there seemed to be all sorts of reasons why she could not see him so often, he always said that it was all right with him, that he expected her to see other men and to go to all sorts of places without him. If he had been more demanding, if he had been more hurt or jealous — but there was no use going into it, even to herself.

She had seldom discussed Bob Tasmin even with Tom, except in the most superficial way, because it never helped to discuss other men who had loved you with your husband, and Tom had always said Bob Tasmin was a Bourbon, who, like the Bourbons, learned nothing and forgot nothing.

Once she had spoken of Bob at greater length to her friend Apples Sandler, but only once. Apples had been spending a night at Pyefield, just a few weeks before she was to marry Arthur Paxton, and Tom went upstairs early. He told Polly to try not to wake him when she came to bed, because Tom said when those two girls got together, even though they declared they were just going up to Apples' room to say good night, they would sit around talking for hours and hours, and God knew what they had to talk about.

It had worked out just that way. They had sat on the bed in the spare room, brushing their hair and eating candy and smoking cigarettes, and talking and talking, just as they had years before. So many things had happened to them and so many more were about to happen, and Polly was so happily married to such an interesting man, with a house of her own, that she was in a position to give Apples all kinds of tips on marriage and husbands and honeymoons, and on engagements too. Apples was saying it was dreadfully hard to be absolutely sure whether you were doing the right thing in getting married even to someone like Arthur Paxton. Now, take Bob for instance — Apples knew that Polly had not been sure for a long while about Bob Tasmin, and possibly Apples felt that way about Arthur Paxton. It was so irrevocable, and you could not tell. It made Polly feel wise and superior when Apples confessed her qualms.

"You mustn't try to pick examples, Apples," she said. "Every situation has different circumstances. Now with Bob, perhaps it dragged on too long. He never did anything definite."

"You mean making love," Apples asked, "in a big way? I don't see how you two could have stood it all that time without forgetting yourselves. He was so romantic, and he always looked so highly sexed. Polly, now didn't you ever — "

Polly would not have dreamed of embarking on such a discussion with anyone but Apples.

"No," Polly said, "it wasn't that way at all. You don't know Bob, Apples, or you wouldn't think any such thing."

"Then he wasn't highly sexed," Apples said. "Or else you aren't. If it had been me, I simply couldn't have stood it."

It was true that Apples probably could not have, but it was not the same thing at all with Bob Tasmin.

"It would have spoiled everything," Polly said.

"Well, I still don't see how you stood it," Apples said again.

"Just get it through your head," Polly told her, "that everybody doesn't have to end up in bed with everybody. It wasn't that sort of thing." Then she found herself thinking of Bob very kindly, a little the way she might think of someone who was dead. "He was so nice," she added. "So damned nice."

"Poll," Apples said, "haven't you ever been sorry?"

"Sorry for what?" Polly asked.

"Sorry that everything didn't go further."

There was no use explaining it to Apples. It would only have sounded smug.

"We'd have both disliked each other," Polly said, "and it wouldn't have been like Bob." She actually found herself defending Bob because he had not done something that he would not have dreamed of doing. "We were awfully busy. He was working, and I was at college most of the time, and then I went to Europe. It kept our minds off each other."

"But what happened to spoil it?" Apples asked.

"Nothing happened." And Polly sighed. "It just went on so long, and there were other men, Apples. You see, we weren't really engaged, except for a very little while."

"What other men?" Apples asked.

"Oh, darling," Polly said. "You know how men keep cropping up. There was Milton Ouerbach, if you want to know."

Apples was fascinated. She had never dreamed of such a thing.

"You don't mean," Apples said, "that you ever went for Milton?"

"He was very clever," Polly said. "I was going through one of those socially-conscious phases then. Bob knew all about it. It never upset him."

Maybe that lay behind it all — nothing ever upset him, or at least he never showed it.

"And then Tom came along," Polly said. "You can't explain it, Apples."

"Do you know what I think?" Apples said.

"What?" Polly asked.

"Well, I guess I won't say it," Apples told her.

Apples had an annoying habit of stopping in the middle of a remark.

"All right," Apples said. "If you'd ever slept with him, I think you'd have married Bob."

If there had been anything to throw, Polly would have thrown it at Apples. Ever since Apples had been psychoanalyzed, all she could think about was sex. To Apples this was the inevitable end for any sort of relationship.

Polly was a senior at Bryn Mawr that winter, and she had only been in New York for odd week ends and for the spring vacation. The courses had been hard — she had majored in political science and minored in English — and the final examinations had of necessity put everything on a sublimated plane. Besides there was such a small sense of pressure about Bob that she had been able to handle it all with him on ice as it were. He fitted into everything she was doing without any crowding.

Whenever she was in New York that spring, Bob always stopped at the apartment around six o'clock. If her mother or B. F. noticed how often he came there, they never said anything about it, and they never made any effort to leave them alone together. Her mother would be in the living room, and B. F. would come in, and Harry when he was at home from school, so that Bob was like a part of the family. She never had to make any effort. She loved to listen to him talking to B. F. She felt that neither of them recognized the fact that the country's whole economic and social system was breaking down, and that there was danger of revolution. They did not seem to care, and it was very provoking. B. F. had tried to read *Das Kapital* by Karl Marx, but he could not get through it. Bob had read it carefully, because she had asked him to, and he said it was as theoretical as Plato's *Republic,* and that it was full of prophecies based on theories.

Bob would smoke one of his straight-grained pipes and B. F. would fidget in a Louis Quinze chair, getting up and pacing about and sitting down again, because B. F. never liked to sit still. Her mother would sit by the tea things, and if Bob wanted it, Timmons would bring him a Scotch and soda.

"You can make predictions from the Book of Revelation," Bob

would be saying, "or you can tell the future by the dimensions of the pyramids. You can prophesy that Communism will be the final social conclusion, but it isn't necessarily true."

"Polly has a lot of queer friends," B. F. used to say. "Now there's this boy, Milton Ouerbach. He knows everything. I wish I knew everything."

Polly never minded when they made fun of her. Instead it only encouraged her to argue.

"Well, you know the system is breaking down," she would say. "Why don't you admit it? Something isn't working."

"Nothing ever works just right," B. F. would tell her.

"Poll's getting to be a Bolshevik," Harry would say. "She ought to go to Russia and see how she likes it."

"You see, Bob," B. F. would say, "Poll thinks I've got too much money. She thinks it isn't right."

"Of course it isn't right," Polly would say. "Why should we be sitting up in this damned French drawing room with everybody starving?"

"Polly, dear," Mrs. Fulton would say, "I don't see why you always have to swear."

"Well, why is it right," Polly would say, "for one half of one per cent of all the people in the United States to have all the money?"

"Poll knows all the facts and figures," B. F. would say. "I'm not saying it's right, Poll, but what would you do? If you were I, what would you? Go ahead and tell us, Poll."

She was always helpless with B. F. and Bob Tasmin because she had never really thought anything through. Nevertheless, she was convinced, though she was only rephrasing things she had read in college and conclusions other people had reached, that she was closer to being right than either Bob or B. F. They were concerned with static principles, while she knew that even principles were changing. Still, it was not fair of B. F. He always made her feel deflated when he asked her what she would do in his place.

"All right," she would say. "I would hand over all your plants to the workers."

"That's a funny expression, 'workers,'" B. F. would say. "Does that mean Bob and I aren't workers? It seems to me we work pretty hard."

"It isn't the same thing," Polly would say. "You're exploiters, you're not workers."

"All right, we'll give the plant to the workers," B. F. used to say, "and then who's going to run the show?"

"The workers will run it," Polly answered.

"Those boys aren't very good at running things," B. F. would tell her. "It takes a lot of training, and what about the stockholders?"

"Never mind about the stockholders," Polly would answer. They were being supported by workers, and they ought to be working too.

"Polly's the little Red flame," Harry used to say.

Those arguments must have been going on in all sorts of places in those days, always ending in blind alleys.

There was no use trying to remember all the things they used to talk about when Bob Tasmin came to tea. The main point was that he was like one of the family, and often he would stay to dinner, and perhaps she and Bob would go to the theater or somewhere afterwards. Then sometimes when he took her home they would stay for a while alone in the library.

"But I wish you wouldn't sit and be so calm," Polly said once. "If you know there's something wrong, why don't you do something about it, or write something, like Milton Ouerbach?"

"Because I don't know what to do," Bob told her. "I'm trying to keep my job downtown. I wish you'd put your mind on me. I'm in the depression too." And then he took her in his arms.

"Darling," Polly said. "Can't you ever take me seriously?"

"There's just you and me, Poll," he said, "and then there's the rest of the world. We've got to do the best we can with what we've got. Don't fly off the handle, Poll."

"I don't know why I feel so — well, so trapped," she said. She sat curled up on the corner of the sofa, and clasped her hands in her lap and stared in front of her. "I keep thinking that I'm being made into something that isn't me. I don't suppose you see what I mean, because everything you do is like you." Bob sat silently looking at her.

"I keep trying to find some way of being useful: I keep trying new systems, but they never work."

"Am I a system?" Bob asked.

"Well, maybe in a way," Polly said and she sighed. "There's nothing I can do for you. You're so much all of a piece, darling."

"You've done a lot already."

"Darling," she said. "Please kiss me."

She could believe anything when he kissed her. It was just what he had said — it was himself and herself, and then all the rest of the world.

"Don't get it into your head that you're different from other people, Poll," he said. "Now when you're married and have a house of your own and children — "

"Is it as easy as that?" she asked.

"Yes," he said, "it will be for you and me. I know it, Poll."

"Then I wish you'd hurry up," she said.

There was never any great sense of haste, though, while she was still at Bryn Mawr. It was during the next winter when she had so much time on her hands that she must have begun wishing for something definite. The spring of 1932 was much the same as the spring of the year before. Not a single new partner had been taken into Bob's law firm, and they still were not engaged.

XXII

She Really Thought She Meant It

WHEN the Fultons went to Gray's Point that spring, Bob used to come down for week ends and stay with his father and mother, and he and Polly would take long walks on Sunday. He said if he ever got taken into partnership he wanted to live in the country, and he hoped she did too. When she told him the family were going abroad that summer, and that she was going too, he said it was just as well. There was no need to ask him to explain that remark, although she did. He said it was not fair to her to have him hanging around all the time.

One Saturday morning when she and B. F. were having breakfast alone in the dining room at Gray's Point, B. F. asked her where Bob was and she said she did not know.

"I've been thinking about Bob," he said.

"Have you?" Polly asked.

B. F. nodded, but he looked completely guileless.

"They ought to make him a partner in that firm," he said. "He's got a good legal mind, and he's been there quite a while. I think maybe I ought to talk to Barstow."

When Polly answered, she was much too emphatic, and not even polite.

"You mustn't do that. Bob wouldn't like it."

"All right," B. F. said, "then I'll take it up with Bob."

The June sun made patches on the floor and the sound of the lawn mower came through the open window. B. F. was in his shirt sleeves. When there were no guests on Sunday, he hardly ever wore his coat, although everyone told him it looked very queer when Timmons was passing things. Polly remembered feeling that every-

302

thing was closing in on her, because she knew very well that all he had to do was to give that firm some of his legal business. She knew that he would not do it clumsily. He could change her future and Bob's in five minutes if he wanted — and everything would be spoiled.

"What's the matter, Poll?" he asked.

Her voice was still too loud and too emphatic.

"Please don't take it up with Bob. Please don't."

B. F. picked up a spoon and looked at it.

"I've always liked these rattail spoons . . . Why not, Poll?"

"I don't know why," she answered, "but please don't."

He looked so pleased that she could tell he had guessed everything about her and Bob. He wanted her to marry Bob Tasmin, and because he wanted it, she was no longer sure.

"Poll . . ." He hesitated and put down his rattail spoon. "Do you think Bob minds your having a lot of money?"

"No," she said, "I don't think so."

Though she had resolved not to discuss that conversation with Bob, she repeated it to him that afternoon when he came over and he listened in such a neutral way that she was not sure how he was going to take it.

"It was nice of him to think of it," he said finally, "but I don't want anything like that."

He said it so definitely that she was ashamed she had ever doubted.

"Darling, isn't it dreadful?" she said. "We'll never be sure about ourselves any more. He may do something, and we'll never know."

"He won't if he says he won't," Bob Tasmin said.

"Darling," she said, "I got you all by myself, didn't I, without anyone's helping? . . . *Please,* don't say I didn't."

B. F. had left word that he was going to be in the library telephoning and that he did not want to be disturbed, but when Polly opened the door a crack, he waved to them to come in. He was seated at his desk talking to Mr. Lovelace in Pittsburgh.

"Then we'll cut the dividends, Homer," he was saying. "I want to see that those boys eat as long as we're eating."

It was usually not wise to interrupt B. F. when he was talking business.

"Hello, Poll," he said. "Did you want to see me, Bob?"

"Yes," Bob answered, "for just a minute, sir."

"All right, if it's just a minute."

"I wanted to thank you for suggesting—"

"About Barstow and Bryce, is that it?"

"Yes, sir."

"Do you want me to do anything?"

"No, sir," Bob said, "but thanks just as much."

"Why not?" B. F. asked. "You'll get in that firm eventually. It might as well be now."

B. F. stood up and walked around the desk. Bob Tasmin smiled.

"Because I've heard you say that there's always a chance for an American boy."

"Well, now," B. F. said, "that's a nice way of putting it, but if an American boy has friends—"

"If I'm any good," Bob said quietly, "I'll get along all right. If I'm not, I'd better know it."

"Well, Bob," B. F. said, "I just thought you might be in a hurry."

Bob Tasmin nodded. "I am, but I'll get along all right."

"Well, I've got another idea," B. F. went on. "I'm looking for a lawyer for the office. How would you like that?"

"Thanks," Bob answered, "but I'd rather keep on where I am."

"I hope you don't mind my suggesting it."

"No," Bob replied. "I appreciate it, sir."

Polly had never been so proud of Bob Tasmin. It was one of the few glimpses he gave her of what he might have been like in the law. If she had ever seen more of that side of him, if she could ever have related it to the rest . . . He was like all those men who led two lives, one in the office and the other at home. If he had told her more about it, if there had been any way in which she could have helped him . . .

She had to admit that spring that, hard as she tried and much as Bob Tasmin loved it, she did not like Gray's Point at all. He kept saying it was great to be out in the country and to get some fresh air.

It was great to see the old crowd at Gray's Point again, and it was swell to get out on the tennis court and bat the ball around. He didn't care whether she played well or not — he loved to have her with him at the Mill River Club. He loved to have her with him when he sat and talked with all those girls in sweaters and all those men in tweeds and flannels. He loved taking her to Sunday luncheons where they talked about horses and the stock market and golf. It may have been that his legal mind was tired on Sundays. Bob said it was great to be with friends again whom you had always known, and that you had more fun with them than you did with intellectual giants. He was at his best on the tennis court playing a hard game. He gave no impression of effort; he was always in position. He always did the right thing.

There was a new real estate development starting there up by Sugar Hill, each house on an acre of its own. There were houses of whitewashed brick or houses with big clapboards, and the rhododendrons and evergreens were all grouped by a good landscape architect. It was just the place, he said, that he had always dreamed of, and a lot of the young married crowd were buying lots. You could just drop in and out there and see everyone, and the houses were small and convenient, all built on slopes so that you could get a garage under them. Of course, they might have an apartment in town for a few months in the winter, but right from spring to late autumn there would be no place like Sugar Hill, just an eight-minute drive to the station and three minutes' drive to the club.

If he wanted it, Polly tried to want it too, though she could not imagine what she would do there all day when he was away. Bob said there would be plenty to do, housekeeping, marketing and all those community things at Gray's Point like the Garden Club; and she could play bridge like all the other girls and brush up on her golf and tennis. If she put her mind on it, Bob said, she could get to be good at tennis. He and Jeff, the professional, had been talking about her, and Jeff could round out anybody's game. Bob could beat him any time, but teaching was an art in itself. It was the same with bridge. If Polly would keep her mind on it and not talk so much across the table, she would enjoy the game and enjoy the way the cards fell. All that spring Polly tried to see herself as a Sugar Hill matron, and it was not inconceivable when Bob Tasmin was around. It was only when he was out of sight that the good life presented itself as a problem.

It was a relief when she sailed with the family to Europe in July, but the relief had nothing to do with Bob, because she missed Bob terribly. She kept thinking of him on the boat and in Paris and in the Dolomites. She wrote him nearly every day, and he wrote to her. It was hot in New York, and he had been to Easthampton. He was not taking an early vacation because one of the cases he had been preparing for Mr. Willoughby was coming up for trial in late August. He had been to Gray's Point and had walked over to the swimming pool. The garden had been beautiful. It had looked for a while as though there might be some recovery from the depression, but everything had slumped again. They were at the bottom and it was bound to get better. He was thinking of her all the time.

She hoped he would be at the dock to meet her — and there he was, right there by the gangplank with B. F.'s shipping man, who had come to take the declarations and get everything through the customs. When she saw Bob in his gray flannel suit, she knew that she loved him more than ever and without any doubt or reservation. She did not care who saw how glad she was to see him, though it was almost like admitting to the family that they were engaged.

"Darling," she said. "Let's go where we can be alone." And before she could think of an excuse to go off and leave the family, B. F. had asked Bob Tasmin to take her out to lunch somewhere, if he had time. They went up to Bob's apartment after lunch, and she kept thinking of all the things she could do to it to make it more comfortable, or at least she did eventually. At first all she could grasp was that he was near her again and that she could touch him.

"Did you miss me?" she asked. "Tell me just how you missed me."

"I'll tell you how," he answered. "Nothing without you is worth a damn."

"Then don't treat me as though I would break. Don't act as though someone might come in."

"Maybe it would be better if someone did," he said.

She did not care what might happen, because this was what they were both meant for.

"Poll," he said, "we'd better cut this out."

"But why," she whispered, "why?"

"Because you wouldn't like it, Poll," he said.

"What makes you think so?" she asked. "Can't we ever be ourselves?"

It was that self-control of his, and she hated it at the moment. It was that damned office and having no right until he had made a certain amount of money. He moved away from her, but at least for once he had been almost natural.

"All right," she answered. "I won't throw myself at you. It must have been the long sea voyage." And she opened her compact and looked at herself in the little mirror. "You're an awful stuffed shirt," she said.

"Yes," he answered, "I guess I am with you. You see, I love you, Poll."

He was hurt and she was hurt, each in a different way.

"Oh, God, darling," Polly said. "Everything is so — so contrived. Everyone's always taking care of me. I'm never face to face with anything."

"You're face to face with me," Bob Tasmin said.

"I'm not as nice as you are," she told him. "I'm a spoiled, disagreeable, maladjusted girl. Why don't you tell me so?"

"Because I'm prejudiced."

"You're so damned balanced," Polly said. "Why can't I be balanced too?"

"I wouldn't like you if you were."

"Do you think it would be biologically safe if you kissed me again?" Polly asked. "I don't want you to put any strain on your better self."

She knew that it would all end suitably because someday they would be married and live happily ever after. She said she was afraid she'd been mean to the family in Europe. When you traveled with B. F. there was a vacuum between you and the rest of the world. There were always suites at the Crillon and cars and chauffeurs, and a lot of subservient people trying to make you happy: persuasive gentlewomen with *bon goût* who took you to the great *couturières* —on a commission basis—scraping *concierges* and scraping little men, too, who wanted to marry you for your money. There had been an Englishman who had followed them about everywhere, proposing and proposing.

"He wasn't like you, darling," Polly said. "He was crazy about B. F.'s money. Perhaps you should have gone to Oxford or something, darling."

No matter what the family said, she was not going to sit around or go to useless parties at Gray's Point or in New York as she had last year. She had a lot of energy—and yet when she had suggested to B. F. that he might give her something to do at the office, he had said that it would upset the whole works if she went down there. Then she had suggested that she might go, with one of those archeologists she had met on the boat, and dig up a town in North Africa or one of those Indian places in New Mexico—but the family objected when she asked B. F. to put up the money.

She was not going to sit around the apartment. She was going to take some courses at Columbia—one in economics, one on the English novel, and one on the history of Europe since 1815. She was going up there tomorrow to see about it . . . And Bob Tasmin said it was a swell idea.

The best thing, they both agreed, was to go on without being engaged, and Polly asked him if he minded if she saw Milton Ouerbach and all those people.

"Of course, Poll," he said. "That's just what I want. I've told you—"

"Stop it," Polly said. "Don't say that you haven't got any right."

"Maybe you'll meet someone you'll like better than me," Bob said. "That's always a possibility."

"When you say that," Polly said, "please smile, darling."

"It wouldn't be funny, but it might happen," Bob said; "but

Poll, keep Sundays open for me, won't you, so that we can walk in the country."

It was the autumn of '32, and Milton Ouerbach was already writing a syndicated column. Milton and all his friends knew that the whole system was going to pieces, and they enjoyed watching poor Mr. Hoover trying to keep it together. Bob said they were all a bunch of crackpots, but Polly saw them more and more, though they all looked upon her suspiciously because she was Burton Fulton's daughter. Instead of liking her they disliked her because of money, and it was a great relief. They took Polly to all sorts of queer speak-easies, and finally to Harlem. When she asked Bob Tasmin why he never took her to places like the Savoy, Bob said he never dreamed that she would like them, and besides, he was too busy to stay out all night. He was so busy that Polly went alone to more and more parties at Washington Square, and finally she had to do something in return.

She invited Milton and Victor Steinhaus, whom Milton called the sculptor, the one who did those queer things that looked like eggs; she invited George Cyst, whom Milton called the explorer, and Kevin O'Rory, the prose-poet. She invited Beverly Pepcorn, the economist, and Dr. Jeannette Sparkoe, who had been indispensable to Freud, and lots and lots of other people. She asked them if they would mind a stuffy evening at the family's, and she was astonished that they all seemed glad to come.

"You don't have to be there, B. F.," she said, and she told Bob Tasmin that he did not have to be there either. She only wanted a buffet supper, and it would be just as well to have it on Timmons's night out.

"Now, listen, Poll," B. F. said. "Don't be shy. I want to see your friends."

"I don't know what they'll think," she told B. F., "and I don't know how they'll behave."

"They'll like it," B. F. said. "I know those newspaper people. They always like food, and this is quite a layout, Poll."

As a matter of fact, they did like it, and a great many more guests came than she had asked. There were a few dreadful minutes at first when everyone tried to be natural, but B. F. said afterwards that it was all like a salesmen's convention — the main thing was to see that everyone had a drink.

"Of course, I have different ideas from some of you kids," she heard B. F. saying. "I believe in the profit motive. It's always worked well with me."

It must have been a very good party, because they all stayed until two. They played the piano and danced in the hall, and Milton thought of one of those word games, and there were some men in the show business who put on an act. Polly had started being embarrassed for B. F., but when she heard him arguing with Milton about abundance, she realized how good he was at enlightened conversation, and as the evening wore on, they stopped calling him "Mr. Fulton."

"I don't know why Poll has kept you all away from me," she heard B. F. say, and at least three of the girls kissed him good-by. When it was all over, she was not even tired.

"Now that was quite a crowd," B. F. said. "Those boys were bright as buttons. Now that boy Ouerbach — he certainly could talk."

"Well, what's wrong with him?" Polly asked.

"There's nothing wrong with him," B. F. said. "It's funny how many people know the answers to everything these days. I wish I knew the answers. Where's Bob? Why didn't Bob come?"

"He had to work," Polly said.

B. F. put his hands in his pockets and leaned against the wall in the front parlor. He looked, as he sometimes did, straight into her eyes.

"Poll," he said. "There's just one thing to remember."

"What?" she asked.

"Bob Tasmin amounts to more than any of them."

"But, darling," Polly said, "it isn't fair to compare them. They are all more like you than Bob Tasmin."

"Yes, I know," B. F. said, "but I wouldn't have them in the office, Poll."

Polly had never felt so in touch with great world movements as she had that winter, and she could thank Milton Ouerbach for it. All those friends of his began coming more and more to the apartment, and they grew to be as much at home there as they were anywhere else. It was discouraging to have Bob say you could always collect freaks if you fed them. Bob was usually tired in the evenings, and he said it was like going to a five-ring circus, and that he could not keep his mind on all those different egocentrics performing. It was like getting drunk on mixed drinks, and as far as he could see, they were only individuals who had failed to cope with ordinary existence.

Then one morning just after Christmas he called Polly early, which was surprising because he hardly ever telephoned from the office.

"Poll," he said, "how are you?"

"Darling, I'm just waking up," Polly said. "I was up awfully late last night."

"I heard you were," he said. "I tried to call you. How's the world situation? How's Russia?"

"Don't be so nasty," Polly said. "What's the matter? Why aren't you busy?"

"I was just asking," Bob said. "I don't have to read any more. I don't even have to ask Milton Ouerbach. I can just ask you, and I can find out anything."

"Darling," Polly said, "do you love me?"

"I'm crazy about you," Bob said. "Listen, Poll, can you be in at six this afternoon? There's something I want to tell you."

His voice sounded forced and unnatural.

"Bob," she asked, "has anything happened?"

There was a pause, a long pause.

"Yes," he answered, "something." There was no sign of elation. Instead he sounded grim.

"Oh, Bob, darling," she said. "They haven't fired you, have they?"

A great many people she knew had been losing their jobs lately.

"I'll tell you about it at six, Poll," was all he said. "I can't talk about it over the telephone."

All that day she felt capable and important. She kept thinking of what she could do for him and how she could show him that it made no difference. He could go into B. F.'s office if he wanted, or perhaps he could have a rest. It meant that at last Bob Tasmin was fallible like other people.

Everyone was there at six, her mother and B. F. and Harry. She wanted Harry out of the way, but when he heard that Bob Tasmin was coming, he said he would wait.

"You can see him any time," Polly said. "There isn't any reason to bother him today."

"I want to talk to him," Harry said. "I want to ask him something about Yale."

"Oh, my God," Polly said. "Why do we have to bring in Yale?"

"If he wants to ask Bob something," her mother said, "I'm sure I don't see why he shouldn't."

"What is it?" B. F. asked. "Something about the Freshman Crew?"

Harry blushed and cleared his throat.

"Well, if you want to know, it is," he said, "but I can't very well talk about it here, Father."

"Why can't you?" B. F. asked. "Is there any chance of your making it?"

"Now, listen," Polly said, "Harry hasn't any more chance of rowing in that boat than a snowball in hell."

"Polly," her mother said, "I wish you wouldn't use those expressions."

"I can't discuss it in the present company, Father," Harry said.

"Don't try to be so important," Polly said.

"Don't try to be so important yourself," Harry told her. "What are you all snaked up for? Where did you get that dress? It looks as though it's coming off."

She was wearing it because it was new and because Bob had never seen it.

Bob Tasmin came in just on time, wearing a new suit too.

"Hello," he said, and he shook hands with everyone. Even then Polly could not tell what was on his mind because he had what she called his "Business" look.

312

"Well, sit down, Bob," B. F. said, "and tell us how everything is."

Bob shrugged his shoulders.

"I'm feeling a little let down," he said. "This has been quite a day — at least it's been for me."

"Oh, Bob — " Polly began, but she did not know how to go on from there. He looked the way he had when he had been beaten in one of those tennis tournaments, perfectly controlled and cheerful.

"I might as well tell you the news," Bob said. "Beginning January, I'm going to be a member of the firm."

Polly drew a quick, sharp breath. Instead of being glad, she was thinking that he might have told her in the morning.

"Of course, it isn't much," he said. "I don't suppose the firm will earn much next year, but there it is."

B. F. shook Bob's hand and slapped him on the back.

"Harry," he said, "ring the bell and tell Timmons to get some champagne."

Then her heart missed a beat, for she saw that Bob had something more to say.

"Now that everybody's here," he said, "I'd like to ask a question."

It sounded so formal that it was silly, and if she could only have known earlier, it would have been much easier. "I'd like to ask if it's all right to be engaged to Poll."

B. F. started to laugh, and so did Harry. They all laughed except her mother, who half laughed and half cried.

"It's about time," B. F. said. "You've had us all worried, Bob."

"You had me worried especially," Harry said. "You ought to see the birds who've been coming around here lately."

"My dear," her mother said, "I'm so glad it's Bob." And then Polly found her voice.

"I wish you wouldn't all look so relieved," she said. "What did you think I was going to do, marry the janitor?" There was no reason why they should have been quite so overjoyed.

That was what she said to Tom Brett not so long afterwards.

"They were all so damned relieved that it was like walking into a surprise party."

There would be an announcement tea now that she was engaged, and she would have to buy clothes, and be saying the same thing to everybody, but in spite of all the boring detail, she thought she was happy. That was what she told Tom Brett.

"I really thought I was. I really thought I wanted to get married. That's what makes it so awful."

"Well, you didn't want to," Tom said. "You needn't have any free guilt. You were trying to get away from him when I came along. You acted as though you were drowning."

It was like a child's wanting something for too long. She had built it up in her mind until it was insipid when she finally got it. It was all very well to say it was a mistake, or you could say it was chance or accident. No matter what the reason might be she felt trapped when she was engaged to Bob Tasmin. If B. F. and everyone, even the servants, had not been so pleased, if Bob had been a little unsure, if he had not been so eternally correct, if Mr. and Mrs. Tasmin and Will had not been so complacent . . . but you could go on thinking indefinitely of reasons. At any rate there was one thing to which she could hold fast: the invitations had not gone out for the announcement tea, and no one knew about the engagement except the family and a few friends; and furthermore, she had found Tom Brett all herself, and no one could say she hadn't, and it was their business and nobody else's — and it was lucky that she met Tom Brett before the announcement tea, for she never would have met him afterwards.

XXIII

They've Got Everything at Macy's

ONCE POLLY heard herself talking about marriage when she and
Tom were somewhere at dinner, and her voice had filled a pause in
the conversation. She was saying that natural selection was not so
natural for a girl as it was for a man, that a girl could not go out
and look for what she wanted. It was a harmless statement, but
then someone made one of those silly remarks about a woman's
having her own way and getting what she wanted always — if she
knew what she wanted.

"She never knows," Polly said, "until it's pushed at her. She has to
wait and see."

"Any woman can marry any man she wants," someone said.

Polly replied that this sounded like something out of Thackeray,
and then, since everyone was listening to her, she had to continue.

"A man goes everywhere, but a girl has to wait until some man
stumbles over her. She has about a tenth the chances of a man. It's
like the double standard of morality."

It was the same as shaking dice. You just went somewhere and
met someone, so why should it be called selection when your chances
to select were so limited? To prove the point you only had to take
the phrases that married women used. "George and I just happened
to meet." "We met in the queerest way." At any rate, that was how
she met Tom Brett.

When Milton Ouerbach called her up a few mornings after that
betrothal scene, if you wanted to call it that, Polly knew it was
going to be awkward explaining her new status. She had forgotten that Milton might be a problem. She had thought everything
would be settled automatically, and it would have been if she had

started right away writing, "I want you to be among the first to know."

There was no reason why Milton should have known by telepathy that his part in her life was over and that she was engaged to Bob Tasmin. She could hear him saying "But — why Tasmin?" and mentally shrugging his shoulders. She had concealed the Bob Tasmin part of her life from Milton because it was outside his sphere of interest, not because she was ashamed of it.

"Hello, darling," Milton said over the telephone. "Milton Ouerbach speaking." Although it meant almost nothing when Milton called her "darling," still it was a complication that must be cleared up quickly, but certainly not over the telephone.

"Hello, Milton dear," she said. "Why have you been neglecting me?"

"You've been in my thoughts every waking and sleeping minute, darling," Milton said. "I'm at Teddy and Adolph's in a vacant and a pensive mood, trying to pull my thoughts together. I go on the air at three. Come on down and have a spot of lunch."

Teddy and Adolph's was a speak-easy in the Murray Hill district and Polly had been there with Milton once before. She enjoyed the mystery connected with any of the places in which Milton habitually ate. It was not an ideal setting in which to tell her news to him, but she had to do it sometime.

She did her face very carefully, and she put on the silver fox scarf that B. F. had given her for Christmas.

"I'm going out for lunch," she told her mother. "I'll be back early."

"Lunch with Bob?" her mother asked brightly.

"No, dear," Polly said, "just lunch."

"Some girls, dear?"

"No, Mother," Polly said, "just Milton Ouerbach."

"Polly, dear," her mother began, "don't you think it looks — "

"It doesn't look like anything," Polly said. "Besides, it isn't announced yet."

Teddy and Adolph's was in a brownstone house on Murray Hill with a glass vestibule and an iron grille door. As Polly walked up the steps and rang the bell, she might almost have been calling on a maiden aunt, but the door was opened by a squat, dark man with a broken nose.

"What you want, lady?" the man asked.

When she asked if Milton Ouerbach was there, the man said he was Teddy and shook hands with her.

"We maka da spaghet' for Milt," he said.

Upstairs she heard voices and a clattering of crockery. The bar was in back in what must have been the old dining room, and it was furnished with chintz-covered chairs and ash receptacles that looked like mushrooms. Some girls stared hard at Polly, and so did some youngish businessmen. Milton, who was always abstemious, was drinking a glass of beer and talking to a pale man in a baggy brown suit. Milton's back was to her and he was gesticulating expansively. Though everyone was speaking in the unconstrained way that was usual in such places, the vibrant quality of Milton's voice raised it above the rest.

"We can make all the changes that are necessary," Milton was saying, "while the trains go in and out of the station."

Milton had often said the same thing before, and she knew that he would go on to a discussion of inequities and special privilege, but he did not have a chance because Teddy tapped him on the shoulder.

"Darling," Milton said, "how devoted of you to venture alone into this *bistro*. I want you to meet a friend of mine, Mr. Brett." And he waved toward the pale man in the baggy suit. That was the way it happened, and her first impression was only one of annoyance because she would not be able to tell Milton Ouerbach about Bob Tasmin before a third person.

"Put your foot on the rail beside us, darling," Milton said, "and be careful of your diction. Mr. Brett is an instructor in English at Columbia, and he is almost in the Brain Trust — Moley, Tugwell, Berle, Brett."

Milton intoned the names, as if in prayer.

"Don't chant, Milton," Tom Brett said, and he twisted his face. "You sound like Eugene Field."

That was the first thing she ever heard Tom say. Her first thought was that someone should have seen that he got his clothes pressed. His soft shirt was wrinkled and his tie was askew. His brown hair was untidy, and his face was pinched and peaked. From the very beginning she wanted to do something about him. Even then she was thinking that he would have looked distinguished if he could have been brushed and put in order. He was drinking rye and ginger ale, his favorite drink, and he had cigarette ashes on his waistcoat, and his hands were slender and stained with tobacco.

"Where's your poodle?" Tom Brett asked.

There was so much noise in the bar that she asked him to say it again.

"You ought to be walking with one of those cinnamon-colored poodles . . ." Tom Brett said . . . "cut to look like an airedale . . . You know the kind I mean. Or did you leave him outside with the chauffeur?"

"You ought to know," Polly said. "You look like a professional dog-walker yourself."

"What's that?" Tom Brett asked.

"You heard me."

His eyebrows drew together, and then he laughed.

"I never thought of doing that," he said. "Maybe I might try it sometime, but the trouble is I hate dogs."

"Well, so do I when you come down to it," Polly said.

"Do you?" he asked. "Do you really? Well, that means that we can't be basically wholesome people. You'll never get far if you're not a dog lover, and yet if you put it in another way — "

"What way?" Milton asked.

"Any way," Tom Brett said, "any way you want to put it. Let's not argue, Milton. I'm hungry, and I want my lunch."

For some reason she felt at home with Tom right from the beginning. When they ate their spaghetti in what had once been the upstairs parlor of the house, he began abruptly to talk about the English novel. He started with Richardson and he touched on Smollett and Fielding. Whenever Milton tried to say anything, he told Milton not to interrupt, and eventually Milton began to grow angry.

"There's no reason to give us a free discourse," Milton said, "and Polly has read Fielding."

"No woman can possibly appreciate Fielding," Tom Brett said. "He was a man in a man's world. He saw women as men see them, but now on the other hand, if you want to take — "

"I don't want to take anybody," Milton said, "and besides I have my broadcast."

"It's good for you to listen to someone else sometimes," Tom Brett said. "You're uncultivated, Milton, basically, and you're a sponge intellectually. When you squeeze yourself, there's nothing left."

"At least I can absorb some more," Milton said.

"That's exactly the point I'm making." And Tom Brett frowned at him. "You can absorb, but you can't retain."

Milton's face had grown red and he had a resigned look.

"I'm sorry, darling," he said. "I've got to be leaving now. I didn't know he would be here. We'll have lunch some other time."

Polly said she really must go too.

"Don't," Tom Brett said. "Please stay." They sat there facing each other across the half-empty dishes and she stayed. Tom Brett leaned back in his chair.

"Well, thank God he's gone," he said. "I'd rather talk myself than listen to Ouerbach. I'm really much more interesting."

"Then why did you have lunch with us?" Polly asked.

"Because you appeared — or do you mind my being personal?"

"No," Polly answered, "if you consider that personal."

"You see," he said, "I'm just a poor boy from the country, educated in the Middle West."

"What's that got to do with it?" Polly asked.

"I don't exactly know," he said. "It hasn't much, has it?"

"People from there never seem to forget it. They always bring it up just the way you do," Polly said. "I don't know whether it's a superiority or an inferiority complex. I suppose it means you're an American boy."

She thought he looked rather like B. F. as he hunched his shoulders forward.

"Now just exactly why do you suppose I'm that?" he asked.

"It just flashed through my mind," Polly said. "It's an expression my father uses. He says Americans have more of a chance than any other boys."

Tom Brett pursed his lips as though he were swallowing medicine.

"Now that you've brought him up, who is your father?"

"The name is Burton Fulton."

"I never heard of him. Should I have heard of him?"

"You're awfully egotistical, aren't you? Who cares whether you've heard of him or not?" Polly asked.

"That puts me where I belong," Tom Brett said. "Was he one of those poor boys from the Middle West too?"

"More or less," Polly answered. She tried to be angry, but at the same time something made her want to laugh.

"He must be one of those grabby American boys who picked up all the marbles and ran," Tom Brett said. "From the way you look, he must be in the chips."

"Very observing of you," Polly answered. "He *is* in the chips, and I don't think he would want *you* in his office."

"That's all right with me," Tom Brett said. "I wouldn't want to be in it. He probably has slogans on the wall like Do It Well, and Make It Come True."

"He's worth any ten of you."

"You wouldn't know," Tom Brett answered, "but it's lovely of you to be loyal. I was never loyal to my father. He was a Congregational minister."

"That explains everything," Polly said.

"You've got a pretty sharp tongue, haven't you?"

"Yes, I have."

"Well, it goes with your hair. It's a wonder you haven't got more freckles."

"Well, I've worked them off," Polly said.

He stared at her and she stared back. His eyes were gray-blue, a little too close together. His eyebrows were so light that they might have been nonexistent. His nose was too sharp, and he looked as though he did not get enough sleep, and certainly no outdoor exercise. That friend of Milton's could stare at her as much as he wanted to, because she had taken care of her face before she went there to lunch. She was wearing a severe smoke-blue dress made for her by Elizabeth Hawes, that went especially well with her hair, and so did the gold clip which Bob Tasmin had given her, not exactly an engagement present, just a present.

"Do you like to play games?" she asked.

"Good God," he said, "why?"

"It isn't any worse than any of your questions."

"Exactly what sort of games?"

"The things people play, the things they build country clubs for — tennis, squash — that sort of thing."

"Good God, no," he said. "Do I look as though I did?"

"No, you certainly don't," Polly said, and she laughed.

"Do you like people who play games?"

"I don't know," Polly said. "I wish you'd straighten your tie."

"Never mind it," he said. "It always does that."

"That's because you don't know how to tie it."

"You're probably right," he said. "I'm not good with knots. I used to try when I was a Boy Scout. I can't make ship models either. Do you think this is entertaining?"

"No," Polly said, "not very."

"Neither do I. Does my tie look better now?"

He had jerked his tie sideways impatiently.

"No, not much," Polly said. "I suppose it's a way of calling attention to yourself. I suppose it's the way you imply that your mind is on higher things."

"That's it," he said. "I've got a lot on my mind. You may have noticed I have a button off my coat, too. I've got it in my pocket. I never could sew buttons."

"I hate sloppy people," Polly said.

"I'm not sloppy," he answered. "I have a very orderly mind, one of the best minds I know. I'm wonderful in a library, very neat with notes."

"Don't try to show off," Polly said. "Anybody can learn to be good in a library. I'm good in one."

"You must be," he said. "It must be beautiful to see you bending over Poole's index. Let's go to a library sometime."

"At any rate, I wouldn't have to hear you talk."

"You'd be surprised," he said. "People pay to hear me."

"Yes," Polly answered, "I would be surprised. Do you talk to women's clubs or just to groups?"

"You would be — actually," he said. "I talk very beautifully, and I love to hear myself. Come to one of my classes someday at Columbia."

"Thanks," Polly said. "I'd rather meet you in the library in the Quiet Room."

"Why not in church?" he asked. "I'm pretty good in churches. I was brought up in them."

"No," Polly said, "because I'd have to hear you sing."

"There's nothing like a good sound hymn to settle your stomach," he said, "with a melodeon. But nothing Episcopal. I suppose you're an Episcopalian."

"And suppose I were," Polly answered.

"In one of those churches made out of rocks and golden oak."

"I wish you wouldn't try to be whimsical," Polly said.

"You're practical, aren't you?" he asked. "Brisk, crisp, efficient. Just a homespun frontier girl. Can you light a fire with one match?"

"If neither of us can talk sense, I'm going home," she said.

"I'm just reaching a sensible basis," he told her. "If you don't like the way I look, why don't you improve me?"

"Why should I want to?" Polly asked. "You're too pleased with yourself already."

"Because all women want to improve men," he said. "It's their one desire, basically."

"I wouldn't know where to start with you," Polly said, "not even basically, and I wish you wouldn't use that word any more."

"Now we're getting somewhere," he said, and he pulled a button from his pocket. "It's just a suggestion, but you could start by sewing this button on my coat for me."

"You mean now," Polly asked, "right here?"

"Why not right here? It would make a very pretty domestic scene."

"I suppose you think I don't know how to sew," Polly said. "Well, I do."

"Well, go ahead," he said. "Here's my coat." And he began to take it off.

"Don't be an exhibitionist," Polly said. "How can I sew on a button without a needle and thread?"

"Let me put my mind on it for a moment," he said. "I have a very good mind."

"It'll be a relief to see you use it."

"Oh, Teddy?" Tom Brett called.

Polly had not noticed until then that they were the only customers left in the upstairs room. Teddy was in a corner talking to a waiter, and he walked over to the table in a slow, muscle-bound way.

"Whatcha want, Mr. Brett?" he asked. "Rye ginger ale?"

"No, Teddy," Tom Brett answered. "This is just a personal, domestic problem."

"We don't do nothing like that here, Mr. Brett," he said. "You gotta go someplace else."

She never knew what she would have done if Tom had not laughed.

"Don't mind Teddy," he said. "Just think of him as an innocent proletarian with a one-celled mind. Teddy, listen to my problem. Have you got a needle and thread?"

"Needle thread," Teddy repeated. "We ain't got nothing here but pins."

"Let's get out of here," Tom Brett said. "There's the whole garment trade outside. We'll find a needle somewhere."

They walked toward the Grand Central Station, looking for a store that sold needles and thread.

"We might try a Liggett's drugstore," Tom Brett said. "They sell practically everything at Liggett's — Teddy bears, odd volumes, everything."

"You might ask a policeman," Polly said, but Tom Brett did not

323

want to do that — he said he might be misunderstood. Now in the country, there would be a dry goods store, selling what they called notions, but there weren't any dry goods or notion stores on Vanderbilt Avenue.

"You could go in somewhere and find out," Polly said. She did not know that he always hated to ask anyone anything. He said he couldn't ask in an antique or an optical store. They might have needles and things at Brooks's or Abercrombie's, but they didn't sell them, and you couldn't go in there and make a fool of yourself.

"I'll tell you what we'll do," he said. "We'll go to Macy's. They've got everything at Macy's. Hey, taxi."

Even then he was quick at getting taxis.

If you just had a definite purpose, he told her as they rode down to Macy's, everything fitted together. Now that they were working on a project, shoulder to shoulder as it were, it made real sense.

They found a spool of thread and a paper of needles at Macy's. Polly was the one who found them because he wanted to walk everywhere without asking, through the pet shop and the grocery department, everywhere. They found the needles and thread at the Notion Counter because Polly asked.

"How did you know they had a Notion Counter?" he asked. "I'd never have thought of that."

"It just came over me," Polly said. "It's because I'm practical."

"Now I'm going to buy you a present," he told her, "that is, if you don't mind."

"As long as it isn't compromising," Polly said.

"I'll buy you a book," he said. "There's nothing in God's world less compromising than a book."

"That would be a beautiful gesture," Polly said. "What sort of a book?"

"Any kind," he answered. "I'll tell you what we'll buy, *The Little Flowers of St. Francis.* I haven't read it, but someone ought to."

"I wish you wouldn't keep on being whimsical," Polly said, but that was what he bought her, and she always kept the book.

"You know," he said, "I've thought of something."

"What?" she asked.

324

"Now we've got those things, there isn't any place to sew on that button."

If you stopped to think of it, there were not many public places in New York where you could make love or sew on buttons.

"I guess I'll have to take you home," Polly said. "We can do it there." The idea had never occurred to her until that moment, and it made her laugh. "You know we could have done it at home all the time."

She forgot that she might have to explain the button sewing if her mother or Harry or B. F. should be there, but in the apartment at four o'clock that afternoon, there was not a sign of Timmons or anyone. When she opened the door there was a fresh smell of hyacinths and azaleas from the hall, and the lights were on above the Gainsborough and the Lawrence.

"Come in," Polly said. "I guess it's early. No one's here."

He stood for a second or two with his felt hat pulled over his eyes. Then he took it off slowly and pulled off his overcoat more slowly.

"Just leave them anywhere," Polly said, and he tossed them on a chair.

"Good God," he said. "Do you live here?"

"Yes," Polly said. "Why not? Don't you remember, my father picked up the marbles and ran."

"That's right," he said. "I'd forgotten that."

He followed her into the French drawing room.

"Good God," he said, "where did this come from?"

"From France, of course," Polly said. "He bought the whole business out of a château. The dining room came from Ireland. Now about that button. Take off your coat."

"Let's forget about that button," he said.

"But that's what we came here for."

"Listen, we can't do it here," he said, "not with all these mirrors."

"Maybe you're right, but there's always the library," Polly told him. "You say you're good in libraries."

"That's right," he said. "I'd forgotten that. Where's the library?"

325

But he was not much better in the library. He stood speechless staring at the backs of B. F.'s books.

"All Americana," Polly said. "All firsts."

"No seconds?" he asked.

"Only a few eccentric ones."

"How do you stand it living here?" he asked.

"You get used to it," Polly said. "I'm perfectly conditioned."

"Well, it isn't like you."

"Well, the same thing's crossed my own mind sometimes," Polly said.

"You know, you ought to get away from this," he said, "or else it will get you down."

"Maybe I will," Polly said, "someday."

"*Shall,*" he said, "not *will.*"

"Well, now we're here," Polly said, "let's sew on that button."

"Suppose someone sees us, suppose someone comes in."

"Don't worry," she said. "B. F. hardly ever wears a coat in here."

"Who's B. F.?"

"My father. B. F. for Burton Fulton."

"Hurry up," he said. "You needn't be so careful."

"I want to show you I can do it right."

She wanted it to be sewed like the others, and she wanted it to stay.

"Well, thanks a lot," he said when she had finished. "That's great. I guess I'd better be going now."

"Oh, please don't," Polly said. "You've only been here a minute. Don't you want a drink or something?"

"No, thanks," he said, "not right now. It's getting pretty late."

They stood there facing each other between a terrestrial and a celestial globe from England, and it was like saying good-by for good.

"Good-by," he said.

"Well, good-by," she answered.

"I've had a nice time. I'm sorry I acted like such a damned fool," he said.

"You didn't," Polly answered, "not any more than me."

"Than *I,*" he said. "Well, thanks."

326

She wanted to follow him to the door. She wanted to ask him not to go, but instead she did nothing. She was sure that it was all over and that she would never see him again.

Her mother was upstairs, and B. F. was not back when Bob Tasmin came in at half-past five.

"God, you look beautiful," he said. "You look radiant."

"Do I?" Polly said.

"What have you been doing all day?" he asked.

"Oh, nothing much, darling," Polly said. "Mostly shopping."

But when she lay in bed that night before she went to sleep, she began thinking of Tom Brett, thinking of what he had said and she had said, going over it word by word, and when she awoke that next morning a terrible thing had happened. She was in love with two men at once.

XXIV

Among the First to Know

THIS WAS all a ridiculous aberration, because Polly loved Bob Tasmin, she had always loved him. Besides, she would never see Tom Brett again. It was an incident that was entirely over. She did not even know where he lived, and it was just as well. She was not going to be so weak as to ask about him — but the memory of that afternoon kept returning to her. Everything was "Why?" Why had they been so congenial? Why had they got on so well together? Why did their minds seem to work in the same way? The first day was terrible, because no matter what she did she could not escape from those questions.

It was like waking from a bad dream when she saw Bob that afternoon.

"Darling," she said, "I wish we could be married right away and have this damn thing over."

He always said the right thing, and he said it then.

"I feel the same way, Poll," he said. "It's awful . . . but they expect us to go through the motions. It won't be long. You were talking about June."

She had been, before she had met Tom Brett. June had seemed very reasonable, and the wedding would be on the lawn at Gray's Point.

"But it's only January now," she said. "Let's make it February. Let's get this over and go to South America."

"Why, Poll," Bob said, "you act as though you were afraid something might happen."

"Of course I'm not afraid," she said, "but we've been waiting so long, Bob. Let's make it February."

In spite of all her rationalizing she had never honestly believed that she would not see Tom Brett again. She found herself waiting for a letter. She was startled by every ring of the telephone and twice, before she was able to stop herself, she asked Timmons whether anyone had called her without leaving a message, but no one had called.

Meanwhile Mrs. Beardhope, who did social things for her mother, was preparing the list for the announcement tea, and Tiffany's had already started on the cards. She had never seen B. F. so enthusiastic. From the way he acted you might have thought he was about to announce his own engagement. He kept checking the lists and thinking of more people until there began to be so many that he suggested they might move the party out of the apartment altogether and have it in a ballroom somewhere. He only refrained when he was told that it would not look well with banks being closed and hungry men selling apples. Even so, he said he wanted it to be right because he only had one girl, and it would only happen once. He went with Polly to Bergdorf's and looked at all the models himself to be sure that there would not be any mistake about her dress, and he began calling dealers about precious stones. She was his only girl, and he wanted to give her an engagement present designed by whoever was the best in the business. Everything was moving as though nothing could be changed, and Polly was moving with it. She wished it would move so fast that she did not have to think.

"You look pale, darling," her mother said. "You always get those dark circles under your eyes when you don't sleep."

"Well, I don't feel pale," Polly said.

"I know it's a strain, dear," her mother said, "but it's a happy sort of strain."

"Did you go through it, Mother?" Polly asked.

"Oh, of course, dear," her mother said. "The night before our announcement party I cried and cried. I was so afraid I would do something awful at that party, like saying that it was all a mistake. I couldn't seem to see Burt in my mind, not the way he was, I mean."

"You couldn't see him in your mind?" Polly repeated. She had not been able to see Bob Tasmin in her mind last night, the way he was, but she had seen Tom Brett just the way he was, and she could see him now.

"It was such a lovely party." Her mother's voice was soft and wistful. "You'd have called it small-town, but it was lovely. It was a bridge-whist party, and there were festoons and bells and streamers and paper flowers all over the room. Do you remember your grandmother at all?"

"Yes," Polly said, "a little." It would have been in the house at Willett in that stuffy little parlor with the horsehair chairs and sofas.

"Mother always had such original ideas. She wrote on the score cards, 'Hearts are trumps for Gladys and Burt.' "

It was silly, but all at once Polly was crying. She wished sometimes later that she had told her mother about Tom Brett then.

"There, dear," her mother said. "I know. You're crying because you're happy."

"I'm crying because it sounds so nice," she said.

On the fourth day after she had met Tom Brett, Polly saw him again, early on a cloudy afternoon. She had been going somewhere to try something on or something, she could not remember what, because it all went out of her mind forever. She had left the apartment building and was walking toward the corner where the same taxicab always stood, and there he was. The collar of his overcoat was pulled up on one side and down on the other, and his hands were in his pockets. She saw him, and everything inside her was weak and watery. She remembered that a cold wind was blowing and that he looked very cross.

"Don't you ever come out of that place?" he asked.

Her heart was beating very fast, and her voice was choked, but she had to appear natural in front of the doorman of the apartment. At least she had to act as though it were not extraordinary that he should be there, not the most surprising thing that ever happened.

"Yes," she said, "quite often. Why?"

"Well, I've been wearing my shoes out walking around here for three afternoons," he said. "Don't look so sour."

"What?" Polly said.

"Don't look so snappish."

"Do I really look that way?" she asked, and she realized they could not stand there indefinitely. "If you wanted to see me, why didn't you ask for me?"

"Up there?" he asked. "Good God."

Someone would be sure to see them on the sidewalk.

"Well, now I'm here," she said, "do something."

"Do what?" he asked.

"Anything — except stay here."

"All right," he said, "all right. Let's do anything. What's anything?"

"Make up your mind. What do you expect me to do, make it up for you?"

"All right," he said. "All right. Let's get in that taxi."

"Not that one," Polly said. "He knows me. He knows everybody."

"Suppose he does. As long as it's got heat in it."

"Don't argue," Polly said. "Get another taxi."

"All right," he said. "But what *is* anything?"

"It doesn't matter," Polly said.

He found another taxi almost instantly. It was an old one with cracked windows, but at least the driver did not know everybody. She observed the most irrelevant details, such as the driver's photograph and license card — his name was Conrad Blitz. It did not much matter what you said in back of someone with that name. She was very glad to sink down on the lumpy seat because her knees were still weak. She sat for what seemed like a long while waiting for Tom Brett to take some sort of initiative, and the driver also waited.

"Well, how have you been?" he asked.

"Never mind," she said. "Tell him to drive somewhere."

"That's right," he said. "Where?"

"My God," Polly said. "You think where."

"Don't snap at me," he said. "Aren't you glad to see me?"

"I'm crazy about it," Polly said. "Tell him where to drive."

"All right," he said, "all right. Take us around the Park."

"No," Polly said, "anything but that."

"Why not?"

"Because everybody always does it," Polly said. "Think of something else."

"All right," he said. "The Metropolitan Museum of Art."

"It's nice your mind is working."

He took his hands from his pockets and blew on them.

"I'm cold," he said.

"Then why don't you wear gloves?" she asked.

"Because I always lose them. I don't like gloves. . . . Well, how have you been?"

"I don't know," Polly said. "How have you?"

"I don't know either," he answered, and they were silent again. They were turning onto Fifth Avenue.

"Where shall we go in that museum?" he asked. "The Etruscan courtyard?"

"No," she said. "I hate Etruscans."

"So do I," he said. "Why do you?"

"I don't know why. Never mind it now."

"Do you want a cigarette?"

"Thanks," Polly said.

He leaned toward her to light it for her and their shoulders touched. He was very clumsy with the match and it went out.

"Give them to me. I'll light it," Polly said.

"All right," he said, and he sighed. "You light it."

It was one of the days on which you paid twenty-five cents to get into the Museum, so there was not much of a crowd. The few people sauntering through the Egyptian Room, the mummies, the miniatures from tombs and the bas-reliefs, all seemed to be in disorder like her mind.

"They certainly concentrated on dying," he said.

"Yes," she said. "Don't you?"

"My mind isn't on it now," he answered. "Is yours?"

"No, not at the moment," she said.

They walked through the hall full of armor without speaking. They wandered through the statuary and picture galleries and the American Wing. They were near a doorway from Salem when he asked her if she was bothered about something.

"Well," she said, "I am. I'm going to be married in a month." He stared at her as though she had said something which was very abstruse.

"Good God," he said. "Do you want to be?"

She looked down at the wooden floor of the American Wing.

"I don't know," she answered. "I really don't know."

"Listen," he said, "not in a month. You've only just met me."

"Yes, I know," she said. "I wish I hadn't."

"I wish you hadn't either," he answered, "but you have."

They understood each other without saying any more. It was terrible, but at the same time it was wonderful to know that he cared and to see him so hurt about it.

"It's ridiculous," she said. "We don't know anything about each other."

"The hell we don't."

"But I don't know why we do," she asked him. "Why?"

"It doesn't make any sense," he answered, "but we do. It's a hell of a situation. I can't get you out of my mind."

"Can't you?"

"Never mind," he said. "We've never made sense."

"I'm so ashamed."

"I suppose you are," he answered, "but it isn't your fault."

"I hate to hurt anyone."

"Look here," he said. "You've got to. You've got to get out of this."

"Well, what am I going to do?"

She glanced at him, but he was not looking at her.

"I'll marry you myself, as long as you're sure you don't like dogs."

That was how he proposed to her, in front of the doorway that had been taken from Salem, and just as he did so there was a clatter of footsteps and they were surrounded by a conducted study group.

"This interior," a pale girl with glasses was saying, "is an example

333

of the mid-eighteenth century period in New England. The wall-paper, which is original, was discovered in a Portsmouth dwelling. The marbleized painting on the woodwork shows Italian influence. Its lack of sophistication is amusing, but effective."

"Who ever heard of a sophisticated house painter?" Tom Brett murmured.

"Let's get out of here," Polly said. "Let's walk in the Park."

"I thought you said you didn't like the Park."

"Not in a taxicab," she answered. "I don't mind walking."

They walked by the obelisk without speaking, and then across the road and up the steps to the reservoir. It was so windy that they could hardly hear the sound of the traffic on Fifth Avenue.

"You need someone to look out for you," Polly said. "You ought to have gloves." She had not noticed until then how upset he was. He was walking very fast and looking straight ahead of him, and that was why she added, "You can take this back, you know."

"I don't know how it will work, but I won't take it back," he said.

Then she took his arm.

"Don't walk so fast," she said, "and don't look so miserable. It isn't very complimentary."

"Well, there it is," he said, and he walked more slowly. "It may not mean much to you, but it's a sacrifice to me. It will cut into my schedule. What are you going to do about it?"

"I told you," Polly said, "that you could take it back."

"I won't take it back."

"But what would we do?" Polly asked. "Where would we live?"

"Uptown somewhere," he said. "Anywhere but Park Avenue."

"That's all right with me."

"I don't sleep well," he said. "I'm apt to wake up and read. People come around and we sit up all night. I like to talk. I haven't any money, except my salary and something extra for lectures."

"Never mind the money," Polly said.

"They say I have a future," he said. "I admit it, I've got a future."

"But why do you want me?" Polly asked. "I don't see why, or do you?"

"I just can't think of getting along without you," he said. "If we're in a hurry, it's your fault, not mine. I'm not engaged."

"So it's my fault, is it?"

"Yes, it's your fault basically."

"Well, it's nice to know it," Polly said. "At any rate, it all might be different."

"Different from what?"

"From anything I've ever known."

"I hope it would be," he said. "Yes, on the whole I think you'd be quite right in assuming that."

"Well, I'll have to think it over," Polly said. "Are you busy to-morrow?"

"No, it's vacation."

"All right," Polly said. "I'll meet you at four at the Altman Collection. I'm afraid we're going to see a lot of that museum. Well, I'll see you tomorrow."

"Don't you want me to put you on a bus or something?" he asked.

"No, thanks," she said. "You make me nervous."

Then he put his hands on her shoulders. They were on that path by the reservoir and no one was near them.

"Try to do what you can," he said. "Won't you? I know it's a damned silly thing to say, and I hate being obvious, but —"

"What?" she asked.

"I love you. . . . Do you mind if I repeat myself? I love you."

While she walked away from him, for a long time she did not know where she was walking. Although nothing was settled, she knew it was all as good as settled. There was nothing that she or anyone else could do about it.

Polly had only one consolation — when she could not understand what was going on inside herself it was pleasant to know that no one else seemed to know what was going on in America, for the machine, or whatever it was that governed the lives of everyone that winter, was grinding to a stop. There were waves of bankruptcies, and there was no work; farmers could not pay their mortgages; people downtown were jumping out of windows. No one, not even people like B. F., knew what was going to happen next, and all that confusion and the growing disbelief in permanence may have influenced her. Besides it was instinctive to blame what you could on something outside yourself.

She had to do something. Every day she was being pushed nearer to the decision of taking it or leaving it. She could not go on indefinitely feeling like a coward every time she saw Bob Tasmin, and also when she saw Tom Brett. She wished that she were rid of them both sometimes, and she often hated herself and both of them because it was all too desperately complicated to be worth the bother. It was the sort of thing that sent people to those retreats where you took long walks and learned how to make mats and ash trays. She was ashamed that she was so incapable of making up her mind, but finally she knew that she had to marry Tom Brett whether it was wise or whether she wanted to or not.

Awake and asleep she kept living through the scene of telling her father, and it was like dying before you died. For some reason it worried her more than telling Bob. She would muster all the arguments and all the facts in logical order, only to have them fly to pieces in her mind. At least she could talk about it to Tom Brett, but he was living in a fraternity house, and he could suggest no place where they could go without being seen by someone, except the art museum in the morning. It made her angry sometimes that Tom took the attitude that it was all up to her, and it was all the more irritating because she knew he was right. They must have talked for hours against backgrounds of Chinese porcelains, against groups of spears and halberds, or against the bare trees in the Park.

"You needn't act like an innocent bystander," she told him. "You're in this too."

"I'm not in the first wave," he said. "You've got to run on the barbed wire first, right through No Man's Land."

"That's where I'm living now," she said, "in No Man's Land."

"Yes," he said, "and you're living there all on account of men."

"I wish you'd shut up," she said. . . . "But you'll have to see him sometime."

"Of course, I'll have to see the Old Man sometime."

She wished he wouldn't call him "the Old Man."

"What else can I call him?" he asked. "I'll see him tomorrow if you want me to."

"No. You've got to be explained."

"I don't think it's going to do any good to explain me," he said. "He won't like me."

"Darling, he's got to like you."

"Well, he won't. You'd be amazed. I'm not the type that anybody's old man would like. What's more, I'm not going to take any backwash from him. He sounds to me like what's wrong with everything."

"You've said all that before," Polly said. "Can't you think of something new?"

"All right. Here's something new. I'll go with you and we'll see him together. It ought to be quite a show."

"No," she said. "I've got to see him alone."

"All right," he said. "Then we're back just where we started."

She wanted to see B. F. in a place where her emotions would not be distracted by old associations, so she went to his office early one morning. Her father's office was on the forty-seventh floor, so high up that you felt the pressure in your ears before you left the elevator. There was no one in the reception hall but the receptionist, a dark girl who looked like a Powers model. She was seated behind a handsome English Chippendale desk. B. F. was interested in the interpretation of industry through art, so the whole place was like a gallery uptown — oil paintings of chimneys, bridges, cranes, grain elevators, blast furnaces, electrical transformers, and of workers wrestling with machine tools.

"I want to see Miss Silver," Polly said. "Will you tell her it's Miss Fulton, please."

"Oh," the girl said, "I'm sorry."

"What are you sorry for?" Polly asked.

"I should have known you right away, Miss Fulton."

"Don't be sorry," Polly said. "It must be nice to sit here with all these pictures."

"Aren't they lovely?" the girl said. "There's the Pittsburgh plant,

and there's Detroit. Here's the catalogue if you'd care to see it."
And she handed Polly a printed card just as though she were an art
dealer. Polly wondered, as she waited, what the girl was like, and
what her life away from the office might be. Here she was a woman
without a man, tranquil, undisturbed, with red fingernails. Polly
glanced at the leather-covered book she had been reading and it
startled her. It was *The Little Flowers of St. Francis.*

"Did a man give it to you?" Polly asked.

"Why, yes," the girl said.

"Well, I hope it wasn't the professor at Columbia who just gave
one to me," Polly said. "Do you like it?" And then they both
laughed.

"I don't like it much," the girl said.

"I'll tell you why men give us those books," Polly said, "because
they think they'll keep us out of trouble."

They both laughed again, but they stopped when Miss Silver
came in. Miss Silver was older with tight lips and clear gray eyes.
No one could have given *The Little Flowers of St. Francis* to her
for a long while, if ever.

"Why, Miss Polly," Miss Silver said — it made Polly feel gauche
to be called Miss Polly — "Mr. Fulton never told me you were
coming."

She followed Miss Silver down a noiseless corridor to a small room
outside Miss Silver's office.

"I suppose it isn't in order yet," Miss Silver said, "but I do want
to congratulate you on your happiness. Mr. Fulton is alone now.
I'll tell him you're here."

Polly sat holding the *Herald Tribune,* but it did not keep her
from rehearsing the forthcoming scene.

In contrast to the reception hall, B. F.'s office looked empty. He
was wearing a brown double-breasted suit which had just come
from the tailor. He was sitting in front of a bare mahogany table
talking over the telephone. There were some blueprints on another
table, and a few photographs hung on the wall near him, one of her
mother, one of Harry, one of her, and one of the house at Gray's
Point. From the windows she could see the East River glittering in

the sun like steel, and buildings in geometrical groups that finally stretched away in a level plain over Long Island.

"I can't tell you why, Jim," B. F. was saying. "You know it isn't personal, and when you've had a good night's sleep, you'll know you had no right to ask me. We'd better leave it that way, Jim."

B. F. set down the telephone gently.

"We've just drawn our account out of one of those Detroit banks," he said. "We've had it there for years. You can't mix friends with business, Poll."

"Is the bank going to close?" Polly asked.

"It can't help it," B. F. said. "What do you think of this suit?"

"It's pretty brown, isn't it?"

"That's what I was afraid of," B. F. said. "I should have got a herringbone or a worsted. Well, sit down, Poll."

"I want to sit near you," Polly said. "I don't want to talk across the table."

"All right," B. F. said, and he pulled a leather-covered armchair beside his swivel chair, but even so, she was not near him. He sat looking down at her, and the light was in her eyes.

"You look awfully pretty, Poll," he said, "as pretty as that information girl out there."

"Thanks," Polly said, "but I'm afraid you won't think so when I'm through." His chair creaked as he leaned back. She hadn't said it yet, she still could avoid saying it, but she went on. "I can't marry Bob Tasmin, B. F. I'm awfully sorry."

She had often heard B. F. speak of putting cork or other compositions on office walls and ceilings to deaden sound, and now she heard her words fall deliberately on utter silence, without a single extraneous vibration to interfere with their balance or significance. Nothing could ever take them back. She had dreaded for days her father's reception of the news, but as it happened, he had no time to say anything before the telephone rang again.

"Excuse me," he said. "Hello. . . . Yes, Bill, I can give you my answer." He sat listening to a voice that came to Polly's ears in a series of undignified squeaks. She could not tell what the voice was saying, but she knew from B. F.'s expression that he had already put out of his mind what she had said. "I understand what you mean, but I'm saying no. I don't want to start anything that I can't finish, and I wouldn't either if I were you. . . . Good-by, Bill."

He set down the telephone gently and stared at it.

"You have to make up your mind fast these days," he said. "Excuse me, Poll." And he picked up another telephone. "Miss Silver, I don't want anyone to get through to me, and I can't see anyone until I tell you. I'm sorry, Polly, I guess you'd better say that again."

The room had that same prefabricated silence again as she said it.

"I can't marry Bob. I know it's awful."

"All right," B. F. said. "Now there's lots of time. Don't get excited, Poll."

She must have spoken louder than was necessary.

"And you can't make me," she said. "I know, because I've tried to make myself."

"Well, I'm glad you've come here." B. F. folded his hands behind his head. "Don't get so excited, Poll."

His voice was usually sharp, but now it sounded as it used to when she had broken something or when she was hurt. She could only tell from the wrinkles around his eyes how seriously he took it. Her own eyes were smarting, and she reached in her bag for her handkerchief.

"Don't cry," he said. "Would you like a glass of water?"

"No, thanks," she answered, and it made her both laugh and sob. "Water won't do any good."

"Don't cry, Poll," he said again. "I'm here no matter what."

"There isn't anything you can do."

"Why not?" he asked. "That's what I'm here for, Poll."

"Because you're always doing everything."

"Yes," he said. "I suppose it's a habit. All right, Poll, but I don't want you to make a mistake. That's all."

"I know how much you wanted it," she said. "That's the main thing I'm sorry for."

His chair creaked again as he leaned still further back, and she could see that he was already trying to break down the problem along practical lines.

"Now wait a minute," he said. "Did you get engaged to Bob because you thought I wanted it?"

"Yes," she said. ". . . No. I don't know."

His eyes looked hurt, and his whole expression grew businesslike.

"It's funny," he said, and his forehead wrinkled. "I thought everything was fine, but then, I guess I'm not a girl."

"I'm terribly fond of Bob," she said. "I know I ought to love him."

B. F. pushed his chair forward, and put his feet on the floor. He was like Tom Brett. He never could sit still.

"I don't understand," he said. "Have you had a fight with Bob?"

"No, he's always so sweet," she said, and she began to cry again.

"You mean he's so sweet he makes you cry," B. F. asked.

"Darling," Polly said. "I don't know how to explain. He's so secure. You can tell in advance how everything is going to turn out. If I married him, it would be just like staying at home." She had not meant to bring that up. "I wouldn't be myself."

"All girls are restless, I guess," he said. "You ought to have someone looking after you. Is that the only reason you don't want to marry Bob?"

"No," she said. "I'm in love with someone else." And she went on quickly before he could interrupt. ". . . But it wouldn't have happened if it hadn't been for other things. I can't always have you and Bob Tasmin looking after me in cotton wool on a yacht."

"How does a yacht come into it?" he asked her. "I haven't got a yacht."

"It's an expression," Polly said, "that he uses, but you know what I mean."

"No, I don't," B. F. said. "Who uses it?"

"The man I'm in love with," Polly began. "He uses it — "

"Now let's get this straight," B. F. began. "How can you be in love with anyone when you're just engaged to Bob?"

"Darling. I'm trying to tell you and you interrupt."

"All right," B. F. said. "This man on this yacht. Who is he, Poll?"

341

"He isn't on a yacht," Polly answered. "He's an assistant professor in English from Columbia, and he comes from Wisconsin and he looks something like you."

"No one ever told me that I looked like a professor."

"His name is Brett," Polly said. "I don't know how it happened, but it did."

"Where did you meet this professor? In one of those courses at Columbia?"

"I met him in a speak-easy if you want to know," Polly said. "A week ago." It kept sounding worse and worse.

"Things don't work that way," B. F. said. "You can't know anything about each other. You've never even brought him home."

"Yes, I did," Polly said, "the afternoon I met him. No one was there. I sewed a button on his coat."

"I don't seem to get this straight," B. F. said, "but then, I guess you don't either, Poll. Try to give me a picture of it. Is he young? Does he wear glasses?"

"I know how it sounds," Polly said, "but we get along with each other. We say the most awful things, and he always makes me laugh. He's interested in politics. He helped with the New Deal campaign speeches — but you've got to see him to know what I mean."

She had to go on telling about Tom Brett, but her words all broke to nothing in that quiet room, and B. F. sat there listening until she had finished.

"It isn't much of a picture," he said. "He sounds eccentric."

"Well, he is," she answered. "That's why I love him."

"Have you told your mother?"

Polly shook her head.

"Have you told Bob?"

"No," Polly answered, "I've got to, but I haven't. You see why I can't go on being engaged, don't you?"

"Well, that's all right," B. F. said. Polly wriggled uneasily in the leather chair and squared her shoulders.

"I don't see how you can say it's all right."

"Now listen, Poll," B. F. said. "I'll tell you what we'll do."

"I don't want you to tell me what to do, because I know."

But B. F. was not listening.

"I'll tell you what we'll do. You're tired, Poll. You're mixed up, and you need to be oriented. We'll tell Bob you need a rest, and you and I'll go out to Arizona. There's H. J.'s ranch in Arizona, horses, cowboys. It's about time you and I had a change. We'll go out there, and you don't write to this Brett or hear anything from him for two months, and then see what you think. That's fair, isn't it?"

"But I'm not tired and that would only make it worse. It isn't the way you think it is. I hate it, darling, but it's something I've got to do."

"You mean you won't go," B. F. said, "even if I ask you? I don't think it's asking much."

"I know how it sounds," Polly said, "but I can't."

"That isn't so," he said. "You mean you won't."

His voice had changed, but he did not appear to be angry, only investigating an unpleasant problem.

"No," she said, "I won't." And then he picked up one of the telephones.

"All right," he said, "you can put calls through now. See if you can get me through to Detroit." And then he stood up. "I don't know what I've done to you, Poll, that you should do this to me. I always thought we got on pretty well together, ever since you were a little girl and Bob was always over. I know you'd be happy with Bob. Well, never mind."

"Darling," Polly said, "you've always done too much."

"Well, never mind," he said.

"Darling, I don't want anyone doing too much for me. Look at Mother, look at Harry. I know you can't help it."

"I remember," he said, "that time you ran away. All right, Poll, what are you going to do?"

"I've got to tell Bob," she said.

"When?"

"When he comes this afternoon."

"Can't you wait until tomorrow?"

"I can't keep waiting," Polly said.

"Well," B. F. said. "I'm always around if you want me, Poll. I'm sorry you don't want me."

Then the telephone was ringing.

"Well, I'll see you later, Poll." He waved his hand to her. "Have they had that meeting yet? I just wanted to get a line." He was still talking when she reached the door, and it closed noiselessly on his voice.

"Now that B. F. has his own private dining room," Miss Silver said, "I know he would love it if you came to have lunch with him. It's always been Polly with B. F. as long as I can remember. It must make you very proud."

"Yes," Polly said, "it does." She smiled at Miss Silver and the girl at the reception desk, but her reactions were very slow.

When she was in the street she wanted to go back to tell him that she was sorry, that she would go with him to Arizona or anywhere. Yet, she knew that if she went back and said she was sorry, she would never be able to do anything by herself again. He had his own way with people because they all expected it and wanted it, and it was not his fault that most people wanted to be led.

He never alluded to that scene again until long afterwards when he was ill.

"Poll," he said, "that time in the office, that time you told me about Brett —"

It all came back to her, the same feeling in the pit of the stomach, the way she stood there on the sidewalk like the erring daughter in the melodrama being sent out alone into the blizzard.

"It was the first time I knew you had guts," he said, "and right at the same time that Ohio crowd was going through the wringer, and I had to decide whether I'd take them over by noon or let them go. It's just as well we didn't go to Arizona — in a business way."

But it was not a matter of guts. Even then it had been some sort of question of personal survival.

"I never told you I almost came back," Polly said. "I just stood there until some man tried to pick me up."

"Someone would have," B. F. said. "Well, maybe it's just as well you didn't come back."

"Maybe," Polly said.

"But I'll bet if you had, you wouldn't have married Brett."

"I bet I wouldn't have either."

"You see," B. F. said, "if you have executive ability, you run things and it's expected of you. It's the way we're made, and you're like me. Maybe you'd be getting along better now if you hadn't run Brett, but you couldn't help it."

"Tom?" Polly said. "I've never run him."

"Haven't you?" he said. "That's what I used to think about myself. You couldn't have run Bob Tasmin, Poll."

Perhaps she could never have managed Bob Tasmin, but her interview with him was not as bad as it might have been. Perhaps she was inured by then; her main idea was to get it over. She had put on a severe, dark dress for the occasion and had looked at herself in the mirror upstairs, surprised that she looked so well.

"Timmons has the tea things ready," her mother said. "Our men will be here soon. Burt called from the office. Isn't it cozy waiting, dear, knowing that they are coming?"

Polly was thinking that she wanted something stronger than tea, and that her mother need not know the worst until after it was settled with Bob.

"Don't you think you might put on another dress, dear?" her mother asked. "That one looks as though you weren't trying to look pretty for Bob."

"It's too late now," Polly said, and everything was too late.

B. F. arrived first, which was unusual, and he nodded to her as though nothing had happened.

"What?" he asked. "Isn't Bob here yet?" And Polly sat up straight in her chair with her hands folded.

"He ought to be here any time now," she answered.

"Have you ever noticed that Polly has a poker face, Gladys?" B. F. said. "She ought to play poker."

"You're looking tired, Burt," her mother said. "I suppose everything's as bad as usual."

"I am a little tired," B. F. said. "I'm going to take tomorrow off. Suppose you and I go down to Gray's Point, Gladys? Just you and me. Gray's Point belongs to us more than this place."

"As long as you don't start planning to build something, Burt," her mother said.

"No," B. F. answered, "I'm not planning to build anything. . . . Just you and me, Gladys . . . I'll tell you what I want . . . a Scotch and soda. Timmons, a double Scotch and soda."

"Burt, dear," her mother asked, "aren't you feeling well? Have you got a cold coming on?"

"Not a cold, just the depression, Gladys," B. F. said. "Polly, get me *Who's Who in America*."

It was no time to tell him that Tom Brett was not in *Who's Who*, and B. F. was still turning over the pages when Bob Tasmin came. He kissed her mother and shook hands with B. F.

"Do you want a drink, Bob?" B. F. asked.

"Oh, no thanks, sir," Bob Tasmin answered.

"You'd better have a drink," B. F. said, and then Polly could not stand it any longer. She said she had something to tell Bob and asked him to come with her into the library.

"What is it?" he asked. "A secret?"

"It is, but it won't be long," she said.

It must have been the way you felt before you murdered someone. Bob Tasmin did not have the least suspicion, even when she closed the library door.

"I'm sorry I'm so late," he said, "but you know what I've been doing? I've been to an architect's office. They've done a sketch for that house on Sugar Hill, just a rough sketch, Poll, for you to go over. Wait, I've left it in the hall."

He was almost out of the room before she stopped him.

"No," she said, "no." At least she was not going to live at Sugar Hill. She was never going to improve her golf. She was never going to drive down to the evening train in a station wagon.

"Why," he said, "what's the matter, Poll?"

"Bob," she said, "we can't get married."

He had never looked so handsome as he had when she did that

thing to him so clumsily and brutally—but then, how else could anyone have done it?

"All right, Poll, dear," he said. "Why can't we?"

"Because I've fallen in love with someone else," she said. "I couldn't help it, Bob."

He did not even ask her who it was. He only stood very straight, looking at her.

"Well," he said, "I suppose you've given me my chance, Poll. If I'm not what you want, that's my fault."

"I wish you wouldn't be so nice about it," she said.

His face was whiter than it had been, but he smiled.

"Why, I couldn't be anything but nice to you, Poll. . . . I've been a little uneasy about it all myself lately."

"Oh, Bob," she began, "do you mean . . . ?"

"Not about me, but about you, Poll," he answered. "But just for future reference, I'd like to know what I've done wrong, if you could tell me."

"Bob, darling," she answered. "You've never done anything."

"I guess that's it," he said. "I guess that's what was the matter. I guess I'm the kind that never does anything and never will. 'Good-bye Girls, I'm through.'"

"Oh, Bob, don't say that."

"All right, I won't," he answered. "I guess I'd better be going, Poll. I know this must be tough for you."

"What about its being tough on you?" she asked.

His face was still white, but very controlled.

"Don't worry about me," he said. "I hope you don't mind if I still love you. I can't help that, Poll."

"Please don't make it worse," she said. "You ought to hate me."

"It doesn't work that way," he said.

"Oh, darling," she said, "I don't know how it happened."

"If you ever change your mind—" he began. "But I hope you'll be awfully happy, Poll."

And then she made one of those dreadful remarks you read about without ever dreaming that you might say something similar yourself.

"Bob, we can keep on being friends, can't we?"

"Why, we always have been," he said, "and we always will be." And then he made a dreadful remark too, which she was never sure that he did not make on purpose, because he was much wittier than you expected sometimes. "If you ever think of it, I'd like to meet the lucky man."

"Damn the lucky man," Polly said.

"That's just the way I feel. Damn him," Bob said. "Well, good-by, Poll."

He always said the right thing, and he did the right thing. He kissed her forehead very gently.

"Good-by, darling," he said.

She stood there watching him walk away, watching him open the heavy library door, but he did not look back.

XXV

He Had to Meet the Family

POLLY FELT like a small neutral nation, explaining her family to Tom Brett by day, and Tom Brett to her family by night. If B. F. and Tom could have met accidentally and unselfconsciously, they might have liked each other very much. If all the embarrassing circumstances could have been eliminated, they would have realized that they came from the same background, and they would have respected each other's brains and abilities.

"Now listen, Poll," B. F. said. "Brett's got to come around. It isn't natural."

"I know he must, darling," Polly said. "He *wants* to, but how would it be if you had him to lunch downtown first, so you two could see each other alone?"

"I don't want to see Brett downtown," B. F. said. "I want to see him up here with your mother and Harry. We've all got to get used to each other sometime, Poll."

It began to sound like a primitive tribal rite from Frazier's *The Golden Bough*. They would all have to meet, and Tom would have to present B. F. with a pig or something — at least verbally.

"But Harry's at Yale," she said.

"Name the evening when Brett can come, any evening," B. F. said, "and I'll see that Harry gets down from Yale."

"I won't have Tom come here if you're not going to be nice to him," Polly said.

She had a suspicion that B. F. was secretly enjoying himself now that he had taken the position that it was her problem and not his.

"Of course, you can do what you want, Poll," he said, "but you can't blame us for being curious, can you? Brett must have something to him to have stirred up all this fuss."

"Now, Burt," her mother said, "don't make fun of Polly. Burt's kind and nice to everybody, and you know it, dear. If you love Mr. Brett, we're bound to like him, aren't we, Burt?"

"We're trying to get right behind you, Poll," B. F. said. "We've all got to stick together."

"Well, don't say it," Polly said, "as though he were something the cat brought in."

"Now, Poll," B. F. said. "Let's all try to be calm. Your mother will write him a note and ask him to dinner, won't you, Gladys?"

"Well, if you'll only be nice to him," Polly said. "Oh, hell — let's make it Thursday."

She met Tom at the corner of Seventy-third Street the next afternoon and they walked along Madison Avenue.

"It's for half-past seven on Thursday," Polly said. "Mother has written you. You'll be sure to answer it, won't you, darling?"

"Now, please get a grip on yourself, Poll," Tom said. "I admit this is going to be a big experience for me. I'm rehearsing for it. I'm remembering to start with the outside fork."

"You can use any damn fork," Polly said, "as long as you like the family, darling. You mustn't mind Mother being obvious — and Harry is only a lay figure."

"Now, listen," Tom said, and he sounded like B. F., "I honestly can get on with people. Try to get it through your head that it's going to be a relief to have this over with."

As early as half-past six on Thursday Polly went over all her dresses. First she tried on the one from Tappé's with the flared skirt and circles that looked like balloons. Then she took out the Fortuny pleated gown that you kept twisted in a knot, but that was too arty, and next she tried the dress that Harry had said looked as though it were coming off. Finally she compromised on a black velvet from Lanvin because it went well with her pearls. Her mother told Polly that she looked sweet, which was not the way she wanted to look, and they went downstairs together. B. F. and Harry were waiting for them, and she might have known that they would be wearing dinner coats though she had asked them not to.

"I don't see," B. F. was saying, "how you can spend as much as that in a place like New Haven."

"I don't like asking friends to pay me back," Harry said.

"Well, that's no way to make friends," B. F. said. "I want to talk to you about this some other time, Harry. Here are the girls."

"Hello, Poll," Harry called. "I didn't know we were going to have to go over one of these jumps again so soon. Give me more warning next time, won't you?"

"That will do, Harry," B. F. said.

"Columbia," Harry said. "I don't know anyone from Columbia."

"Don't be embarrassed," Polly told him. "Don't let it make you unnatural."

"I don't have to go to college or anywhere," Harry said, "to learn about love and life. You can teach us, Poll."

At least it kept her from wondering whether Tom would be late.

"I could," she began, "if you could learn anything."

"Timmons is answering the door, dear," her mother said.

She could hear Tom murmur something in the distance. He must have asked whether he was expected because she could hear Timmons saying—

"Oh, yes, sir, you're expected."

"Father," she said loudly and unnaturally, "those pictures of yours in the office . . . why didn't you get Grant Wood to do one?"

"Grant who?" B. F. asked.

"Why, Father," Polly said. "Do you mean to say that you never heard of Grant Wood?" At least there was conversation and not a silence when Tom came in, and furthermore he did have on a dinner coat, although she had particularly told him not to bother. He would have looked almost distinguished too, if his shirt had not kept buckling in the middle and if his tie had not ridden to one side.

"Hello," she said. "Now you have to meet everyone."

"How do you do, Mrs. Fulton?" Tom said. "How do you do, sir?"

"This is my brother Harry," Polly said.

"How do you do?" Harry said.

Then there was a momentary silence that seemed much longer

351

than it actually was. She never forgot how Tom looked in that lopsided tie, with B. F. watching him.

"Good," B. F. said, "here come the cocktails. Will you have a cocktail, Mr. Brett?"

"Why, thanks," Tom said, "I wouldn't mind one at all."

"Well," B. F. said, "I'm glad we've got together, Mr. Brett."

"So am I," Tom said. "I'm glad to see everybody."

"Naturally, we've heard quite a lot about you," B. F. said, "but Poll's never very good at giving a word picture."

"Don't call him Mr. Brett. Call him Tom," Polly said.

"Oh, yes," B. F. said, "Tom."

"I think Polly exaggerates her descriptions," Tom said. "Well, it's my weakness too."

It had not started badly, but she still could not tell how Tom and B. F. would get on.

"Have another cocktail, Tom," Polly said. "Just before you came in we were talking about Grant Wood."

"These modern painters all seem the same to me," her mother said, "all cornfields, barns, and silos, don't you think so, Mr. Brett?"

"They do have a lot of silos where they have cornfields," Tom Brett answered. "I was brought up in the Middle West."

"I'll make a note of that man," B. F. said. "I don't know much, but I try to keep an open mind. How about you, Mr. Brett?"

"Call him Tom," Polly said.

"Oh, yes," B. F. said. "Tom."

"It's a funny thing," Tom said, "how seldom tolerance goes with an open mind. They ought to go together, but they don't."

"That's too complicated for me," B. F. said. "I always thought they were one and the same thing."

It was a relief to see Timmons standing in the doorway.

"Burt," her mother said, "dinner's ready."

"Good," B. F. said. "What are we having?"

"You'll find out when you come in, Burt," her mother answered. "Women have to know what there's going to be, but men shouldn't ask. Don't you think so, Mr. Brett?"

Polly was much too nervous to follow the talk at dinner. It

slipped through her mind without sticking, and she was on everybody's side, swayed by every different emotion. She did not realize that a perennial design for family dinners was in the making, and that on later occasions her thoughts would move as erratically as now. She hoped Tom was not thinking that the table was set too elaborately. She hoped B. F. and Tom would not start arguing, and that the subject of the profit motive would not crop up. Her memory of Tom at the family table was exactly what it would be in the future. He would always have the same shirt and tie trouble, he would invariably forget his food when he was talking, and again and again she would suffer the same dread that B. F. would think he was brash and juvenile, and that Harry would think he was too Western. Then she would begin to worry for fear B. F. sounded moss-backed and didactic, and yet when B. F. was silent, she would be afraid he was being taciturn and disapproving. She would always experience the same surprise and relief when Tom was sweet to her mother — but even this did not make it possible to enjoy those family dinners.

Polly rolled her napkin into a ball while her mother was telling Tom of a lecture she had attended that had something to do with giving shares of stock to workers so that they would all have a partnership in the companies where they worked. Tom listened very attentively, and Polly could not understand how he could be so polite about it, but when B. F. began to talk about labor, there was a new sort of tension, not that Tom was not still polite. Then she was afraid that Tom was talking too much as he always did when he was bored, and his shirt was bulging more, and she could not keep her eyes off it. One of the first things she must do was to get him some evening shirts which stayed flat like B. F.'s and Harry's. She was sure if he kept slouching in his chair and hunching forward that one of his dingy gold-washed studs would give way. It was impossible to follow all that they were saying.

First there were oysters which B. F. always liked, and she knew that Tom did not. Then there was clear soup and then there was pheasant. Her mother was saying that she hoped Tom liked pheasant, and Polly was sure that Tom had thought it was chicken.

"I admit a lot is wrong with the general picture," she heard B. F. saying, "but I wish all the reformers would understand that the fundamentals are sound. You can't monkey with economics."

"A lot of people have in the past," Tom answered. "Don't you think the corporations do?"

"What they do is nearer control than monkeying," B. F. said. "I don't like big corporations myself, but there's got to be control."

"Yes," Tom said, "but why not let the government try it? Isn't that what government is for?"

"I don't know whether government could do better," B. F. answered. "It takes experience to run business. I don't know why a lot of people should tell me how to run my affairs if they don't know how themselves. I wouldn't tell you how to teach boys at college."

"What about girls?" Polly asked.

It was a silly question, but she had to say something to change the subject — and then Tom's shirt came undone in front just as she knew it would. "Oh," he said, "I'm sorry. It always does that." It did not disturb him in the least, and he wriggled in his chair and began working at the stud.

"Now let's put it this way," he began. "How free is enterprise?"

It was not as bad as it might have been. In fact, those dinners never were, because they had each given up trying to convince the other. B. F. began to tell a story, and then he learned that Tom had been to Hyde Park, and B. F. always liked to hear about people.

"Well, let's go into the library and have a cigar," B. F. said. "Do you like cigars?"

She knew that Tom disliked cigars, but he and B. F. went into the library while Harry stayed with them in the living room.

"They'd better have a little talk, I guess," Harry said, and he grinned at Polly. "Their minds met, didn't they?"

It was unbearable waiting, wondering what B. F. and Tom were saying in there.

"He wasn't so bad," Harry said. "I couldn't stand up and argue with B. F."

Even though no one said anything critical, Polly felt that they were trying hard to look on the bright side. Her mother was saying that she thought Mr. Brett was very nice, but then her mother always tried to think that everyone was. Tom did not belong in a business office or in that apartment either. He never would, and neither would Polly, and that was why she was going to marry Tom no matter what any of them thought. Her surroundings had never seemed so oppressively elaborate or so far removed from reality. She did not care whether Tom Brett could support her or where they were going to live, as long as it was simple.

"Of course," Harry said, "I'll admit he's got something. He's different."

"Your father was different, too, dear," her mother said. "Mr. Brett told me about his family. You never mentioned his mother, Polly. Mr. Brett spoke very nicely about her."

"Mother," Polly said, "he's very civilized."

"And you never told me he had a sister teaching in high school."

"No," Polly said. "He never told me."

"Well, it sounds as though he came from nice people."

"He comes from about the same people we do, Mother," Polly said, "small-town."

Harry winced when she used the phrase.

"Well, don't sit on a cracker barrel and pretend you're small-town, too, Poll," Harry said.

"That's my problem, not yours," Polly said.

"All right," Harry said. "I feel sort of sorry for Brett. He can't know what he's getting into."

"Why can't he?"

"Getting married to you," Harry said, "and having you push him around."

"I'm not going to," Polly said. "I'll do just what he wants."

"Well," Harry said, "just the same, I'm sorry for him. He's a fly when he walks into this parlor."

"That's where you're wrong," Polly said. "He isn't going to walk into it."

She and Tom were going to walk out of it into a life of their own, magnificent and new. They were going to leave materialism behind for a world where money did not matter, and they were going to make their world all by themselves without anybody's help. The family would understand Tom better as time went on, when he had achieved what he wanted. She did not know as yet exactly what he wanted to achieve, but she did not care. She believed in him and he was going to take her away from the French drawing room and from Park Avenue, from the Mill River Club and from Sugar Hill — as far away as possible.

When Tom and B. F. came out of the library, she could not tell what had happened. They did not seem any more friendly, but B. F. was serene and courteous.

"Well," B. F. said, "we've covered a lot of ground."

Polly exchanged glances with Tom.

"We had to," Tom said.

"I hope you saw Mr. Fulton's books," her mother said.

"Yes," Tom said, "we opened all the books." And then B. F. laughed.

"That's one way of putting it," he said, "and we won't have to do it again. I don't like being a bank examiner." At least B. F. did not look disturbed.

"He hasn't many prospects, has he?" Polly asked.

"I don't know," B. F. said. "Tom and I are in different lines, but we know a lot more about each other than when we started." At least he had called him Tom spontaneously. "This sort of thing makes me thirsty. Let's have a Scotch and soda, shall we?"

"I'd like one very much," Tom Brett said, and he slumped into one of the chairs.

"You see," B. F. said, "our ideas don't often mesh, but that doesn't matter, as long as Tom knows I have a few human instincts. Poll, where's the whisky?"

She had not seen B. F. drink so much for a long while. He had tried his best to find some sort of common ground with Tom Brett, and it was not the fault of either that they never found it. It was the price she had to pay for Tom, and it had been worth it once.

When Tom left she stood with him outside the apartment door in the little hall waiting for the elevator.

"Darling," she whispered, "I know it's been dreadful, but it couldn't help but be."

"I hope I did all right," he said.

"Darling," Polly whispered, "you were awfully sweet. You won't have to see them often."

He held her hand tight, but he did not answer.

"You mustn't worry about the money," Polly went on. "We don't want any of it, do we?"

Tom Brett sighed. "It isn't as easy as that," he said. "We were talking about it. It would be selfish of me to make you uncomfortable, Poll."

It sounded gentle and sweet at the time. It was only years afterward that Polly sometimes thought Tom should have taken a stand in line with his convictions. It was only afterward that she thought of Tom as being weak, and even then, when she tried to put herself in his position, it was hard to blame him for letting B. F. give her an allowance.

"Darling," she whispered, "we'll talk about it later, and tomorrow I'm going to get you some new shirts and some pearl studs that won't pop out."

"Oh God, not pearl studs," Tom said.

Not pearl studs perhaps, but she was going to see that he had a new black overcoat and new pumps that were not cracked. She was going to do everything for him, everything.

"Darling," she said, "I don't want to change you. I love you the way you are."

They were all silent when she came back.

"Well," she said, "don't stop. Go ahead."

"Well," B. F. said, "that was quite an evening."

"Didn't you like him?" Polly asked. "Didn't you like him at all?"

"Well," B. F. said. "I can't make him out, Poll. I don't know where he fits."

"But did you like him?"

"Of course, we were both embarrassed," B. F. said. "He's intelligent, Poll, but he's got a lot of fixed ideas."

"Well, so have you. That isn't anything against him, is it?" Polly asked.

"Not unless they're too fixed," B. F. said. "Anyway, I made him see that you had to have some money. He was reasonable about that. I don't know, maybe we'll get to like each other."

"I know it was an ordeal," Polly said, and she looked at them hopefully, "and you've all been awfully sweet about him, even Harry."

"Why, thanks, Poll," Harry said, and her mother added: —

"You know we want you to be happy, dear. That's all we care about."

No one spoke for a while, and then B. F. coughed.

"Are you sure you want to marry him, Poll? Absolutely sure?"

"Why do we have to go over it and over it?" Polly asked. "Don't you know we both must want to or we couldn't have gone through this?"

"You still want to get married? I want this double-checked."

"Yes," Polly said, "we still do."

"All right," B. F. said. "That's all I have to know, Poll. Harry, what time is it?"

Harry looked at his wrist watch. It was ten-thirty.

"Seven-thirty on the Coast . . ." B. F. said. "I've got to call the Coast."

XXVI

Money Was No Problem

In the autumn of 1940 Polly had been at another dinner party,
in Washington this time, talking to a stranger from the State Department about marriage. It was during the "on hand" and "on
order" days when Washington was first beginning to be called a
madhouse, and when they were first beginning to send for Tom
frequently to work on propaganda projects. Tom had spent the day
in a series of conferences, and she had been looking up something
for him in the Library of Congress. It was exciting to be so close
to what was going on, and Tom liked it too, but he took a dim view
of the State Department.

Tom said the State Department boys in striped pants considered
social graces and an independent income more important than
ability. It did no good to explain to him that if you needed social
finesse anywhere you needed it in the diplomatic service, and that you
had to have your own income because the Government never gave
you enough. Tom himself had been offered a State Department job
recently, a very good one, though the offer had been so confidential
that Polly could not breathe it to a soul, but he had turned it down
because he had said the Department and all the people in it reminded him of the fretwork on the old United States Hotel at
Saratoga. Polly was sorry because she would have liked to help with
the entertaining, and she would have been good at it too, but Tom
said he was not going to spend his life juggling teacups.

Polly could see Tom at that dinner eyeing the State Department
man in a tepid, superior way he had cultivated lately. Polly had even
hoped for a little while that Tom was jealous, and he may have

359

been, but not of a man who was attentive to her. He was only jealous of the advantages that went with a privileged childhood — a preparatory school background, a chance to acquire tennis form and a golf swing, experience in trapshooting and sailing. He was still jealous of this side of Bob Tasmin.

If Tom had wanted, he might have acquired some of these skills, but it was easier to ridicule them, and lately there had been a bitter, almost offensive, note in his humor. His eyes and his co-ordination were bad, though he did not admit it, and if ever he and Polly were in some place where there was a good tennis professional or a guide who might have shown him how to cast with a light rod, Tom always said he did not want to make a monkey of himself. B. F. had never been good at those things either, but he had never been as sensitive as Tom.

The State Department man was full of information about skiing in Japan and polo on those little Mongol ponies in Peking. He touched on Antibes and mountain climbing in the Tyrol, on the social life in Bagdad and on country life in England. His information added up to a desperate effort to show off. Polly had been bored until he began to talk about marriage, and then she gathered that he must be in the State Department because he had a rich wife. He said there were two sorts of marriages which were predestined to fail. The first was the international marriage with its conflict between alien cultures and traditions. The second was the marriage of a poor man to money.

When Polly asked what was wrong with this, he said that a woman with money always dominated the whole situation. If she wanted something she would buy it, and the man in the end must accept. It made her realize that she and Tom had been very lucky. Tom had contributed more than anything her money had to offer. Right from the first day of their honeymoon she had always followed where Tom had wished to go, and you never could be sure what he wanted next. Money had been no problem because it only gave him what he needed. Tom would not be in Washington now if he had not been able to give up that position at Columbia which he had never liked anyway. He would never have been able to spare time for writing, though it was true that his own restiveness interfered with it. They could go to Pyefield when they wished to be alone. When they wanted company, they could entertain just the friends he liked best. If he wanted to do something absurd, he could drop everything and do it, like the time, for instance, when they had suddenly flown to a jungle in Central America. There was nothing to tie them, no children, no steady work, and it had always been that way right from the very beginning. Tom was not spoiled by money.

If you were at all skeptical you could take their honeymoon, and you know what was always said about honeymoons — that they consisted of nothing but stress and strain and readjustment. Polly could not recall anything of the sort in theirs, because it had all been so delightfully unpredictable. They were not married until June, and by then, Tom had said, he was run ragged between Columbia and Gray's Point. He said he was tired of jumping through hoops and he wanted to vegetate. He supposed they ought to see his mother and sister, but not during any honeymoon. He wanted pellucid peace. He wanted to be outdoors and to get some health because he said he was physically depleted after that emotional winter, what with being a great lover and teacher and at the same time all mixed up with politics.

He had once visited a lake on the border of Minnesota and Ontario where you could rent an island with a cabin on it. He had been there with some boys when he was in college and he remembered that you got off a train at a place called Three Forks, where an old Swede named Svensen had a general store; and Svensen owned the island with the log cabin. He would write to Svensen. All you needed to do was to bring some groceries and sit on the island, and that was all he wanted, because he was run ragged. His first letter to Mr. Svensen was returned, and when Polly got out a map, Tom said of course, it wasn't Three Forks, it was Portage Farouche where the old trappers used to camp in the days of the fur trade. That was where Svensen was, at Portage Farouche, except his name wasn't Svensen either. It was Holmquist, Sigurd Holmquist. Sigurd was quite a character, just an old Swede who bought pelts from Ojibway Indians, and Sigurd would take care of them. All they needed to take from New York were two suitcases. It was lucky that Polly went to the camping department at Abercrombie & Fitch and bought them some warm clothes.

They had a drawing room on the Century, and just as soon as they were inside it, Tom took off his coat and his vest and his tie, and then he took off his shoes.

"Well," he said, "thank God all that is over. Let's get some setups for our rye." And then he looked around him wildly. "Oh, my God," he said.

"What is it now?" Polly asked.

"The tickets. . . . I left them in that room where I changed my clothes."

"You couldn't have," Polly said. "Don't you remember just before we went downstairs, before people started throwing things, I asked you about the tickets?"

"I've got a damned good memory," Tom said. "You never did."

"I did too," Polly said. "You went back and got them. I saw you put them in your pocket."

"Where are my shoes?" he asked. "We've got to get off at Harmon."

"Give me your coat," Polly said.

The tickets were just where she had seen him put them.

"Well, by God," he said, "they were there, weren't they?" Somehow everything on that trip was funny, even the worst parts of it. "Be a good girl and keep those damned things yourself. I'm feeling emotionally unstrung, Poll, and I think I'm going to be ill."

"Oh, darling," Polly asked, "where are you feeling sick?"

"Everywhere," Tom said. "I'm having a very bad reaction. I think I'm going to have a chill."

"That's because we're alone together," Polly said. "I feel that way too."

"Well, let's not be alone," Tom said. "Let's get the porter and get those setups, and get out *The Oxford Book of Verse* and see if there isn't something by Swinburne."

"Swinburne?" Polly repeated. "I thought you hated him."

"I do," Tom said, "but now I feel exactly like him at his worst."

When Tom did not feel well ever afterwards, he had her read him works of poets he hated. When he wanted to hear "Hiawatha," she always knew that he was seriously indisposed. He asked for "Hiawatha" then, but it was not in the *Oxford Book*. Tom leaned against the window and sighed and closed his eyes when she started Swinburne. He told her to read it more theatrically, and then the buzzer sounded.

It was not only the porter with the ice and ginger ale, but the train conductor and Pullman conductor as well, and a man from the Passenger Agent's office. They wanted to congratulate Mr. and Mrs. Brett, and they hoped that they had everything they wanted, and nothing was too good for relatives of Mr. Fulton. She was afraid this might upset Tom, but instead, he asked them to sit down and have a drink. The train conductor and the passenger agent began telling anecdotes of other newly married people on the Century, and finally Tom asked if they had some aspirin. You never could tell what would happen next with Tom.

When they got to Chicago, Tom said it was not as bad as it might be, considering it was a honeymoon. They had a room at the Drake where they waited between trains instead of going out, because Tom said that the city reminded him of his boyhood and of the Democratic Convention, and he wanted to get away from memories.

"You just take over, Poll," he said, "and see about the train and the baggage. This is all a very great strain on me."

"What about me?" Polly asked.

"Don't tell me you don't like it," he said. "Don't make things worse than they are. I'm going to lie in a hot bath for a while. I think I'm going to have another chill. Just sit outside the door and read me Rossetti. That's a good girl, Poll."

Of course she liked it. She knew he would not have behaved that way unless he really loved her, and unless he knew she liked it.

When they arrived at Portage Farouche late the next afternoon, it turned out to be nothing but a group of unpainted shacks by the side of a lake. A high wind was blowing, and it was so bleak and so far away from everything that Tom was sure it was not the place he had been on his college vacation. He could not even remember where Mr. Holmquist lived until Polly found the name on the front of the General Store.

"Oh, yes," Tom said, "I remember. He's got skins and fishhooks inside. I'll buy you a bearskin if you like. There's nothing like a good bearskin."

"For what?" Polly asked.

"So you won't have a bare skin," Tom said.

It made her laugh and laugh. Everything was funny. It did not matter what you did or said when you got to Portage Farouche. Her matched luggage looked funny there, but even that was not as funny as some of the things she had bought at Abercrombie & Fitch.

"Now, listen, Poll," Tom said. "From now on I'm taking over because this is a man's world. We're up against primitive forces and you'd better leave everything to me. You let me talk to Svensen."

"But it isn't Svensen," Polly said, "it's Holmquist."

"Who said it was Holmquist?"

"You did," Polly said. "Don't you remember?"

"Do you see that man down by the dock," Tom said, "the one in overalls who looks drunk? He's an Indian."

"But it's Holmquist," Polly said, "it isn't Svensen."

"All right," Tom said. If you were in the right mood nothing mattered.

It was all outside her experience — the air, the weathered buildings, the damp smell of fresh water beating on round rocks, the Indian, who knew where Mr. Holmquist was, and Mr. Holmquist in his patched trousers and frayed sweater. He took them in his dirty white motorboat, several miles down the lake to the island, and helped them unload the canned goods they had bought. The island was a granite, moss-covered ledge sprouting Christmas trees in every crevice. It had a miniature harbor with a beach and a dock and a path leading to the log cabin. There were two bunks in the cabin and a rusty stove, a pot, a frying pan, a pail and a dented axe.

Polly had never seen anything that looked so lonely, and she had never felt as lonely as when she saw Tom's bewildered expression.

"I don't seem to remember it this way," he said. "Is this the only island you've got, Mr. Svensen?"

"Holmquist," Polly said.

"Don't be so bright with names, Poll," Tom said. "You leave this to me and Mr. Holmquist."

The mattresses looked dirty, but there were some brown Army blankets.

"How can we get off if we don't like it?" Polly asked.

"I can come tomorrow morning," Mr. Holmquist said, "to see if you be all right."

"But what if your boat breaks down?" Polly asked him.

"You leave this to us," Tom said. "This is a man's world, isn't it, Holmquist?"

It was funny to see Tom in that man's world trying to light the fire in the stove and going down to the beach for water. It was funny to hear him say that they ought to try to catch a fish, and his expression was excruciating when he finally said he didn't know it was going to be so bad.

"Oh, darling," Polly said, "it's wonderful."

It was wonderful feeling that it belonged to them and thinking of possible improvements. It was silly for anyone to say that it wasn't a very good thing to be married to a girl with money.

After Tom got the stove going he was very tired, and next he cut himself opening a can of tomatoes. He looked like an injured Boy Scout when she bandaged his hand from the First Aid box she had bought.

"Let's see," he said. "How do we make coffee?"

"You put it in the pot with water and boil it, don't you?" Polly asked.

"I don't know," he said, "I guess so. Mother always made the coffee."

"I didn't know you had a mother complex," Polly said. "Did you marry me because I'm like your mother?"

"Let's not talk about it now," Tom said. "It's getting dark and we've got to eat somehow."

"There must be a lantern somewhere," Polly said, "and dishes and forks and things. See if you can find them."

"Where?"

"Anywhere," Polly said. "Look around, darling, while I try to do this coffee, and you'd better give me that can opener."

It was a relief that the cabin had only one room so that there were not many places to look for anything. Tom found a rusty lantern in a box and also some tin plates and knives and forks and spoons. He said leave it to him, that he knew how to handle lanterns. He said his father had a horse and buggy, and there used to be a lantern in the barn. He knew all about lanterns. You just pushed something and the chimney went up and then you lighted it, and then you gave a pull and the chimney went down . . . but he could not find what to push.

"God damn," he said. "This must be another kind of lantern. Maybe we'd better get a pine knot and light it. There are too many gadgets in the world."

"Don't keep hitting it," Polly said, "you'll break it."

"All right," Tom said, "I want to break it."

"Give it to me," Polly said, "and get some more water."

She had seen several lanterns at Willett, though only at a distance, but she had never known until she examined this one in the dusky cabin that she must have inherited B. F.'s instinct for gadgets. If you looked at a piece of mechanism, without getting mad at it as Tom always did, you could see that it had a principle. She never forgot the soft glow of the kerosene flame through the smoky glass, or the way the light spread over the board table and lost itself in the shadows.

"Look, Tom," she said. "I've done it." And Tom looked as though he could not believe it.

"Who taught you to do that?" he asked. "It must be a gift. You're wonderful."

She never forgot her sense of competence, of being alone with

Tom and able to manage things. She never forgot the smell of the coffee, or that she was making coffee. She never forgot the sound of the wind and the splash of water on the rocks of the island, or the gathering coolness of the dusk, and she never forgot that Tom was happy.

"Just Mr. and Mrs. Thoreau," Tom said. "You never knew you'd married a Thoreau, did you? Or maybe I'm Daniel Boone."

"Yes," Polly said, "you look more like Boone." He had thrown his coat onto the bunks and he had unbuttoned his vest. "There's one of those plaid shirts in the bag."

"That's right," Tom said, "Old Trapper Brett. And there's some rye in the bag. How about some rye and lake water?" But Polly did not need any. He sat drinking rye out of a tin cup, watching her and talking while she opened the can of tomatoes and began slicing some bread and bacon.

"We should have brought Parkman," he said. "*The Jesuits in North America* or *The Conspiracy of Pontiac*. Of course, Parkman was a Boston snob. He was basically an overprivileged, social misfit on the Oregon Trail, but occasionally he forgot himself. I'll tell you what we'll do. You get the supper, and I'll have another drink and tell you about Parkman."

"Oh, darling," Polly said.

"What is it?" Tom asked. "Have we forgotten something?"

"I don't care if we've forgotten everything," she told him. "Darling, I'm so happy."

She had never felt so sublimated, getting all over grease and tomato juice and frying bacon for Tom Brett. She had never done so much for anyone, nor had she ever belonged so much to anyone. For a little while at any rate the whole island and the stove and the coffee were only his and hers. His mind and all the things he thought and wanted were hers, and they always would be, no matter where they were. They had bacon, bread and butter, warm tomatoes and that coffee. It was full of grounds, but still it tasted like coffee. She had used so much that it was black as pitch and that must have been why they stayed awake for such a long time. While she lay in Tom's arms not able to sleep, she still kept making plans for the island. It was theirs to do with as they wanted — for a little while at any rate.

"I'm going to fix this all up for you, darling," she said. "You won't know it in another day."

"That's all right with me," Tom said. "I'm Thoreau. I'll tell you what I'll do; I'll tame a chipmunk." And he told her for the first time about the book he was going to write some day on American literature.

"Oh, darling," she said, "I'm so happy."

"That goes for me too," Tom said. "It's great to have things simple. It makes you understand what life's about."

"Oh, darling," Polly said, "say it again. Are you really happy? Concentrate on it. Are you really?"

"Of course I am," Tom said. "Why, you and I have everything."

They had so much that it almost frightened her. She lay very still, but she could not go to sleep as soon as Tom did because he was used to black coffee. She was thinking about everything that she was going to do for years ahead, everything.

Money never interfered with marriage if you used money right and she was learning how much you could do for someone you loved. When Mr. Holmquist came next morning, Polly had a shopping list all ready and she went back with him to Portage Farouche. There she hired a car and drove to a town called Port Haynes where there were pulp mills and larger stores. Tom did not go with her, which was just as well, because he would have distracted her. He said he would sit in the sun and read a little and perhaps go for a swim.

"But, darling," she asked, "what are you going to do about lunch?" He had not thought about that, and so she got it ready for him before she left — a cheese sandwich, canned tongue and canned peaches.

He told her to go out and run the world but not to get lost in it because he would miss her, and he stood by the dock while she went away. All that day she thought of things that might happen to Tom alone on the island. He might get a cramp if he went swimming, or ptomaine poisoning, although she had taken that tongue out of the can, or he might cut himself with the axe. It seemed years before she got back, and she had never had so many things to tell him. She could see him waiting on the dock when she was half a mile away.

"My God, Poll," he said, "you're like Balto bringing the serum to Nome."

Considering how hard it had been to get anyone to hurry, she had done a lot in a single day. She had hired a cabin cruiser for their own use with a man named Joe to run it. It had two bunks in case they cared to sleep aboard, and Joe would bring it for orders every morning. She had telephoned New York for books to be sent out by Air Express, and a portable typewriter in case Tom wanted to write. She had bought sneakers for him and a pair of high boots and a sweater. She had bought bedding, brooms, soap, aluminum kitchen things, a gasoline lantern, a hot water bottle, aspirin, cigarettes for Tom, ginger ale, rye that had come from Canada, and some camp chairs and a folding table and finally a canoe. She had arranged with Mr. Holmquist's son-in-law, Mr. Hansen, to come with his wife Gertrude to clean the whole cabin and to chop some wood. She had bought a new axe, a raincoat, more canned provisions, two dozen eggs, and had arranged for Joe to bring meat, milk, butter and eggs. She had even bought a cookbook, and everything was aboard that new boat with Joe to unload it.

When the cargo was all in the cabin, it had not disturbed Tom much. He loved the gasoline lantern although he could never work it. He only asked once how much it all had cost, and he only said once that he ought to pay for it himself, because he was paying for the trip; and she only had to tell him once that it was her party, and only to remind him once that he had said he wanted her to be comfortable.

It may have worked so well because money never interested Tom. He never asked for anything, and so it was pleasant to do things for him. He loved the boat and he got on well with Joe. He loved the way she learned to cook. He liked it when they went on overnight trips and had Joe cook for them. The best of it was seeing how much better he looked every day. His color was better and he must have gained five pounds — and Polly had done it all herself. You would not have known that island after a few days, and she had done it all herself.

"None of it would be any fun at all," she told him, "if you didn't like it. You're the boss."

He told her that it was almost too easy to take, but Tom never took anything without giving more back. Somehow his simply being there with her gave her complete security. There was more and more to marriage, a happy one, all the time. All the things they did together contributed — swimming in the lake, trying to fish, paddling the canoe, talking about his books and his lectures and reading things together. It was hard to believe, and yet every day there was always something more.

That was why, when they went to the little town in Wisconsin where his mother and his sister kept house, it seemed as if they had always been married, and as if everything that had happened before were meaningless. Polly loved Tom's mother because she told her about Tom when he was a little boy. She loved walking with Tom through that flat, dull town, because, as Polly told him, it was like Willett and she had always wanted to live in Willett. Sometimes when he was quiet and she asked him what he was thinking, he said he was thinking that she was wonderful.

One night there in Wisconsin when it was hard to remember that they had not been married always, they walked to see the high school where Tom had graduated at the head of his class.

"I don't know where you've been all my life," Tom said. "I don't know how I ever got on without you."

"All right," Polly answered. "I don't know how I got on either."

"There's only one thing," he said.

"What thing?"

Tom stood looking at the high school, one of those brick buildings that could only have been a public school.

"I used to have a lot of ideas when I was here," he said. "I used to think I was going to leave here and run the world. 'The thoughts of youth are long, long thoughts' — Longfellow."

"Stick to the point," Polly said. "What thing?"

"What thing?" he repeated. "Oh yes, there's just one thing. Your sewing buttons and opening cans. I mustn't get too dependent on you, Poll."

"That's the way I want you to be," she said, "dependent, so you won't run away. I want you to want everything about me."

"Yes, I know," he said, "but you've got to watch it, Poll, or else there won't be any me."

She laughed because he was such a definite character that he could never be anything but himself.

"Don't worry," she said. "You've got too many bad habits. You're too damned selfish ever to get like that."

"I know," he said, "but I want you to promise me just one thing. Give me a good kick in the pants, will you, if I ever do get that way?"

"You can't," she said, "because I'm good for you, and you're good for me. We're just what the psychiatrist ordered. You'll see."

"Well, maybe," Tom said. "But just kick me the hell in the pants if I get soft."

"All right, I'll practise tonight," she told him, "in front of a mirror."

And then he put his arm around her. He had never done any such thing before in public.

"You see, I'm giving you everything I have," he said, "not that it amounts to much, but it's everything. I've got to trust you, Poll."

"That goes both ways," she said. "I'm giving you everything, too."

"All right," he said. "Now let's go to the drugstore and see if we can get some shaving soap. That's something you've forgotten."

"No," she said. "I got it for you yesterday. Didn't you see it? It's on the bureau, darling."

Polly was thinking of all this at that dinner party in Washington while the man from the State Department talked interminably. It was absurd to say that the wife's having money could break up a marriage. If two people gave each other everything, if they enjoyed each other's company more than anyone else's, no matter what conflicts there might be between them — and there were getting to be a few with her and Tom — they were not important, not if two people gave each other everything. If you got through the first of what were called adjustments, you formed a habit of give and take.

When the men came back after dinner, she spoke to Tom as soon as she could.

"You're right about the State Department," she said. "Who was that man beside me at dinner? He says he's shot bustards near Peking."

"Damned if I know," Tom said. "Are you sure he said bustards?"

"They're some sort of bird," Polly said, "and you're better than all these other birds, darling. I wish you'd run out and pull down your shirt. It's bulging."

That was the way it used to be. That was the way it had been even in 1940 before the war fixed it so that no one had time for anything. What was it that Norman Bell had said? Nothing counted that had happened before the war? Most of Europe was knocked flat, and so too perhaps were the bustards in Peking, but New York was there and Washington. A lot of boys were dying, but a lot still were not dead. She and Tom were still living. The war had hardly touched them physically. So what was it within themselves that had vanished? It was fantastic to believe that all that two people had shared, all that two people had meant to each other, could be turned and twisted, blown to nothing by a war.

XXVII

A Quarter before One, Miss James

THE LEAST that Tom could have done was to have wakened her and given her some idea of his plans before he left the hotel suite that Monday morning. It was no excuse that he had started early, because he knew very well that she did not mind being wakened. In fact, it had once been a part of their routine. Tom's temperament never allowed him to sleep in the morning especially after a late party the night before. He awakened almost automatically, always full of ideas requiring an immediate audience. Although he never actually aroused Polly, he used to be deliberately noisy so that the result was the same. Normally he collided with chairs, splashed in the shower, wrestled with bureau drawers (he never could pull a drawer out of any bureau without its sticking) and delivered sharp expletives when he could not find things, and these grew louder and more plaintive until she awakened — but Polly had not heard a sound from him that Monday morning.

He had gone leaving his black trousers where he had dropped them the night before. The closet door was open and his pajamas were in a heap in the middle of the passage to the bathroom, just where he stepped out of them. Obviously, Tom had left hastily without wanting to talk to her, which perhaps was just as well under the circumstances. He had not even ventured to have his breakfast in the living room, but he had left a note balanced against a soda bottle on one of those white pickled tables. Polly picked it up gingerly as though it were an old rag and scowled at Tom's small, crabbed, but very legible writing.

"DEAR POLL: All right, I'm saying it again, there's a war on, and I've got to be out there backing the attack. How do you like that one? I'm going to be backing the attack until late tonight, so don't count on me for anything all day — Tom."

Polly crumpled up the sheet of hotel stationery on which it was written, and as she could not see any wastebasket in the modern suite, she threw it on the floor. There had been a restless hiatus of sleep, and now she was right back where she had started. The rain had stopped; the cloudless sky was a soft transparent blue, and the sun would be shining somewhere, although not in that room. She was right back where she had started, and she had a great deal to do. The main thing was to list all the items in her mind just as though it were a normal day, one of those beautiful sunny days in Washington, when you knew that spring, like prosperity, was just around the corner. That was what they used to say just before she and Tom were married, that prosperity was just around the corner.

Only God knew what was just around the corner now. Some optimists called this unknown "the world of tomorrow," and the world of tomorrow was nothing but a vague, pious wish, though it was Monday and the sun was shining. She remembered one of those institutional advertisements with which big companies were filling the magazines, presumably to avoid taxation — a picture of a soldier in combat overalls, seated on a landing barge. The soldier was delivering a short pep-talk written for him by someone safe in an advertising agency. He was telling the world that he was not playing for marbles. He was telling the world that he was fighting to keep America just as it had been when he had left it, a place where a good Joe could get a good job and bring up his kids as he had been brought up without any people with foreign isms telling him how to do it. He wasn't playing for marbles. She supposed he was what B. F. would call an American boy, and apparently no one had told him that the world of tomorrow was not going to be like that. You had only to look at other advertisements to see it — the ones for refrigerators that could freeze things into the shapes of your desire, stoves that did the cooking and washing machines that did the ironing while you went to the motion pictures and relaxed and enjoyed

374

the finer things of life, radios that did not squawk, prefabricated homes C.O.D. anywhere, furniture all colors of the rainbow made out of soybeans, sawdust, corn husks, and perhaps a little milk and water, runless stockings made out of glass, roach powders that would kill anything unpleasant, penicillin and all those vitamins. They weren't ready yet because they had all gone to war, but just wait. Buy your War Bonds and Stamps now, but just wait. You'd be amazed, those things were just around the corner. There was so much around that corner that she had no time to guess what. Besides, she had a lot to do.

It would be a good idea to make an appointment at the hairdresser's now that it was Monday, provided always she could get Miss Rosalind. Also, she must tell her mother that she could not be back at Gray's Point when the executors started on the inventory. If they needed her, they would have to wait a few days. There were a number of other people whom she should call up, and then there was That Other Thing. She was going to do That Other Thing and not stay in the dark.

Polly was dressed by the time her breakfast came up, again in her black dress with its gold belt and the topaz clips. The newspapers had come with her breakfast, the *Times-Herald* and the *Washington Post*. The Marines were still fighting on the southerly end of Iwo Iima, and the Germans had flooded a river valley near Cologne. By the time she had finished her orange juice and toast and coffee, she was ready for That Other Thing, but first she called the hairdresser and then she called her mother.

Polly sat curled on the corner of the sofa holding the telephone, thinking of the days and the hours of her life that had been spent that way. She was like B. F., always telephoning, until sometimes voices were clearer in her mind than faces. She could see her mother sitting by the little telephone table in her dressing room, all neat, up hours ago reading some helpful book.

"I can't come back today, dear," she heard herself saying, "I simply can't. Something has happened down here. It isn't anything I can speak of over the telephone. It's something I have to have settled."

She had to give some half-reason which would seem important, or her mother would be hurt, but as always when she was trying to be devious, she might as well have told the whole story.

"Is it something about Tom?" her mother asked, and Polly made an exasperated face.

"It's something," she said, "or else I'd be back with you, but never mind it, Mother."

"Oh, dear," her mother said, "Burt was always afraid of it."

Polly found herself tapping her foot on the soft carpet.

"I wish you wouldn't jump at conclusions," Polly said. "Never mind what Father was afraid of."

"I do think," she heard her mother saying, "you ought to tell me frankly, dear, whatever it is that's the matter. Burt always said —"

That was the way it would be — as long as her mother lived she would be telling someone what Burt had always said.

"Polly, dear," her mother said, "it isn't — another woman?"

"It isn't anything, Mother," Polly said.

"But it must be something. I can hear it in your voice."

"Oh, Mother," Polly said, "never mind my voice. Tom and I are having an argument. We're not *getting on together,* but that isn't news, is it? You knew that, Father knew it. Please don't worry."

"Polly," her mother said, "don't you think it would be more dignified if you came home?"

"I told you, Mother," Polly answered, "there's something I want settled before I come home. Now, Mother, please."

"I do hope," her mother said, "that you and Tom won't do anything you'll be sorry for . . . You're both so impulsive, dear."

"I hope so, too," Polly said, and she looked at the penciled notes on her lap. "Now Mother, about the Gray's Point inventory . . ."

She was not being impulsive. She was being as cold as ice with everything under perfect control. When she had finished with New York she stood up and turned to the breakfast table and drank a glass of water very slowly. She was almost finished with it when the telephone rang behind her. If it weren't for telephones, she might be able to run her life without being everywhere at once and without changing her mood and manners every second. It was Mildred Tasmin, the last person she wanted to cope with at the moment. Polly recognized the bell-like tones of her voice, and Mildred, too, was under control.

"I hope I haven't interrupted you, dear."

"How could you interrupt me?" Polly asked. "I've just been sitting here mulling over the *Times* and the *Post* and making a date for my hair."

"Well, you had that exasperated, interrupted sound."

"It's only because I'm being efficient, dear," Polly said. "Have you heard any word from Bob?"

"Oh, no, but I don't expect to. No news is good news. I just had an idea."

"What idea?"

"I've just been talking to Mother."

"Have you?" Polly asked. "So have I. My mother."

"I'm going up to Connecticut to visit her for a day or two, and I'm taking Ned. I just thought — how long are you going to be down here?"

"Well, it depends." In spite of herself Polly found her voice was growing more careful, more precise. "Just for a few days." And she laughed. "It's the only way I can get a glimpse of Tom."

"Well, here's the apartment," Mildred said, "and we have a treasure of a maid. I don't know how I ever found her. Why don't you and Tom use the apartment for a few days, if you'll use *her* carefully. I don't like it to be empty."

"Why, Mildred, that's awfully sweet of you," Polly began, "but I don't really think — "

"Don't say 'No,'" Mildred said. "With everything so crowded, it might be a change for you. I really mean it, dear. I'd love it. I'll tell you what let's do. Come up to tea at five, and you can see it for yourself. We're not leaving until tomorrow. Remember, you promised last night to come to tea."

"I'd love to come," Polly said, although the last place she wanted to have tea was in the contented atmosphere of Mildred's apartment.

"Five or fivish," Mildred said. "Fivish" was in itself a banner of security.

You never particularly envied security in others until your own was gone. In fact, if you possessed it yourself, you gave it a different name when you observed it in other people. You called it complacency or dullness or unawareness. Mildred Tasmin's conviction that everything was right in her world seemed to Polly now a priceless possession. It was all very well to tell herself that everything was falling to dust around Mildred, poor thing, without her knowing it, but when the news reached Mildred Tasmin, as Polly was certain it would, that Lieutenant Colonel Tasmin's plane was overdue and he might be presumed lost, Mildred would still be secure with his memory. It was exasperating to Polly that Mildred should not have shown that she valued what she had. If *she* were Mildred, she would have stayed right there in Scott Circle, instead of going to Connecticut. She would have been making a nuisance of herself getting in touch with officers who might have news of Bob Tasmin. She would not be sitting waiting, saying that no news was good news.

She wished Mildred had not called, because Bob Tasmin was back in her thoughts again. Wherever he might be now, if he were still alive, he would fit — never saying too little or too much, always looking as though he were meant to be there — and if he was afraid he would not show it. Even if he were dead, his memory would be as clear as Burton Fulton's, without any smudges or shadows. If there were any women, Bob Tasmin would not be mixed up with them. Bob Tasmin would not need sedatives for insomnia, and if he threw cigarettes at the fireplace, they would land there. His trousers would be neatly folded on a chair, and he would not leave his pajamas in a heap on the floor.

Polly slammed the bedroom door shut so that she would not see Tom's evening clothes or his pajamas, and then she picked up the telephone again. When you had made up your mind, there was no use waiting, and it was better to do something than nothing. The exchange for Tom's office was Monroe. All those Washington exchanges were as resounding as the names on Pullman cars — Monroe, District and Executive — and she did not need to look in her notebook to remember Tom's extension. 27816 — no wonder the lines were always jammed. She sat tapping her foot on the carpet again while she listened to the hotel operator dialing it; then she gave the extension number clearly and pleasantly, but incisively. The building where Tom worked would be jammed too — with its occupants filing past guards who checked their identification badges, pushing through the polished stone hallways of the ground floor to the rabbit warren of halls and offices above.

"Would it be convenient," she was asking, "to speak to Miss Winifred James, if she is in the office?"

"This is Miss James speaking."

Polly caught her breath. There was no longer any time for her to collect herself; it was too late to be deliberate.

"Oh," Polly said, though there wasn't any reason to say, "Oh."

"This is Mrs. Brett. Good morning."

"Oh . . . good morning, Mrs. Brett."

At least the James woman said "Oh" too, so they both were even.

It was undoubtedly the same voice that had called yesterday with the same slightly artificial inflection. Polly found herself smiling icily.

"It's so nice to hear your voice," Polly said. She waited smiling, but there was no response. "I wonder whether you're too busy to have lunch with me?"

There was another pause, and then there was that melodious, artificial voice again, but perhaps it was a telephone manner. If she talked that way always, Polly did not see how Tom could stand it.

"Oh, luncheon, Mrs. Brett?"

"In my suite here at the hotel," Polly said, and it *was* her suite because she was paying the bill. "I hope you can arrange it. I think we ought to meet, don't you?"

There was another pause, and Polly could hear the distant rattle of a typewriter.

"Oh . . . I think it would be very nice. Thank you for thinking of it, Mrs. Brett. What time?"

"Any time that's convenient for you," Polly answered, and she laughed in a friendly way. "I know there's a war on. I should hate to take you away at the wrong moment, Miss James, and have us lose the war."

Polly was pleased that her laugh was not too loud or too long. It had just the tinkling, composed sound she wanted.

"Let me just look at my calendar," Miss James said . . . "Shall we say a quarter before one?"

"A quarter before one," Polly repeated. "I'll have lunch ordered. Is there anything you especially like, Miss James, or anything you don't like?"

"Oh, anything, as long as it isn't much. I never eat much lunch."

"Neither do I," Polly said. "It will give us more time to talk. Just come right up."

"A quarter before one. I'll be there, Mrs. Brett."

"I'm looking forward to seeing you," Polly said; "good-by."

It had not been a long conversation, but all her muscles must have been tense, and all her energy must have gone into it, because she felt cramped and tired when it was over, and the room felt stuffy. It was only ten o'clock and she could not wait there for two hours and three quarters. She picked up the telephone again. She wanted everything to be absolutely right. She would give the room waiter five dollars and another five dollars to the maid, and she wanted fresh flowers too. Then she would go for a walk alone in the sun.

While Polly waited out there again for one of those elevators to stop at the fifth floor, she suffered a heightening of any ordinary mood of preoccupation, not unlike that of the absent-minded professor. It was the way she had sometimes felt when Bob Tasmin had been teaching her to dive in the pool at Gray's Point. You would be out in the air with everything as you had known it, and the next instant you would hit the water, and the water would compress your world until everything that existed would be confined to your own being. Then you would be at the surface again, and your whole range of consciousness would widen. She might have been under water. When she thought of Tom and herself and this Winifred James, she was aware of nothing around her.

That phrase of Tom's kept repeating itself like a theme in a disorderly symphony. There was a war on, *a war on,* and now she had stepped deliberately into her own war. She had landed on her own Normandy beachhead or whatever you wanted to call it. Her armored columns were advancing in good order across a line which she never had thought she would have to pass. She looked at the dial above the elevator doors, and smelled that carbolic smell of the hotel corridor, and heard the distant whir of a vacuum cleaner, and the tinkle of china on breakfast trays. But she still seemed to be under the water.

There was a war on. Polly knew that Winifred James would be organizing now that the line was crossed. Winifred James would be in communication with Tom by now, telling Tom the news, gathering information. She was sure Tom would not like it, she hoped he would not, but there was a war on.

"Good morning, Mrs. Brett."

Polly felt herself coming to the surface. She was back again on the wavy modernistic carpet waiting for the elevator. It was the young flying officer who had asked her on Saturday night to join the boys, and it seemed years since Saturday night. It was Lieutenant Meek, back from Burma with malaria, the one who reminded her of Bob Tasmin. He was dressed in his combat jacket, holding one of those soft, floppy caps that showed he was a flyer. He looked thinner and yellower than he had on Saturday night.

"Hello," Polly said. "What have you been doing all week end?"

He was smiling at her exactly like Bob Tasmin, and it was a great relief just then to feel that someone was glad to see her.

"I've been adjusting myself like crazy," he said. "I'm due at the Walter Reed at one o'clock."

"Oh, I remember," Polly said.

"Somebody up there will be taking me apart," the lieutenant said. "That's all they do. They really love it, and then I'll get the word." He cleared his throat and twisted his cap uncertainly. "I thought I'd go outside and get some air. It couldn't be that you'd have time to take a walk?"

"Why, yes," Polly said, "that's just what I was going to do."

It was pleasant to see how delighted he looked.

"That's awfully kind of you," he said. "I don't want to be alone, but I don't want to be with anybody I used to know either, until I know what the score is."

"Well, I feel the same way," Polly said. "I don't want to be alone."

"Well, that's swell," the lieutenant answered.

"But you mustn't let the score bother you," Polly said. "No one knows what the score is these days."

"Don't you know it either?" the lieutenant asked.

"No," Polly answered, "not any more."

It was a beautiful day, and the air was fresh from all the rain. There was the usual group of Army officers and civilians with brief cases in front of the hotel waiting for taxicabs, and, as usual, there were too few taxis. The doorman was busy loading them, calling out the names — Union Station, Pentagon, Munitions, Social Security.

"Where shall we walk?" Polly asked.

"I don't know," the lieutenant answered, "but let's see if we can get away from Social Security."

Polly laughed. There was no security that morning. Not even at the State Department or the Red Cross or the Pan American Building or the Hall of the Daughters of the American Revolution. The people on the sidewalks, the taxis, the trolleys and the busses, swirled around these buildings like a tide washing at their foundations. Lieutenant Meek was walking just as Bob Tasmin used to walk, with his back very straight, taking long, easy strides.

"Everybody's talking around here," he was saying, "about things they know aren't true. Have you noticed that?"

"Yes," Polly said, "but they can't help it."

"I guess that's why I don't seem able to talk much," the lieutenant said. "I can't seem to get things straightened out."

As they walked down Constitution Avenue, he stared at the wireless antennae above the Navy buildings, and blinked at the glare from the white marble of the Public Health Building, the Federal Reserve and the Academy of Science.

"They call them Healthy, Wealthy and Wise," Polly said. That was what Tom called them.

"There didn't used to be so many people here," the lieutenant said. "This war is all crowds. Have you noticed that?"

Polly put her hand on his arm.

"Yes," she said, "but don't look so unhappy. You're right, there are a lot of new people."

382

"Crowds," the lieutenant said, "all moving. It's the same way in London, Cairo, Calcutta — people who have never been there before, all moving. Do you know what I wonder? It's a funny idea."

"What?" Polly asked.

"I wonder whether any of them know what they're doing? I wonder whether we know. Did you ever think of that?"

"It doesn't matter," Polly said, "if no one else knows."

"Maybe," the lieutenant said, "but don't you think they used to know? I used to — just what I was doing, and what I was going to do."

She thought of Norman Bell and she thought of telling the story about the officer in the Pentagon, but she checked herself.

They were walking back to the hotel, and the lieutenant still looked unhappy.

"You've been awfully nice to me," he said. "I wish — " He stopped. "Well, never mind."

"I hate people who say 'Never mind,'" Polly answered. "What do you wish?"

"Never mind it," Lieutenant Meek said again, "but I'm glad you don't know what the score is either."

"We'll know sometime," Polly said. "Well, good-by." And she held out her hand.

He must have said good-by to all sorts of people a great many times without any hope of ever seeing them again. He must have often been thrown accidentally with strangers in an enforced intimacy. When she looked up at him, he did not have to tell her that there was a war on. She knew he did not want to leave her, and she did not want him to, but they both knew there was nothing one could do. Suddenly he looked desperately uncertain.

"I wonder what I'm going to do if they wash me out?" he said.

"Why, you can go back home," she said, "and have a rest."

"And just sit there?"

If Polly got washed out, she could go back home too and just sit there, but there was not any home. He had been to Burma, and Kunming and all those places, and she had been through a dozen years of marriage. They both had their combat ribbons, she and Lieutenant Meek. You could not arbitrarily drop experience and go home.

"Let me know what the score is," she said. "Maybe I can help you if you get washed out."

If you could be useful to someone, nothing was as bad as it might have been, but it revealed a pathetic state of mind to be clinging to a nice boy like Lieutenant Meek.

"Well, thanks a lot," he said. "I'll depend on it. We could have a drink or something. Yes, I'll let you know."

"Happy landings," Polly said. "That's it, isn't it?"

He laughed, and for once he looked no more than his age.

"That's it," he said. "Happy landings."

Then Polly was alone, and it was exactly twenty-three minutes to one o'clock.

There was just time to take off her coat, and to put on lipstick and to glance about the sitting room. She did not look badly, and the room did not look badly either. The five dollars for Room Service had helped so much that a waiter was there already with the cocktails, and the spring flowers were there — snapdragon, iris, and narcissus, jammed awkwardly into three vases.

"Everything looks very nice," Polly said to the waiter. That was what you always said. ". . . If you could bring the lunch in at five minutes to one?"

She did not want the waiter there for a few minutes. She wanted the sitting room to look efficient and yet at the same time lived in. She dropped a copy of the *New Republic* and one of the *Nation* carelessly on one of the sofas. She moved two of the chairs, opened the window a little, lit a cigarette. She picked up the *New Yorker* and sat down, as she had the night before, the way she had been taught to sit at Heatherbloom Hall, knees close together, one foot a little behind the other, her back uncompromisingly straight. After a second she got up and opened the door into the hall a crack because she did not want to have to open it later herself. She wanted to be sitting reading. She wanted to toss the *New Yorker* aside and stand up.

384

XXVIII

Take It All Away

"OH, my God," Polly whispered. It was ten minutes before one, and if Miss James made her wait in front of those cocktails on the little table, she would never forgive it, never. She began to look attentively at the advertisements in the *New Yorker,* as you did under a beauty shop dryer. There were liquor advertisements, and then there was a perfume advertisement, a hazy picture of an insolent, pouty, bony-looking girl with smoldering eyes and half-parted lips. "*Je rends,*" was what the perfume was called, and in case you were unfamiliar with French, it was translated. "The evanescent distillation of Riviera moonlight, a bar of music that knifes a turgid silence, the sweet, throbbing solace of surrender. *Je Rends (I Surrender)* — $5.75." She was just thinking that a higher figure might have been asked, considering, when she heard a knock. Though Polly had been ready and waiting for the last three minutes, it made her angry to discover that her throat was dry and taut, and that she had a hollow feeling of inadequacy.

"Come in," she said.

When Winifred James stood in the doorway, Polly found herself rising gracefully without using her hands to push herself from the sofa, as she had been taught at Heatherbloom Hall, instinctively going through the finishing school pantomime of receiving the welcome guest.

There she was, and without meaning to appear vulgarly curious Polly was observing those details that in combination make women able to read the backgrounds and instincts of other women. She was certain that Winifred James had gone home and had changed her clothes. Her dress was gray and too light in color for an office, and her small gray openwork hat and her black suède pumps were too elaborate. When Polly took her mind off the clothes, she had to admit that this Miss James was a pretty little thing, and not so little either. She had well-proportioned legs, but her hands were plump and her fingers stubby. Her curly brown hair made her face look round, but still she was not overweight. It might not last, but now she had a pretty figure, a large, good-natured mouth, an indifferent little nose and alert bluish eyes.

It was fascinating to watch her for that second and to wonder honestly what it was that Tom saw in her, a mediocre girl in her early thirties, almost mousily dressed — but then, this might have been done on purpose. It was fascinating to stand there smiling, waiting for her to speak, because her voice and her first words were needed to complete that first impression.

"I do hope I haven't kept you waiting, Mrs. Brett."

It was not quite her telephone voice. It was more natural, but still careful, and sweet without being saccharine. It made Polly wonder whether this girl had ever been in the theater, but on second thought Polly was sure that she could not have been. She was only another of those women whom you could not exactly place.

"Waiting?" Polly said. "Oh, dear, no. I just had everything ready because I knew you'd be busy." And then she heard herself laughing very naturally. "It's so nice to see you after hearing you."

Miss James laughed too, very naturally.

"I know," she said. "Seeing is believing, isn't it?"

"That's just what I was thinking," Polly said. "Do sit down anywhere if you don't mind getting cast in this upholstery — and you'll have a cocktail, won't you?"

"Oh, I really shouldn't," Miss James said. "If I have a cocktail at lunch, I feel sleepy all afternoon."

"One wouldn't hurt you, would it?" Polly asked. "My dear, you look so wide-awake."

"Well, just one," Miss James said. "I know it's weak-minded, but just one."

"It's so nice to be weak-minded at odd moments, isn't it?" Polly said.

"Yes," Miss James said, "at odd moments."

"I don't mean to imply that this is one of them," Polly said. "It's an occasion, and it's so sweet of you to come." She lifted the carafe from the bowl of ice and poured two cocktails. "There."

"Oh, thank you," Miss James said. "It's so good of you to have me, Mrs. Brett. You make it a lovely occasion."

Polly's sense of adequacy was returning — she was feeling contemptuous of Tom simply because Winifred James had used the word "lovely" in the same way as that Air Force colonel.

"I've heard so much about your little house in Georgetown," Polly said. "Georgetown *is* lovely."

For just a second she thought that Winifred James had a surprised look.

"Oh," she said, "it isn't anything much. It's just one of those cute little old houses, very little. We bought it before the war."

Polly must have looked surprised herself, and Miss James went on quickly.

"My husband and I. He's a Navy man."

"Oh," Polly said, "are you married?"

"That was before Pearl Harbor," Miss James said. "Henry's married again now. He's in the South Pacific."

"Oh," Polly said. "Tom never told me. How about another cocktail?"

"I really shouldn't," Miss James said, "but if you're having one — "

"Yes, I'm having one," Polly said. "Tom is always so interested in old houses in out-of-the-way places."

"Yes, I know," Miss James said. "He's told me about your home away off in the Berkshires. It must be charming. He says you worked so hard over it."

"Oh," Polly said, "did he? He exaggerates sometimes." And she poured her second cocktail. The door was opening noiselessly. It was the Room Service waiter, and he had come at exactly the right moment. It gave her a chance to drink her cocktail slowly and to look undisturbed at Winifred James. The waiter wheeled in the table, and after it one of those tin ovens. He set out clear consommé and bread and celery and olives.

"I brought everything up together, Mrs. Brett," he said. "That was right, wasn't it?"

"Yes," Polly said, "that's very nice." He was moving about the room placing two straight-backed chairs at the table, while Polly watched him, glancing now and then at Winifred James. It was what she needed, time to think, because she wanted to be civilized. Many questions had been answered without their ever having been asked as soon as Tom's name was mentioned. You did not have to be told some things about men and women. There had been those purely unintentional pauses, not embarrassed pauses, but short, indescribably watchful little interludes of silence. There was self-confidence in that woman's bright face, a possessive sort of satisfaction which she could not help but show. It was obvious what was going on between Tom and Miss Winifred James, and she might as well have confessed it. They were living together, and you could even tell that it was not an eccentric or transient relationship, but something that had been going on for a long while, as long as the war perhaps. There existed a prosaic aura of familiarity, an ingenuous admission that Winifred James knew Tom as well as Polly did, and some sides of him perhaps better than she did. There was only one question left unanswered, that devastating question of *why*.

Polly knew Tom well enough to know what other women saw in him, but what did he see in Winifred James? What was there in that synthetic girl? That was the word — not cheap, but synthetic. The girl in dove gray, with those brown curls, which were natural at that, was not nearly as bad news as she might have been. If she had been worse or better, Polly could have taken it more tolerantly. It was this mediocrity that made her angry. Her reaction was not jealousy, but a sort of anger caused by disillusion at Tom's bad taste.

"I ordered a thinning lunch," Polly said. "I hope you like chicken and asparagus."

"Oh, I adore them," Miss James answered. "You guessed just right."

That was what it was, comfortable mediocrity. It would not be long before Winifred James would have to be careful of her figure.

Instead of keeping her mind clear and alert, instead of manipulating the conversation, Polly was obsessed by details. She observed with intent, academic interest the manner in which Miss James's blunt little fingers grasped her soup spoon. Tom had once said that the hands of a good portrait were more important than the face, and she wondered whether Tom had ever noticed Miss James's hands. There was nothing wrong with the way she held the spoon, no stylized crooking of the little finger, but at the same time the way she held it competently and firmly evoked a picture of Winifred James stirring things in pots over a cute little gas stove in that cute little house in Georgetown; and loving to cook for a man.

But then Polly herself could cook when she had to. She could have made a better soup than the hotel consommé, and she could have done better with the asparagus and the chicken. There was no great mystery about cooking if you worked at it, and it was ridiculous how a little plain cooking could impress a man, particularly Tom, when he was in a certain mood — but this was not the time to be going off on tangents. The main thing was not to let emotion get the upper hand, but to be aloof and relax, the way everyone relaxed nowadays — at parties, in chairs, and with Camel cigarettes. All the girls like Apples Sandler were always saying, "Darling, just take your hat off and relax." That was how Winifred James looked holding her spoon, relaxed, and she even looked relaxed when she nibbled at her asparagus.

"I envy your being in Washington all the time," Polly said. "It must be so exciting."

Winifred James looked up from her asparagus and smiled.

"I wouldn't be anywhere else for all the world," she said.

"There must be so much going on, so much you can do to help. I wish you'd tell me exactly what it is you do — that is, if it isn't a secret." She was wondering how much Tom had told her about their marriage, and she wished that her voice did not sound nervous and edgy. "But then it must be nice to know secrets."

"Not if you know too many," Winifred James said. "When I was in the War Department, I knew too many. I like working for Army officers. Of course, what I do now is mostly screening."

"Screening?" Polly repeated. "Is that hard?"

"Not if you're used to it," Miss James answered. "I was in Personnel before the war. It's largely a matter of learning who the Chief needs to see and who he doesn't, and how long he needs to see them." Miss James laughed, though it was more of a giggle than a laugh. "You know how Mr. Brett is."

"Yes, I ought to," Polly said, "but don't you call him Tom? You must if you've been — thrown with him so much."

Winifred James's curls bobbed alluringly as she shook her head.

"Not in office hours. Everything is strictly formal in the office. But you know the way Mr. Brett is. He gets talking with everyone who comes in. He likes to hear himself, and he hasn't any sense of time, especially when he's tired. It's all we can do to keep him quiet."

"Can you keep him quiet?" Polly asked. "I never could."

Then the room waiter was back.

"I forgot to ask," he said, "if you care for coffee with your lunch." He was late in asking because they were finishing the mixed green salad, and there was nothing left but a compote of fruit.

"Oh, I'd love some coffee," Miss James said. "A large cup, please. I'm a great coffee drinker. That's what comes of having been mixed up with the Navy. You know in the Munitions Building they have coffee cooking all the time just like the wardroom of a ship. I've introduced it in our office. Of course, it's nothing but tea with the British on Lend Lease."

Polly nodded to the waiter.

"If you'll just clear away everything but the dessert," she said, "and the coffee, that will be all for now."

When the dishes and the portable oven were gone, Polly sighed, leaned back deliberately and lighted a cigarette. She had learned all she wanted about Winifred James. She had caught enough little glimpses of her daily life. She had concentrated on her so hard that she felt tired. If Tom wanted mediocrity and efficiency with a touch of pedestrian obtuseness, there it was, and Polly could not give it to him. There it was, and she did not know why he wanted it, and to her astonishment she no longer particularly cared. He could have *her* and that cute little house in Georgetown too. Holding Tom any longer did not seem worth the struggle or in the least rewarding. As she leaned back in her stiff, straight chair and looked at Winifred James across the table, she had a complete sense of severance. She could no longer understand what Tom had meant to her, or why she had put up with him so long; Winifred James had made her sick of the effort — she simply did not care. . . .

"We've said a lot without saying anything, haven't we?" Polly said. "Just seeing you explains so much. I suppose we ought to get down to brass tacks."

She watched Miss James and waited, but Miss James did not reply. Perhaps her personnel and screening experience enabled her to sit so quietly. Or it may only have been that she had Tom.

"You've known my husband quite a while, haven't you?"

At least the girl did not shift ground, and she was not a little bitch. She folded her hands efficiently on the table as though it were an office desk.

"Oh, yes." She spoke like a clever schoolgirl who knew her homework. "I've known Mr. Brett for three years."

"Let's call him Tom," Polly said, "just as a point of convenience. Don't you think it would be easier?"

"Why, yes," Miss James answered, "if you want me to, Mrs. Brett."

Polly coughed a little. She smoked her cigarette too fast, and she dropped it in her coffee cup, an unpleasant habit she had learned from Tom.

"I don't suppose I've done all I could about Tom," Polly said, "but I'm not entirely sure. I've been rather out of touch with him these last three years — necessarily. I've lost my influence, haven't I? There isn't much chance for a wife when there's a war on. Perhaps you've noticed — I mean in other cases."

"Yes," Miss James answered. "I think I know what you mean, Mrs. Brett."

She reminded Polly of that girl at the reception desk in B. F.'s office long ago. She had the same detachment, the same impersonal kindliness.

"Of course," Polly said, "he's particularly attractive when he's working; so you've seen the best of him, and he's seen the best of you, while he and I have been having the worst of each other. I don't know how it could have been helped, and I admit there must have been something else wrong between us — I don't know what — but you've helped me realize it."

Miss James unclasped her hands and examined the red manicure on her fingers.

"How did you know?" she asked.

That direct question was disconcerting because it cleared away all pretense and verbiage, and nothing was civilized any longer. Miss James seemed to have surprised her half-dressed.

"Know what?" Polly asked, and her voice was very sharp.

"About Tom — and me."

"Because I'm not a fool," Polly said. "Any wife knows when there's someone else if she isn't a fool."

"Did Tom tell you?"

"No," Polly said, "he didn't have to."

Miss James raised her hand daintily and pushed a curl from her forehead.

"Then I don't see how you knew, I mean who it was — about me."

"I don't suppose Tom's very clever about these things," Polly answered, "and maybe you aren't either. People are always stupid when they're in love."

When she said the last word, her voice broke, in spite of every effort. Her eyes were smarting because she was thinking of the time when she and Tom were in love. She pulled another cigarette from the pack on the table, and picked up a paper of matches. She could read on the paper, when she lighted the match, *For Sea Food — Go to Jack's*. Tom must have left those matches.

"He should have told you," Miss James said.

Polly blinked and lighted her cigarette.

"Yes," she said, "he should have, if he'd had the guts."

"I told him he ought to," Miss James said. "I'm awfully sorry." And then her own voice was uncertain. "You see I'm good for him, I'm what he needs . . . but that sounds mean, and I don't want to hurt you."

"You're not hurting me," Polly said. "How long has this been going on?"

"I wish you wouldn't ask," Miss James said. "It's been going on so long that we're both sure. I only wish he'd told you."

"He's absent-minded sometimes," Polly said.

She was thinking of that afternoon in front of the apartment on Park Avenue, that cold afternoon when Tom Brett had waited for her. She could see his hat and that thin overcoat with its turned-up collar. She could even remember exactly the way his hands were jammed into his pockets.

"It doesn't mean he isn't very fond of you," said Miss James. "He really is, and he has such respect for you. He knows you've done so much for him. We both know."

"Oh, stop it," Polly said.

What she had done for Tom belonged to her, and it was none of this girl's business.

"I'm awfully sorry — " Miss James began again.

"There's no use being sorry," Polly answered, "no use at all. Do you want to marry him?"

Miss James nodded, and Polly wished that she would not speak in that kind, consoling way.

"I wouldn't want to if I wasn't positive I could make him happy . . . You're being so nice about it, Mrs. Brett, so adult, so integrated."

"I'm old enough to be," Polly said, "and please don't say you're sorry again, if you don't mind, because I've stopped being sorry. Why do you think you can make him happy?"

She told herself she did not care. She did not want to show how upset she was. She told herself she did not care.

"I hate to be personal, Mrs. Brett," Miss James was saying. "I know you once meant so much to each other, and you still do in some respects. It seems wrong of me to say anything, but I think . . ."

At least Miss James was not enjoying it. She clasped her hands and unclasped them, and her face looked flushed and mottled. ". . . I think he needs someone to look after him . . . in an unpossessive way, I mean."

"That's true," Polly said. "He isn't the lone wolf type. He's always been a . . . sort of sophisticated Peter Pan."

"That's it," Miss James said. "That's what I thought when I saw him first. There's something in him that's still so — so fresh and boyish. He so needs someone who — well, *appreciates* him."

"That's true," Polly said. "I suppose I've got out of the habit of long-term appreciation."

"Someone," Miss James was speaking more eagerly, "duller than you, Mrs. Brett, who doesn't — well, keep him stirred up. Someone not quite as lovely — without as many definite ambitions for him. I mean someone common. That is what he needs." She raised her hands and dropped them gently on the table. "Like me."

It was so embarrassing, that self-portrait of Winifred James, that Polly could find no answer.

"You see, Tom's common, too," she went on ". . . in a nice way, I mean. He's just from the Middle West like me. He needs someone he doesn't have to compete with. You're so brilliant, so charming, such a rare and lovely person, Mrs. Brett. I think you're too good for him really. I know I'm saying this badly, but he just needs someone who loves everything he does without so many perfect standards. I do hope you know what I mean."

The words of Winifred James kept buzzing around Polly's head like flies in meaningless, distracted parabolas . . . those Midwesterners always got back to that Midwest.

"I suppose he's always had an inferiority complex," Polly said, "but I've never thought of his feeling that he had to compete with me. I'm sorry about that."

"I've said it badly," Miss James answered. "It's so hard to say, and no one knows what there has been between two people, does one? Competing isn't the right word really. I suppose I mean living in a certain — well, atmosphere, according to high standards, with so much money."

394

"Money?" Polly frowned. "Did he mention money?"

"Only to say you were very sweet and generous," Miss James said. "Why, once he said — " She stopped.

"Please go on," Polly told her. "You're the only one who can tell me these things. Aren't you?"

At least Miss James looked hot and unhappy.

"Once he said that he was the boy in the toy store and that you would buy him an electric train when all he wanted was marbles. You know the way he says things . . . but he's so fond of you, Mrs. Brett."

Polly felt her face growing red. She was tired of being adult and tired of being a sweet, generous person.

"Does he want to marry you?" Polly asked.

Miss James was silent for a second. Perhaps because she had started being frank she could not help but continue.

"I don't know," she said. "You know how indefinite he is. It's hard for him to make decisions."

For an instant a bright light of elation burned in Polly. It was just like Tom, and if she wanted, she knew that she could take him by the ear and lead him back. She knew that she still had a stronger hold on Tom than Winifred James, and she would always have it. Polly dropped her second cigarette in her coffee cup and stood up.

"Well, my dear," she said, "you can have him if you want him. I've tried it long enough. Take him away if you want him." And then she laughed. "And good luck and happy landings."

She had not known what she was going to do that afternoon until she had done it — she had not realized how close it all was to irrevocable. Winifred James had begun to cry and it was a horrid, sticky little scene — those last minutes. Winifred James had been so surprised and then so grateful in a doglike way, although she was not a bitch. There was something cloying and mawkish in the way she had said thank you, that Mrs. Brett had been so generous, so adult and understanding. Miss James had never known that anyone in the world could be as wonderful as Mrs. Brett, and Polly had told her that she had better go to the bathroom and wash her face and stop crying. Polly had finally accepted the conclusion, but she still could not grasp its implications. When she was alone all she wanted was to forget those final minutes.

"Room Service," she said over the telephone. "You can clear away the luncheon now."

You could clear away dishes and empty ash trays, but you could not clear away years of living with a man. You could not close off those years as if with a closet door because parts of the years, in shreds and tatters, would always be drifting through the cracks. There was bound to be reaction, and she was facing it already. The best thing was to put it off as long as possible. All that she was sure of was that she was quite alone and that she had arrived on some new plane.

She must think as hard as she could of other things and of what she had been going to do before That Thing had happened. There was the appointment at the beauty parlor at three o'clock — her hair did need attention — and afterwards there was tea with Mildred Tasmin at Scott Circle. That was almost too much to go through with, but it was better to go through with it for just this reason. It was one of those tatters of all she was leaving behind, and it was time to learn how to behave with them.

"Is this the Bell Captain?" she was asking over the telephone. "My bags will be ready in twenty minutes. Will you have them taken to the Check Room?"

XXIX

Dear, I'm Dying for a Drink

THE APARTMENTS that had been built in Washington shortly before
the war had always confused Polly because their glass doors and
plate-glass corner windows made them modern, and so did the air-
conditioning in summer; but once you were inside, they had the
overcarpeted corridors, the smell of cooking, the stodgy atmosphere
of a family hotel. She was sure that the Tasmins would not have
stayed at Scott Circle if they could have found something more
like them.

An Army officer living in one of those apartments could always
make arrangements with another officer who had a car to drive out
to the Pentagon, or to Gravely Point if he was in the Chemical
Warfare Service, and Scott Circle was within walking distance of
most places, a great advantage with the gas rationing. Mrs. Tasmin
was on the fifth floor, the girl at the telephone switchboard said.
Just push button Five on the elevator — the doors would open automatically when it reached its destination — and then turn to the left
and take the second corridor to the right.

The second corridor to the right was painted a seasick beige. A
colored girl, that wonderful girl whom Mildred had found but who
did not look wonderful to Polly, opened the door. The apartment
must have been rented furnished, for the Tasmins would never
have owned a hat rack or a carved Chinese camphor chest. An
Army officer's overcoat was hanging on one of the hat-rack pegs,
with a boy's overcoat beside it, and some rubbers and a pair of
roller skates were on the floor beneath. The roller skates raised a
lump in Polly's throat. They made her wish, now that it was too
late, that she and Tom had had children.

"Just rest your coat on the rack, ma'am," the colored girl said, "and step right in."

It was not very far to step. There were two doors on the left leading to the bedrooms, and the living room was right ahead, a smallish room with plate-glass windows and Venetian blinds and furniture that must have been collected quickly from secondhand stores — a studio couch, a bookcase with glass doors, some easy-chairs with chintz covers, and some small Oriental carpets. There was a painted table in a dining nook near the kitchenette. The only traces of Bob Tasmin that Polly could observe were some pipes in a brass bowl beside a tobacco jar.

"Well, here it all is," Mildred said. "There's not a bit of use trying to do anything with it. We're just camping out for the duration."

"It must be a relief," Polly said.

"There's a double room," Mildred said, "and a little hole of a room for Neddie, where he has his fun with electricity and his chemical set. We all get in each other's hair in the morning, but you're right — it's wonderful not to have to bother."

It was not hard to make polite conversation with anyone like Mildred Tasmin. Polly could talk and see and think quite effectively with one lobe of her brain, while at the same time she endeavored to smooth the turgid upset of her mind. She could cope with the unanswered question of why she had done what she had done, and simultaneously, she could wonder which of those stuffy chairs had been Bob Tasmin's favorite and how he could have endured the reproductions of Matisse on the cream-colored walls beside the purple window curtains.

"There's no use shortening your life over something that isn't permanent," Polly said.

Yet, if that apartment had been hers, she would not have tolerated for a minute the imprint of other tasteless, vulgar occupants. She could not have lived there without doing something about those breakfast-nook chairs with hearts sawed out of their backs. At least she would have got rid of that combination portable bar-and-victrola and those aniline-dyed Oriental rugs.

"When I first came here," Mildred was saying, "I was so indignant with Bob for thinking I could stand it, that I wanted to throw up my hands and scream. He was determined to bring Neddie and me down when he found he might be here for the duration. So I'm just an Army wife like the old campaigner in *Pendennis*. You know how stubborn Bob is. When he puts his mind on something, he looks like a Roman coin."

"Not like Nero, darling," Polly said.

"Oh, no," Mildred said, "Marcus Aurelius. Bob has an affinity for Marcus Aurelius. He keeps reading the *Meditations* before he goes to sleep. You'll die when you see our bedroom."

"Well, as long as the beds are comfortable," Polly said.

"Twin, ivory-enameled beds," Mildred was saying, "with pink flowers painted on them and pink crepe-de-Chine lamps. Of course, I didn't realize at first, coming fresh from New York, how lucky Bob was to find any place at all for us. He literally had to snatch this up before I could see it. It belongs to a colonel who has gone overseas — Colonel Elmendorff."

"Who?" Polly asked.

"Elmendorff," Mildred repeated. "Isn't it queer when we're fighting the Germans that so many officers have German names? There must be hundreds of them. Eisenhower, Wedemeyer, Kimmel, and who else?"

"Oh," Polly said, "Nimitz."

"Oh, yes," Mildred said. "You're always so quick, Polly, Nimitz — and then there was that admiral at dinner the other night — the one on my left, who had something to do with that thing called Special Projects."

"Oh, yes," Polly said, "Krankhaus."

One part of her mind still worked on one thing while the rest of it was able to wander elsewhere. Mildred was asking Polly if she wanted something stronger than tea, and indeed she did, though she said that tea would be perfect. Mildred might not have bothered about the apartment, but as she sat there pouring, in the precise way that all nice girls had been taught, it was obvious that Mildred had bothered about herself. She was beautiful in her

399

periwinkle blue wool dress with its box shoulders, with long flowing sleeves buttoned tight at the wrists, and a bow in a soft knot at the neck. Periwinkle was a color that Polly had always wished she could wear herself, but could not.

"It's such fun seeing you again," Mildred was saying. "And Polly, how chic you look — not that you don't always."

"It's my hair," Polly said. "Do you know Miss Rosalind at the hotel? I wish I could give her a knockout drop and take her to New York."

"And how's Tom?" Mildred asked. "I don't suppose you get more than a glimpse of Tom."

"Only a flash of his coattails," Polly answered, "occasionally, like the White Rabbit hurrying to meet the Duchess."

"I never thought of Tom as a rabbit."

"Neither did I until right now," Polly answered, "but then I don't always know what I think of Tom."

It was natural that Polly's curiosity should be piqued by Mildred Tasmin and that Washington apartment, because Polly might so very easily have been pouring tea there herself instead of Mildred. It was Dover Beach revisited, it was a line from "Locksley Hall" — as the husband is, the wife is, though Mildred was only like Bob Tasmin in a superficial way. Perhaps you always thought that no girl was quite good enough for a man you had once loved.

Polly would have done a lot to that apartment if she had been married to Bob Tasmin, but then perhaps he would not have cared. She remembered how much she had wanted to fix up that bachelor apartment of his in New York. It had also had a temporary quality, and she knew that he had wanted permanence, which for Bob Tasmin meant a house in the dreadful real estate development at Sugar Hill. He had wanted permanence, and Tom had wanted impermanence — no children, nothing to tie him down; and she had wanted — what was it she had wanted? If you got what you wanted, did you always want something else? "Leave me here, and when you want me, sound upon the bugle-horn."

"Husbands are so unstable in Washington," Mildred was saying.

"How do you mean." Polly asked, "unstable?"

"I mean," Mildred said, "the poor things work so hard. Up before it's daylight, and always back late. Now Bob is the most reliable person in the world, but I've hardly had a glimpse of him for years. He's only stable now when he's asleep — and then the alarm clock rings. All I get is a glimpse of him at breakfast reading the *Post*. 'Good-by, darling, I'll be back late. . . . Hello, darling, what's there for supper? Hello, Neddie, how was school? I can't go any-where, dear, I've got to work on a report.' It's like the law in New York, only ten times more so . . . and then these trips."

Mildred Tasmin was not a very good mimic, but she gave the illusion of Bob Tasmin's voice.

"Wars are men's business," Polly said. "Women don't belong."

"I wonder if that isn't why men like war so," Mildred said. "It does give them a vacation from women, and yet they seem to want women around. They want their women to call on each other, according to rank."

"I suppose Bob is just made for the Army," Polly said.

"He adores it," Mildred answered. "You know Bob — and he adores these trips — London, North Africa, the Pacific."

Mildred was smiling, tolerantly amused.

"Aren't you worried about him?" Polly asked.

Mildred still smiled and shook her head positively.

"No, dear, he has something to do with planners, and nobody shoots planners, although Bob says someone ought to. Besides he's with a three-star general, General Bogart. I wish you could see his wife, dear. She looks as though she lived on atabrine and an occasional pickled lime. Mrs. Bogart's not worried, so I'm not."

Mildred should have been worried, and should have been more loyal — in front of her, of all people.

"I know you don't mean it, Mildred," she said, "but don't you think you sound a little hard on Bob?"

"Oh, dear," Mildred said quickly, "I only meant to sound inured to it. You see, dear, we've been pinned right down here — ever since before Pearl Harbor."

"But darling, the war's pinned everyone down."

"Well," Mildred said, "I'm not pinned down any longer because

Neddie's school is closed by measles, and we're going up to Mother's for a week. That's why I'm asking this of you." She lowered her voice and glanced meaningly at the closed door of the kitchenette. "Minnie. She's the last pin to pin me, and if you could be here, you could keep an eye on Minnie. You and Tom can move right in tomorrow morning."

"It's awfully sweet of you," Polly said, "but I think Tom's going away too."

"Oh, dear," Mildred said. "Then won't you come alone? Please." There was a gentle click as Mildred set down her teacup. "Why don't you come up tonight? You can sleep in the other bed."

In that apartment no one would be able to find her for a day or two. It was a God-given opportunity to be alone until she could face people again.

"I wish you would," Mildred was saying "I know it's a left-handed invitation when I'm running away and leaving you."

"Could you really have me tonight?" Polly asked.

"Don't be silly, dear," Mildred said. "It would be such fun."

Such fun was what Mildred said. Polly knew that if she did not do something very quickly she would begin to cry. Already Mildred and the apartment were making the tears well up in her, not tears of gratitude but of enraged frustration, for it was not fair that Mildred should have so much without being at all aware of it. She was blind and she was stupid, and Polly wanted to shake her physically. She wanted to tell Mildred that she had everything that mattered, and that Polly knew. She knew because she had been so blind to it herself. She wanted to tell Mildred not to take it for granted — that it might vanish into thin air.

"Mildred," Polly said. She could tell that something was wrong with her voice from the startled, curious way that Mildred looked at her.

"Why, dear," Mildred said, "what is it?"

Polly was groping blindly in her bag for a handkerchief.

"It isn't anything," Polly said. "I'm just so damned tired."

"I know," Mildred said. "It's your father, isn't it, dear?" And she placed her hand over Polly's for a moment.

402

"No —" Polly shook her head. "It's everything."

Right in front of Mildred Tasmin she was blowing her nose and dabbing at her eyes.

"Don't mind, dear," Mildred said, and that was the worst of it all, having Mildred be so kind. "Wait, I'll get you a glass of water."

Why was it in God's name that when you cried all anyone could think of was to get you a glass of water?

"No," Polly said, "never mind. . . . Mildred, I wish you wouldn't go away until you get some news from Bob."

"But why, dear?" Mildred asked. "There won't be any news. They'd tell me right away if anything were wrong."

At any rate Polly had stopped crying.

"I know I'm being a damned fool," she said. "It's really none of my business." And she blew her nose again.

"It wouldn't make sense, dear," Mildred said. "It would be different if Bob weren't Bob. It would only make him uncomfortable to think of me mooning around. You know he's the least demanding person in the world."

"Yes," Polly said, "I know."

"Bob has an expression for it," Mildred said. "He says we have to go on living."

There was the sound of a buzzer at the apartment door. "That isn't anyone," Mildred said. "It's only Neddie. He's been down the hall at the Rysons'. Do you know the Pat Rysons from Greenwich?"

"No." Polly shook her head.

"He has something to do in the State Department. They have a boy just Neddie's age."

It was the war again. The men one knew were out being shot at if they were young and well enough, or if they weren't, they were in the State Department or the O.W.I. or something. Polly would have taken a war job herself, but Tom always said he wanted her right there behind the scenes. She could have gone overseas for the Red Cross, except that Tom did not want her overseas. He had even put his foot down when she wanted to take some English refugees. Once she had told Tom she was going to join the Wacs, but Tom had told her that she was distinctly over-age. She had asked him what about Hobby, that colonel woman who ran the Wacs, and Tom had explained that Polly couldn't very well be a colonel, and she had answered that some of the stupidest men she knew were colonels. It had not helped when Tom had started addressing her as "Colonel." He had always been jealous and upset when she tried to do anything on her own.

"This is Mrs. Brett, dear," Mildred was saying. "You remember. She gave you that lovely Christmas present."

Neddie Tasmin was standing there in front of her, the only thing in the room except the pipes which she was sure belonged to Bob — and Polly could not remember what she had given him for Christmas. She was never good with little boys, but now she was shaken by the sight of Bob Tasmin's little boy. He looked about as her brother Harry had when Harry had been nine — knee-length trousers, bare knees, wool stockings, a brown pullover sweater; and he was out of breath, just as she remembered Harry.

"How do you do?" he said.

His hand was limp and grubby like the hands of other little boys, and Bob and Mildred had obviously taught him to stand up straight and look people in the eye when he was introduced.

"Why, hello, Neddie," Polly said. It was like touching the might-have-been when she held Neddie Tasmin's hand. Though he had Mildred's mouth, he had his father's eyes and forehead, and he held his head and shoulders like him, too.

"How would it be," Polly asked, "if you called me Aunt Polly?"

She knew it was a mistake as soon as she saw Neddie Tasmin's stricken look. Children's eyes were so utterly truthful. They were saying that she was another of those women whom one met who made fools of themselves, and she was not his aunt, so why should she bring it up?

"When I was a little girl," Polly said, and her voice had a cloying playful note, "I used to live almost next door to your father at Gray's Point." But Neddie Tasmin did not give a Continental who she was, and she did not blame him for it either.

"Now, run along and get washed, Neddie," Mildred said, "and then you can ask Minnie to get the cocktail things. What do you think? Aunt Polly's going to have supper with us and spend the night."

"My father's in the Army," Neddie said. "He's overseas."

"Yes, I know, darling," Polly said.

"Now, Neddie," Mildred said ". . . please. Run along . . . or wait, I'll go in with you and see you wash" — she laughed — "so the dirt won't come off all over the towel." She turned to Polly. "There's some gin in the cellaret, dear. Would you mind taking it out, and the vermouth?"

Polly had never felt as much like a refugee as she did when she opened the door of the combination phonograph and bar. Down the narrow hall she could hear Mildred and Neddie Tasmin talking, and she could hear the water running in the bathroom.

"Can I take my chemistry set?" she heard Neddie call. "Ouch! It's too hot."

It sounded like Harry's voice and it was like her own bathroom experiences with her English governess. The water had always been too hot, and Miss Pembroke had always brushed too hard with the Kent nailbrush. Polly's mind was wandering back to that perpetual world of childhood, living in it again through the life of Neddie Tasmin. . . . If they had only had a child there would have been something left. . . .

But what could she have done differently even if she could have turned the clock back and attempted it all again? She would have still tried to create an environment for Tom. She had tried in their apartment at University Heights, that stuffy building with all those college wives. It was not her fault that Tom did not get a permanent appointment, and she was right in getting him to leave; but there was no use reviewing the bidding when her thoughts were not in order. She would have to see Tom, she would have to get it over with. They would both have to sit trying to explain their positions, when there was nothing left worth explaining. The war — you had to put a date on it — that was when everything went sour; but what had she left undone? There had been the British War Relief, Bundles for Britain, the committee to help America by aiding the Allies, that time she helped Tom before Lend Lease . . . *We are in the war and don't know it.* . . . *They* were at war, but at peace with themselves. . . . *We* are at peace, but at war with ourselves. . . .

There was that evening at the Garden when Tom had made a speech — he would have collapsed if it had not been for her — and she had to feed him brandy. The Office of Facts and Figures . . . Washington, Pyefield, New York, Washington . . . the Speakers' Table at the Waldorf, the White House for dinner, Fight for Freedom . . . Studio A at the N.B.C., the Committee for a Just Peace, Freedom House — she had helped Tom with all those damned committees. Dorothy Thompson, Dr. Kingdon, Lowell Mellett, Archie MacLeish, Elmer Davis, Herbert Agar . . . she had helped Tom with all of it . . . Mr. Litvinov, Field Marshal Sir John Dill, Steve Early, Harry Hopkins, J. Edgar Hoover, Paul V. McNutt — she had helped him with all of it, and he needn't say she hadn't. He needn't say she was indifferent. If it hadn't been for her a year ago in Washington . . . she had backed him up, and just let him say she hadn't.

"Polly." It was Mildred's voice. "Did you find the gin and vermouth? Minnie's working on the ice cubes. It's funny . . . I never was brought up on cocktails, but every afternoon now I'm just dying for a drink."

Polly moved swiftly in her chair and squared her shoulders. Those were the things that you had to bury deep inside you . . . The March of Time — Time Marches On. He needn't say she had not been there whenever he had wanted her as time marched on . . . the galley proofs from Harper's and that other book, *The Home Front — America Fights,* the Victory Loan, and that thing he wrote: "Do You Hear That, Mr. Hitler? Twenty Million American housewives . . ."

"Yes, dear," Polly said to Mildred, "so am I. I'm dying for a drink."

XXX

A Little off the Beam

THERE WAS one thing about traveling with General Bogart — you were not on bucket seats. It was a plush job all the way — the same plane that had carried them for a month, the general's own C–54. Now they were going back as quickly as they could go — Kwajalein, Johnson, an hour's stop at Hickam Field to take another crew aboard and to gas and check the plane, another hour at San Francisco for another crew and another check. The Old Man did not want to wait around shaking hands — and then there was security. The fewer people who knew about the trip the better.

They had left Guam hours ago, blacked out, and Bob Tasmin was still glad he was alive. He must have been asleep in his reclining chair when a sound awakened him. The door forward had opened, and a member of the crew holding a dim, red flashlight was walking down the aisle. They were getting into Kwajalein, letting down from nine thousand feet.

Kwajalein was a very active airport now, and though it was two-thirty in the morning, the repair shops by the field and the field itself were brightly lighted, a clear enough reminder that the Japanese left on those other atolls near Kwajalein were dying on the vine. One could still distinguish the gaunt trunks of coconut palms decapitated by the preliminary bombardment. As the plane came to a stop, the lights inside were switched on, and the occupants began tightening belts and buttoning shirts. General Bogart was looking for his cap and Gilkey, his aide, was helping him find it.

"All clear now, sir," Gilkey said, and the general rose and walked down the aisle.

The island's commanding officer and two or three guards were out to meet them, and the commanding officer's car and three jeeps were beside the plane. There was no waiting traveling with the general, except a pause for a formal exchange of courtesies. The general was saying that he was sorry to get anyone up at this hour. All they wanted was some place to wash and a cup of coffee, and there was no reason at all for the commanding officer to take them to his quarters. It was what the general always said on such occasions, but everyone knew that there was a good reason for the commanding officer to do everything he could. Bob Tasmin could hear the commanding officer telling the general that it was no trouble at all, that things were still a little sketchy, but there was time for a bite to eat. He was used to being up at all hours. It was his business and his pleasure. Then the general and his chief of staff and Gilkey climbed into the commanding officer's car and the rest of them followed in the jeeps. It was clear from the way the island officers acted that they were making a special effort for a Very Important Personage. A commander beside Bob Tasmin in the jeep gave a briefing on Kwajalein which Bob had heard on the way out; it reminded him of those monologues that colored drivers in Bermuda used to give when he and Mildred had gone there sometimes in the winter. He would not have been surprised if the commander had started discoursing on the flora and the fauna, but of course the only fauna he mentioned were the Japs. Patrols went over the enemy-occupied islands once a day just to take a look, and Bob Tasmin asked if there was any ack-ack, and the commander said there was only a little sometimes if you went too low.

"They know how to use anti-aircraft when they want to," Bob Tasmin began, and then he checked himself, because there was nothing he disliked more than hearing others boast about personal exploits. It was the way people used to talk about gall-bladder operations. He had been obliged to remind himself several times that his flight over that beach was something a lot of kids were doing every day, and yet it still was something. They had been at tree-top level in a B–24 with everything being thrown at them that could be thrown. The fuses had not been set for that level, but there had been the automatic fire. He could remember the shattered plexiglass, and that there had been too much noise and motion to leave any space for fear. . . . This had been *it,* and when you were face to face with it, the reality had not been as bad as the waiting.

"Have you had a good trip, sir?" the commander asked.

Bob could tell from his politely condescending tone what the officer thought of visitors from Washington, rubberneck tourists who interfered with routine, who pushed you out of your quarters, who had to be entertained and instructed, and who then turned around for home while you were stuck out there indefinitely.

"Yes," Bob Tasmin answered, "we've had a swell trip up to date." Again he had to repress his infantile desire to tell that Navy man, whose face he had hardly seen, that, by God, he had been over that beach in a B–24, taking low, oblique photographs.

"You ought to stick around and see this show out here," the commander said. "It's going to be something."

His companion was coming close to gossiping on future operations, and Bob Tasmin answered curtly.

"I wish I could," he said, "but I can't." Then he realized that he might have been discourteous. "On second thought that isn't so," he added. "I don't wish I could. I'm damned glad I'm getting back."

"You said something then, sir," the commander said. "Anybody's island-happy who doesn't want to get the hell back. If you'll duck into my place for a minute, I can offer you a drink."

"Thanks," Bob Tasmin answered, "but you ought to save it for yourself, and I'd better stay with the general."

"That's all right," the commander said. "The C.O. said for me to take care of someone."

They were in the hall of a small wooden shack, walking softly so as not to disturb the other occupants. The commander had a room of his own which reminded Bob Tasmin of a cubicle in school. As Bob sat on a bench watching the commander uncork a bottle, the vibration of the plane still ran through his body.

"Well, here's looking at you," the commander said. "You're going right through, aren't you?"

"Yes," Bob answered. "The general's in a hurry."

It was bad rye whisky and warm water, but as he drank it the ten-

409

sion inside him relaxed, and though he and the officer would never see each other again, Bob Tasmin felt that they would have gotten on well together if there had been more time.

"I wonder if you'd mind doing something for me?" the commander asked.

"What?" Bob Tasmin asked. "Carry a letter?"

That was what they always wanted, and the officer had picked up an envelope from the table near the washbasin.

"If you wouldn't mind . . . it's for the little woman."

Tasmin was still alive and he felt very obliging.

"If you'll give me another drink," he said, "I'll call her up and tell her all the news."

The commander took his glass, and he was very careful filling it.

"I don't know that she'll want any more news," he said. "The letter will be enough."

Under the circumstances it did not seem appropriate to ask what the commander meant. Bob Tasmin took the letter and unbuttoned his shirt pocket, and as he did so his fingers encountered the letter he had written to Mildred and had left with Gilkey to deliver. It was that François Villon letter, that Last Testament, for which there was no longer any need, and Gilkey had handed it back to him in the plane. He tore it across, and then tore it into quarters.

"Is there any place where I can throw this?" he asked. "I'd like to be sure it's out of the way."

"Is it classified material?" the commander asked, and Bob Tasmin found himself laughing.

"It's one of those post-mortem letters. You can make a damned fool of yourself writing them. Did you ever try?"

It was a strange thing to ask a stranger, but it was natural there at Kwajalein.

"Yes," the commander said, "I've written them. I read one of mine over once at Biak. It broke me of the habit. It was lousy."

"What made you want to read it?" Bob Tasmin asked.

"Egotism," the commander said. "I thought it would sound swell. God, it was lousy."

"It's funny," Bob said. "Maybe I was unconsciously saving this to read. It's the only natural composition I ever wrote, but it's probably lousy too."

"To your wife?" the commander asked.

"Yes," Bob said. "It was a summary."

"Well," the commander said, "I'll tell you what you'd better do. Just put it in the basin here and burn it. Have you got a lighter?"

Bob sat watching the yellow flames and bits of paper growing blacker while he held his drink, and it meant that he was right back where he had been before. What he had considered the past was becoming the present, and all the present in which he had been living would be buried in the past. In a day or two he would be back with his wife and son. He would be helping Neddie with his lessons when he had time. He and Mildred would be going over the household bills together, and they would go out together to play bridge — Mildred played a very sound game of bridge — and they would walk together in Rock Creek Park discussing their friends and Neddie. She would be asking him not to read so late at night, and he would be asking her why she couldn't write letters instead of telephoning to New York, and she would be asking him whether he liked her new dress and to please be frank about it because she would send it back if he did not like it. They would be involved again in all those unexciting details that make up any marriage. He felt a sudden pang of contrition that he had thought so little of Mildred since he had written that letter.

"I suppose I ought to have brought back some souvenirs," Bob Tasmin said, "but there aren't many gift shops around here, are there?"

"You mean a present for your wife?" the commander asked.

"Yes," Bob Tasmin said, "a sword, or a flag, or a scroll. She might not care, but my boy would. I should have brought a souvenir."

"Didn't you see any Marines?" the commander asked. "They always have souvenirs."

"I didn't think of it," Bob Tasmin said.

"It's hard, isn't it," the commander said, "to feel domestic out here — to think about fixing the furnace and letting the cat out?"

"Yes," Bob Tasmin said, "but it's coming over me again. I want to see my wife. I want to see my boy. I want to let the cat out."

It was coming over him so strongly that he obeyed one of those war-theater impulses and pulled out his leather wallet.

"Here's the family album," he said. "Here she is."

"She's very pretty," the commander said. "She looks like a Powers model."

"She's a good girl," Bob said.

"The kid looks like you," the commander said. His glance shifted across the room to his valpack. "Look . . . I've got a sword and a scroll if you want them. Take them along. I don't think I'm going to need them. . . . Well . . . down the hatch."

As soon as they had taken off from Johnson and gained their altitude, the general had ordered boards to be set in front of him with maps and papers. There was no use twiddling their thumbs and reading Agatha Christie, the general said, when they could have a five-hour "skull" session. The general wanted to get those beaches in his mind, and now was the time to start, so he kept calling to Bob Tasmin for more and more maps and reports and photographs. It was like being in two places at once because they were moving away from those beaches so fast. The general went through the intelligence line by line, and then he doubled back. He only stopped when he was told that they would be at Hickam Field in twenty minutes.

"Now, gentlemen," the general said, "we'll all stay on the field and no one is to try to get out personal messages."

A flight eastward over the Pacific against the tide of time gave a staggering sense of distance and interfered preposterously with the normal processes of thought and digestion. The sun had hardly risen, for instance, when they took off from Johnson, and the flying time from there to Honolulu was only five or six hours. Nevertheless, the sun was very low when they let down at Hickam Field. It was disturbing to have passed through a day in six hours, and it gave Bob Tasmin the idea that if you could speed up the plane the general and all the rest of them might get into next week or next year without knowing it.

Sometime in the middle of the night they were high over a sea of cloud that a headwind had worked into ripples like the sand marks on a beach, and the moon shining on the cloud made it like a silver curtain that shut them from the earth. He could not rid himself of a feeling that he had been given a glimpse of a new dimension, and that it was not important whether he had lived or died. That sense of unimportance must have soothed him into sleep — because there he was, back at Gray's Point carrying his Quackenbush air rifle, back at Prout's Brook by the fir trees and the rocks, and a man with sandy hair in gray flannel trousers was speaking to him. Of course it was Mr. Fulton, and Mr. Fulton was asking him to come over and see his place. They were walking through the gardens, and Mr. Fulton was saying that he had made them all himself, all himself.

"Everybody's got to make things for himself," Mr. Fulton was saying, and then he disappeared for no good reason, and there was Polly Fulton near the swimming pool in a print dress with tortuous flowers on it like the flowers that grew in Honolulu. Her hair was in disorder because the wind was blowing. When he moved toward her, slowly, as one did in dreams, she began to run away, and he was running after her, not near the swimming pool, but through a wood. His feet were like lead, and he was calling to her to stop. Her voice was the clearest part of all the dream — that unmistakable husky voice — and it was still in his ears when someone shook his shoulder.

"I can't stop, darling," she was calling. "I've got to get away before B. F. finds me. I'm awfully sorry, darling, I've got to get away."

"Wake up," someone was saying. "We're letting down." It was broad daylight in the plane, late morning or early afternoon.

"Down where?" he asked, and he pulled himself together.

"Frisco."

"Don't call it that," Bob Tasmin said. "Call it San Francisco. The citizens don't like it."

He must have been asleep for hours. It was time to get into woolens if they were in San Francisco.

*　　*　　*

413

They arrived in Washington at one-fifteen in the morning. As he stood there in the dark feeling the sharp cold, the events of the trip were fading away — left behind in the plane. They were already Classified Material — period.

"Tasmin," the general called.

"Sir?" Bob Tasmin answered.

An Army car would drive him to Scott Circle, and he need not report until two in the afternoon — period.

"Sleep it off first," the general was saying as they shook hands. "It's been a good trip, hasn't it?"

"Yes, sir," Bob answered, "a fine trip."

He climbed up the apartment steps with his baggage, and there were the same dim lights, the same somnolent, stuffy aura, and the same man on night duty dozing by the switchboard. You pushed the button, and the elevator doors opened automatically. You pushed the button for the Fifth Floor, waited until the elevator stopped, and then the doors opened automatically again. Those tedious details fascinated him because he had felt so definitely that he would never be there again. The relentless beige of the corridors made him remember how Mildred had complained of the apartment, but it all seemed a long while ago.

When his latchkey fitted and when he saw the carved camphor chest and the hat rack in the hall under the single light that had been left burning, it was like awaking from a deep sleep. He walked softly down the hall and switched on the living room light and set his canvas bag down carefully on the Oriental rug. The room was as garish and impersonal as it always had been. He took off his cap and dropped it on his valpack. He took off his trench coat and dropped it beside the cap. There was the bridge lamp by the chair where he usually sat, and the bar-victrola which had always amused him somewhat, and the dinette with those impossible tearoom chairs, and the reproductions of Matisse. Then he saw his face reflected in the overdecorated mirror above the bar-victrola. Although his eyes were tired, he was unchanged, like that room, except for his free Navy haircut and his need for a shave. The face that looked back at him bore no imprint that he could see of anything that he had been through. He wondered whether it was a stupid face, incapable of receiving impressions like other people's. It looked too precise, too carefully molded, and devoid of any of the bewilderment he felt. When he saw Mildred and Neddie, he knew that everything would come into focus, but now he was still spread over everywhere.

There was a piece of petit point lying on the table by the sofa, and he remembered that Mildred had been working on it at odd moments all that winter. It was one of those tight, antique patterns of flowers against a russet background, and he picked it up without knowing he had done so until he found himself examining it. Though Mildred had said that she would finish it while he was gone, there were still bare stretches of inked design, and the needle with a piece of purple thread still through it was plunged into the embroidery exactly as she had left it. He could think of her bending over it, her face pleasantly intent, while Neddie sat in the armchair beneath the bridge lamp reading *Ivanhoe*. He had his first real sense of homecoming, because the embroidery was as traditional and devoid of mistakes as the pattern of their lives. He was back with Mildred and his son, back to the strongest ties that anyone could have, and he felt a deep sense of gratitude for having been permitted to return. He had not felt so close to Mildred for years. He would be seeing Neddie in a moment, and Neddie was the most important person in the world. They all belonged together, and nothing else counted except that sense of home.

He heard a footstep on the bare floor of the hall behind him, the unmistakable click of a woman's mules, and he began to speak before he turned around.

"Hello, dear — " he began. "Mildred — "

Polly Fulton, in a blue quilted silk dressing gown, was standing on the other side of the room. He had only seen her in a dressing gown once, and that was after a week end at Gray's Point when he had taken a very early train on Monday morning and she had come out into the hall to say good-by.

"Bob," she said, "is that you?"

There was no mistaking her voice, because it sounded exactly as he had remembered it in that dream. He drew a deep breath.

"Why, yes," he said, "I'm under that impression, Poll. Where's Mildred?"

"She and Neddie are gone," Polly said.

He tried to consider the idea carefully, but he still could not understand why Polly Fulton was there.

"Gone where?" he asked. "For God's sake, Poll?"

"To visit her mother in Connecticut."

He saw Polly tighten the belt of her quilted silk dressing gown, and he shook his head again. He had no clear idea of what happened next, but he heard her saying —

"Oh God, I was so sure you were dead."

"Well, you were damned near right, Poll," he heard himself answering.

Then she was pressed close against him, sobbing in his arms, without his ever knowing how she got there, but at the time it all seemed natural. His cheeks were wet with her tears and her face was buried on his shoulder.

"I thought everyone was dead," she was saying.

The words made no particular sense, and it did not seem to matter what he answered either.

"Poll," he said, "my darling Poll." And he said it again, "My darling."

He had never in any flight of fancy thought of holding Polly Fulton in his arms again.

"Say that again," she said.

"Darling Poll," he said.

"No," she answered. "Say it even if it isn't true. Say 'My darling.'"

When he kissed her neither of them seemed to be anywhere in particular, but no such oblivion could last long. It was not Gray's Point or New York; it was Scott Circle and it was the present. He was holding Polly in his arms there in the center of his own living room, and it was time to find out how she had got there.

"Look here," he said. "Where did you say Mildred was?"

She drew away from him when Mildred's name was mentioned as any nice girl would have.

416

"There were measles in the school," Polly said. "She's been away five days and she planned to stay a week."

"Oh," he said. "Neddie's school. Was he exposed?"

"What?" Polly asked.

"Not that it's important," Bob said. "Was Neddie exposed to those measles?"

"Bob dear," Polly said, "I don't remember. Why didn't you send some word?"

"There wasn't much chance," Bob said. "Where's Tom?" He remembered what Harry had said at Guam about Polly and Tom.

"I was with Tom at the hotel," Polly said. "I couldn't go home, darling. I wanted to be alone — and Mildred asked me here."

"Well," he said, "I guess it wasn't such a good idea."

"No," she said, "it wasn't. I suppose I'd better pack up and go somewhere."

"Don't be a damned fool, Poll," Bob said. "Let's put it down to combat fatigue. I'm a little off the beam tonight."

"That sounds just like you, darling."

"Yes," he said, "I suppose it does. I'm usually just like myself."

"All right," Polly said, and she stood there smiling at him. "Let's write it off the books. I wouldn't have gone off the deep end if I hadn't thought you weren't alive."

"Do you know what you look like?" Bob asked.

"No," she answered. "What?"

"You look like Botticelli's 'Spring.'"

She had that same half-smile, and her hair was rumpled, and she must have thought about her hair because she had pushed it from her forehead.

"Do I still?" she asked. "I don't feel that way. You make me feel deflated."

"Yes," he said, "I suppose so. That's the way I've always made you feel, isn't it?"

"No," she said, "not always." And she put her hand on his shoulder. "You look so queer with that haircut."

"Poll," he said, and he took her hand, and kissed it. "I want to tell you something."

"What?" she asked.

"I may as well admit it," he told her. "Don't you know I've always loved you?"

"Yes, dear," she said, "I know."

Polly put her hand back on his shoulder.

"Darling," she said, "you look so different."

"Do I?" Bob said. "I feel different. But then I ought to. I've been through quite a lot." And then he smiled. "A very valuable emotional experience. . . ."

XXXI

As Long As You Know What You're Doing

It NEVER would have happened at any other time or place. It never would have, Polly was sure, if she had not been through a series of scenes with Tom, if she had not been broken all in pieces. She had never felt so alone with Bob Tasmin, so close to him or so dependent. In those other years, he had never held her or kissed her in that way.

"Darling," she said, "why don't you take off that Army coat and sit down? It makes you look like General Marshall."

"All right," he said. "That's a pretty good idea. Listen, Poll, you'd better tell me about Tom. Where is he?"

It was time to try to pull herself together.

"He's moved in with a little floosie," she said, "in Georgetown."

"Oh," Bob said, "has he?"

It was time to pull herself together.

"I've left Tom," she said. "I've kicked him out."

"Oh," Bob said, "have you?"

"Yes, if you want to know," Polly answered, and her voice broke. "Out on his pants."

"On his pants?" Bob repeated. "Does that mean you're through with him?"

"It's a coarse expression," Polly said, "but what else can it mean?"

"I don't know," Bob said. "I wouldn't be exactly sure. You have so many bright ideas, Poll."

"Oh, darling," Polly said, "let's not talk about it now. I'll tell you later but not now. Bob, where have you been?"

He seemed to have a hard time thinking where he had been.

"Out to Guam," he said, "and further. It was quite a trip."

"Why don't you ever say anything?" Polly asked. "Why do you always keep everything inside you like a ship in a bottle?"

"I can't, Poll," he said, "but it was quite a trip. I'm not quite over it. That's why I say I'm a little off the beam."

"Darling," Polly said, "aren't you awfully tired? Don't you want to go to sleep?"

"No," he said, "I'm not sleepy, Poll, not now."

"I don't know how to handle soldiers," Polly said, "but I'll tell you what we'll do. I'll cook some bacon and eggs and coffee. I got a pound of bacon yesterday."

"I didn't know you cooked," Bob said.

"I had to, darling," Polly said, "with Tom."

"Well," Bob said, "that's a very good idea, and I'll tell you what I'll do. I'll call up Mildred in Connecticut. I guess the circuits will be open."

She had seen enough other women, and men too, to know that people in her position were dangerous both to themselves and others, because once you lost your sense of security, you began seeking security elsewhere. It was a process of adjustment, she supposed, of which no one was wholly conscious. Even in the kitchenette as she looked for the frying pan and the eggs and bacon she had a perilous feeling of elation mingled with relief because Bob Tasmin had said that he had always loved her. It appeared to make no difference at all that he was married to Mildred because nothing made any difference except that he still cared about her. She even knew this passage between them would inevitably reach some sort of climax and that it would be her fault. Nevertheless, it all seemed as natural as though it had been providentially intended — that she should be there alone with him in the small hours of the morning cooking eggs. It was natural to turn to him, and she felt no sense of strain or sense of wrong. He was strong enough to lift her burdens and resolve her doubts, and that was what a man was for. It was as though they had always been together, and perhaps they had been really, for there were some things you could never outlive or forget.

The water in the percolator began to boil, and while she was taking the dishes and the cups off the shelves, she could hear him saying that he would speak to anyone at the Connecticut number. She could hear him saying that he would hold on, when she was frying the bacon.

"How do you like your eggs, darling?" she called to him.

"Sunny side up," he called back.

It was wonderful to be doing something helpful for a man again. She tried not to listen to what he was saying because it was the only discordant note, but she could not help hearing.

"Hello. This is Bob . . . Yes, I just got in . . . Oh, I'm all right, thanks. Tired, but fine otherwise" — he sounded a little like B. F. at the telephone — "I don't know whether I should have waked you up or not, but I thought I'd better call and check in with Mildred. Is she there?"

She could not help hearing. If he was not speaking to Mildred, she supposed it was Mildred's mother.

"Oh," he was saying. "Do you know her number in New York?" . . . And then she heard him laugh. "Why, it doesn't make a bit of difference. That girl always forgets to leave numbers, doesn't she? . . . No, really it doesn't make any difference. Just tell her to call me when she calls in the morning." And then he laughed again. . . . "Well, I wouldn't call it alone in a lonely apartment. Polly Fulton — I mean Polly Brett's here whipping up some coffee and eggs. Didn't Mildred tell you? . . . Unconventional, but eminently proper. . . . Why, I'll sleep in Neddie's room. . . . When she calls in the morning, just tell her to call me here. I'll be in until half-past one, and then I'll be at the office. . . . Give Neddie a kiss for me. . . . Oh, and one thing more. He hasn't got measles, has he? . . . Well, it certainly is — swell to be back."

Polly was looking for forks and getting the eggs on a warm plate, and by the time she started to set the table in the dinette the conversation had ended. Bob had taken off his tie and had opened his shirt collar and was sitting by the telephone with his hands on his knees examining the pattern of an Oriental rug.

"Bob," she said, "isn't everything all right?"

She knew from the quick way he smiled and raised his head that he had not heard her come in with the eggs and coffee.

"Oh, yes, everything's fine," he said. "She forgot to leave her number. She'll be calling in the morning." And then he stood up. "Well, it's nice to see some food. It's kind of you to be a cook."

"Why, darling," she said, and she laughed. "I'm just a homebody at heart."

Bob smiled down at her; at least his lips were smiling.

"It's funny," he said. "All women think they are. It's a sort of reflex, isn't it?"

She could almost believe they had always eaten together in that dinette, except that he pulled back her chair for her instead of slumping down first the way Tom would have done. He suddenly seemed gay and careless, and he told her that they couldn't make coffee like that in the Army, or in the Navy either.

"Poll," he said while they were eating, "do you remember the swimming pool?"

"What about the swimming pool?" she asked. "I remember no one could ever keep the frogs out of it, not even B. F. He never could forget those frogs."

Polly had been worried because he looked tired until the swimming pool at Gray's Point was mentioned, and then his whole face had brightened.

"Coming there in the summer," he said, "with the heat, and everything around it so still. Do you remember when you came back from abroad and brought me those pipes?"

"I thought it was going a little too far," Polly said. "Perhaps it was."

"Do you remember that dinner dance at the club?" he asked. "I mean that first one, when you were at that party with those pimply boys and that little Hollister number? You looked so frightened and so pretty. When I danced with you, I got you over being frightened, didn't I?"

"God, I was frightened," Polly said. "You looked like Sir Lancelot at the time — to me you did, but then you do again, right now."

"Sir Lancelot," Bob said. "I used to think a lot of Lancelot until I heard about Guinevere. I'd rather you'd put me down as Arthur, Poll."

"Arthur," Polly answered. "Arthur was a stuffed shirt."

"Well," Bob said, "why not?" And he laughed, and she laughed too.

"Oh, darling," Polly said. "It's funny to think of being here, isn't it?"

It was very funny if you thought of the beginnings. Everything stretched back like threads, tied to fragments of their childhood.

"It's a lot funnier to me," he said, "to be anywhere at all."

"Darling," Polly said, "you look so handsome. The war's done you a lot of good."

"Just an answer to a maiden's prayer," Bob Tasmin said, and he tilted back his chair.

"And I'm not a maiden, darling."

It didn't matter what she said sitting there watching him. He was more mature, more defined, and yet at the same time she could see him all over again as he used to look.

"Poll," he asked, "what made you think that I was dead?"

"There was a broadcast."

He stopped tilting his chair and sat up straight.

"Now what do you mean by that?" he asked sharply. "What broadcast?"

"It was Milton Ouerbach," Polly said. "He was talking about you. Tom had turned it on. Eleven o'clock last Sunday."

She remembered the whole scene with sharp distaste — breakfast in the hotel, Tom twiddling the dial and Milton Ouerbach's voice.

"Ouerbach?" Bob said. "Good God."

" 'This is Milton Ouerbach at the front,' " Polly said, " 'speaking from our advance base at Guam.' He was telling about a friend of his whom he called Joe, darling, and I knew it was you, because he sounded just the way he always used to when he talked about you — an overprivileged boy in top-drawer clubs. He disapproves of overprivileged boys. He said you were going to do something dangerous which he could not describe, and that you were debonair. He was very sweet about you."

"Oh, good God," Bob said.

423

"Sweet and patient, and a little patronizing because of your social attitude. He said your plane was now overdue, and he was very humble in the face of your bravery. He said, 'God bless you, Joe.'"

"Well, God damn him," Bob Tasmin said, and it was startling because it did not sound like Bob. "God damn him, I wish he'd been with me. We had the hell shot out of us."

"And besides," Polly said, "he called you a gentleman unafraid."

She had never seen him angry in all the time she had known him. She knew he was not angry at her, but she could not tell whether he was angry at Milton Ouerbach or himself. He pushed back his chair and walked into the living room.

"But, Bob," Polly said, as she followed him. "He's right, you know, and you're about the only one he's ever known — I mean the only gentleman unafraid."

"All right," Bob said, and he drew a deep breath and turned and faced her. It frightened her to see the way he looked, without a vestige of his usual self-control. "All right," he said. "I've always been a goddam gentleman, and I've always been afraid not to be one. Let's put it on my tombstone. That's my whole obituary."

"But, darling," Polly said, "don't you want to be one?"

He took a step toward her and then he stopped.

"Hell, yes," he said, "I want to be one, and I wish I didn't. How about our having a drink?"

He jerked open the door under the victrola and pulled out a bottle of whisky and two glasses.

"I'd love to have one," Polly said. "I'll get some ice."

"Ice?" Bob Tasmin said. "Why ice?" And then he was polite again. "Not unless you want it, Poll."

"Oh, no," Polly said, "I don't want it."

"Well, let's take the bottle over here and let's sit down," Bob Tasmin said. "We've got all night, or morning. The time's all twisted up. I'm sorry."

He sat down on the sofa behind the coffee table, and she sat beside him and rested her hand on his head and stroked his hair very gently, but he gave no sign of being aware that she was near him.

He was staring straight ahead of him holding his half-empty glass.

"I'm sorry, Poll," he said.

"But darling." She took his hand and pressed it with both of hers. "What for?"

"Never mind it now," he said. "It's all the way we've been brought up to live, and maybe we've both been brought up impossibly, but never mind it now. I saw Harry out in Guam. The Corsairs kept going over when we talked. He was trying to look like MacArthur, but he didn't have that pipe. I'm sorry — Harry told me — about B. F., Poll."

He paused and she held his hand tighter.

"Do you remember when he took me up to the town where he used to live? He was wonderful to me. I gave him a good talk about church schools. What was the name of that town?"

"Why, Willett," Polly said.

"That's it," he answered, "Willett. It's always been a little hard on Mildred, Poll."

"Why, darling," Polly said, "why should Willett be hard on Mildred, particularly if you can't even remember what it's called?"

"I've never been able to live down you and Willett entirely," Bob Tasmin said. "Let's skip it, Poll. You'd better tell me about Tom."

Tom had not been on her mind since she had fried the eggs in the kitchenette. Her surprise at Bob Tasmin's sudden self-revelation made Tom seem momentarily like an unpleasant incident that she had faced when she was younger, but as soon as Bob Tasmin mentioned him her humiliation came over her in a wave that flooded and obliterated everything else.

"I'm a cast-off woman, darling," she began, but she could not continue in that vein and she doubled up her fists. "Everything's so smashed. I'm such a failure, and I don't know — I can't decide why."

"All right," Bob said, "maybe we all are, up to a point. Take it easy, Poll."

If he had been sweet and sympathetic as he should have been, she did not think she could have stood it with everything inside her hanging by a thread.

"I've always run away from everything, haven't I?" she said. "I'm

425

leaving him because I can't stand being with him for another minute. I'm doing what I've always done, all over again."

"Maybe that's so," Bob said. "Maybe."

"You don't have to be so smug," Polly said, "just because you've never run away yourself." But he sat there without answering. "Don't be like a psychiatrist," Polly said. "Don't act as though you knew all the answers."

He put his arm around her shoulders and drew her nearer to him.

"I know a lot more answers than I did," he said. "That place Willett. . . . I remember when you ran away."

Then her reserve melted away, because he was close beside her. She was telling him things which she had never dreamed she would tell anyone. She was telling him everything again just as she had years ago at the swimming pool.

She started with the house at Gray's Point, with her nurse and the governess, and with Timmons and the second man. She told him how ashamed she used to feel as a little girl, because they had so much money, and how she felt when B. F. kept building more and more. She told him how she loved B. F., and yet at the same time how she could never do what she felt he wanted. Her words were like the stone blocks in one of those great boxes from the toy closet in the nursery at Gray's Point, those German blocks that were blue and green and yellow, fashioned in cubes, arches, pyramids and cylinders and cones. You never knew what sort of a thing you would build when you started with those blocks; and now when she tried to explain herself, she did not know exactly what she was building either.

She always felt, she was saying, that nothing at Gray's Point was hers, not even her books or her dresses or her dolls. Everything in the house belonged completely to B. F. and no one else. He wanted to give them, but he could not, at least not to her.

"Oh, hell," Polly said, "no one cares what happens to a girl if she's on a yacht."

"Who said that?" Bob asked.

426

She had curled her feet under her and she was leaning against Bob Tasmin's shoulder.

"That was Tom," she answered. "Tom was always saying that."

"Well, he had a yacht of his own," Bob Tasmin said. "Everybody has some sort of yacht."

But she didn't want someone else's yacht.

Heatherbloom Hall, she was saying, at least gave her her first opportunity to be herself; and parts of college had been exciting too, because she was away from home; but there was always the same ending, back to the apartment on Park Avenue or back to Gray's Point. That apartment on Park Avenue did not belong to her either. It all belonged to B. F. It was not that she did not adore B. F. It would have all been simpler if she had not.

"That's why I ran away to you, darling."

But then, she said, he had been like B. F. There had been nothing she could do for him, at least that was the way she had felt. That was why she ran away to Tom. There was so much she could do for Tom and she had done everything, and no one could say she hadn't. All she had wanted was to have Tom amount to something. She told about that camp on the island, and Columbia and all their new friends, though it was all like whistling in the dark. She told about the house at Pyefield and their trips abroad and that book of Tom's. He was always talking about writing, but you could never make him write. She wanted honestly to be fair, she was saying. Of course she had known for several years that things weren't going well, but there came a point, a point . . . it was no longer like building blocks because it was all too fresh in her mind. . . . She had never known that everything would break when she came down to Washington. Of course, they had been quarreling and bickering, but there was a point, a point beyond which you could not go, and she was describing that point step by step until she was tired of it, deathly tired.

"Bob," Polly was saying. "Do you remember a boy named Norman Bell?"

"Yes, I know him," Bob Tasmin answered. "Are you telling me that you've got yourself mixed up with Norman?"

"Don't be stupid," Polly answered. "I'm only mixed up with you at the moment."

"Well, then," Bob asked, "why bring in Norman Bell?"

"I just happened to meet him over some cocktails," Polly said.

"That's the easiest way to make friends," Bob said. "How else would you meet him?"

"That was last Sunday," Polly said, "just when I was finding out about that girl of Tom's. Norman was let out with a doctor from Bethesda. Do you know what he said? He said nothing matters that happened before the war."

He put his arm around her again, and she rested her head on his shoulder. Neither of them spoke for a long while.

"I'm awfully glad I've told you so much," Polly said. "It's been very therapeutic." She sighed. "It's like the ending of a case history, isn't it?"

"That's a silly thing to say," Bob said. "There isn't any ending to anything until you die. I know, at least I ought to."

"Darling," Polly said, "I want to ask you — I know it's a silly thing to ask, but there's no one else — "

"All right," Bob said; "go ahead and ask it, Poll."

"What am I going to do now? Someone's got to tell me."

It was like climbing a high mountain with a heavy burden and letting it fall from her when she reached the top. It was like giving away something which she valued more than anything. It was the first time in her life that she had ever surrendered to anyone, and all at once she was very happy, just when she had thought she could never be happy again.

Everything she had said about Tom had the familiar, tiresome ring of someone else recounting her marital difficulties, but it made no difference now that her eyes met Bob Tasmin's. Nothing mattered that had happened before the war, absolutely nothing. Nothing mattered except that she trusted someone absolutely for once in her life. It was a new, complete sort of fulfillment.

"Bob, dear," she said, "please tell me what to do."

428

"All right," Bob Tasmin said. He stopped, and he seemed to have difficulty speaking. "I'll tell you what you'd better do first. You'd better go in there and get some sleep."

"Oh, darling," Polly said, "you and I don't need to be alone tonight."

She could not imagine herself saying such a thing or underlining it in such a way, at any other time.

"We're always alone," he said. "Don't forget that, Poll. Everyone is, always."

Then she pushed herself away from him.

"Oh, my God," she said. "What's the matter with me, darling? Don't you think I'm attractive? Most men do."

"Well," he said slowly, "then I'm like most men."

"No you're not."

Bob Tasmin put his glass on the table. "Through it all I'm still a goddam gentleman," he said. "I've had the same idea as you for about an hour, but it wouldn't do any good, Poll. I wouldn't consider it — not here and not when you're in this mood."

"Oh, my God," Polly said.

"I agree with you," Bob Tasmin answered, "absolutely." And he reached for the bottle. She saw that his hand shook as he poured himself another drink.

"Poll," he said, "Poll, darling."

"Oh, shut up," Polly said, "and don't think I'm ashamed. I said I wanted to sleep with you, and don't say it wouldn't do any good again, because you don't know."

The infuriating part of it was that he looked almost amused.

"Do you still want to?" he asked.

"Oh, stop it," Polly said, "it isn't funny. You do, too, and you know it."

"Yes," he said, "I know it."

"Well, then — " Polly began, but his voice rose over hers.

"Listen, Poll," he said, "let's try to think, if it's possible. You want me to tell you what you ought to do. Frankly, I don't know."

"That's a big help," Polly said, "thanks for working on it, darling."

At least he was disturbed, at least he had stopped being so sure of himself. He stood up and crossed the room and turned on his heel and walked back toward her. He had never looked so handsome. His shirt must have been made to measure, and even with his collar open it looked perfectly neat. His waist was very slender, and every motion he made was beautifully co-ordinated. He picked up a book from the table and dropped it back with a little slamming sound.

"Listen, Poll," he said. "I almost got myself killed the other day. I wish to God I had. It would have been so much easier."

"Oh, darling," Polly said, "please don't say that, and please come back here and sit down. I didn't mean to upset you, but I'm so upset myself."

"All right," Bob said, and he sat down again beside her. "I won't say that. I wish I could express myself all over the place the way you can. I was saying I damn near got myself killed. We went right in over the water at fifty feet, to photograph a beach. But never mind it."

"You've got to tell someone, darling," Polly said, and at least she had forgotten herself again.

"I mean never mind the details," Bob Tasmin said. "The point was —" He was leaning forward looking at the floor again. He pointed to it, and his hands were slender and beautiful. "It wasn't so bad to be thinking that there wouldn't be any more. It was all so easy, so out of my hands. I don't suppose I'm being clear."

"Yes," Polly said, "you're being clear." And Bob Tasmin smiled at her.

"It was quite an experience, at least for anyone like me, to be picked up suddenly out of a soft, comfortable world. I suppose you might get used to it after a while, like the kid who piloted the plane, but I wasn't, I'm still not. That's why you've got to excuse me, Poll."

"Excuse you for what?" she asked.

"Oh, well," he answered, "for everything. You'll have to excuse me if I don't see things quite the way I used to. I'm still in two places at once. I was thinking all this over when you were talking about Tom."

"What were you thinking, darling?" Polly asked.

"That things don't look quite the same . . . Of course I never liked Tom much. There's no reason why I should; but when you went to work on him, I began feeling very sorry for Tom — and I still am sorry for him."

It was so unexpected that Polly felt her face stiffen.

"Oh, you are?" Polly said.

"Yes, in a way," Bob answered. "I'm sorry for him with you running his life. Of course that is why you married him — now, wait a minute." And he raised his voice before she could speak. "I think it's all right you got rid of him, but I can be sorry for him, can't I?"

"But I told you." Her own voice was high and sharp. "I did everything for him, everything he wanted. Don't you believe me when I tell you?"

"Yes," Bob Tasmin answered, "I believe you think you did."

She knew her face was growing scarlet.

"I never thought you'd take his side," she said.

"I'm not," Bob answered, "but I can see what unsettled him. You're like your father, Poll, except he had more outlets for his energy."

She felt her body tingle as it always did when she was furious.

"I wish you'd leave B. F. out of it," she said.

"I knew you and B. F. pretty well," Bob answered. "You both of you had quite a lot to do with my life, you know."

"Well, I wish we hadn't," Polly said. "Why did you keep coming around? I wish I'd never known you."

"I've had that idea sometimes too," Bob said, "but the fact remains you're like your father, Poll. You were saying you wanted to run away because everything belonged to him."

He sat there watching her with that half-smile of his, and it looked almost like a smirk. She picked up a cigarette and lighted it and smoked it too fast as she always did when she was angry.

"Well, what of it?" she asked.

431

"You're like him," he said, and everything had become coldly impersonal. "I don't say either of you could help it, but you don't know yourself, Poll. I know myself better than you do. You did the same thing to Tom that your father did to you. You built up your own world, and he ran out on you. You had too much personality. He couldn't take it, Poll. He was like you, he ran away because nothing belonged to him. You had it all."

It was like a dash of cold water in her face. She felt as cold as ice.

"Don't get mad, Poll," she heard him saying. "You have to run things, like B. F. It's all right as long as you know you're doing it, but you don't know."

Polly drew her breath through her teeth because they were clenched together tight, but before she could say anything he was speaking again.

"You're a very dangerous girl because you don't know what you're doing or why — a very dangerous girl, darling."

He stopped, and Polly drew another breath.

"If you know so much about me," she asked, "why did you want to marry me?"

"I didn't know much when I wanted to marry you, Poll," he said, "but you wouldn't have ever stepped on me. You wouldn't have made me dependent the way you made that poor guy. Maybe you should have married me."

"Well, thank God I didn't," Polly said. "Is that all you've got to say?"

"About all," Bob said. "You're very attractive when you're angry, Poll, and now you'd better go to bed."

"All right," Polly said, and she flung herself off the sofa. She was in the hall and opening the bedroom door before she thought of something else to say.

"Thanks for the free lecture," she called.

"You asked for it," Bob said.

"Don't be so damned complacent," Polly said, and she slammed the door behind her.

She stood there in the dark for a long while before she opened the door again. Bob Tasmin was still sitting where she had left him.

432

"Bob," she said, and when he looked up, he looked very tired.

"You're wrong about one thing," he said. "I'm not complacent, Poll."

"Bob," she asked, "why didn't someone ever tell me?"

"Don't worry about it, Poll," Bob said. "It was only an idea of mine."

"It isn't such a bad idea," Polly said. "If only someone had told me so I could have understood it. Darling — "

"What?" Bob asked.

"Do you think I ought to go back to Tom and try it all again?"

"That's up to you, Poll," he said. "But if it isn't Tom, there'll be someone else in the brave world of tomorrow. Nothing matters that happened before the war."

"Well, darling," Polly said, "if it makes any difference to you, I'm not licked yet."

Bob Tasmin looked very tired, but he laughed.

"You never will be, Poll," he said. "You're a damned good girl."

XXXII

Farewell Address

POLLY had slept very soundly, and this surprised her because she had not been sleeping well for weeks. It had not been the sort of sleep induced by those pills that Tom was always taking from which you awakened with a feeling that you had been hit over the head. It had been a natural, dreamless sleep which she was afraid had carried her late into the morning. She could tell by the quality of daylight coming through the Venetian blinds before she even looked at her little diamond wrist watch. She had awakened naturally without bewilderment. She was in that ugly bedroom in the apartment at Scott Circle, and as she lay with her eyes wide open, she could see the mirror-top dressing table and the other, unoccupied twin bed, the pink crepe lamps, the bureaus and the light-colored carpet, and the full-length mirror on the bathroom door. It was five minutes of eleven, and that colored maid of Mildred's, that treasure, never came before half-past twelve. Polly was perfectly clear about the present, but she was vague about what had happened the night before. At first there was nothing but uneasiness in her mind like the uneasiness she had felt sometimes when she had awakened after a party in New York at which she had talked too much, as she sometimes did, or had lost her temper with Tom in public. She was not sure what she had said, except that she must have said too much.

Yet, in spite of it, she was feeling very well. When she took an ice-cold shower in the cabinet that looked like an aquarium, she felt well and young and deeply relieved, and it was not right after the way Bob Tasmin had behaved. She sat brushing her hair as hard as she could brush it, thinking that no one had ever treated her as he had, and then she realized that Tom had said the same thing often enough when they had quarreled. Even the words had been almost identical, but she had not accepted them. She was looking at herself in the mirror on the bathroom door. Her hair was not rumpled, nor were her eyes the proper color. She looked too competent for Botticelli's "Spring." She was putting on her black dress again and buckling the gold belt. She had been through enough in that dress, and she would throw it away when she got to New York. She would go to Valentina's and find something new, and then — she did not know what then, but she was not afraid. It was very peculiar what people said to you about yourself. They might say the same thing for years without its conveying any meaning, and then all at once, for no good reason, you would have lived the truth — not heard it. Know thyself was what the Bible told you.

She had thought that Bob would be in Neddie's room, but instead he was on the sofa, dead asleep, still in his uniform, his shirt unbuttoned, his coat still on the chair as he had left it, and it was not fair to encounter him in such a defenseless state. She supposed that people traveling in war zones were used to sleeping in strange places, in tents, on benches in station waiting rooms. He was lying on his back with his hands clasped over his chest like a figure on a Crusader's tomb. His lips and eyes were closed tight, and his face had that Roman coin look that Mildred had mentioned. He looked as neat asleep as he did awake, and she was thinking of what Milton Ouerbach had said about Club men and children of privilege. Bob Tasmin, she was thinking, was on his own yacht, and by God, asleep or awake, Bob Tasmin knew how to sail it. You could laugh at him if you wanted, and you could say in the merriest sort of way that you would be safe with him anywhere, but then, you would be.

Damn him, she was thinking, he was not kind last night; but she knelt on the floor beside him and kissed his forehead.

"Bob," she said, "you'd better wake up, dear."

His eyes opened very quickly and he looked up at her without any expression of surprise.

"Hello, Poll, darling," he said. "What time is it?"

"It's a quarter after eleven," Polly said. "We're right back where we started. I'll do some more bacon and eggs and coffee."

She was still kneeling beside him, and he raised his hand and touched her hair.

"Poll," he said, "do you know what you look like?"

"Yes," she said, "so don't repeat yourself."

"All right I won't," he said. "Did you sleep well, Poll?"

"Yes," she answered, "and I don't know why."

"I'd better get a bath and shave," he said. "Is it all right for me to go in there and get some clothes? What are you laughing at, Poll?"

"At you," Polly said. "Why shouldn't it be all right? Darling, I know what I'm doing this morning. I thought you'd like to know."

Bob Tasmin sat up.

"Do you?" he asked. "What are you doing?"

"I'm going to pack my overnight bag," Polly said, "just as soon as I've cooked your breakfast, and get to hell out of here. That's what you want, isn't it?"

He always did the right thing. He leaned over her where she knelt beside him and touched her hair with his lips.

"No, it isn't," he said, "but it's a pretty good idea. Then what are you going to do?"

"I'm going to New York and see a lawyer," Polly said. "I can't go back to Tom."

"Think it over first," Bob said. "That's what we always tell them at Barstow, Barstow and Bryce."

"You needn't be so austere," Polly said. "Oh, Bob, can't we both be natural? I'm not going to try to break you down. I want to make a little speech . . . We'll call it a Washington Farewell Address."

"Don't you think we said enough last night?" Bob asked.

"I'm going to make my speech. . . . Darling — we should have got married, shouldn't we? . . . And I want to say I'm awfully sorry we didn't."

Bob Tasmin shook his head.

"I'm sorry too," he said, "but it wouldn't have worked, Poll. It was all bad timing."

"Well, it would work now," Polly said, "or we wouldn't be able to talk this way."

"Well, we'd better stop talking this way then," Bob Tasmin said.

"I'm going to finish, darling," Polly said, "because I know what I'm doing. . . . I really know. I just want to say — "

"Poll," Bob Tasmin said, "please stop."

"I told you it was a Farewell Address, darling," Polly said, "and no matter what happens, I'm glad about something. I'm glad I've known someone once in my life who can make me feel the way you do, someone I can honor and obey. . . . I should have known I wanted that."

Her voice broke in a sharp sob, and she brushed the back of her hand across her eyes. Bob Tasmin was staring down at her, and she dropped her head on his knee.

"Poll." His voice made her look up and she saw him bite his lower lip. "Poll, if I were only just a little different. I wish to God I were . . . but, Poll — "

"No," Polly said, "I don't wish it. I wouldn't love you if you were."

Then the telephone was ringing.

"That's Mildred," Bob Tasmin said.

The telephone stood on the little table in the corner with bars of sunlight coming across it through the Venetian blinds. When she saw him turn and take a slow step toward it, she was grateful that he belonged to her even in the way he did. He was himself. He did not have to pose, like other men she knew; he did not have to dramatize himself in little ways like Ouerbachs or Bretts. He did not have to be conscious of externals, because he was himself. The telephone rang again.

"I'd better go and pack, dear," she said.

"Don't go," he said. "There isn't any reason." She was glad there was no reason, but she did not want to listen. She hurried down the hall. She did not want to leave anything of hers in that bedroom, and she had the list of her possessions carefully in her mind, her comb and brush, her face powder, the Chanel No. 5, the diamond clip that B. F. had given her, the toothpaste, the aspirin, her nightgown, her wrapper, her mules. She was laying them all in her suitcase very neatly and efficiently, because if there was one thing she understood it was packing. She had left the door open though she had not intended to, and now it would look obvious to close it. Even when she tried not to, she could hear his voice, with a pause for Mildred's voice and then his own again.

"Hello, Mildred," he was saying. "How are you, dear? . . . Don't give it a thought. . . . I'm fine, I couldn't be better. . . . Yes, it was quite a surprise. She's just packing. . . . Is Neddie there? . . . Well, get the suit in at Brooks. You know the one to ask for. He always looked after Will and me. . . . I'm going down to the Pentagon at two. . . . Get something on the Congressional. I'll meet you at the station if the Old Man lets me off. . . . I don't think anything of the kind, dear. You'd just have been here sitting with your knitting. . . . Yes, I'll tell her. Now let me speak to Ned."

His voice changed to a tone that she had never heard.

"Hello, Neddie," he was saying, "how's the boy? . . . It was a C–54. We'll ride in one some day, and I was on a B–24 too. Do you know that one?" Then she heard him laugh. "I didn't. I didn't have a gun, but I saw a few. . . . Wait till you see what I've brought you. . . . I've got a lot to tell you. . . ."

He had finished with the telephone when she came back into the living room. She set down her suitcase beside his valpack and tossed that mink coat over it.

"That was Neddie," Bob Tasmin said. "He's up in New York to buy a suit. He hasn't got measles. Neddie's quite a boy."

"He looks like you, darling," Polly said. "I hope he'll be just like you."

"Don't wish that on Neddie."

"Darling . . . I guess I'd better be going now."

It was the only thing to do.

"Don't go," Bob said. "You haven't had any breakfast."

It was just what he should have said, but he looked so terribly alone.

"Please don't ask me," Polly said, "please, darling. I'll get a taxi. . . . I'll get some breakfast at the station."

Bob Tasmin nodded. "Give me that suitcase," he said, "and I'll go down with you and whistle for a cab."

Polly picked up her suitcase and coat.

"No," she said, "please, I couldn't stand it now, and I'm used to carrying this damn bag. Don't you know there's a war on? Good-by, darling."

She did not want to come nearer to him or to touch him. She just wanted to say good-by.

"Well, good-by, Poll," Bob Tasmin said, and then just as she was turning away his voice stopped her. "Poll."

"Yes, dear," she said.

"Thanks again for telling me what you did. It makes the whole damned show worth while."

"Does it, dear?" Polly said. "Well, don't forget a word of it. Good-by."

He did not speak again until she was at the apartment door fumbling with the knob.

"Poll," he called.

Her back was to him, and she did not dare to turn around.

"Just one thing more. You and I. . . . I wish — but we're going to be all right."

"Good-by," she said, "darling." And the door was open. She wished that there were some other word besides "darling," some word that she did not use indiscriminately in badinage, in anger or in love. She was out in the stuffy corridor, and she had closed the door tight shut. She was walking to the elevator very fast carrying her coat and her suitcase. She was sure that she had not forgotten anything.